SQUEEZE

SQUEEZE

Play

JANE LEAVY

Doubleday

NEW YORK   LONDON   TORONTO   SYDNEY   AUCKLAND

PUBLISHED BY DOUBLEDAY
a division of Bantam Doubleday Dell Publishing Group, Inc.
666 Fifth Avenue, New York, New York 10103

DOUBLEDAY and the portrayal of an anchor
with a dolphin are trademarks of Doubleday,
a division of Bantam Doubleday Dell Publishing
Group, Inc.

Library of Congress Cataloging-in-Publication Data

Leavy, Jane.
    Squeeze play / by Jane Leavy. — 1st ed.
        p.   cm.
    I. Title.
PS3562.E2619S65   1990
813'.54—dc20   89-16861
                                         CIP

ISBN 0-385-26300-7

This book was printed on acid-free paper.

For Peter
Who goes the distance

I guess I knew it was going to be a long, strange season the first time I called the front office and a voice answered, "Washington Senators, praise the Lord." This was the day Sal, my sports editor, told me I was going to be covering the team for the *Trib* and a week after Reverend Jimy Boy Collins acquired the franchise. This had all the makings of lunacy right up front: nice Jewish girl covers expansion baseball team owned by right-wing televangelist. Something told me it might be a good idea to write this all down just in case. So here it is. In the raw, so to speak.

A. B. Berkowitz, October 1989

Opening Day

April 3 You see a lot of penises in my line of work: short ones, stubby ones, hard ones, soft ones. Circumcised and uncircumcised; laid-back and athletic. Professionally speaking, they have a lot in common, which is to say they are all attached to guys, most of whom are naked while I am not, thus forming the odd dynamic of our relationship. They are athletes who believe in the inalienable right to scratch their balls anytime they want. I am a sportswriter. My job is to tell you the score.

Generally I try not to look at their penises, which is why I always carry at least two felt-tip pens and a steno pad. This way I can take notes without staring at the glans of some poor son of a bitch who has just been demoted to Triple A. But the fact is: penises have a way of intruding upon your field of vision, especially if you are five feet one, which I am. One time I was hiding behind my steno pad talking to Tyrone Jackson, the basketball player, when my notebook began to shake. After that, the line on Tyrone was he really gets off on being interviewed.

So I pretty much thought I had seen it all, until today.

My name is A. B. Berkowitz and I have been a sportswriter at the Washington *Tribune* for nine months now. The initials stand for Ariadne Bloom, which is why everyone except Mom calls me A.B. and why the Washington Senators were a bit surprised the first time I showed up in their locker room. Generally, when people find out what I do for a living, they want to know one thing: who has the biggest schlong in America? You'd be surprised how many different ways there are to ask this question. Dolly Mitchell, the wife of the publisher, showed up at the Christmas party at Duke's, ate forty shrimp balls, blushed, and said in that Betty Boop voice of hers, "So tell me, A.B., honey, just between us girls, who *is* the most impressive ath-uh-lete you've ever met?"

Sal practically hurdled the raw bar to get me before I could say anything. They didn't make him sports editor for nothing.

Two weeks later, he called me into his office and said, "You got the Senators beat. Don't say a fucking word to Mrs. Mitchell."

Today I got the answer to her question.

The answer, Mrs. Mitchell, is the Stick.

It was three hours before game time and everyone was working the room: reporters, agents, assorted hangers-on, everyone who ever made the A list in Washington or thought they should have. The clubhouse was strictly SRO. Opening Day is always a zoo. But everybody in town wanted to be able to say they were there the day baseball returned to Washington. I talked to five senators (elected), three congressmen, Duke Zeibert, the restaurant guy, Lynda Carter, who used to be Wonder Woman, and Dick Bosman, who started the last game at RFK eighteen years ago and learned belatedly the aerodynamic impact of tears on a major league fastball.

Bosman gave up five runs and eight hits in five innings that night, including three home runs, all of which he chalked up to tears. Still, the Senators were winning, 7–5, with two outs in the top of the ninth when the last crowd to see major league baseball in Washington raged onto the field and refused to let the game end. Jim Honochick, the umpire, declared a forfeit at 10:11 P.M., and with that Washington surrendered its right to be called a major league city.

Then last year the Reverend Jimy Boy Collins cut a deal to throw his considerable religioso support in the direction of a particular right-wing presidential candidate, the quid being a promise of an expansion franchise should said candidate get elected. The candidate is now President of These United States, as Jimy Boy likes to say, and the Reverend Collins is owner of the Washington Senators. He calls his born-again Nats a divine reincarnation.

Everybody figured when and if Washington got another team, it would be a National League franchise, what with the Birds in Baltimore. But the American League expanded first and the President kept his promise, using his influence to get Jimy Boy the franchise after the initial ownership went under.

Jimy Boy is also founder of the Christian Fellowship Entertainment Network, the slogan of which is "Jesus rocks 24 hours a day!" and Super Stars Ministry, a Christian outreach program aimed at the spiritual needs of athletes. Jimy Boy says that of all God's children, ballplayers are the most tempted, the most fallen, and the most needy of "getting right with the Lord." On this much we agree. He also believes that ballplayers will be the vehicle by which the Gospel of Jesus Christ is proclaimed worldwide, sports being the one thing, other than Jesus, we all have in common. This is why he bought the Washington Senators. "My mission," he says, "is to soothe 'em, save 'em, and make 'em stars in the Lord's starting lineup."

I'll never forget the first time I met him. This was last winter, just after I got the beat. He kept me waiting in his office at RFK for a half hour. Leaving a reporter alone in your office is a stupid thing to do. I made sure to check out the place. There was a Bible open to Hebrews, with Chapter 12, Verse 1, underlined, a platinum record from Jimy Boy's former career as Christian rocker, and a baseball autographed by all the newly signed born-again members of the 1989 Washington Senators. There was also this smell. Like Muzak in an elevator, it was *everywhere*. And it was awful. It smelled as if somebody had poured a bottle of Chanel No. 5 on a pair of sweat socks after a doubleheader and then boiled them with onions and cloves.

After about ten minutes, my head was pounding. After twenty minutes, I was beginning to gag. By the time Jimy Boy wafted into the room, I was in tears. "Like my new cologne?" he said. "Clubhouse, it's called. I feel perhaps it will help me get closer to the boys."

We got along fine as long as I breathed through my mouth and didn't try to interrupt or leave. When I finally got up to go three hours later, he grabbed my hand and held it till my knuckles cracked. His palm was clammy, his voice soft but urgent. "A.B., I want you to consider the man, Jesus Christ, Who He was and what He says. Either He is Who He says He is or I'm wasting my life."

I told Jimy Boy I was sure he wasn't wasting his life but probably he was wasting his time where the Lord and I were concerned. He said, "I'll pray for you, A.B."

There wasn't much he could do about the Senators' roster except pray. (He actually told me in spring training, "The meek will inherit the outfield." Trust me. It's on tape.) So Jimy Boy put his heart and soul into the locker room. A year ago, this clubhouse was a storage space called the Elephant Room, where visiting football players went to get high before playing the 'Skins. When the renovations began, workmen dug up all sorts of Senators memorabilia—scorecards, pennants, even an old usher's uniform (Number 6), which now hangs behind glass outside the administrative offices. The Elephant Room was a regular archaeological find, all right; buried inside were the hopes and dreams of the faithful.

It's hard to know what to call the present accommodations, which, according to the 1989 Washington Senators media guide, are covered with 240 square yards of plush Dacron polyester custom-made stars-and-stripes two-inch pile. The ceiling is stenciled with amber waves of grain. And over the door to the showers is a trompe l'oeil rendering of Mount Rushmore. "Unbe-fucking-lievable," Monk said the first time he saw it. Monk is the manager. He is also a very religious man.

The players hold court on these little Naugahyde thrones separated by red, white, and blue chain-link fence. Their names are inscribed above in gold leaf: NO. 36 SEN. "STICK" FULLER (DH), and so on. Over the doorway there's a plaque that says IN GOD WE TRUST. Somebody inserted the words AND HIS FASTBALL after GOD, which, Rump says, sort of puts the Almighty in His place.

Rump is the catcher and my best source on the team. Hell, he's everybody's best source on the team. He's what sportswriters call a *talker*, which means he's a godsend. Rump is a guy who can find nuance in every 6–4–3 doubleplay; a one-man Greek chorus, the conscience of the game. He is also a perennial All-Star on the downside of a Hall of Fame career. His locker occupies a place of honor just inside the clubhouse door, beside the bulletin board, where everything of importance that he doesn't say is posted for general consumption.

An hour before the game, Rump and I were standing by his locker reading a story from yesterday's Boston *Globe* predicting that Roger Clemens would open the season by tossing a no-hitter, the weather and the Senators' lineup being what they are. Underneath it were the words NO HITTER MY ASS. And underneath that in smaller letters were the words UNLESS HE'S GOT *HES* GOOD SHIT.

I was too busy laughing to hear the crackle of the Secret Service man's walkie-talkie and the cackle of Jimy Boy Collins announcing, "Ladies and gentlemen, the President of These United States." A flying wedge of blue suits and earpieces surged across the threshold, knocking me on my ass and scattering the A list right quick.

Jimy Boy had been bragging for days that the President of These United States would show for a pregame prayer session. Of course, no one believed him. No President has set foot in RFK since Jimmy Carter. The special presidential elevator, with the buttons 2–3–P–4, and the special presidential holding room have been vacant ever since. People have become skeptical about Jimy Boy's predictions ever since he issued a press release on the first day of spring training guaranteeing that the Lord God will rise up the Nats into first place by September 14. Rump has been wearing a SEPTEMBER 14 T-shirt ever since.

Anyway, there is some debate about what happened next. All I remember is the look on the President's face when he saw Stein standing over an eighty-pound pastry likeness of Old Glory (courtesy of Duke Zeibert) with a fungo bat in his hands and a twisted look in his eyes. "Yaaaa-hah!" Stein said.

You have to understand a little bit about Stein. Until a couple of years ago, he was known primarily around the league as the founder of Jewish Jocks for Jesus (the JJJ). Not that Stein is religious. I wasn't even sure he was Jewish until he announced he wouldn't play on Passover. He just started the whole thing to aggravate Lawson, who is otherwise known as Brother John. Stein and Lawson have more in common than you'd think. They share first base and ex-wives, whom they traded back when they played in Milwaukee, where, Stein said, there was nothing else to do. Soon after, Brother John got religion and Stein got himself a JEWISH JOCKS FOR JESUS T-shirt.

Stein is as vain as he is sacrilegious and worships only at the temple of Stein. Every day you can find him flexing his triceps in front of the clubhouse mirror. Last year he was voted best white body in baseball, which is why the brothers call him White Body when they aren't calling him Dickhead. I overheard Demetrious and Mug Shot talking about him one day in spring training. They are outfielders and two of our seven "men of color," as Jimy Boy likes to call them.

Demetrious says to Mug Shot, "What you call a white boy with a good body?"

Mug Shot takes a minute to think about this. His real name is Michael, but everyone calls him Mug Shot because of his cheerful demeanor and the five-year hitch he served for armed robbery, the majority of which he spent memorizing Webster's Third New International Dictionary. Nowadays he tries to use forty syllables whenever one would do. After carefully considering Demetrious' question, Mug Shot says, "Experientiallywise and tangentiallywise, I call him unusual."

"Must be some blood in there somewheres," Demetrious says.

Stein said it was the nicest thing anyone ever said about him. Now he thinks he's a black, born-again Jewish samurai. He's been hell on cakes ever since.

Anyway, Rump swears Stein could have checked his swing. But I'm not sure. Stein always swings from the heels. I think he had committed himself.

I want you to know how impressed I was by the Secret Service guys. They were awesome. Bat met cake and they hit the floor, shielding the forty-first President of These United States from a hail of chocolate mousse and red, white, and blue icing. "Make sure you put in the Grand Marnier filling," Duke told me later while I was trying to nail down the particulars.

Suffice it to say, there was enough cake to go around. Wonder Woman looked like Whoopi Goldberg. Bosman looked like Al Jolson. And later, in the bottom of the sixth inning, with the Senators losing, 13–0, Mug Shot found the forty-ninth and fiftieth stars in his protective cup while scratching himself on national TV. Sal, who had the binoculars, swears Mug Shot licked his fingers before striking out on an 0–2 pitch out of the strike zone.

Anyway, you don't have to be in Washington very long to know a photo op when you see one. It took the President's aides about thirty seconds to decide that the Chief Executive would make the rounds of the locker room as planned, which he did, except, of course, for a smidge of Grand Marnier filling above one eye. I'm still not clear whether no one wanted to tell the guy about it or whether it was a policy decision to allow him to look human.

The President praised Geronimo Guttierrez, the Nicaraguan shortstop, for his commitment to freedom, which was odd considering three of his brothers died for the revolution fighting the Contras. But Geronimo, who speaks approximately two words of English, beamed and said, "Sí, sí, sure, sure, Your Presidency."

He shook hands with Mancusi, the third baseman with the slipped disc. "Yo," Mancusi said, which is all he ever says, though he did accuse me of misquoting him once in spring training. "What I said was 'Yo, momma.' "

And then the President came to the Stick. But there was no Stick.

There was this awkward moment as the President, the President's men, and this reporter stood together waiting on Kentucky's favorite son, the Louisville Slugger.

"Yo," Mancusi said.

"Yo," Stick replied.

There's a reason they call him the Stick, and quite suddenly all twelve inches of it were preceding him into the locker room toward yours truly and the President of These United States. The Stick was in full throb. Harder, he likes to say, than Chinese arithmetic.

"Unbe-fucking-lievable," Monk said.

"Praise the Lord," Stein said.

"Holy shit," Rump said.

There's been a whole lot of talk for a whole lot of years about women in the locker room, and frankly the whole thing bores me. There are guys, God Squadders like Lawson and Pentacost, for whom this is a true moral dilemma on a par with cheating on their wives. There are guys, the Stick chief among them, who have no such ambivalence, for whom my presence is a challenge and a provocation. And there are guys, maybe one per twenty-four-man roster, for whom nakedness is a metaphor, who understand that the issue is not so much being seen but being seen for what you are. Rump is one of those rare individuals. He is also a catcher from New England, which means he has a sense of honor as well as the absurd. His real name is John Fitzgerald Doubleday.

Like most of the 1989 Senators, Rump has seen better days. I have a picture of him squatting behind home plate at Yankee

Stadium when he broke into the majors sixteen years ago. He hasn't changed much except for the surgeon's tracks on his knees and the perpendicular fingertips. He still has eyes as blue as my grandma's and a bushy red beard. I think he looks like Robin Williams, but it's hard to tell under all that hair. In the picture, he is alone in the Stadium, the way I always wanted to be. The stands are empty and in the distance you can see the original scalloped frieze that Jake Ruppert built. It's not really a dignified way to spend your life, squatting, but Rump knows this and suggested I hang the picture in the bathroom, which I did.

After sixteen years behind the plate, Rump's knees are shot. But he's still got the best arm in the league. And when he grabbed that towel, which like the rug and the cake was in a stars-and-stripes motif, and cocked his arm, well, I had a feeling he was going to cut the Stick down to size.

Rump was standing maybe thirty feet from the Stick, half the distance to the pitcher's mound. He balled up that towel, measured his target, so to speak, and let it rip. The throw was straight and true, guided if you will by some unseen moral radar. Down, down, down, the towel fluttered, coming to rest atop the proud Louisville Slugger, the owner of which suddenly resembled some neo-demigod with his privates sheathed in Old Glory. Monk, Duke, Jimy Boy, Wonder Woman, and the President of These United States watched as the Stick's hard-on succumbed to the first high hard one of the season.

And all the time I was thinking, "How do I get this in the fucking paper?" Which means, I guess, I'm for real.

April 4 I'm sure by now you're asking, "So how did you get to be a sportswriter?" which is what everyone asks after they ask, "So what do you do?" which is what everyone in Washington asks instead of saying hello. This makes me very popular at cocktail parties. "Yes, I go in the locker room. No, I don't *look*. Of course my boyfriend doesn't mind."

I should carry a sign: THIS ISN'T SEXY! THIS IS WORK!

Most people, guys, get this dreamy look on their faces like I've won the lottery or something when I tell them what I do. A few people are simply grossed out. Either way, the simple answer is: my father didn't have any sons. He had to teach somebody how to throw. My older sister was a complete wuss. And my baby sister was into soccer. That left me. I wanted to grow up to be a Yankee.

I wrote some sports in high school and college. But frankly, I really only wanted to play. Looking back, I guess it was natural that I would end up being a writer, since what I wanted to do most I was consigned to observe. But I think also that's why I resisted it. Writing about baseball was second-rate; a violation of intent. Writing meant giving in. And besides, all the sportswriters I ever met were slobs.

In retrospect, you could say newspapers and me were inevitable, though I never thought of it that way until once I was talking to Dad and he said something about the time Mom's father, Grandpa Dave, took us all on a tour of the *Journal-American*, where he worked in the composing room for a couple of years, and how all the girls except me started to cry when he took us down to see the paper running off the presses. I barely knew Grandpa Dave. He died when I was six, soon after he left the paper. We didn't spend much time with Mom's family anyway. But it all came back to me: the roar of the presses, the grease, the deaf men talking to each other in sign language, and the papers, crisp and black and white, rolling off the huge machines. Dad says I took a line of type home with me and kept it under my pillow along with my transistor radio. Funny, I don't remember that.

I do remember my first day of journalism school, when some hotshot handed in his story just as I was getting my margins set and later how I sank lower and lower in my chair while the teacher read my story aloud and said, "This person really needs some work on who, what, where, when, and how." I drank seven gin and tonics, told the president of the university he looked fat, and cried all the way home on the bus.

I also remember the swelling crater in my chest the morning my first story appeared in print. Some of that was just plain ego, of course. But also there was this giddy sense of being part of a vast, energized continuum that turns fact, or in the case of the Washington *Tribune*, what passes for fact, into something irrefutable that lands with a thud every morning at your door.

It was a six-inch story on a party at the Guatemalan Embassy. They told me to file ten inches and they would cut from the bottom. I gave them thirty-six. They didn't just trim it. They scalped it. I didn't care. I woke up at five and went out to get the paper. I was so new in town my subscription hadn't started yet.

The corner store wasn't open, so I walked three blocks in my pajamas and my Burberry raincoat until I found a Washington *Tribune* newspaper box.

One of the many things wrong with Washington is the presence of news boxes where honest-to-God-newsstands ought to be. There are no newsstands in Washington except those stalls in spanking-clean hotel lobbies or stores that call themselves newsstands, all of which are owned by guys named Muhammad and sell the London *Observer* along with *Architectural Digest* and greasy croissants. The corners here belong to guys who peddle Redskin T-shirts and sour grapes.

I remember the first time I got off the train at Union Station and seeing this queue of newspaper boxes: the baby-blue *New York Times,* the gray *Wall Street Journal,* the yellow New York *Post* (yellow journalism!), not to mention boxes for *The Learning Annex, The City Paper,* the Washington *Blade.* It looked like a goddamn cemetery for print journalism.

Newspapers should be delivered, flung with abandon from bicycles by boys with voices that crack, or hawked by guys with a century of newsprint on their fingers. I was five when I bought my first newspaper from one of those smudged men. His name was Monte and he ran an honest-to-God newsstand outside Yankee Stadium by the entrance to the IND. I remember the feel of the nickels, wet and clammy in my hand. I remember the headline too: BOMBERS LOSE! Monte gave me a peppermint with my purchase, a World Series edition of the *Journal-American.* For Grandpa Dave, I guess.

Monte's place was one of those old green shacks that looked as if it was about to collapse on itself. I never saw all of him, just the grizzled cheeks that peered out from beneath the girlie magazines dangling from clothespins over his eyes. Monte always had one hand outstretched and the other in the pocket of his blue printer's apron. He turned giving change into a science. He had an economy of motion that I have envied ever since. Monte was the champion of change, an athlete with dimes and nickels and quarters. And he kept his place neat: the *Times,* the *Post,* the *News,* the *Trib* all stacked crisply beneath lead bars. Grandma took the *News,* my parents the *Herald Tribune.* I never quite understood what it meant to *take* the *Trib* as opposed to reading it or buying it. But I liked the sound of the construction even then. I thought Monte was magic. He had to be to make all those papers inside that little green shack. I guess that's where the mystery of newspapering began for me. And even though I know better now, I have to say that the fact of the morning paper will always be one of the seven wonders of the world in my book. I still tingle when I walk through the newsroom just the way I did the first time I saw it. I wish Monte had been there to sell me the paper the morning my first story hit the streets. He wouldn't have short-changed me.

Anyway, I got the job right out of journalism school, answering phones in the Today section of the *Trib*. Or, I should say, not answering phones, because we all thought we were too good to answer phones and specialized in putting people on hold. The paper was in trouble then and offering buy-outs to former ace reporters now deemed deadwood. So lots of us copy aides got to write. After a year, they offered me a staff job for the exalted salary of $13,000, which was illegal or something, but I didn't care. I did a little bit of everything—party stuff, of which there is a disgusting amount in Washington, talking heads (celebs doing five minutes per in hotel suites), and the feature angle on any particularly revolting local crime, which is how I officially met Michael last April, fighting over who got to ask a grieving widow how she felt.

Actually, I had met him once before, collided with him, really, during a softball game four years ago. It was the night I became the *Trib*'s starting pitcher. Sal is my battery mate. He makes an interesting target, Sal. You might even say an inviting target. Sal is the Ichabod Crane of sports editors—six feet six and 140 pounds. Nonetheless, he insists upon catching. It's actually painful watching him get into his crouch. He kind of collapses like a tire jack. His knees come up and his elbows come down and there's nothing in the middle to aim at. Pitching to him is like pitching to a cipher. He isn't even as wide as home plate.

We were playing the *Post* down at the Ellipse. It was 19–19 after six. In the top of the seventh, I gave up a leadoff double to some hotshot named Michael Holliday. The next batter hit a wicked line drive to my friend Ruth, who was playing shortfield that day. Michael did not hesitate coming around third. Sal did not hesitate and set himself at the plate. Ruth's throw and Michael arrived simultaneously. The collision was fierce. Michael had not even bothered to slide. He simply put his shoulder down and knocked Sal backward into the picnic area. However, the force of the impact also carried Michael past the plate, which, I noted, he had not touched. I was backing up on the play. There was a scramble. Michael dived for the plate. I dived for the ball. I landed on top of him for the first time and tagged him out.

"Heads up," he said.

I accepted the compliment but not the allusion or the invitation for a drink. We didn't meet again until last spring when the Today section called me off the ball field to go cover the murder of a poet up on the Gold Coast.

Anyway, for the last four years, Sal has been yelling, "Hum it on in there, babe!" at me and nudging me to come over to Sports. Finally, one day last spring after we combined for a nifty twenty-two-hitter, we all went out for crabs and beer and he said how he had to go hire himself a baseball writer now that Washington was getting a franchise.

That got me thinking. I was almost twenty-nine. I'd been writing Today stories for five years; and all my ledes were beginning to sound the same. Suddenly "baseball writer" didn't sound like heresy. Besides I figured it was now or never. Not that I was contemplating quitting to write a novel or anything. It's just that women sportswriters, like fecund careerists, operate on a unique biological clock. You're okay as long as the naked person on the other side of the notebook is a peer. Once you're old enough to be his mother, locker room interviews get to be a real problem.

I told Sal I might be interested. He suggested I write a couple of pieces to see how I liked it before making up my mind. It was just before the NBA playoffs. Sal had this great idea about jocks getting all pretty and sissified. Despite the fact that athletes still spit and scratch and share their bodily fluids with almost anyone on the planet, vanity is hardly a new locker room development. Maybe this was news back in the sixties when Joe Pepitone got fined for bringing a hair dryer into the Yankees' clubhouse and Jim Bouton filled it with baby powder. But there's no arguing with an editor who thinks he has thought of something new. So I said, sure, sounds great, and went off to interview some professional basketball players with Marcus Johnson, the NBA beat guy, who is himself a handsome young black dude.

Marcus left me standing at the threshold of the Bullets' locker room at the Capital Centre and the damnedest thing happened: I couldn't make myself cross it. After a lifetime of being on the outside looking in, suddenly I wasn't sure I wanted to go inside. I wasn't sure what I was relinquishing or what I was getting myself into. Of course, it wasn't exactly as if I had any choice.

I was still cowering by the door when Marcus returned from interviewing the Lakers and grabbed my arm and dragged me in.

You know what I did my first time in the locker room? I stared at the walls. They are cinder-block walls, much like the cinder-block walls you find in college dormitories and penal institutions. I looked at those cinder blocks like I had never looked at cinder blocks before. They had strength. They had mass. They had structural integrity. At that particular moment, cinder blocks struck me as the single greatest development of Western civilization and I could have studied them forever.

I felt an arm around me. It was a very long, very wet, very white arm. It belonged to Gordo Conally, the whitest man in the NBA. Gordo is known for his forty-six-inch shirt sleeve and his ability to block any inbounds pass. His arms are approximately as long as me.

" 'Scuse me," Gordo said. "But is this your first time?"

I checked the cinder blocks and thought about lying. But the handwriting was on the wall. "My parents didn't raise me to embarrass people," I said.

Gordo nodded. His very long, very wet, very white arm was still around me. When I say around me, I mean: all the way around me. It was like being encircled by a long, wet, white noose. "Well," he said, "I just want you to know you're doing very well and we all appreciate it."

Then he was gone. Then all the other reporters were gone. And for the first time in my life I was alone with a locker room full of naked men I did not know. I was still standing there five minutes later when Gordo returned, as wet and as white as before. "By the way," he said, "what are you doing here anyway?"

I explained the pretty jocks angle. Gordo is from Iowa. He is not a pretty jock. Marcus says threadwise he is the biggest geek in the league. He hasn't even heard of the Aqua Velva man. But he understood what I needed.

Across the room, Xavier Starling, the flashiest ball handler in the league, sat rubbing cocoa butter into his thighs. "Hey, Star," Gordo said. "You got some smells?"

"Smells?" Star said.

"Yeah, you know, smells."

Star got up from his bench, opened the lid on his trunk, and began extracting smells: Paco Rabanne, Chaps, Hero, and Andron by Jōvan; Woodhue, Dallas, Timber Line, Sweet Sweat, and, of course, Sex Appeal. "Now you don't have to be born with it." Gordo tried them all, prancing back and forth stark naked except for his smells. The conflagration of aromas smelled worse than the Bullets ever did.

"What do you think of this, man?" Gordo said, sniffing his wrist like one of those overrouged ladies in Saks Fifth Avenue. "What kind of statement would you say this makes?"

"Red," Star said. "Definitely red. I myself am definitely in a red mood tonight."

By this time, Gordo had sprayed himself with twelve colognes, slapped his cheeks with eight after-shaves, moisturized his skin with six moisturizers, dabbed himself with four fragranced sun blocks, perfumed the air with Consort hairspray, massaged his scalp with Right On Curl, a Wet Look activator moisturizer, and saturated his very long, very wet, very white arms with Ambi cocoa butter in the name of racial equality.

"What's this, man?" Gordo said, reaching for a little plastic bag with a cap inside that looked vaguely like a yarmulke.

"It's a doo rag," Star said.

"A doo rag?"

"You know, for your *doo.* Your hair, your *doo.*"

Gordo put it on his head and shrugged. "Yeah," he said. "But ain't you got nothing for the pits, man?"

That was the day I decided to become a sportswriter. That was the day I decided after years of insisting otherwise that it was okay to want to be just one of the guys. Everybody thought it was a great idea except Mom, who would have been happier if I was writing for *Vogue,* and Ruth, the feminist junk bonds reporter, who would have been happier if I was writing about sexual harassment in the workplace. I promised her I would. And thanks to the Stick, I already have.

The day I came over to Sports, which was last June 25, Dad called and said, "Finally." Michael, who was new at the paper and new in my life, called and said, "You know why we're meant for each other? We both cover a bunch of stiffs."

And that's why I'm sitting here at Marcus's desk, staring at a Day-Glo orange sign that says SIT ON MY FACE and trying to find another euphemism for a twelve-inch erection.

I sent out a system-wide message to the newsroom asking for help. I got a lot of good suggestions, but I liked Michael's best: "I just call mine 'sir,'" it said.

Today is an off-day and we'll probably get rained out tomorrow, so we won't play again until we get to New York Thursday.

That means Jimy Boy and Monk have forty-eight hours to decide what to do with the Stick and I have another story to write about him without using the word "penis." I used "manly protuberance" at least six times yesterday. I can't think of what else there is to say. But Sal can. Sal's got what you call a nose for the news, especially if it involves schlonging and donging and especially if it happens to be a slow news day. He'll milk this baby for a week.

Jimy Boy is off on retreat praying for Stick's soul and trying to decide how much to fine him. (Somehow I don't think your basic eye-for-an-eye methodology is going to work here.) All Monk has to say is "Unbe-fucking-lievable." And everyone else, including the Stick, has only one comment: "The Stick's gotta be the Stick." In sports everyone talks about themselves in the third person as if they're all having an out-of-body experience. I think it's their way of saying they're not going to take any more responsibility for what they say than for what they do.

I've got nothing.

Except an anecdote about the time the President went to an Orioles game last season and somebody's protective cup set off the alarm on the security system when he tried to get back into the clubhouse.

"Make some calls, Berkowitz," Sal said. "You ever hear of legwork? I want sixteen inches by three."

To which Roth, the high school editor, replied, "He should live so long." And Dr. Deadline said, "Yeah, that's why they call him the Little Guy."

Around here, everybody is either a Big Guy or a Little Guy. Occasionally, someone is both, though usually that's ironic. Athletes are always Big Guys, as in "The Big Guy came to play." Editors, no matter how big they are, are always Little Guys unless you're talking to them, in which case they immediately become Big Guys. The reverse is true of friends.

Stick is definitely a Big Guy today. He's front-page all over the country. It's days like this that make me glad I work for a feisty little tab like the *Trib*, which is to say a scummy rag specializing in boobs, bodies, and baseball. The *New York Times* ran a story on A1 with a carefully cropped picture and an even more carefully crafted lede about a "pregame locker-room display of sexual preparedness." We had a 360-point headline BONER! and a full-page picture of the Stick fondling his bat. Sal loved my lede. "On the day baseball returned to Washington, the Stick rose to the occasion. And as a result, no one will remember that Roger

Clemens pitched a no-hitter in the first major league baseball game in Washington in 18 years. The Senators lost, 19–0. It was the ultimate laugher."

I guess I should have expected as much from the Stick. The first day of spring training he pinned me against the outfield wall, bellowed, "Women, that's for me," and sucked on my jugular until Rump pulled him off. He's a type, all right. He's the guy you've seen in the corridor of every high school in America with one arm draped around an unopened stack of textbooks and the other pulling on an unsuspecting bra strap. Once he had a flattop; now he has a rat's tail. But he really hasn't changed. He's still the Jock. He still has the same flat, pasty, featureless face that could be one thousand other faces; a face that will age and jowl and degenerate into something approximately as distinct as a pig's ass.

The Stick divides women into two categories. Either you're a mullion, which is to say a dog, or you're fuckable. One thing you can say for the guy—he doesn't set impossible standards. He goes to bed every night with his bat and only refers to himself in the third person or occasionally as the Louisville Slugger. He also wears a necklace of the great god Priapus. They are very big around the league this year. From a distance, the copper pendant looks sort of abstract, like a tortured figure from Dachau. It's only up close that you can tell it's a guy with a hard-on.

It was the third day of spring training when the performances began. Every day the same thing. I come into the clubhouse, the Stick goes into the shower. Three minutes later the Louisville Slugger is parading around the locker room at full mast. "Like clockwork," Rump says.

Even some of the other players started to get grossed out. I figured the best thing to do was ignore him. I never thought it would get this far. I mean, I've heard all the stories about women reporters who get hit on, and dumped on, and get dead rats in the mail. But this?

Sal keeps telling me I'm gonna have to suck it up and play hurt before it's all over. "It's us against them, Berkowitz," he says, "and the jockos are winning." I don't know if he's trying to scare me or what, but so far I'm inclined to laugh or at least fake it.

Like the other day before coming north. I was standing talking to Billy Blessing, the rookie, when the Stick presented himself in all his glory.

"I also give good phone," he said, winking.

So I asked for his number.

"Jesus," Billy said.

I called it this morning and got the Stick's machine. He pants until the beep.

April 5   My grandmother, Delia Bloom Berkowitz, lived one block from Yankee Stadium in a building called the Yankee Arms. In all the time I knew her, she never set foot in the Stadium whose shadow crossed her parlor at five o'clock on summer afternoons. I told my friends you could see the outfield wall from her front window, which was a lie, and that you could hear the crack of the bat in her living room before you could hear Mel Allen's voice on the radio, which may or may not have been true. Exaggeration was a way of life for me then.

Delia Berkowitz was a small woman with large breasts and lots of rose sachet in her dresser drawers. I am her size and Mom says I have her shape. When she died the only thing I asked for was the porcelain heart in which she kept her rose sachet. I keep paperclips in it now.

Sometimes when I think about how I ended up here, standing in a locker room full of naked men I do not know talking about good skull, which is what the Washington Senators call a blow job, I think about her. I think probably she'd laugh but only in private, the way she did when I was three and told an old maiden aunt to buzz off or I'd shoot my airplane up her vagina. I can still see Grandma peering through the glass french doors trying not to laugh, or at least I think I can.

I think somebody gives you permission for the things you do, permission to put paperclips where once there was rose sachet. Somebody gave me permission to do this and that somebody was her.

When I was four, she put on her open-toed shoes and I put on my Mary Janes and we took the CC train downtown to Saks Fifth Avenue to buy me a baseball glove. A few of the trains still had those old straw seats then, and the bristles caught in my tights and we almost missed the stop while trying to get me untangled. I always got tangled up when I tried to be a girl.

We bought a glove, the only one they had, a Sam Esposito model, and though no one including me had ever heard of him, I told Grandma he was a Yankee. Many years later, I looked him up in the Baseball Encyclopedia and found he retired the year we bought the glove that bore his name. What did Saks know?

Sammy was my first hero. He played ten years in the majors, all but eighteen games for the Chicago White Sox, and retired in 1963, with a career batting average of .207, disappearing into the fine print of the Baseball Encyclopedia, where everyone is created equal even if they only hit eight home runs lifetime.

I took Sammy with me everywhere, including to Temple on the High Holy Days. Services were held in the ballroom of the Concourse Plaza Hotel at the corner of 161st Street and the Grand Concourse up the hill from the Stadium, where visiting teams stayed in Babe Ruth's day. Delia Berkowitz was a religious woman, but she loved her grandchildren more than she loved God. And so she hid me and Sammy and my transistor radio inside her mink coat until we got past the old men downstairs in their prayer shawls and yarmulkes. I told everyone she got the coat two sizes too big because she wanted to make room for Sam and me. My mother says she got it two sizes too big because it was on sale. Maybe. But that isn't why she wore it to Temple on warm fall afternoons.

The drapes in the ballroom were thick burgundy velvet with gold-braided ties. Any self-respecting five-year-old could get lost in the folds of those drapes, which I did, watching a fraction of the 1964 World Series from the ballroom window while my grandmother prayed and sang for my future. I heard the shofar in one ear and Mel Allen in the other.

The hotel sat just high enough upon the hill that a forty-inch person standing on tippy-toes in her best Mary Janes could see over Joyce Kilmer Park, where black men still called Negroes sold towers of undulating balloons to white children, past Addie Vallin's ice cream parlor, where Grandma ate one too many ice cream sodas and consigned herself to an adulthood of diabetes, to the concrete and copper of the outfield wall, which parted just enough to allow a glimpse of centerfield and a flanneled figure running hard after an unseen ball. This was how I saw things then. This was my reality—a swath of vision cut through a gap in the outfield wall.

By the time I was nine I knew I was going to grow up to be Joey Proud, the Yankees centerfielder. My parents, who had other faults, never bothered to tell me this might be a problem. Every afternoon I practiced against the garage door of their home at 5234 Eldridge Court in New Rochelle, New York. Bending, scooping, making the throw; one knee to the gravel, hands caressing the ball in the pocket of my Sam Esposito glove, making the peg from deep centerfield to an X chalked on the middle of the garage door. It was the only house in the neighborhood painted pink. Every day when the sun went down, the whole damn thing vibrated. I couldn't believe they had done this to me. My father was sympathetic but all he said was, "Your mother is bored."

Every night I stood in front of the television watching the game and practicing my swing. I always swung for the seats. I even practiced fouling the ball off my foot. Mom would come in the den and find me limping around the rug, walking off the pain. I never said a word and neither did she. By the time I was nine I knew you gotta play hurt.

Joey came up in 1968, the summer of Bobby Kennedy and the riots. Everybody said he was the next Mickey Mantle, which of course was the kiss of death. Like the Mick, Joey was a white boy who could run black. And like the Mick, Joey didn't stay whole very long. Mantle was a hick with a blond cowlick and unspeakable dreams. Joey was a city kid with curly black hair who grew up playing sewer ball in Sheepshead Bay and running for the BMT. "So much for country hardball," he used to say.

Guys who knew him when talk about the time he hit one twelve sewers. The legend prospered, and by the time he showed up at St. John's his freshman year, it was commonly accepted fact that he had decimated a pink Spaldeen one June afternoon with a swat that left half the ball on Avenue X and other half on Avenue Y. They called him the Sultan of Spaldeen.

His looks were as prodigious as his stroke. He was Cupid in flannels: with smiling green eyes, the longest lashes you've ever seen, and brows that met above his nose and made him look more serious than he ever was. He was a kid from the nabe; a hang-out kind of guy. *"Che si dice,"* he always said. What's happening? What do you say? *"Che si dice?"* the writers asked after every game.

He was born Joey Provenzano, the only son of Anthony and Juliana, who made the best pizza crust in the borough and wanted something better for their son. Joey promised to get a good education. And he did. His first week at St. John's, the athletic director changed Joey's name to Proud. "Marketing," he explained.

Joey's mom, who never learned to speak English, went to

church and prayed for forgiveness. Joey kneeled beside her and whispered in Italian that it would be okay. Years later, long after baseball made it easy for him to stop going to Sunday mass, Joey still crossed himself every time he stepped into the batter's box. Needless to say, so did I.

St. John's also tried to make Joey a switch-hitter so he would be even more like Mickey Mantle. Joey was a pure left-handed swinger; a natural for the Stadium's short rightfield porch. He told the coaches: *"A-fan-culo."* Joey never told anyone to get fucked in English.

Everybody thought he was just being proud. But that wasn't it at all. Mickey was Joey's hero just as Joey was mine. Unlike me, Joey didn't try to imitate Mickey's every gesture. Joey refused to presume he was going to be as good as the Mick.

He signed with the Yankees the day his freshman season ended and received an unprecedented bonus worth almost as much as Mantle made that year, his last in the majors. Joey also negotiated a special clause in his contract allowing him to wear his own tailor-made flannel uniform. Joey was the real thing, all right. He was also allergic to polyester.

In his first major league at bat, he hit a home run, a soaring, majestic shot that seemed to foreshadow the arc of his ambitions. The Stadium went crazy. All those Yankee haters from Brooklyn cuckolded by Walter O'Malley purged their pain with a whoop of delight for one of their own. Joey rounded the bases and found his hero, the Mick, waiting for him at home plate. He went 3 for 4 that day with 3 RBIs and was deep into a postgame oration when Pete Sheehy, the clubhouse man, came and whispered in his ear that his father was dead of a heart attack, at age forty-three. Dropped dead in the stands as Joey rounded the bases in the bottom of the first.

Joey went home to Brooklyn that night, buried his father a day later, and was in the starting lineup when the Yankees opened a three-game set against the Red Sox the day after that. "You gotta play hurt," Joey said.

From then on, he played every day as if his heart might break. Sportswriters are very big on heart. If a guy doesn't choke on a 3–2 pitch in the bottom of the ninth, they say he's got heart. Joey Proud made "heart" a cliché. He said he had never seen things so clearly; had never seen the ball so well. He had an eternity to decide what to do with every pitch. After three months in the majors, he was hitting .391, with 17 home runs and 51 RBIs. He was zoned with the angels.

In those days, my grandparents spent their summers playing bingo on the boardwalk in Long Beach. They wanted no part of the heat of the Bronx or the pennant race. So it was late September before I got to see Joey for myself at the Stadium. We had box seats along the third base line. It was a cold, raw night. By the end of the fifth, dew was embracing the outfield grass. I clenched my teeth so they wouldn't chatter. By the bottom of the ninth, the stands were almost empty and my mother was agitating to leave. Chocolate cake was waiting at Grandma's. Joey Proud was waiting on deck.

The game meant nothing except on its own terms. Win or lose, the Yankees were still going to finish fifth. Joey was still going to be Rookie of the Year.

I can close my eyes and see that uppercut swing as he pointed the bat again and again at the pitcher. He had a habit, between swings, of curling his fingers around the bat, one finger at a time, the way you play an arpeggio on a piano. It was as if he couldn't quite get a grip on something; as if he knew everything was one swing from flying out of his grasp.

He lunged at the ball, which was low and away, and turned instinctively toward first. A slow roller, they call it, a slow roller to short. It had infield hit written all over it. In moments like this, baseball forces you to make a choice. You can watch the shortstop charging, or the path of the ball, or the runner racing down the baseline against the geometry of aerodynamic flight. You cannot watch it all.

Joey was maybe a yard from the bag, straining to beat out the inevitable, when his leg caved in. The violence of the injury was oddly beautiful to see. He was a dancer in mid-leap, his legs extended beyond reach or reason. He hung there for an instant, or so it seemed, before the force of gravity sucked him to the ground, splayed in the basepath, covered with chalk. His fingers kept feeling for the bag.

"*Cretino,*" he said, "*cretino.*"

They carried him off the field on a stretcher and into the hospital, where surgeons cut off his tailor-made flannel uniform and tried to reconfigure his shredded Achilles tendon. He promised he'd be back. And he was. But he was never really the same.

Two years later, they moved him from center to first, and then finally to designated hitter. Joey said they cut off his balls the day they told him to put away his glove. My father said Willie was better anyway and maybe even Mickey, which was supposed to make me feel better, but it didn't. Joey was my guy. One time, Grandma and I stood outside the Stadium waiting for an autograph for an hour. Joey farted as he walked by.

I read his bio, *Proud of the Yankees*, and committed his stats to memory. I knew his wedding date and the birth weight of his two daughters and his only son, Joey Jr., who was born two months early and frail. But it was the unknowns that consumed me. What if Joey hadn't tried to beat out the throw on a meaningless bouncer to short on a raw September night?

They say that every great slugger has a hole in his swing, a vulnerable place in the arc of presumed contact. Joey had a hole in his leg and another in his heart. He was a real-life hero with a real-life Achilles heel. I couldn't have known it then, but I think maybe that's what I liked so much about him, that prodigious what-if.

In the spring of 1972, Dad was transferred to Richmond. I couldn't get the Yankee games on the radio anymore, which was probably just as well considering I was entering puberty surrounded by magnolia trees and blossoming Southern belles. Then Mom left, and Grandma died a year later, without ever having set foot in the Stadium, without ever regretting it, without teaching me how to be a girl. I dialed her number every night and listened to the ring, waiting for someone to answer. Finally someone did and I stopped calling.

That fall they tore down the House That Ruth Built, demolishing the green copper frieze that cast a shadow over my childhood. In his last at bat before the wreckers came, Joey hit a ball out of Yankee Stadium. The Yankees were playing the Orioles that night, so I was listening with the transistor under my pillow. I remember the silence before the pitch. "Proud steps in. McNally rocks and deals. The pitch is swung on and . . . it's going. It's going. It's *still* going! Holy cow! It's gone *out* of Yankee Stadium!"

Joey had done what no one, not Ruth, not Gehrig, not Mantle, had ever done before. And all it did was rekindle all those what-ifs. A kid found the ball later on 158th Street, half a block from Grandma's window.

The season ended. The Bombers finished fourth and I got my period. My career as a Yankee was over.

I want to get to the Stadium early tomorrow. I haven't been there since Grandma died.

New York

April 6   Well, I finally made it to the Yankees' locker room.

Talk about a letdown. I don't know what I was expecting. Something. A welcoming committee headed by Casey Stengel or at least a scent of history. But there wasn't anything in that room that smelled of Yankee pride or tradition unless you count the picnic table where the Bambino overate fifty years ago. There wasn't any smell at all, except Mr. Clean. The carpet was this reddish blue, not pin-striped. The walls were Georgia Pacific. The locker room was empty except for two Latin ballplayers I didn't recognize sitting on leather sectionals playing cards and scratching themselves and screaming at each other in high-pitched Spanish.

It was 2:00 P.M. when I arrived. No one gets to the ballpark at 2:00 P.M. unless they're injured or divorced. I'm always getting places too early, or too late, depending on your point of view. Last year, when I was still writing for Today, the paper sent me down to Florida to go to one of those fantasy baseball camps and to do an Opening Day piece on Doc Gooden. I showed up at Port St. Lucie around 9:00 A.M. for a 7:35 P.M. game and couldn't figure out why none of the Mets were there. So I asked someone in public relations. "On game days, they drift in around noon," the girl said. I guess I must have looked confused. "It's a job," she said.

I stood there in the Yankee clubhouse looking stupid, just as I had stood there looking stupid last spring. I didn't really want to ask anybody anything. I didn't even know who they were, or care.

I just wanted to see where Joey put his pants on one leg at a time, where Reggie flashed his wad, where Wally Pipp nursed his headache. I wanted to commune with the Babe and the Clipper and the Scooter and the Mick. But the Latinos didn't know that. All they knew was that they didn't want to be looked at sitting there in their underwear playing cards and scratching themselves. They certainly didn't know I was looking for ghosts, not them.

"Hey, lady *sportwriter*! You want some *white ink*, lady *sportwriter*?"

One of them grabbed his crotch just to make his point clear. Halfway down the hall to the visitors' locker room I could still hear him cackling.

Monk said he wanted to see me at two-thirty. He was sitting in the manager's office wearing his civvies when I walked in. Civvies are what baseball players call regular clothes. Civvies are serious. Civvies mean business. I was tempted to ask if he had ever heard of white ink, but thought better of it. Monk is a very religious man. His real name is Elmo, which explains why everyone calls him Monk. Also he has these little hooded eyes and a few wisps of hair that emerge from the side of his head at right angles to his scalp.

There was a copy of Tuesday's *Trib* sitting on the desk in front of him and he had it open to my Opening Day game story. I could see a whole lot of red ink from where I stood, which was better than white ink, I guess. He didn't look up. He didn't say hello. He just began to read.

" 'The Washington Senators began the future by reclaiming the past yesterday. They lost to the Boston Red Sox, 19–0, which means, if you count the last time they played in Robert F. Kennedy Memorial Stadium in 1971, the Senators haven't won a game in 18 years, the longest losing streak in the history of professional sports. The Senators didn't so much begin anew as start right where they left off.' "

Monk has a two-packs-a-day voice, gravelly yet strangely high-pitched. It's a voice that's ridden too many buses on too many back roads. You can hear the miles in his voice, and the bumps, too, especially when it cracks, which it does every time he gets truly pissed. And Monk was truly pissed.

"This is a horseshit story," he said.

"Gee, I kind of like it, Monk."

"It's horseshit. And I don't need no horseshit writer for a horseshit paper coming in here and getting my boys upset with negative fucking horseshit. Ain't you never heard of positive fucking horseshit?"

Until he was named manager of the Washington Senators, Monk McGuire was known chiefly for three things: his twenty-three-year tenure in various coaching boxes around the major

leagues, his disconcerting tendency to sit on a bat with its handle
stuck in the crack of his ass, and the foulest mouth in the major
leagues. I've heard the bootleg tapes of some of his famous rants.
This one had the makings of a classic. His voice cracked every
time he said "horseshit," shooting up an octave between the
"horse" and the "shit." It was hard enough to keep a straight
face, much less think of something that might appease him. So I
told him the only thing I could promise him was fair fucking
horseshit, which didn't help.

Tobacco juice and spittle were running down Monk's chin
the way creamed herring used to run down Grandpa's. He spat
at the paper and for a moment I thought it was involuntary until
he aimed a practiced chaw at me and started reading again.

" 'The Senators, who set a major league record for spring
training losses, were held hitless by Roger Clemens, who spared
them the indignity of a perfect game by walking the leadoff batter in the bottom of the ninth. The Washington defense was
worse, committing six errors, three on one play. In the fifth,
centerfielder Mug Shot Hackett turned a single into a double by
kicking the ball to the outfield wall. Rightfielder Demetrious
Mourning retrieved the ball and overthrew the cutoff man.
Third baseman Joe Mancusi then heaved the thing over the
catcher's head into the Boston dugout, where it landed in a duffel
bag of practice balls.

" 'For 18 long years, the nation's capital has yearned to have
baseball back in Washington. On Opening Day of the season,
whatever it was that was back in town wasn't baseball. It was
theater of the absurd.' "

Monk methodically ripped the paper to shreds and glared at
me. "You call that *fair* fucking horseshit?"

"Well, Monk, I call it unbe-fucking-lievable."

His voice cracked and soared. "Unbe-fucking-lievable? I'll
give you unbe-fucking-lievable. Some fucking horseshit reporter
who don't know horseshit about squat comes in my fucking clubhouse and calls us unbe-fucking-lievable? What major fucking
league did you star in, missy? I'll tell you what. You are horseshit.
You write horseshit. And your paper is horseshit. You got that?
Horseshit! Now get outta here before I say something I might
regret."

At which point, Monk spat out his chaw and crossed himself. Monk is a very religious man.

"Horseshit" is ubiquitous in the locker room, as is religion.

27

Horseshit game. Horseshit pitch. Horseshit food. There is almost no bullshit in the locker room. For some reason baseball players prefer horseshit to bullshit. I always thought it had something to do with the old horsehide. But Rump says no. "Just always been horseshit," he says.

"Horseshit" is an all-purpose modifier, the adjective of choice, except of course when used as an exclamation meaning you're full of it. In the *Trib*, of course, it is transmogrified into that other ubiquitous entity, "horsespit" or "horsebleep," although "bleep" is much more commonly used as an exclamation ("Oh, bleep!"), a verb ("Bleep you"), or an adverb ("You bleeping bleepsucker") or in Monk's case ("Unbe-bleeping-lievable"). "Bleeping" and "horsespit" have been staples of the sports page for some twenty years now since a bleeping horsespit columnist (now deceased) for a New York paper discovered he could not cover a bleeping horsespit baseball game without "bleep" and "horsespit." This was not so much a reflection on the modern ballplayer as it was an editorial judgment that said ballplayers had something worthwhile to say. Baseball players have always been full of horsespit and bleep. It's just that nobody ever quoted them that way. Nobody ever quoted them at all. Nowadays we are very precise about quoting these bleepers accurately, which is why every locker room story begins with "Hey" (a contraction of "Hey, man"), unless, of course, the sentence begins with "Horseshit." I have never heard a ballplayer say, "Hey, horseshit." There is no antecedent to "horseshit."

Anyway, it's 4:00 P.M. now and I'm alone in the press box. The shadows are drifting across the pitcher's mound. Dirt has never looked so brown or grass so green or sky so blue. It's like discovering the original of something. Out beyond the center-field fence, the monuments to Ruth and Gehrig and Huggins are still bathed in a warm spring sun. George Steinbrenner once threatened to build a waterfall out there as a gesture to the youth of the South Bronx. But he never did. Probably spent the money on a .500 pitcher instead. Just over the wall is the building where my grandmother lived for twenty years in the shadow of the copper frieze that Jake Ruppert built. You can still see the Number 4 train for an instant as it leaves the 161st Street station, and in the distance the Bronx County Courthouse, where old men still sell towers of undulating balloons to young children. Thank God, some things remain the same.

I just got off the phone with Sal. I told him about Monk,

though not the white ink. He wants verbatim notes on everything Monk says. "Tape the mother" were his exact words. He
also says he wants more bleeping horsespit in my stories.

April 7 I got back to the hotel late, maybe 1:00 A.M. Two
games, two losses, and already I'm having trouble thinking of
things to say. I was ten minutes late on deadline and had to take
the subway back downtown.

I came through the revolving doors feeling very glad to be
alive and saw security guards swarming all over the lobby. Piggy,
the bullpen coach, who is the bullpen coach only because he is
also the father of Stretch McCarthy, our fireballing young right-
hander, was standing at the front desk screaming, "Where the
fuck is Beanie?"

Beanie is Jimy Boy's flak. He played a couple of years in the
St. Louis minor league system until he got beaned leaning into a
3–2 pitch. That's when he stopped being a player and started
being a baseball man. There's a difference between ballplayers
and baseball men. Players stay young in the game. Baseball men
grow old with it. Beanie is a baseball man. He wears loud plaid
sports coats and a beeper so Jimy Boy can find him at all times. I
knew right away if Piggy was screaming for Beanie, there had to
be some bleep involved. Like Sal says, "You gotta have a nose for
the news." Also for bleep.

Sure enough, over in the corner by the newsstand, there was
this pile of blue-shirted security guards writhing around on the
floor, and at the bottom of the pile a muffled voice was screaming, *"No! No! Stop, you bitch! No!"*

I wandered over and saw a whole bunch of players, Rump
and Stein and Billy Blessing and Al Brawn, the reserve outfielder, standing around listening to the pile groan.

"What's up?"

"Stick's in love," Rump explained.

"So?"

"She's not a nice girl."

"So?"

"She's not a *girl* at all," Billy said.

"You think he knows?" Brawn said.

"Nah," Stein said. "Me and Stick were out hounding the
beef—"

"Hounding the beef?" I asked.

"An act of courtship," Rump explained.

"Yeah, you know, chasing some skank, wool patrol," Stein said impatiently. "But nothing. So we had a few pops and come back to the hotel. Well, maybe more than a few pops. Anyways. Stick sees this girl just standing there. At least, he thinks it's a girl. But like I say, he's had a few pops. And before you know it, he's all over her. Uh, him. You know the way Stick gets. 'Come on, baby. Come to the Stick. My Louisville Slugger is as hard as Chinese arithmetic.' "

The pile began to quake and heave. There was an eruption of taffeta and tweed. Now two voices were bellowing, both husky and indignant, "*No! No! No!*"

It was hard to tell which of them was yelling louder but I think it was the Stick, who was being pulled kicking and screaming from the manly object of his affections. Piggy dragged him away to the elevator and Stick began to sing "My Cherie Amour."

A deep, unmistakably male voice interrupted the serenade. "Somebody gonna give me a hand?" he said tartly.

He was lying there spread-eagled on the lobby floor, a vision of loveliness in a heap of peach taffeta. His skirt was up around his thighs, his bun had come undone, and there was tangerine lip gloss all over his bosom. Yet somehow his dignity was intact.

"A fine figure of a woman," Rump said.

"A fine figure of a man," Billy replied.

Gallantly they hoisted him to his feet. He was a stately creature: six feet tall and well built, if you like the type. He rearranged his skirts, asked for his purse, and opened his compact. Evidently he didn't like what he saw. "The brute," he whimpered.

Beanie arrived just about then, a wad of bills clutched in the palm of his hand. Apparently Piggy had told him the nature of the bleeping problem. "You aren't gonna press charges, are you, mister . . . ?" Beanie said, counting out four fifties. Beanie's a real subtle guy.

"Dale," he said. "My name is Dale."

"Well, Mr. Dale," Beanie said, peeling off another two bills.

"Just Dale."

"Well, Dale?"

"Well," said Dale. "He *was* a humpy little number."

Beanie handed him the rest of the roll, which Dale demurely tucked inside his ample brassiere.

"The charges," Beanie said.

"Honey," Dale said, "transvestites don't press charges." And with that he swept up his skirt and was gone.

Everyone was feeling merry, so we decided to get a drink. I was pretty beat, actually. But it's my policy not to turn down any respectable invitation from these guys. So Stein and Rump and Billy and Brawn and I went to get a beer. They were pretty impressed by Stick's performance, judging by how much they went on about it and his three-year $2.1 million guaranteed contract. The Stick has two subjects of conversation: his money and his dick. When he isn't fondling himself, he's fondling his billfold, which he says is as thick as his Stick is hard. I guess in his mind they're sort of interchangeable.

"Best part is Stick even offered to *pay* the guy," Stein said. "You know how he is, always peeling hundreds off his wad."

"Oh my God," Rump said. "You mean Stick paid a transvestite?"

"Gotta be a first," Billy said.

"Nah," I said. "It's been done. Guy in our department, Vito Marchese, did it three years ago."

I was not just making idle conversation. It was a calculated decision telling them about Vito, just the way it is every time I say "fuck" around them. It's weird, but it's the only way I know to make them feel comfortable with me. So I curse more than usual and use a lot of double negatives, and if I get the chance to indulge in some macho one-upmanship, I grab it.

Vito is our hockey writer. One night, three years ago, he got rolled by a transvestite at the NHL All-Star Game. Only Vito could end up in bed with a transvestite who called himself Canuck. Anyway, the guy rolled him, tied him, and, believe it or not, painted Vito red, white, and blue. Just like a barbershop pole. Vito, who's no rocket scientist, actually called the cops and filed a report on his missing wallet. Honest to a fault, he dutifully reported all the details, including his red-white-and-blue-striped organ. A night editor on the city desk saw this lively little item come over the wire and wrote a nice twenty-inch story for the morning paper, not realizing that Vito was one of our own. So the next day, the trials and tribulations of Vito Marchese appeared on page 3 of the *Trib.* Vito has been known as Old Glory ever since.

Stein's eyes got real big as I recounted the tale. No doubt

about it, he was impressed, which is just what I wanted. I think I'm making progress with these guys. I can't wait to tell Michael.

Boston

April 10 No answer again tonight. I guess I can't expect the guy to pine for me every night of the week, though I'm not above wishing he would. He's probably knocking back shooters in some dive on Capitol Hill while I'm sitting here waiting for them to call this sucker on account of rain. Michael's middle name is Damon, after Runyon, which is just about the only thing he takes seriously other than dead bodies.

Michael Damon Holliday is a hard-news guy in a city of party stories. In a roomful of collar pins and braces, he's the one with the loosened knit tie. He hates press rooms, all national political reporters, and anybody with an American Express Gold Card. The last time an editor sent him to cover an embassy party, Michael came home with the blue velvet ropes they use to keep the reporters from contaminating the guest list. At stately Washington functions, members of the media stand behind these ropes yelping questions at glazed VIPs like dogs on a kennel run. If they behave, they are allowed out to mingle with the glitterati for exactly one half hour and snarf up Ridgewell's crudités and crab claws while probing a member's mind for some evidence of life. As legend has it, Michael stood behind the ropes at the Australian Embassy for ten minutes trying to get Mike Deaver's attention. "Mr. Deaver!" "Sir!" "Mr. Deaver!" "Yo, Mike!" Something snapped and Michael stepped forward, unhooking the velvet ropes from their gilded stanchions and draping them about his neck like a feather boa. He found Deaver sucking on a crab claw next to an ice sculpture of a koala bear and asked, "Do you ever think of the homeless at a time like this?"

The velvet ropes now set off Michael's bed from the chaos that is his bedroom, a fact I discovered our first night together, which was one week after he came over to the *Tribune* and one week before I came over to Sports.

Michael is a legend in town because he's the only person ever to quit the *Washington Post* to go to work at the Washington

Tribune. He was hired away with a promise of lots of money and lots of space. Michael can get anything in the paper he wants. He has more clout than any of his editors. He also has a Pulitzer Prize for local reporting; they're lucky if they can spell their names.

We met on April 11, 1988, exactly a year ago tomorrow. That was the night they called me off the baseball diamond to go cover the murder of that distinguished black poet up on the Gold Coast. Michael was still at the *Post.* Today sent me to do the feature angle. I knew I was in trouble when the cops lifted the yellow CRIME SEARCH SCENE barriers to let Michael in. Michael is that good. He knows every cop worth knowing in the city. He has a police radio in his car and another beside his bed. Sometimes he gets to crime scenes before the backup car does.

Michael comes by this honestly. His father was a City side columnist for a Boston tabloid who never got tired of chasing cops or fire engines, which explains why Michael quit the *Post* for this dump. Michael Holliday, Sr., called himself a boy reporter just the way Michael does. And when his only son turned five, he took him downtown and introduced him to the roar of the presses. But he didn't live long enough to see his son win a Pulitzer Prize for local reporting. The night Michael told me all this was the night it first occurred to me that maybe we really are meant for each other.

I think if he had been born two centuries ago, Michael would have been a pirate, though he more resembles Billy Budd, which is probably the secret of his reportorial success. His dad was Irish and his mother is Italian. He's got all this blond curly hair, which is going prematurely gray, and these huge blue eyes and this skin that turns gold in the sun. He looks like an Irish Modigliani painting. It's not surprising people tell him things. This is a man priests would confess to. Also, he tap-dances for exercise. He learned how when he was six and conned his mother into letting him do that instead of the waltz at Arthur Murray.

Anyway, Michael ducked under the police barricade and I followed him. It was 8:30 P.M., and the police lights were going around and around and the red kept flashing in my eyes. A detective grabbed my shoulder and demanded some I.D. I just nodded toward Michael and said, "I'm with him." Michael must have liked that because he just shrugged and said okay.

33

He was already kneeling at the widow's feet looking at her with those big baby blues by the time I got my notebook out of my purse. I decided to let him run with it. I wanted to see him work. Also, I figured I had taken enough liberties for the night. And maybe I was just a little intimidated.

He asked the poet's wife to describe the events of the evening and what kind of man her husband was and if she had any ideas who might have wanted to do this, pretty prosaic stuff. He kept calling her "ma'am" and nodding sympathetically. But he wasn't getting anywhere. I wasn't impressed.

Finally, after about ten minutes of this, I introduced myself and asked if I could get her a cup of coffee. She said, "Oh yes, that would be nice, I haven't eaten all day. My husband was going to make us dinner. He was a wonderful cook, you know." I went off to the kitchen to get her coffee and a bite to eat, and when I came back I asked how they had met and how old they were when they got married. She ate and cried and showed me the first love letter he ever wrote her, a poem. Michael took lots of notes.

The next morning I made sure to read his story before mine. I couldn't help noticing he had the poem in the lede. But my story was on the front. His led the Metro page.

Two months later, he came over to the *Tribune*. He was not exactly greeted with open arms, except, of course, by our publisher, Ross Mitchell, who hired him. We had all read the figures in the *Washingtonian*: HOLLIDAY DEFECTS TO *TRIB* FOR $100,000 PER. This is approximately $70,000 per more than the rest of us are making. I posted the story on the staff bulletin board by the front elevator.

It's not that I hated him. I just assumed the worst: that he was a pompous, self-important *Postie* with an overinflated salary and an equally exaggerated view of himself. I mean, he didn't exactly knock me dead with his interview technique the night we met, even if he did break the story of the killer the next day.

Anyway, I found him sitting on my desk reading my mail one morning about a week after he arrived at the *Trib*. I told him to mind his own business and acted quite put upon even though he was only reading a mailer from some PR firm. He said his salary was private, too, and that the *Washingtonian* had it wrong and I might have checked with him before posting it on the bulletin board. Obviously, he had checked me out. This time I was impressed.

"So I guess you're busy for lunch, huh?" he said.

"Yup."

"Dinner?"

"Yup."

"How 'bout breakfast?"

The thing about Michael is that he looks so innocent, he can ask anything including whether you have company for breakfast, and it doesn't occur to you you've been skewered until long after you've answered his question. The truth is, he only *looks* buttoned-down. But I didn't know that then. I only suspected as much.

"Look, Berkowitz, you owe me one." He meant the barricades. "The least you can do is show me the ropes."

So we had dinner the next night. We drove out to the most romantic restaurant in Virginia, the Auberge Chez François (where nobody but Michael can get reservations that fast), in his old Triumph, listening to the crackle of police talk and burglaries in progress.

"It's not $100,000 per," he said right off. "It's $80,000."

"Too bad."

"You want to know why I really left the *Post*?"

I shrugged.

"They don't like bodies," he said. "When they talk about knowing where all the bodies are buried, they're talking about undersecretaries who've been getting a little on the side. They don't want stories that ooze and bleed."

He was eating snails and the butter was dripping down his chin and settling in its cleft. His chin glistened and so did his eyes. He was so blond, his passions so dark. Who wouldn't fall for a tap-dancing choirboy with a thing for corpses with familiar faces? I reached over and dabbed his chin with my napkin. It was a gesture of presumed intimacy and I regretted it immediately.

"*They* want scandals. Give me an ax murderer anytime. Give me feet in concrete. Give me something tangible. *Fraud. Procurement scams.* They're polite crimes. I don't do stories with manners."

We skipped dessert and he took me home and introduced me to his cat, Copy, who was asleep at the foot of his bed on his old paper-route delivery bag. He poured some brandy from a bottle he keeps inside the *New York Times* box by his side of the bed. He has two of them: matching night tables. He stole the first one on a dare from the UDC campus one night back in '79. That's the liquor cabinet. The other one some guys at the *Post* gave him the night he left the paper. He uses it to store his yellowed clippings. He changes the paper in the window every time he gets on the front, which is all the time. Now that I've pretty much moved in, he puts my stories in the window on my side of the bed. But I don't get out front near as often as he does.

I asked my older sister once how she knew to hold on to the guy she married. She was only nineteen when she met him and too young to know any better. She said she knew that he would never bore her and that there were some things she would never have to explain. I looked at the headlines in Michael's *New York Times* boxes—IT LOOKED LIKE HIS FACE WAS SHOT OFF and NUDE COUNTESS DEAD OF CANCER—and knew there were some things I would never have to explain about the locker room. I think finally it was his enthusiasm for gore that swept me off my feet. I was over the velvet ropes before I knew it.

"You wouldn't believe the body I saw last night," he said.

"And you wouldn't believe the one I saw."

"Seen one, seen 'em all," he said.

"Same with stiffs."

"No way," Michael said. "My guy was so bloated he looked like one of those balloons in the Thanksgiving parade."

It was an odd kind of foreplay, but effective. Live bodies being what they are, one thing led to another and all I can say is it was a relief not to have to hide behind my steno pad, which sat atop Michael's *New York Times* box where I could reach it just in case Sal called.

We have been a newsroom item ever since. Schedules permitting, of course.

April 12   As of tonight, the Senators are 0–7. They've given up twice as many unearned runs as they've scored and haven't yet had a lead. Still, no one's panicking. They have a long way to go before anyone will take them seriously. After all, the Baltimore Orioles lost twenty-one straight to open the season last year. As Mug Shot said after making three errors in one inning tonight, "I categorically deny myself the inalienable right to get upset because that would cause me undo worriation."

Toronto

April 16 0–11. We lost four in New York, two in Boston, and four in Toronto. So far, we have been zapped, thrashed, trounced, shellacked, whipped, ripped, rocked, burned, blown out, and nipped (twice). Nobody ever just loses in the Washington *Tribune,* especially not the Senators. At this rate, I'm gonna run out of verbs by the end of the road trip.

The Senators are in a serious early season funk. At least, that's what I wrote yesterday. The team batting average is under .200 and the team ERA is over 7.00. Rump is hitting .047, Mancusi can't bend over to field a ground ball and Brother John Lawson, who went 0 for 4 today, striking out three times and leaving five runners in scoring position, said, "God works in mysterious ways. No matter how many times I strike out, I'm still gonna walk with Jesus."

"Amen," his buddy Pentacost said.

"Unbe-fucking-lievable," Monk said.

All things considered, the players don't seem particularly depressed. Half of them expect to lose and the rest think it's God's will, including the entire starting rotation, all of whom are earnestly hoping the Lord will add another foot to their fastballs. What we've got here, baseball fans, is a roster of God Squadders, bush leaguers, and has-beens, who, as Monk says, "used to be what they once were." Or as Stein puts it, "We are in the Twilight Zone of our careers."

There's no one who can throw a yakker and no one who can hit one either. As for foot speed, it only manifests itself in how quickly these guys get into their baggy Bermuda shorts and out the door once the game is over. The God Squadders accept this as God's will. The has-beens gratefully accept the per diem. And the bush leaguers need a little more seasoning. Like maybe twenty years.

Stein is trying to keep everyone loose by putting heat balm in their jocks, giving hotfoots, and telling blow-job jokes: "What do eggs Benedict and a blow job have in common?"

I was stumped.

"You can't get either one at home."

Stein is an anomaly in the game, a rich kid from Shaker Heights whose father sells Mercedeses. He wears a Benz hood ornament around his neck and reflector shades. He's a wiry guy, especially for a first baseman. He looks as if someone plugged him into an electrical socket and left him there through puberty. His muscles bulge. His eyes bulge. His veins bulge. And his pants bulge. But that's only 'cause he stuffs them. Also, he's hairy. He's always pulling errant hairs and buggers out of his nostrils and leaving them dangling from people's name plates over the lockers.

Stein got Demetrious pretty good the other day. Cut the crotch right out of his new Ted Lapidus suit. Demetrious was not amused, especially since Monk fined him $250 for violating the dress code, which requires ties and jackets on road trips. Demetrious does not have much of a sense of humor. Mug Shot says that's because of his legs, which look as if they belong on a baby grand instead of a six-foot-three, 180-pound outfielder. Also, Demetrious had bad acne as a kid, the scars of which remain. Yesterday Stein named him to his all-time, all-star, all-ugly team. "His face looks like a melted Nestlé Crunch," Stein said. "He'd be ugly even if he was white."

So Demetrious was not pleased when Stein followed that up by ruining his five-hundred-dollar suit. He stomped around the locker room for an hour after the game, yelling "Mo'fuck," and finally went back to the hotel in his underwear.

Stick isn't saying very much to anyone, least of all me. Turns out Sal told the Schnoz, our gossip columnist, about Stick's encounter with the taffeta queen. The Schnoz printed a blind item that said: "What prodigious hunk of man about town tried gallantly to deflower a six-foot lovely with all the wrong equipment in the lobby of a chic New York hotelerie? Boys will be boys, but come on now. *Sticky* situation, eh, sports fans?"

Beanie brought the item with him to Toronto and showed it to Stick, who categorically denied he was involved, saying, "There's no doubt about it, but you can never be sure."

Lawson read it and decided more prayer is in order. Yesterday he stood up in the clubhouse and announced that henceforth there would be daily chapel services before batting practice. "Why don't you leave us alone and go get laid?" Stein replied.

Stein's the only guy on the team who knew Brother John

before he began his sober Walk with the Lord. The Steins and the Lawsons were pretty good friends, and one night at a barbecue things got cozy and Mrs. Stein ended up going home with Mr. Lawson and vice versa. It was very big news around the league. Wife swapping always is.

It's easy to see that the former Mrs. Stein got the better of the deal. Lawson is undoubtedly the best advertisement for God in the major leagues. He is a hunk. Apparently, his religiosity is in direct proportion to the amount of beef hounding he used to do. He is long and lean and elegantly muscled; blond in the way that seems the sun is always shining through his hair. He even looks reborn. His skin is as pink and soft as a baby's. I know it's only 'cause the blood vessels are close to the surface. But he really does look as if he's in the presence of God. He grew up in some Gulf town in Alabama and prays with a sincere drawl. In full thrall, he looks like he's having a heart attack.

Brother John is going into the ministry full time when his career is over. In the meantime, he conducts chapel services in the toilet. "It's my calling," he says.

In the off-season, he operates the Cruise for Christ Ministry, which offers one-week vacation packages of Bible study and fun in the sun where fans and ballplayers can get to know one another in Christ. He keeps a jar of TRY GOD buttons in his locker and a stack of baseball cards in his pocket with his personal testimony on the back. The other day I asked him why he had never learned to hit a curve or a slider and he said, "I'd be happy to share that with you." He's very into sharing. Sharing is a lot friendlier than proselytizing.

Every day since spring training, he's been going locker to locker campaigning for the Lord. The last day or so, he's been hitting on Billy Blessing pretty good. I guess he figured with that name, Billy was a shoo-in. Billy is a utility infielder, the twenty-fourth man on a roster that has a whole lot of candidates for the position. He only made the team because he's white and can run the forty under five seconds.

Billy's a California kid with surfer curls who's always singing "Born to Be Bad." He's a slam dancer masquerading as the All-American boy, or maybe vice versa. Only his eyes, which have a perverse and continuous glow, give him away. "I can pass," he says.

The first day of spring training, he showed up in Sears work boots and a tuxedo he bought at the Salvation Army. He has the best collection of death metal in professional sports, including all of Metallica, Slayer, Texas Metal Massacre, and Suicidal Tendencies. Billy says, "I'm a devout American. I'm just a little more aggressive on the basepaths now."

He wears his eye-black deep and his stirrups unfashionably low in honor of his hero, Bill Mazeroski, whose 1961 baseball card he keeps tucked inside his cap. "It's a little symbolic of how I like to play," he told me in spring training. "I like to play hard and get dirty. Like Maz did. This is his number I'm wearing on my back. I like to think of myself as hard-nosed. I don't go for that courtesy slide type thing. Last year I broke my finger and sat out nine weeks. Maz probably would have spat on it and said, 'Let's go.' "

Of course, Billy doesn't yet have a major league at bat, but he does have an autographed copy of the Dead Kennedys' first album in his locker at RFK and a blood-red Satanic poster that reads: THE DEVIL IS DUDICAL! SATAN LIVES!

No wonder Brother John is worried about Billy's soul. A couple of days ago I heard Billy explaining "dudical" to him by the batting cage. "You know, like *dude,*" Billy said. "Like *radical.* Dudical."

"You don't know who you're messing with," Lawson replied.

"If you don't believe in God, then you don't believe in Satan either," Billy said.

I don't think that possibility had ever occurred to Lawson. Today Billy brought him a copy of the Stryper *Isaiah 53:5* album. Lawson thinks he has a convert.

The one I'm worried about is Rump. For sixteen years, Rump Doubleday has been the best catcher in the major leagues. For sixteen years, he has batted .300, caught at least 130 games, and hit at least 20 home runs. For sixteen years, he has called the game, deciding what to throw, when to throw it, whom to throw it to. Pitch by pitch, game by game, season by season, baseball has expanded for him into a limitless trove of decisions and situations and possibilities. For sixteen years, he has called the game his own. He is as sturdy as baseball. He endures.

Last year when his contract ran out, the Mets offered him a three-year deal, but only the first year was guaranteed. Unlike most great athletes, Rump does not believe he will know when to quit. He says the great ones never do, that their talent deludes them into believing they can do it forever. He says it's the marginal guys, the Billy Blessings and Sammy Espositos, who know when it's time to go because they know what it took to get there.

But Rump is as proud as he is sturdy. And he is in love with the game. So he told the Mets to shove it and accepted Jimy Boy's offer for the same money, guaranteed, knowing he was accepting the responsibility for making the Senators respectable, which meant knowing he would fail.

Every day he looks worse at the plate, flailing at pitches over his head and in the dirt. Every day it's harder for him to get down in the crouch. To give you an idea of how baseball people feel about him, all you have to know is there are guys who won't bunt on Rump because of his knees.

Today he went 0 for 4 again. "Oh well, it's early," I told him. Rump just shook his head. "Wrong," he said. "It's too late."

I couldn't think of what else to say to cheer him up, so I told him Dr. Deadline is going to meet us in Detroit and put everything in perspective. It was the first time I've seen him smile in a week.

Dr. Deadline is a legend among scribes. He makes everyone smile, except, of course, his editors. He was the *Trib*'s baseball writer until Washington got a team, whereupon he was immediately replaced by me. I use the term "baseball writer" loosely because the Doctor hasn't actually filed a game story of any sort in eight years.

Dr. D covered NBA hoops until 1982, when the Cleveland Cavaliers lost twenty-four straight games over two seasons to set a modern record for futility—a feat that may soon be equaled by our own Washington Senators. Dr. D was there the night the Cavs finally won, but he never filed. He blew all six editions, and when he got home Sal pulled him off the beat. He's been known as Dr. Deadline ever since. For the last seven years he has been a baseball writer in a city without a baseball team, which was perfect, because if there aren't any games there aren't any deadlines. He was all over the "Baseball in '87" campaign and specializes in MVP award lunches, which is how he got to know Rump. The last two years the Doctor has filed the exact same stories except, of course, for the names of the winners.

"Maybe," Rump said, "we'll win a game by the time he makes a deadline."

Detroit

April 18–19 It's 11:50 P.M. and I'm sitting in the press box freezing my butt, waiting on Dr. D. Sal sent him out here to gauge the mood of the team. Sal is very big on mood and scene, especially if the mood is horseshit. But this morning Juan Arroyo's wife found his birth certificate in the attic of their family home in Baja. Turns out the ace of the pitching staff is forty-four, not thirty-four. So Sal called and said he wanted a Mr. Juanderful featurette for the daily in addition to the mood thumbsucker for Sunday. This set the Doctor back a piece. The Doctor doesn't need any setbacks. As we speak, Dr. D is clutching his forehead, which has broken out in hives, and humming the Columbia University fight song, "Roar, Lions, Roar." It's a tic he has. He hums it whenever he's on deadline, which is strange considering he's a Princeton man and has never been seen in the press box without his club tie and his Phi Beta Kappa key.

In addition to deadlines, the Doctor is also allergic to fried food, which is a life-threatening disease for anyone who spends any time in a press box. Colonel Sanders gives him hot flashes. Popeyes gives him hives. Any amount of fried food gives him the chills, which in turn cause his teeth to chatter. I am sitting next to a man who is sweating, scratching, and humming, between chattering teeth, the fight song of a team that has approximately one win in the last decade. And there isn't a damn thing I can do about it.

Half an hour ago he said he'd be done in fifteen minutes. Fifteen minutes ago he blew the third edition. Ten minutes ago he said, and I quote, "I can't fucking write it. It's too fucking big."

As far as I can tell, he's written one sentence: "Time does funny things to a man."

It's 1:25 A.M. now and D just blew the replate. I offered to write it for him, but he thinks he's Shakespeare. Besides, he says the lions

are really roaring now. "Great," I said. "The press box attendants are leaving." I was tempted to go with them, but the Doctor doesn't drive, and if I leave, he stays. Permanently. That's
another thing you should know about the Doctor: he's the only
sportswriter in America who does not drive, which is a good
thing for the driving public considering his 20/400 vision, but
not such a good thing for the rest of us who serve as his chauf-
feurs. Dr. Deadline once showed up an hour late for a game at
the Cap Centre in a limousine after calling his entire Rolodex of
friends and failing to find anyone home. "Sal won't pay for any
more cabs," he explained, stepping out of the stretch. "But he
didn't say shit about a limo."

1:40 A.M. The Doctor swears all he needs is a kicker. I told him,
"Fuck the kicker. Zeke cuts from the bottom anyway."

Well, it's an hour later. It took the Doctor fifty-seven minutes to
write the kicker. He made the final edition by exactly one minute. Dolly Mitchell, the wife of the publisher, and approximately
thirty-five thousand of her closest friends and relatives, who get
the final delivered to their doors four and a half hours from now,
will have the benefit of Dr. Deadline's wit and wisdom. The
other two hundred thousand or so readers will read an AP
roundup. D's getting his things. I'm getting out of here.

5:00 A.M. Dr. Deadline is asleep in a corner on a bed of quote
sheets and peanut shells. Goddamned son of a bitch. We're locked
in the press box of Tiger Stadium and he's snoring like a baby.
The security guards must have figured everyone was gone when
the press box attendants left. A reasonable assumption, I might
add. We banged on every door and dialed every number we could
think of. When I finally called the cops, the desk sergeant
laughed so hard, I thought he was gonna choke. "Sure, lady,
sure," he kept saying. "The press box. Tiger Stadium."

The Doctor shrugged and hit the hay. He's slept in press
boxes before. And besides, he said, "I've got a mood piece to do
tomorrow."

At least he isn't sweating and scratching anymore.

I called Michael two hours ago and woke him up. At least I

got him on the phone. "I'm locked in the press box with Dr. D," I said.

"That's nice," he said. "Who won?"

I figured he had to be kidding. Then I remembered he was asleep. "Who won? The Tigers won. Twelve straight losses. Stick struck out three times and hit a home run in the top of the ninth to avert the shutout. Later I asked him where the pitch was and he says, 'Right down the cock.'"

I read Michael my lede and I told him I missed him. "Too soon," he said. "It's only April."

So I'm sitting here eating a hot dog I ordered nine hours ago and drinking flat beer. What else do you do at Tiger Stadium at five in the morning?

When I was very young, I used to wonder what happened to ballparks late at night when everyone went home, the way I used to wonder if certain things would have happened if I hadn't been there to see them. Would Joey Proud have ripped his Achilles tendon running down to first base on a routine grounder to short if I hadn't been sitting along the third base line hugging my Sam Esposito glove? Would he have hit that home run out of Yankee Stadium if I hadn't been listening to the muffled sound of a transistor radio under my pillow?

No, I decided. Definitely not.

Baseball fell into the category of things so much a part of me that they were completely dependent on me for their existence. Ballparks could not exist in the absence of my consciousness of them. They evanesced while I slept. Fenway, Candlestick, the Stadium, they weren't structures, though I could tell you their dimensions, right, left, and center, and the number of obstructed seats in each. They were places of the soul, located within; constructs of imagination and will, not iron and molded plastic. Thus the national pastime became a consequence of me. Looking back, I guess that's 'cause for me baseball was always an interior monologue.

It's five in the morning. My hot dog's cold. My beer is flat. The ballpark is asleep. But Ariadne Bloom Berkowitz is awake and so Tiger Stadium stands. From where I sit, you can just see the upper deck in rightfield where Joey once hit a ball so far it sailed over the wall and into imagination. The only thing that stopped its flight was the bank of lights that hovers over the façade and staves off the night. Those lights are shining now (I can't imagine why), illuminating the silence and the dew. It looks as if there's a halo over the stadium.

April 19 The Doctor overslept. He was still snoring like a baby at 9:00 A.M. when the guy showed up to sweep out the peanut shells and the stat sheets. It took the two of us ten minutes to rouse the Doctor, who kept murmuring "A little to the right" every time I shook him. There was just enough time to get to the hotel, pack, shower, and get back to the stadium for batting practice. "Let's talk mood," D said in the car as we headed back to the ballpark.

"It sucks," I said, which pretty much ended the conversation.

He lit a joint and smoked it all the way there. The Doctor never writes straight, which may explain a thing or two. He left me standing in the press lot with all my things while he set off in search of a trend.

You know how it is when you get so tired everything seems as if it might just dissolve? Well, Dr. D was atomizing before my eyes and the ballpark looked like a mirage. Nothing was tangible except my luggage, which kept falling off my shoulders. I hate getaway day. You try balancing a computer, a briefcase, a suitcase, a dress bag, and a pocketbook large enough for two felt-tip pens and a steno pad on your shoulders. Me, I'm only 112 pounds. I caught a glimpse of myself in the side-view mirror—a short person with dirty blond hair still wet from the shower and circles under her eyes. It was not a pretty sight.

"Let Buck help, miss."

Never have I been so happy to see the team bus. Never have I been so ready to relinquish my practiced self-reliance. Never have I been so glad that Ruth was not around to chide me. I dropped the bags at Buck's big feet and murmured, "Thanks."

Buck Buchanan, our rookie leftfielder, grew up in Nuba, Louisiana, a town with manners and one stoplight and a history of crosses burned on front lawns. His given name is Eleazer after his granddaddy, who was a preacherman with a mean curveball. His grandpa died some years back but not before informally rechristening his grandson Buck. "I don't believe there's ever been an Eleazer in major league baseball," he said. "I do believe the Lord will understand."

The other day, Buck told me he is homesick for his grandma

and her red beans. He also told me she made him promise "to keep everything in perspectus." Buck doesn't say much, and what he does say tends to come out a bit scrambled even if it does make a lot of sense.

Last year Buck played Class A ball in Macon, Georgia. His manager was an old black guy who told stories about having guns stuck in his face at truck stops during road trips in the 1950s. Buck wasn't sure whether the guy was trying to tell him how good the modern ballplayer has it or to shut up and behave. Either way, he scared the shit out of Buck, who bolted the team a month into the season and went home to his porch in Nuba. His grandma finally talked him into going back. And when he did, he was a different player. He hit .299 for the season, with 48 home runs. Jimy Boy didn't flinch. He awarded Buck a starting job the day he signed him, applauding himself in the process as an equal-opportunity employer. "Buck's my boy," he said proudly, thereby prompting two thousand black season ticket holders to turn back their seats.

The signing took place in January in Jimy Boy's office at RFK. The Senators flew Buck up from Nuba. It was the first time Buck had ever seen a major league ballpark. He took a piece of sod from the outfield and wrapped it in Saran and took it home to Louisiana with him. But he left it on the radiator and it dried out and he had to throw it away before spring training. "It died a hard life," he said.

The day he left, his agent, a former local D.A., took Buck aside and told him he ought to take some condoms with him. Buck said not to worry, he was going to rent.

Everything about Buck is big except his mustache, which is young and straggly. It's a pathetic growth and it just makes everything else about him look that much bigger. He has the biggest thighs, bar none, on the planet. They are surely, each of 'em, as wide as my waist. Try to picture a twenty-eight-inch thigh. A thigh so thick, so defined, so taut that it would make redwoods tremble. I know I'll never persuade people I'm not in there checking out the dicks. But let me tell you, I checked out Buck's thighs. They were undoubtedly the cause of my most unprofessional conduct to date. This was back in spring training. I was midway through asking Buck some benign question about his minor league career when he dropped his pants and suddenly these things came into view and I completely forgot what I was saying. I couldn't take my eyes off them. "Miss, miss," Buck said, finally. "Huh?" I replied. "You was asking something?" My eyes were glued to his legs. "Beats me," I said. "Well, then, miss, Buck best go hit."

Now Buck was reaching down for my luggage. He is six feet six, which makes his burgeoning bald spot hard to see, and I had to run through the parking lot just to keep up with him. I thought I ought to make conversation. So I asked him how he felt after his first two weeks in the majors. He stopped, having reached the press gate, and said, "Buck is in a state of shockness."

The smile faded from my face right quick when the big old white guy standing guard at the players' entrance put his hand against Buck's chest and said, "Whoa, boy."

His name tag said: JAWORSKI. His face was red and his nose was pickled. One look at him said trouble. One look at us told him the same thing. Here was this big black guy in a cheap black leather jacket carrying all this pretty luggage and this little white girl racing along after him trying to catch up.

"Where you going in such a hurry, boy?" Jaworski said.

It wasn't a question. Not the kind a black kid from Nuba, Louisiana, wants to hear. So Buck didn't say a thing. But he straightened up real tall. "You got some I.D., boy?"

I introduced myself. I introduced Buck. I said he was the rookie leftfielder for the Washington Senators and I was a reporter for the Washington *Tribune,* and if he didn't let us through, his superiors were going to hear about it along with the reading public. I tried to sound impatient. I tried to sound patronizing. I think I only sounded small.

At the elevator there was another big old white guy. His name tag said: O'MALLEY. "Whoa, boy, where's the fire at, boy?" O'Malley said. The guy at the entrance to the press box was named Hawkins. All he said was "Hey, boy!" At each checkpoint, Buck stood a little taller and the noses on the security men got a little brinier and my "sirs" got a little louder. I pleaded with Buck to put the bags down. I told him I'd be fine. But Buck just kept walking faster and standing taller until he saw me to my seat.

He put the bags down at my chair and said, "Buck stops here."

As he left, Bernie Squire, a columnist from one of the Detroit papers, tried to tip him and Mac MacKenzie, from the Washington *Times,* said, "Who said you can't get good help anymore?"

47

And all I could think of to say was "You guys are really horseshit."

Home Stand

April 20   When Buck got to the ballpark today, there was a bellhop's uniform hanging in his locker and shit in his spikes. Shit is a staple of ballplayer humor. Dr. D says he once got a can of it in the mail from a basketball player who didn't like something he wrote, with a note that said: EAT SHIT AND DIE.

Buck spent the better part of an hour in the shower. When he came out dripping wet, there was a mountain of junk, dirty towels, dirty jocks, dirty plates, piled inside his locker. His brand-new Armani suit was at the bottom, soaking in watermelon juice and cantaloupe seeds. The legs were cut off below the knees.

"Yo! Bellhop," Mancusi said.

"Oh, boy!" Stein said.

It took Buck an hour to clean it all up. Rump gave him a hand, and so did Guttierrez, the shortstop, who was working as a bellhop in Nicaragua when he was signed by Hymie Richter last summer. "Nice, clean work," Guttierrez said.

Buck never said a word, but when he went out to hit he put on quite an exhibition: five hacks, five dingers. "Looks like Wonder Boy, don't he?" Rump said.

And he did. The next time he came up, everybody gathered round to watch. "Big Fly, Big Fella! Big Fly!" someone yelled. Buck swung so hard at the pitch that I ducked when it collided with the back of the cage.

Bonk!

The cage shook for three minutes. My hands stung for half an hour.

Buck fouled back another and another. *Bonk! Bonk!*

It's one of those baseball noises like the crack of the bat and the thud of horsehide against leather and the crunch of spikes in soft dirt that you take for granted until it's gone. There were no thuds, no thwacks, no bonks, no tonks, no binks, no dinks, no dingers, here a year ago or for the last eighteen years. For eigh-

teen summers there were no bingles, no safeties; no *"Charge!"*
Two decades without *"Hey, peanuts!"* or *"We want a hit!"* A gener-
ation came and went in the nation's capital without hearing the
sound of rhythmic clapping that begins deep in the bleachers and
envelops the stadium and unsettles the pitcher until he gives up a
single, a double, and is gone. Washington heard nothing while
baseball was away.

It's hard to believe that it was just a year ago that the Mets
and the Orioles played the final exhibition game of spring training on a make-believe field with a 23-foot wall in left 265 feet
from home plate. Fat Sid Fernandez, the Mets pitcher, hit a
three-run home run over that silly fence and giggled and jiggled
all the way home. He was laughing at Washington. Who didn't
then? Who isn't now?

Ruth and I were sitting in the first row right behind the
makeshift screen that was more hole than screen. It took a hell of
an effort to get her to come to the game. She loves baseball. It's
just baseball players she can't stand. We met five years ago on the
Ellipse at softball practice. Ruth can pick it. But she doesn't give
a good goddamn about major league baseball. I never could separate the players from the game. She insists upon it. Her love is
purer than mine and harsher. But she's a hell of a ballplayer.

Anyway, there was a foul-back. *Whack!* It came straight at us
through the screen, heading for my face. Ruth reached out and
bare-handed it, spilling my beer but saving me from plastic surgery. She got a big hand for making the catch and we all had a
good laugh at Washington. I pointed to the sign in leftfield that
said: BASEBALL BACK IN D.C. "Like hell," I said.

That was a year ago. Now baseball is back. Sort of. The
hapless Washington Senators have come home to try to win a
game. Buck's obviously going to try to do it alone. And he may
have to.

Cr-rrack! Pffft!

Buck hit a shot that dented a seat in the upper deck and Billy
Blessing spat at my feet. As Billy says, if you're going to chew,
you better spit. *Pffft!*

"You hear 'bout the clubhouse meeting?" he asked.

I nodded, though of course it was a lie.

"Seems like Jimy Boy hisself is going to come down and
preach us some hellfire and brimstone." Billy did two years at
Auburn, so he can talk some country when he wants to.

"Praise Jesus."

"Yup," Billy said. "He's going to preach some hellfire and brimstone and then we're going to go out and kick some ass in the name of the Lord."

"I'd like to be a fly on the wall for that one."

Billy nodded. "I was kinda thinking maybe this sermon ought to be preserved for posterity. What do you think, A.B.?"

"Absolutely."

"You want maybe I tape it for you?"

"You serious?"

"I'm always serious when it comes to Jesus."

Billy's a crazy bastard, but this was the dumbest thing yet. I'd like to tell you I was going to be honorable, do the right thing by the rookie. But I work for Sal. I handed Billy my tape recorder, which he stuffed in his back pocket with the bubble gum and round tin of Copenhagen and his batting gloves. "Dudical," he said.

"Rad," I replied.

Tell an editor you've got great stuff and he'll tell you space is tight. Editors always say space is tight. Space was tight until I called Sal and told him Billy was going to tape our born-again baseball owner preaching hellfire and brimstone to an 0–13 team. "We got an extra column," Sal said. "Anybody else have it?"

"I don't think so," I said.

"Well, make sure they don't."

Billy was waiting for me at his locker after the game, the fourteenth straight loss. He handed me a three-album set by the Skinned Cats with my tape recorder inside. "Praise the Lord," he said.

It was late. I had an hour to transcribe the tape and write the story. The press box was empty except for Myron, the press box attendant, and me. Myron was snoring, so I figured it was safe to forget the headphones. I turned on the tape and the voices of the saved wafted through the empty stadium on the wings of sweet Jesus.

"Listen up, men." This had to be Monk. He always says, "Listen up, men," except when he says, "Listen up, boys."

"Listen up, men. Jimy Boy here has a few words of inspiration he'd like to share with us this afternoon. I personally would like to thank Jimy Boy for coming down here to pray for us. I mean, pray with us. And I personally would like to suggest we all hold hands."

Giggling obliterated his last couple of words. That had to be Billy. Though I thought I could make out Rump's voice, too.

"Let us worship Jesus, men, and let us not be afraid to be boys in the eyes of the Lord."

This was how Jimy Boy began. "Boys, it is tough to be a hero. Who knows that better than you? Who, I ask you, who?"

Jimy Boy waited for an answer that did not come. "Jesus, that's who! Je-sus! Think about it, boys. He was a winner. He was a champion. One day He was a hero and one day He was a bum. And they crucified Him. Just like they're crucifying you.

"But what did Jesus do? What can we learn from His divine example? Jesus went to bat for what He believed in, and so should you."

"Amen!" This was Stein, who is 0 for 12 in his last three games and struck out with the bases loaded in his last at bat.

"Tonight," Jimy Boy said, his voice hushed and husky, "tonight when you're waiting in that on-deck circle, reaching for the pine tar, I want you to reach for something more. I want you to reach for something that will stick to you for life, our Savior's love."

"Hallelujah!" Stein again.

"And when you're kneeling in the on-deck circle, kneeling for the Lord, I want you to ask Jesus to be your Savior, your personal coach. I don't just want you to take Jesus into your heart. I want you to take Jesus into the batter's box! I want you to go to bat for the Lord! And, boys, I promise you this. If you go to bat for Jesus, Jesus will go to bat for you!"

Jimy Boy was on a roll. He had the spirit. And so did Monk: "Help me, Je-sus! Love me, Je-sus! Take me, Je-sus! I am slain in the Lord! Oh! Holy Ghost! Holy Ghost! *Ahh baah daah baah daah!*"

Monk was speaking in tongues again. He was in ecstasy. Billy was in stitches.

Jimy Boy took a deep breath and collected himself for a socko finish. No coach had ever given a pep talk quite this good. "If that pitcher offers up four balls, I want you to walk with Jesus. And if he gives you something good to hit, I want you to take an extra base for Je-sus! I want you to go to the wall for the Lord God, Jesus Christ!"

"Jesus fucking Christ," Billy said into the microphone.

"Repent of your boneheadedness! Relinquish your slump. And know this: you will always be safe in the Lord!"

"Go for it, Jesus!"

Thank God for Stein. He had given me my lede. I began to write: "Go for it, Jesus!"

There was a message on my tape when I got home from Michael's in the morning. It was Beanie O'Neill saying Monk wanted to see me in his office first thing.

April 21 "You ever read the fucking Bible?"

Monk wanted to talk religion. He was standing in his long underwear in the middle of the locker room, his cheek bulging with Red Man, brandishing King James in one hand and scratching himself with the other. Usually the locker room is a cacophony of noises: lots of "fuck you's" and rap music and color commentary from ESPN. Suddenly it got real quiet, as if somebody had turned down the sound on life.

"Hi, Monk," I said.

This did not slow him down.

"The Bible says, 'For everything there is a season.' And this is my fucking season. Twenty-three fucking years in the coaching box and one horseshit month as an interim manager in Milwaukee and now this!"

I wasn't sure how he meant that. Considering the record (0–15 after tonight), he could have meant it either way. But he didn't.

"And you know what, Berkowitz? Every day I get down on my knees and praise Jesus for giving me, Monk McGuire, His humble fucking servant, this chance to lead this horseshit team out of the fucking wilderness. And I believe God will raise us up. Yes, I do. I believe it because a lot of good men on this horseshit team have taken a stand for God. And He will exalt us.

"God is great, Berkowitz. God is a great guy who laid down His life for us. But He can't tell you whether to put on the hit-and-run with a man on first and a .213 hitter at the plate, now, can He?

"That's *my* job, Berkowitz. And you is getting in the way."

A stream of tobacco splattered my stockings. Spitting is more than a way of life with Monk. It's punctuation. I've noticed that by the end of the sixth inning, his white sanitary hose are completely brown. One time in spring training, George Bailey, the *Sports Illustrated* guy, came by to do some legwork for a piece on the rebirth of the Senators. He's standing there in the dugout in his Gucci loafers talking to Monk, who's doing a lot of spitting and very little talking. Monk goes left. Monk goes right. Finally Monk goes right up the middle on Bailey's Gucci buckle. Monk is not known for giving good quotes, unless, of course, he's quoting the Almighty or something scatological. Sal swears he once saw Monk do a whole postgame press conference speaking in tongues. Some guys even took notes.

I looked around the locker room. My colleagues were scribbling furiously, taking down every word Monk said. They were his first intelligible quotes of the season. It hadn't occurred to me that I might become a story. And God knows I didn't want to be one. But I reached for my tape recorder, wishing like hell I had bought a voice-activated one.

Suddenly Monk was quoting Genesis, ribs and all. He was begatting this and begatting that and looking me up and down just to make sure where I fit in the genealogy, I guess. The players just kept going about their business, farting and scratching and getting undressed. I'm getting the shit kicked out of me and they're eating baloney. I guess it figures.

Monk thundered on, doing his patriarchal best. " 'And the rib which the Lord God had taken from the man he made into a woman.' It don't say horseshit about making her a motherfucking Judas sportswriter!"

He spat again for emphasis.

"Now, this ain't the Garden of fucking Eden," he said, getting to the point. "And you ain't Eve. This here is a major league baseball club and I am a religious fucking individual. I wouldn't let the Holy fucking Mother in this locker room unless the commissioner said so." He paused to cross himself here. Monk crosses himself so often, the coaches decided to make it the take sign, which may explain why nobody swung away for three innings on Opening Day. "Now, I got here a piece of paper saying I gotta let you in. So I'm gonna. But that doesn't mean I'm going to say horseshit to you. And neither are any of my boys. Right, boys?"

"Amen," Stein said, falling to his knees naked before God. "*Hallelujah!*"

At which point, Monk crossed himself again and stalked back into his office, scratching his behind.

The only sound in the locker room was Fast Eddie Hernandez shuffling a deck of cards, which he believes is the key to the release on his knuckleball. I guess they were all waiting to see what I would do, which, as a matter of fact, so was I. All I can remember thinking is "So this is a hot flash."

I turned to Rump, who was standing by his locker wrapped in a skimpy red, white, and blue towel, and reached for my steno pad.

"The Angels' pitcher . . ."

Who *was* the Angels' pitcher? My mind was blank. I had no idea who the Angels' starting pitcher was. I looked at Rump.

"McKeckney," he said.

"McKeckney, yeah. What does he throw?"

Rump opened his mouth to answer, but before he could, Stick darted across the locker room and snatched the towel from Rump's waist, snapping it against his ass. It's an ancient male gesture of domination, a rat's tail, I believe they called it in high school.

"Show her your machine!" Stick bellowed. *"Show her your machine!"*

I looked at Rump. Rump looked at me. We both looked at his machine.

Then Rump tucked the towel around his waist again and Stick grabbed it again. His voice had become a chorus. *"Show her your machine, John! Show her your machine!"*

"McKeckney," I said. "What does he throw?"

Stick snatched the towel again, and this time Rump didn't bother with modesty. "Rising fastball. Wild high. If you're patient, he'll give you something to hit."

As the door slammed behind me, I caught a glimpse of Rump chasing Stick across the locker room and a new hand-lettered sign by the clubhouse entrance: WHEN THIS DOOR IS CLOSED, STAY OUT! (P.S. THAT MEANS YOU, BERKOWITZ!)

All the way down the hall, I could hear Stein singing "Amazing Grace."

April 22 Sal is a happy camper this afternoon. Nothing like a shit storm to improve his mood. This is just what he hoped for, just what I feared. I guess he was right. It is us against them. I don't know which makes him happier: knowing he was right or being able to write lots of gonzo headlines bashing them for being sexist, religious fanatics, not to mention losers now of 16 straight. No doubt about it, Sal was in his up-yours mode when he gave me the beat. The man is Italian but not exactly what

you'd call devout. Davis, the 'Skins beat writer, says Sal has a real
thing about God Squadders. He loves locker room dissension
stories, especially if the Almighty is in the middle of it. A couple
of years back, when one of the born-again Capitals wouldn't fight
some guy from the Rangers, Sal's headline was: CAPS TURN OTHER
CHEEK. Which is nothing compared to what he did to me. Jimy
and Monk can't banish me from the locker room, but they sure
can make life a bitch. So can Sal.

I was still sleeping when Ruth found me at Michael's. He's
in Miami tracking down a dead guy, but I'm staying at his place
anyway. Easier to feed the cat this way. Also, you never know
when Michael might show up again.

"Check out this morning's headline?" she said.

"I'm asleep," I said.

"Shall I read it to you?"

"Yeah, sure, what."

"HOLY WAR!"

"Oh God." I had called in what I had, but I didn't think they
would do *this* with it.

It seemed to me Ruth enjoyed my discomfort just a little
more than perhaps was warranted. She disapproves of my career
choice. She read on and I could almost hear her smirk. " 'The
management of the faltering Washington Senators declared war
on *Trib* reporter A. B. Berkowitz yesterday when skipper Monk
McGuire announced that neither he nor any of his players would
speak to Berkowitz for the remainder of the season on religious
grounds.

" 'I wouldn't let the Holy bleeping Mother in here unless
the commissioner said so,' McGuire told Berkowitz. 'He says I
gotta let you in. So I'm gonna let you in. But that doesn't mean
I'm going to talk to you. And neither are any of my boys.'

"*Trib* publisher Ross Mitchell said the paper was considering
legal action against the club. 'We stand by our reporter,' Mitchell
said. 'You would think that the Senators would stick to baseball,
considering how much trouble they're having mastering that. We
will not allow religious intolerance and sexism to determine our
assignments. This is a case of sexual harassment clothed in religious vestments.'

"In the aftermath of the tense locker room scene, catcher
Rump Doubleday said he would continue to talk to Berkowitz in
defiance of the manager's decree. A handful of players, including
utility infielder Billy Blessing and rookie outfielder Buck Bu-

chanan, said they have no problem with women in the locker room. Several players said they had no comment. The majority of the team, however, agreed with first baseman John Lawson, a lay minister in the off-season, who conducts the team chapel services.

" 'Basically, I guess to me, it's a number of things,' Lawson said. 'Number one, it's a matter of privacy. Number three, to me there's certain boundaries I think are good and that I don't think are discriminating. For the moral aspect of it, it just upsets me that the boundary isn't there. It's no big deal. But it's a small reflection on a lot of boundaries that are depleted. Like a chalk line blowing away. Poof, it's gone.' "

Ruth paused. "That's almost poetic," she said.

"It's also the first simile I've ever heard in the locker room," I replied.

"Obviously, you bring out the best in them. You want to hear more?"

"Yeah, sure. Like number two. What happened to number two?"

"There is no number two," Ruth said. "But get this. 'To me, this is not an occupation a woman should be in,' Lawson said. 'To me, in God's society, a woman was created in a role of submission. It's not that a woman is beneath me. But, to me, she shouldn't be in an aggressive mode. And besides, a man's locker room is his castle.' "

You could say I wasn't exactly looking forward to going to the ballpark. All the beat guys were standing around the batting cage waiting for me when I arrived. "Well, if it isn't Saint Berkowitz," said Mac MacKenzie of the Washington *Times.*

"The Holy fucking Mother," said Pete Girard of the *Post.*

"You got any comment?" said Herm Brenner, who had to do a write-through for the AP. I shook my head, and Paul Giordanno of the *Sun* kissed my hand. "Read all about it. The Holy fucking Mother has no comment," Brenner said.

I guess a word about my colleagues is in order here, if you can call them that. "Colleagues" implies we have something in common, which I fervently hope we do not. Mac MacKenzie is an old fart with a flattop who doesn't wear anything unless it's a freebie. Today he was wearing a yellow DICK BUTKUS/NUTRA-SWEET/LINEBACKER INVITATIONAL golf tournament sport shirt, a SENATORS sweater, golf spikes, and a pair of lime-green madras pants that were left over from last year's Jack Nicklaus collection. Mac wears three watches at all times, all of which he got in media goody bags at big events. One is set for the time zone he's in; one is for the time zone his deadline is in; and one is for the post time of whatever racetrack he's got the most money down at that day.

Lots of guys wear two watches so they never blow a deadline. Personally, I like to be rooted to one time, one place. I wear one watch: the Cartier tank watch Grandma gave me just before she died with my name and the New York Yankees logo engraved on the back.

Anyway, according to Mac MacKenzie, there are two kinds of people in the world: hacks and flacks. Lucky for him, he never had to choose. All you need to know about Mac is that Jimy Boy offered him Beanie's job before Beanie took it.

Pete Girard covered Maryland state politics for us until he got sick of writing corruption stories and tired of wearing a suit and tie. I didn't like him then and I don't like him now. These days he wears the same pair of jeans every day and covers baseball as if a missed pick-off is a scandal. Rumor has it he hasn't changed his pants in six months. He's also had the same cold since the 1986 season, evidence of which can be seen in his Fu Manchu. He does not believe in fraternizing with the competition unless it's one of his buddies with whom he trades quotes.

Herm Brenner covered the Senators for the AP from 1954 until the day they left town. Herm was still a young man at the time and Sal says he had all sorts of offers. But Herm turned them all down for a job as a rim rat on the graveyard shift. He swore he wouldn't leave the rim until the Senators returned to Washington. On Opening Day, Myron found Herm sitting in the exact same place he was sitting eighteen years ago, eating the exact same thing he was eating the night the Senators left town: baked ziti.

Danno writes for the morning *Sun*. He won't travel with the team unless they lose sixty straight, which is beginning to look possible. Danno was an English major and once actually referred to Yankee Stadium in print as "the *locus amoenus* in the Bronx." He also throws like a girl and wants to go to bed with me. I like Danno.

It is baseball etiquette that beat writers go to the manager's office right after the game for comments, even if all he ever says is "Unbe-fucking-lievable." So, this afternoon, after the sixteenth straight loss, I followed Danno, Brenner, Girard, and MacKenzie into Monk's office.

"Well, Monk," Mac said. Mac always goes first and he always says, "Well, Monk."

"Unbe-fucking-lievable," Monk said.

He was leaning back in his chair, rubbing his beady little eyes and wheezing, "Unbe-fucking-lievable."

"What about shaking up the lineup, Monk, bringing some kids up from Triple A?" Brenner said.

"They're already here," Girard grunted.

Monk opened his eyes to confront the traitor but saw me first.

"That's it, boys," he said. "I ain't saying horseshit with Berkowitz here."

The boys looked at me. I looked at Monk. "Sorry, boys," I said. "I ain't leaving."

"C'mon, Monk," Girard said. "You can't do this to us."

"Sorry," Monk said.

"C'mon, A.B.," Girard said.

"Sorry."

"I'll do your legwork for you," Danno said.

I shook my head and we all shut our notebooks. "Close the bleeping door on the way out," Monk said.

I figured I might as well get it over with all at once. I went up to Stretch, the losing pitcher, who was eating tacos. "No can do," he slurped.

I tried Stein. "The skip is the skip," he said.

Mancusi. "Yo," he said.

And Mug Shot. "More so," he said.

From what Danno told me later, nobody had much more than that to say, so I guess it doesn't matter that no one in the stadium, including Girard, MacKenzie, and Brenner, is talking to me. Rump, Buck, Billy, and our nifty double-play combination, Guttierrez and Duvalier, who do not speak English, are the sole exceptions to Monk's vow of silence. My sources are not exactly impeccable. Guttierrez calls me La Conchita and smiles whenever I see him. Jean-Claude (Mini-Doc) Duvalier, our diminutive second baseman, is a fourth cousin once removed from the legendary Baby Doc. He's got the worst hands in the league, but he always kisses mine. One of these days, I swear to God, he's going to miss. Blessing still doesn't have a major league at bat. And all Buck says is "Buck be bad" whether he goes 5 for 5 or 0

for 5. Rump is 0 for 29 and just shrugs a lot. Oh I forgot: the
Stick. The Stick has only one thing to say to me and he says it all
the time: "Are you getting enough?"

So I wrote a lede that said: "It's beginning to look as if the
Washington Senators may go 0 for April."

Sal liked that so much, he didn't even notice there were no
quotes in the story. He says he's going to start a reader's poll.
"Will the Senators go 0 for April? Just call 1-800-U-LOSERS."
Anybody who guesses the date and the score of the first Senators
win gets a season ticket.

April 23 Today Stein microwaved Mr. Smith and I got
my first scoop of the season. Mr. Smith was an alley cat who had
lived in RFK for as long as anybody could remember, subsisting
on moldy chili dogs and flat beer. As a result, Mr. Smith had a
problem with flatulence and Stein had a problem with Mr.
Smith. Stein has a problem with any flatulence that isn't his own.

It was ten minutes after the game was called for rain, and
the cat, who was fairly huge, maybe fifteen pounds, was parading
back and forth through the locker room looking for leftovers and
rubbing himself against Stein's legs. Stein was not in a good
mood. Nobody was in a good mood. The Senators were winning,
6–0, when they called the game at the end of three and a half,
which meant that Stein's first home run of the season went for
naught and the record is still 0–16.

Stein has a well-documented history of animal abuse. He has
been known to torture bugs with ethyl chloride, the stuff trainers
use to freeze an injury. In baseball, the rule is you never rub.
Part of that is macho bullshit. Also guys know that the faster
they get down to first base, the faster the trainer will get there
with the ethyl chloride, which numbs the pain and makes the
hair on their arms stand straight up like icicles. I've seen whole
arms practically defoliated by this stuff.

Anyway, Stein likes to chase bugs around the locker room
spraying them with ethyl chloride and providing appropriate
death rattles. He's particularly good at the death rattle of a water
bug. Nobody really objected to his methods of pest control until
today. But then nobody thought he would off Mr. Smith.

Admittedly, Stein had had a bad day. First he was fined $250
for not being in the dugout when the umpire said "Play ball." He
was on the clubhouse phone at the time getting down on the

third race at Pimlico. Monk did not take well to the embarrassment of having to ask for time while Piggy went in search of their first baseman. Then Stein lost his dinger. So he was definitely not in the mood for Mr. Smith's advances. Two things are true about Mr. Smith: first, he sheds, or I should say, shedded. Also, he was never fixed. So every once in a while when Mr. Smith got really worked up, he would spray the locker room and Rube, the trainer, who kind of looked after Mr. Smith, would have to call in the fumigators.

Stein was pulling on his new Polo jeans and telling Girard to get fucked when Mr. Smith sprayed Stein, Stein's new Polo jeans, and Stein's new imported Italian leather jacket. Stein went crazy. "I'll kill him," he said. "I'll fucking fry him."

He grabbed a can of ethyl chloride from inside his spare protective cup and chased Mr. Smith all over the clubhouse, screaming, "You fucking spray me, I fucking spray you," until he caught up to him under the buffet table, where Mr. Smith was lapping up a major glob of Sloppy Joes. It was Mr. Smith's last supper. At least he died happy.

Stein froze him where he crouched, then picked him up and carried him into the trainer's room, where Rube had thoughtfully installed a microwave at the beginning of the season. Stein opened the door and placed the numb, dumb cat in the revolving oven. Most guys were still in the shower. So a lot of them didn't know what was going on. I happened to be talking to Buck, whose locker is next to the trainer's room. Buck started to protest, but Stein told him to get fucked, that this was between him and Mr. Smith. Buck is a rookie. Buck shut up.

Stein punched up the code for the Auto Sensor Cycle A-3 (cook beef, lamb medium) and stood guard, bat in hands, warding off any potential saviors. Stein had previously experimented with the microwave on his freeze-dried bugs. He was disappointed to find that neither ants nor roaches snap, crackle, and pop. Mr. Smith did not disappoint. He mewed and stewed and a crowd gathered outside the door as word passed of Stein's treachery.

"What's happening?" Stick said.

"Oh man, Stein's fryin' the cat," Demetrious said. "That's one po' mo'fucking cat."

"Oh man, Stein," Stick said.

For a moment I thought someone had finally found a way to offend Stick's elusive sensibilities. But I was wrong. Stick wasn't offended. He was merely jaded. "Microwaving is retro, man. It's old."

Stein looked stricken, the flush of innovation drained from his face. "Whaddya mean old?" he demanded. "You ever microwave a cat?"

"Nah, only a poodle," Stick said.

"When?" Stein demanded.

"Last year in Seattle. You were in Japan eating raw fish, if I recall."

Stick and Stein went round and round. Mr. Smith went round and round. The digital clock showed that twenty minutes of the allotted sentence had passed. "I'm telling you, man, it's been done," Stick said.

Just then there was a sickening *ka-boom*, the force of which rocked the table and shook Stein's bat. But he stood firm. The players peered inside the oven window. But you couldn't see anything except blood and fur. Mr. Smith had exploded. Only Al Brawn seemed surprised. Brawn looks and sounds pretty much the way you'd expect someone named Brawn to look. "I thought cats had nine lives," he said.

Still no one thought to turn off the oven. At the end of the cooking cycle, the oven beeped five beeps. The death knell of Mr. Smith.

Stick hummed taps, Rube shed a tear, and Lawson offered a prayer for Mr. Smith's soul and another one for Stein's. Piggy shrugged and said a black cat was bad luck anyways and maybe this was what we needed to get things turned around.

No one seemed particularly revolted, including me, which I think is a bad sign. One month with these guys and nothing gets to me. It's like, "Oh yeah, Stein microwaved a cat." This is not a healthy way to be.

Anyway, Rube got a garbage bag and poured Mr. Smith's remains into it and when the rain stopped he carried the bag out of the locker room, down the tunnel, and onto the field. I headed upstairs to the press box trying to decide just how tongue-in-cheek to write this. When I got to my seat, I could see Rube and Chester Doyle, the groundskeeper, standing at the mound. Rube was gesturing and pointing at the pitching rubber and Chet was standing there with his hands on his hips, shaking his head and also pointing at the mound.

Finally Chet disappeared for a while and Rube sat down, clutching the garbage bag to his bosom. Chet came back a little later with a shovel and a hoe and started to dig. When the hole under the pitching rubber was deep enough, Rube emptied the bag and said farewell to Mr. Smith. I wrote sixteen inches and sent it in. Zeke, the night editor, said it was too gross to print. But Sal overruled him and even ordered a black border around the story, which ran under the headline: MR. SMITH LEAVES WASHINGTON. When I left, Chet was still down on his knees shaping the mound with his hands, putting the finishing touches on Mr. Smith's final resting place.

Baltimore

April 24 Rain delay again tonight. There was no infield, no BP—nothing whatsoever for the players to do except play cards and watch "Oprah!" and refuse to talk to me, which they have been quite adamant about except, of course, when they're asking me to go to bed with them. It was Arroyo's turn today. Mr. Juanderful looks like a candidate on "The Price Is Right." He has four identical leisure suits, aqua, peach, beige, and lime, all with that decorative topstitching that was popular at Robert Hall's back in the sixties, and four identical pairs of blue suede shoes. All the hair on his head, except for a dainty fringe, has migrated to his cheeks, which sport the most miraculous pair of mutton chops you've ever seen. Arroyo thinks he is a looker. Actually, he looks a lot like the super in my grandmother's building when I was a kid. Anyway, he called me over to his locker and said, "I'm in room 1321," and pressed a key in my hand. Nice, huh? Arroyo doesn't have a place in D.C. He hasn't had a place in any of the nine major league cities he's called home. Hotels are a lot more convenient than a wife and kids.

My all-time favorite "How do ya do" was Call Flowers's. Call's a Hall of Famer. I met him my first day of spring training last year, the same day I met Rump. He is a roving instructor for the Phillies. You find that really bad teams always have a whole lot of Hall of Famers at spring training. It sort of helps make them forget about the prospects for the present. Anyway, the Phillies were playing the Mets and there was this group of reporters standing around, so I joined them. Call starts looking at my shins and *keeps* looking at my shins. So finally I say, "You like that white skin, huh, Call?" And Call says, "I *always* liked white skin. How long you stayin' anyways?"

Guy's seventy-seven years old and still hitting fungos and still looking for action. Just goes to show you never really lose the reflexes. Most guys are less cheerful about their rejections than Call and less imaginative in their come-ons, too. "What's your boyfriend think of this?" they say. I tell them all what I told Arroyo this afternoon. "He trusts me. And besides, he knows I have too much taste to sleep with men who aren't talking to me."

"Okay, okay, Berkowitz, so I talk to you, I talk to you," Arroyo said. But by then I was eavesdropping on Brawn and Duvalier.

Brawn is the fifth outfielder and he doesn't get a whole lot of playing time. So he's taken it upon himself to tutor Mini-Doc in English. To give you an idea of Brawn's qualifications, he ordered pie à la mode at dinner the other night and then asked the waitress if he could also have some ice cream on top.

Anyway, what got Brawn motivated was an incident last week. He was starting in right again in place of Demetrious, who took himself out of the lineup on account of a cold. Twice during the game, Brawn called for a short fly to right only to have to catch his second baseman as well as the ball. Mini-Doc doesn't speak much English except that which he learned from his hero Joaquin Andujar, who expressed his philosophy of life in one word, "Yaneverknow." Andujar is a pitcher, however. He never mastered "I got it."

So Brawn went to Piggy, whose French is just a tad more elementary than his English, and asked him to translate "I got it." What they came up with was: *"Je l'ai."* Brawn went around the locker room all day practicing. *"Je l'ai. Je l'ai."*

The next day, on the first ball hit to right, Brawn stands out there screaming, "I lay, I lay." Mini-Doc got the idea anyway and stopped dead in his tracks and watched as Brawn was blind-sided by Mug Shot, who came running over from center to help. "In actual point of factuality, he never called for the fucking ball," Mug Shot said.

The damnedest part of the story is that the same thing happened to Richie Ashburn when he was playing center for the '62 Mets. You could look it up. These guys are so bad, they can't even be original about it. It's sort of creepy really. I wonder if it's an omen. Can the 1989 Senators really be *that* bad?

Anyway, Brawn decided a rain delay was as good a time as any to start the lessons. So there they were in their birthday suits, Mini-Doc and Brawn, blowing smoke rings and practicing "A,E,I,O,U."

"Now repeat after me," Brawn said. He said it very loud and very slow, as if Jean-Claude was deaf as well as a French-speaking Haitian.

"We're pressing."

"We're pressing," Jean-Claude bellowed. He was a serious student and intent upon mimicking the teacher perfectly.

"We're due."

"We're due."

"Okay, now, bud, here's a tricky one," Brawn said. *"Our backs are up against the wall."*

"Our backs are up against zee wall."

"All right, guy! Okay!" Brawn was pleased. As well as ambitious. They had gotten all the way through "There is no place to go but up," "It's do or die," "There's no tomorrow," and "I come to play" when the rain stopped.

So play they did. The game started at 8:45 P.M. and ended with their seventeenth straight loss at 12:31 A.M. Mini-Doc made two errors, his tenth and eleventh of the season, which led to four unearned runs and to a new moniker in the Washington *Tribune:* Dr. E. Afterward, Brawn consoled him. "It's okay, bud," Brawn said. "There's no place to go but up."

Brawn is the Truth.

April 25   Monk benched Jean-Claude today, giving Billy Blessing his first major league start. Monk said he was hoping to light a bleeping fire under some bleeping asses. However, the only fire was set by Jean-Claude, who torched his locker in protest. Seems he hasn't been benched since third grade. He did what he did the last time he was benched. He took everything in his duffel bag and stuffed it in a garbage can and lit a match.

The firemen were just leaving the clubhouse when the game was once again called because of rain. The pungent odor of burned jockstraps filled the air. When I got downstairs, Dr. E was sitting on the shelf above Brawn's locker, coughing and bellowing, "I come to play. I come to play."

Piggy and Monk had a conference about what to do, and it was decided that everyone should ignore him except Brawn, who

speaks the same language, sort of. It took Al half an hour to coax
Jean-Claude down. The magic words were "Eeets steel earlee."

For once, Brawn really hit it on the nose. It is still early.
Which, of course, is a problem. We're already twelve games out
of first place and April isn't even over. Panic and lethargy are
beginning to set in. Monk practically punched out Demetrious in
the dugout after our fleet (i.e., black) leadoff man declined to run
out a routine grounder to short, which the infielder obligingly
threw into the stands. Mancusi trashed Mug Shot's boogie box
after he played an old Tommy James and the Shondells album six
times in a row. And Rump's wife, JoAnne, has made an appointment for him to see the First Lady's hypnotist Friday about his
slump. JoAnne is thrilled. Rump is obliging. "She says it usually
takes a year to get in to see the guy," Rump said. "I told her,
'JoAnne, the first seventeen games have felt like a year.'"

Home Again

April 29   The Washington Senators' relentless march toward oblivion has once again been halted by rain. You think God
is trying to tell us something? There was a big advance sale,
thirty thousand or so, for this game, so they are determined not
to call the sucker unless absolutely necessary, especially after last
night's rain-out, the fourth this week. They've covered and un-
covered the field twice so far and even sent out a guy to spread
sand on the mound an hour ago. He did a lovely job, and just as
he finished, the skies opened up again and it began to pour. Now
it's the bottom of the seventh and we're in our second rain delay,
with the Senators behind 6–5. It's 10:30 P.M. and the home plate
umpire hasn't been seen since he stuck his head out of the dugout
a half hour ago. The tarp is down and the scoreboard lights are
shining through the mist. I feel as if I'm seeing the world
through a scrim.

Also, I'm writing my fourth story in six days about the
Streak. I think people in town are finally starting to get excited
about this. It took a while, what with the Orioles having lost
twenty-one straight last year. But I think this team is starting to

make believers out of Washingtonians. Who woulda thunk there would be another team this bad again so soon?

When the Orioles won their first game exactly a year ago today, they had been outscored 129–44, outhit .311 to .200, and outpitched 1.93 to 5.96 ERA. So far to date, the Senators have been outscored 152–32, outhit .337 to .191, and outpitched 1.67 to 6.89 ERA. The O's did a lot of dumb things. But I don't think they ever had a second-string catcher who could throw a ball over the second baseman's head, only to have the centerfielder play it off the wall and hit the catcher in the balls with an incredible throw home.

But Baltimore did set a standard. They even had a party at Harborplace to celebrate their own ineptitude and sold out Memorial Stadium. "Civicwise," Mug Shot says, "they was awesome."

The nation's capital is not to be outdone. Everyone said Washington would never support another losing team. Everyone who said it was wrong. All over town there are posters proclaiming Washington's nostalgic losing past. FIRST IN WAR, FIRST IN PEACE, AND LAST IN THE AMERICAN LEAGUE—AGAIN! A parade down Pennsylvania Avenue is promised by the mayor when the Orioles' record is smashed. No ifs, ands, or buts about it. And every two-bit pol who ever lost an election is summoning the team to take courage in its time of trial. A resolution was introduced on the Hill yesterday by some congressman from Idaho: "Resolved that the Senators take heart from their defeats and know they are loved for their frailties."

Fact is: everybody's talking Senators. A D.C. funeral parlor arranged for a local mortician to send over leftover floral arrangements from some hot-shit funeral. My favorite was a horseshoe that spelled out DEARLY DEPARTED in pink carnations. Bobo the Bebop Queen, who calls himself the Drive-Time Deejay in D.C., has promised to stay on the air until the Senators win. His motto is "Baseball back in D.C. in '89!" which is particularly bitchy considering that was the battle cry before we got a franchise. He has also started an "Adopt a Senator" contest. "Take one of these cuddly creatures home as a pet," he says. "Otherwise, he might be put to sleep in the morning."

The Georgetown University Senators Fan Club has vowed to abstain from sex until the team wins, which upset the Fathers plenty. Not to be outdone, the George Washington University him when I get blocked. I read him my lede and he tells me it's fine and I'll be fine and they can't possibly keep it up all season. I'm not sure whether he means the silent treatment or the way they've been playing.

So with Michael away and all this rain I'm spending a lot of time at the office. Beat writers never go to the office. Sal keeps saying, "Go home! Why don't you go home? You're always bitching you're never home."

I should have taken his advice. But I didn't. And so I left myself wide open to Captain Fuck-up.

Captain Fuck-up is a fixture here, like the six televisions (four color, two black-and-white) that are always going at once, each tuned to a different channel and each louder than the next. But no one is louder than Captain Fuck-up, who is also known as Zeke Dombrowsky. Zeke has been the night sports editor at the *Trib* for the last twenty-nine years. He is a mean little cocksucker who learned the basics of who, what, and where so long ago he can't remember when anymore. He is a newspaper stiff. He not only believes in the inverted triangle, he looks like one. In fact, he looks like a Polish Danny DeVito with padding.

Around the newspaper, Zeke is known as Captain Fuck-up because that's all he ever says to anyone: "You fucked up."

If there are fifteen people in the office screaming "Cocksucker" into fifteen phones, you can bet that the one yelling loudest is Zeke. "You fucked up, you cocksucker."

I remember the day I came over to Sports, some reader called in to ask, "If you go to sleep in the snow, will you wake up dead?" Zeke took the call and told the guy to get himself a frontal lobotomy. Which kind of gives you an idea of the milieu.

Anyway, I'm sitting here at Marcus's desk, staring at his Tina Turner pinup and his December 1987 *Playboy* centerfold and listening to two grown men debate the merits of the Atlantic Coast Conference versus the Big East Conference in perfect Lefty Driesell dialect. I used to have my own desk, but Sal gave it away when I left for spring training.

Baseball writers do not come into the office unless they have to write an obituary or something. That's why I'm here. I just finished writing an appreciation of some former Senator great nobody remembers who's supposedly fading fast. Guy wasn't very good, so there isn't an office pool on when he'll kick the way there usually is. Dr. D still talks about the time he won a hundred bucks on Joe Louis.

Senators Fan Club has promised to screw until the team wins. They're even keeping score.

Jimy Boy has opened a special "Prayer-a-thon" telephone bank. For a fifty-cent toll call, you get the latest score and a daily homily for the team. Then an operator gets on the line and tries to sell you season tickets.

There is a lot of talk in the press box about whether these new Senators are as bad as the old Senators. There is no consensus on that. But everyone agrees they are as funny as the old Senators. Brenner was reminiscing a little while ago about one time back in the fifties when the Nats actually managed to get a man on first. This was a rare occasion and called for extraordinary measures. The manager sent in a pinch runner. His name was Julio Becquer, and he was fast of foot but slow of tongue. In point of fact, he spoke no English. So when he actually got all the way to third, the Nats had to call time again to remove him for a second pinch runner because Julio couldn't understand the third base coach's instructions.

That ain't bad. But I'll take the hidden-ball trick Stein pulled in the fifth anytime for sheer humor. He had the thing in his cup, for Christ sakes. God knows how long he had it there. Suffice it to say, when the moment of truth came, he had trouble getting a handle on the ball, which is how the go-ahead run scored.

Gotta go. It's clearly up. They're taking the tarp off the field. I guess there's no postponing the inevitable.

11:30 P.M. Number 19 in the books, 6–5.

April 30 I've been home more or less twelve days and Michael has been here for exactly three hours of them. I got back from Dulles at 4:00 A.M. He left for National at 7:00 A.M. I thought about letting him sleep. Now I'm glad I didn't. It was nice while it lasted.

Michael had gotten a tip from a cop he knows that some luggage had been circling the Delta Air Lines carousel at National for five hours when some porter grabbed it and $100,000 fell out. So Michael went out to the airport and ended up taking the first flight to Miami. By the time Michael found the guy whose name was on the bag, he was dead. Turns out the guy was the major crack supplier in D.C. So the City desk told him to stay in Miami. By the time he gets back, I'll be in Milwaukee.

We've been talking pretty much every night. Usually, I call

Today is the last game of April. The Senators are 0–19 and going for the collar. I'm not sure who's had a shittier month, them or me. Ruth keeps saying, "What did you expect?"

I guess it was stupid to tell her about the Yankees and the white ink and Stick and his date with the transvestite. "Isn't that wonderful?" I said. "Wonderful?" she replied. "It's disgusting. I don't see how you can spend your life talking to these people."

I reminded her that they're not speaking to me.

"You know what I mean. You used to be a serious person."

"Too serious," I thought but I didn't tell her that. Ruth doesn't have much of a sense of humor about certain things. One day last fall she and Michael and I were standing around reading the wires and this bulletin comes across about a Senate page who was raped in the Folding Room under the Rayburn Building by the legislative aide to a congressman from Alabama.

"Great rape," Michael says.

"Great rape!?!" Ruth says. "There is no such thing as a great rape. Have you ever been raped? What do you know about rape? Oh God! Oh, *men!*"

She won't forgive him for that or me for my charity toward the Washington Senators. But she would have known what to say to Captain Fuck-up. Me? I don't think of my best rejoinders until the next fiscal quarter. She would have told Zeke to fuck off.

Being night editor, Zeke is in charge from the time Sal goes home to Manassas at 7:30 P.M. until the paper goes to bed at 2:39 A.M. Basically, since I write at night, this means Zeke runs my life.

I had just gotten in this morning when he came by and said, "Berkowitz, you fucked up. You were fifteen minutes late, you were seven inches over budget, and you shoulda had the score in the goddamn lede."

"Hello," I said.

"I said, 'You shoulda had the score in the lede.'"

"Nice to see you too, Zeke."

"Sal says you fucked up too, Berkowitz."

I groaned.

"Now, see here, R.B.—"

"A.B."

"The score's gotta be in the first paragraph."

"Look, Zeke. It says they lost. It says they lost their nineteenth straight. It says two more and they tie the Orioles' record for the worst start ever, eight more and they break the record for the most consecutive losses in history. That's the story, Zeke. That and Buck. He's only 17 for 23 since Stein put shit in his shoes. He had three pumps yesterday. Three home runs! That's the story."

"But it don't say they lost, 6–5, till the third graph."

"What's the difference? They got shellacked, didn't they?"

Zeke is big on getting shellacked.

"Yeah," he said. "But it's got to be in the first graph."

He was stomping his foot and waving his cigar and clutching his head with his hand. Also, he was frowning. Zeke's always frowning. He's got a permanently down-turned mouth that makes him look like he's grimacing whether he is or he's not. He also has a full head of oily black hair that is pasted to his scalp by some foul-smelling tonic that could be Shoe Goo, for all I know. Anyway, he was standing there pulling his hair when I heard Milo say, "What's happening?"

Milo McHenry is the only daily sports columnist left in America. He also writes game stories in a pinch. The guy probably writes 300,000 words a year. And not one of them is "horse-spit" or "bleep."

I wasn't sure how long he'd been listening. Guys around the league say the same thing. Somehow you don't notice he's there until you see it in the paper the next morning.

"I was just explaining to R.B. here that she's got to have the score in the first paragraph," Zeke said.

By now Roth, the highs guy, Davis, the Redskins guy, Rocky, the racing guy, Vito, the hockey guy, and Pincus, who smells, were all standing around listening. None of them ever put the score in the first paragraph, except maybe Vito, who once wrote a lede saying the Capitals had fought to a 5–4 tie and it went in the paper that way 'cause Captain Fuck-up didn't catch it.

It's quite unusual that all of us would be at the office at the same time, especially on a Sunday morning. These guys know enough not to come in even if I don't. None of them would have been there except that Sal had issued a memorandum saying that if all 1988 expense accounts aren't in by today we will forfeit all moneys due us.

There isn't a single one of them that hasn't been reamed out by Zeke. And there isn't a single one of them that doesn't share some of his less lofty sentiments about me. Liberated these guys aren't. But they aren't exactly what you'd call independent thinkers either. They were waiting on Milo.

Milo is God. Milo named Sal sports editor when he gave up the job five years ago to focus on the column. Milo hasn't missed a deadline in thirty years. In the old days, when he was a cub reporter, the nicest thing you could say about a newspaper guy was "Nobody can carry his typewriter." Well, nobody can carry Milo's McHenry's lap-top either unless he's very drunk, in which case he regards it as a professional courtesy.

Milo looked at Zeke. Everyone else looked at Milo. My fate hung in the balance.

"She can play, Zeke," Milo said. "She can play."

I can tell you right now what I want on my tombstone: SHE CAN PLAY.

It began to rain at 2:00 P.M., five minutes before game time. Beanie called the weather service and they said there was a front coming through. So we waited and waited for fair weather to arrive. It was the beginning of the longest day of the longest month in Washington Senators history.

The game didn't start until 7:30 P.M., and when it did it was as slow and as boring as a close game can possibly be, full of stranded runners and fidgety batters and pitchers who shook off too many signs. Then, at 9:15 P.M., the showers came again.

The umpires did everything they could to avoid covering the field. They played the seventh in a drizzle, the eighth in a gale, the ninth in a downpour. The Senators were one strike away from their twentieth straight loss when the home plate umpire finally called time. Bases were loaded. The Mariners were winning, 5–4. The count on the Stick was 3–2.

It rained and rained. Twice the umpires came out to check the field and twice they refused to call it. Girard, MacKenzie, and Brenner sat in the press room drinking beer and telling rain delay stories. I figured maybe this would be a good time to make amends. So I chimed in with this story about Nigel Lamb, the tennis player, who used to circle the locker room before a really big match eyeballing everyone's genitals. When he got to his opponent for the day, he would stop and say, "You don't think you're going to go out and win with *that*?" It's a great story, and true. But Girard, MacKenzie, and Brenner didn't think so. They went back to their conversation without even acknowledging me.

I went back to writing my American League notebook, cursing them under my breath, and promising never again to try to be one of the guys.

An hour passed. Two. And still they wouldn't call the game. Finally, at eleven-thirty, Chet Doyle and the grounds crew came out and started pouring sand on the basepaths. Centerfield was a swamp. First base was an isthmus. The home plate umpire put on galoshes. Ten minutes before midnight, he signaled it was time to play ball.

The pitcher, who looked half asleep, kicked the dirt from his spikes and went to the rubber. The Stick stepped in. The runners took their leads. There were maybe two thousand people left in the stadium, historians who wanted to see for themselves if the Senators would become the first team in history to go 0 for an entire month.

The pitcher went to the stretch. The Stick took three mighty practice hacks and never took the bat off his shoulder again. He looked at a called strike three, a fastball right down the cock. And at 11:59 P.M. the Washington Senators lost April.

Milwaukee

May 1 Zeke called at 1:25 A.M. Needless to say, I fucked up.

"Windy Bragg signed a fat Jap. Some guy named Ricky Himeshi. Plays for the Hiroshima Toyo Carp. He's supposed to be the next coming of Sadaharu Oh or some such shit. It's on the wire. The *Post* has it, too. Where the fuck are you?"

"In bed," I said.

"Don't give me that shit," Zeke said. "Sal don't like getting beat on news stories. And they beat your ass. You better make some calls."

Make some calls, the man said. What the hell. They don't talk to me all day. Maybe they'll talk to me at one-thirty in the morning. You never know, Sal says.

So I made some calls. Monk hung up on me. Rump wasn't in his room. And Windy Bragg, our voluble general manager, had his phone off the hook. It took three minutes to find that out, which meant there were twelve left to deadline. I was playing catch-up all right. The first rule of catch-up is you gotta get just enough stuff so they can stick a staff byline on the sucker and say they hadn't gotten beat, which they had. *I* had. Under the present circumstances, this was not exactly what you'd call an upset. When the owner, general manager, manager, and three quarters of the twenty-four-man roster aren't talking to you, you might get beat on a story or two, especially one about a Japanese slugger who doesn't speak English. But Zeke didn't want to hear about that. And neither would Sal.

I was desperate. I called Stein. Stein played in Japan last year for the Yomiuri Giants. "Paid me a million bucks to eat fish and hit dingers out of bandboxes," he told me when we were still on speaking terms. "They called me their Gaijin. I think it means 'alien' or something. They were nice little cocksuckers. But the only English words they know are 'Sony' and 'Mitsubishi.'"

Stein was in bed.

"What do you know about Ricky Himeshi?"

"I'm not talking to you."

"Give me a break, Stein."

"Ricky Himeshi? He's a fat little fucker who thinks he's Babe Ruth. Ask him yourself. He's down in the lobby waiting for someone to ask for his autograph."

Stein does not lie. Ricky Himeshi is a fat little fucker and he was down in the lobby, though as far as I could tell he was only waiting for a room, along with thirty members of the Japanese sporting press. I introduced myself. He bowed. I asked him a question. He bowed deeper. I showed him my Baseball Writers Association of America press card. He bowed as deeply as he could, straightened up with considerable difficulty, and shook my hand vigorously. "Press! Press! Very nice press," he said.

I asked him how it felt to be in America. He bowed and smiled and shrugged. So I started acting out America, crossing my heart and pointing to a flag on the television with a station that was signing off for the night. It was 1:35 A.M. and I was playing charades with a fat Jap in the lobby of the hotel. "*Oh* yes," he said, smiling and nodding and bowing as if he was bobbing for apples. "Gaijin so very happy to be here."

I bowed and smiled and begged a quote from an English-speaking reporter who writes for the Gaijin's hometown paper. Zeke grunted and hung up, which I think was his way of saying I was a lucky bastard who had just missed sucking the big one. For once he was right. One of these days, my ass will be grass.

Captain Fuck-up and I haven't exactly seen eye to eye since December, when he inserted the words "out indefinitely with cancer" into the first sentence of my story on Ron Grant, the Redskin tight end who has leukemia. Here I am writing about this guy who's lost all his hair and 90 pounds and will probably also lose his life to a disease he can't spell and Zeke changes the lede to say: "Grant, the 245-pound blocking tight end, is out in-definitely with cancer." Nice, huh? The telephones really rang off the hook on that one. I even won an award for the tackiest lede of the month. I was truly honored. But I figured if I didn't say anything, Zeke would maybe see how I was just one of the guys, sucking it up and all. But Zeke didn't see it that way. He just thought it was a wily feminine ploy to show him up by suffering in silence.

If I remember exactly, what he said was "Whaddya think this is? The fucking *New York Times?* You wanna write poetry, do it on someone else's shift."

Maybe he's right. Maybe I'm not cut out for running and subbing. Last time I used a four-syllable word in a story, Zeke told me it wasn't in the *Trib* style book and to keep my fucking microcosms to myself.

Well, anyway, trade rumors are rampant in the microcosm. Stick is going to Baltimore, Stein to the Braves. And everyone else is going to hell. Tempers are getting frayed. Demetrious hung a No-Pest Strip over his chair yesterday and taped a NO TRESPASSING barrier around his locker. "Shitfuckpiss, I don't talk to no mo'fucking bugs," he said, before disappearing into the john. Girard ripped Rump in the Sunday *Post.* They stripped the sucker across their page: WHAT'S REALLY WRONG WITH RUMP! Girard quoted unnamed team sources as saying Rump is jaking it in order to force a trade. Now Rump isn't talking to Girard, which just about breaks my heart.

Windy finally issued a statement this morning saying it's too early to panic and that all trade discussions are on hold. Windy is the only baseball man I've ever met who doesn't like to talk base-ball. He issues statements instead. At least he looks like a baseball man even if he doesn't sound like one. He's got a thinning white flattop, so thin, in fact, that all you can see is his scalp. He's so fat that he's got a roll of flesh that circles his neck like an orthopedic collar. No one knows exactly what he did to earn the job of general manager, having been out of baseball for eleven years when Jimy Boy hired him. But he sure can eat. Anyway, he went around the locker room today, clomping guys on the back and grunting and handing out these Xeroxed copies of his statement, which said: "I don't want the players worrying about getting traded with so much else on their minds. They don't need to get any more depressed than they already are."

Stein read this and just about collapsed laughing. "Worried?

Depressed? Women and children better look out. We're talking *Titanic* here. It's every man for himself."

Stein has decided to talk to me, but only off the record. Today he wanted my opinion of the worst way to die, dehydration or immolation?

"Try covering you assholes," I suggested.

Anyway, tonight the Senators tied the Baltimore Orioles' record for the worst start ever in the history of baseball, twenty-one consecutive losses. Tomorrow we go for immortality. It's getting to be like *The Invasion of the Body Snatchers* around here. Loss by loss, our following grows. There are now fifty reporters detailing the daily agony of the Washington Senators, including one from Bangladesh, and one from the Washington *Blade*. The gay community has taken a big interest in baseball ever since Stick's encounter with the taffeta queen. "A fucking death-watch," Billy calls it.

Beanie has become the most popular man in America. He does twenty interviews a day and says nothing in all twenty of them. He says he's been getting a lot of calls from people with jobs that end in *ist*, including one from a paleontologist, whom he put on hold while he went to look the word up in the dictionary. Miss Lisa, the palm reader, offered to read twenty-four palms. Madonna's astrologer sent a team chart. A statistician at the University of the District of Columbia told him not to worry, the odds of two twenty-one-game losing streaks two years in a row were 8.7 in a million. So much for math. This afternoon a medium named Rex showed up at the stadium and offered to contact the spirit of the dead bats. For a small fee.

Benny Albani, who does sports for Channel 8, is leading an 0–162 campaign. He did his stand-up live from the batting cage tonight wearing an 0–162 T-shirt, which are going for $10.95 each in Georgetown. "C'mon, people, we're talking awesome, people. We're talking a feat unequaled in history, and you'd have great attendance, too. Everybody comes out to see 0–162. Who comes out for 2–160? C'mon, guys, get with the program. If you can't win 'em all, let's lose 'em all! Am I right?"

Don't tell this to Monk. Monk is in a funk. Every comedian in the country has called to cheer him up—Henny Youngman, Bill Cosby, Robin Williams, Richard Pryor. Quick: What do Michael Jackson and the Washington Senators have in common? They all wear gloves for no apparent reason.

Or, hear the one about the boy who ran away from home

because his parents beat him? "Where ya going?" the cop asks. "RFK," the kid replies. "The Senators don't beat anyone."

But Monk ain't laughing. And he isn't taking any calls either, not even from Wayne Newton and Donna Summer. "He only talks to God," Rump said. "And not even Him if He calls collect."

Lawson called a special chapel meeting before the game. Billy Blessing happened to be indisposed at the time. Not wanting to be rude, he sat on the can for twenty minutes trying to decide what to do. Finally he flushed the toilet and marched naked through the Twenty-third Psalm. "They sounded like real nice guys," he said. "Thanking God and all. Lawson was really pumped up. He kept saying how Jesus really gutted it out on the cross. And Pentacost said, 'Yep, He really played hurt.' I was just trying to get out of there. Lawson yells out, 'Billy Blessing, what do you believe?' It's like he's trying to sell you the Encyclopaedia Britannica or something."

When we got to the ballpark, there were boxes of Surpass on every stool and a note from Jimy Boy suggesting that everyone drink ten ounces a day for the rest of the season. Some health fanatic who owns a combination laundry and workout studio had donated a lifetime supply of the stuff.

"What is this shit?" Stick said, spitting pink goop on Stein's sanitary socks. "A potion of vitamins, electrolytes, and amino acids," Piggy replied.

"Well, it tastes like shit," Stick said. "It tastes like we play."

After the game, which was routine in every respect except that it was the twenty-first straight loss, Monk chugged ten ounces of the shit and said, "It's not how bleeping good you play when you play good. It's how bleeping good you play when you play bad. And we play bad as bleeping good as anyone in the bleeping league."

Danno gave me the quote.

May 2   The Gaijin made his locker room debut today. He was sitting in his cubicle wearing a white silk kimono with Babe Ruth's Number 3 on the back, a jockstrap, and a Nikon around his neck when the team bus arrived. He had taken a twenty-six-dollar cab ride to County Stadium, which is five blocks from the hotel. As the players dressed, he went from locker to locker, bowing and smiling and taking a picture of each of his new teammates. "So very happy to be here," he said. "So very happy to be here."

He was trying to get Lawson to smile when Stein emerged from the trainer's room, also in a kimono and a jockstrap, with a fungo bat raised ominously over his head. Stein is still trying to keep things loose. "I have come to vanquish you, Gaijin-San!"

"Why, if it isn't Samurai Stein," Rump said.

The Gaijin looked puzzled, but only until panic set in. Stein advanced on the Gaijin, backing him into the buffet table with the pregame meal and pinning him against a platter of Sloppy Joes. "Yaaaa-hah!" Stein said.

"So very happy to be here," the Gaijin said.

"Yaaaa-hah!" Stein said again.

It was quite an accomplishment. He actually got the Gaijin to bend. He was in fact doubled over backward into a vat of Gulden's Extra Spicy and the Sloppy Joes. His hair was dipped in relish. His white silk kimono was suddenly Sloppy Joe red. The Gaijin was no longer so very happy to be here. Luckily for him, Rube, the trainer, arrived just in time with his uniform and told Stein to fuck off. The Gaijin looked quite relieved until he tried to put the sucker on. It wasn't even close. Baseball players have this saying about everybody putting their pants on the same way, one leg at a time. It's their way of saying they're just regular guys. Well, let's just say the Gaijin is an exception to the rule. You couldn't have hoisted him into those pants with a crane. So he stood there stark naked at his cubicle, his once white kimono at his feet, while Rube went to look for something bigger. Like the infield tarp.

Now, I know what I've said about not looking at guys in their wherewithal, which is why I always carry a steno pad and two felt-tip pens. But I confess I could not take my eyes off the Gaijin. And neither could anyone else. His triceps hung. His chest hung. His belly hung so low you couldn't see his protective cup. The Gaijin was 280 if he was a pound. Monk had asked for a right-handed bat with pop and he got an entire outfield.

"I think he ate a Datsun," said Stein.

"I think he ate a Sumo," said Billy.

Brawn looked perplexed. "I thought Japs only ate fish."

The Gaijin tried on uniforms for an hour: 46, 48, 50, 54. He even tried Piggy's warmups. It was no go. He was still standing there stark naked when the public address announcer announced him as a pinch hitter for Guttierrez in the top of the ninth. He went to bat wearing a SENATORS cap, his HIROSHIMA TOYO CARP road uniform with the SENATORS logo taped over it, the biggest jockstrap ever seen in major league baseball, and a chance to win the Senators' first game of the year. He struck out. But at least he went down swinging. I mean that literally, by the way. He swung from his heels on an 0–2 pitch and landed with a thud in the dirt in front of home plate. It took the bat boy, the umpire, and the Brewers catcher to pull him to his feet.

So now the Senators hold the record: 0–22, the worst start ever in the history of baseball. The record for the longest losing streak is 23, held by the 1961 Phillies. Of course, that's only the modern era. Louisville lost 26 straight in 1889. Don't put it past us.

In the press box after the game, Beanie released a statement from Jimy Boy saying Rube would provide the Gaijin with an immediate "body transition plan" of 800 calories a day. Also, all golf clubs and backgammon sets have been banned from the team plane. In a separate announcement, the club designated Billy Blessing for reassignment to the Senators' Triple A team in order to make room for the Gaijin on the roster.

"They'll have to reassign the whole middle infield in order to make room for him," Billy said when I found him sitting by himself in the dugout. He was still in uniform. The eye black was still smudged under his eyes. He was alone in the stadium except for the guys sweeping out the peanut shells and two little boys, sons of one of the Brewers, practicing their home run trots. "That's when the game was easy," he said. "You didn't have any worries, pressures. You'd just go out and play and not worry about getting sent down. You were excited just to pick up the ball.

"My sister and me made up our own field, our own rules. Anything over the elm was a home run. But the hitter had to go get it. We hit with a tennis ball. Even I hit a few. But there was a big old dog in the neighbors' backyard, and we lost a few tennis balls that way."

"You ever feel like that now?"

"I'm too nervous to feel like a little kid. But once you put on the uniform, I'll tell you what, you don't want to take it off. Sometimes I watch how guys go about their business as they put on the uniform. They get younger. They start changing. They come in old and sore and they metamorphose. They change into little kids and they're ready to go play baseball again. It isn't till after, when you're sitting around like this, that you know you hurt again."

I pointed out that the Triple A club is 13–7 and he'll be playing every day. Billy nodded. He's a realist. You can't be too secure if you're the twenty-fourth man on a club that's lost twenty-two straight. Still, I can't help but wonder if they know who gave me the tape. Also, I can't afford to lose any more friends. Or sources. Especially ones that know the word "metamorphose."

May 3 Today I called Sammy Esposito.

I was surprised how easy it was to find him. I guess I didn't really think of him as a person with a job and a phone number and bills to pay. Sammy was history to me—an entry in my Revised, Updated, and Expanded Baseball Encyclopedia, right there on page 938 between Alvaro Espinoza and Cecil Espy, the only Esposito ever to play major league ball.

ESPOSITO, SAMUEL
B. Dec. 15, 1931, Chicago, Ill. BR TR 5'9" 165 lbs.

That's where he began for me and that's where he ended with the last year under his name:

2 teams CHI   A (1G—.000)   KC A (18G—.200)

He was a name in fine print, a signature in cowhide on a child's baseball glove. He was the first man I ever took to bed.

I never expected him to answer his own phone.

"Esposito," he said.

"Ari Berkowitz," I replied.

Sammy told me about his life after baseball, coaching college ball in North Carolina, teaching kids the fundamentals of the game. I told him about my grandmother, Delia Bloom Berkowitz, and the Sam Esposito glove she bought me at Saks Fifth Avenue in the spring of 1963.

"Do you still have it?"

I could be wrong, but I thought I heard a note of expectation in his voice. "Nah," I said. "My mother threw it out years ago."

"Oh, too bad," he said. "I don't have mine either. I went looking for it in my locker last year. I was gonna give it to my son. A couple of years ago I gave it to a kid 'cause he didn't have one. I never have seen it since. Kid swears he gave it back to me. I feel kinda bad about it. It was the last one I had."

"I'd give you mine if I had it," I said.

"I believe you would," Sammy replied.

"I've got a Dave Parker now. But I never have slept with it yet."

Sammy laughed. There was a pause while static occupied the line. "Saks Fifth Avenue, you say. That's kind of shocking, really. It's not like I was Joey Proud or Mickey Mantle."

"It's not like my grandma would have known the difference."

He laughed again. "So tell me. Were you any good?" Sammy wanted to know what kind of ballplayer was wearing his glove.

"I could throw some leather around. I had soft hands."

"You probably still do," he said.

"You know, 'Good field, no hit.' That was the book on me."

"Tell me," he said.

Sammy played ten years for the White Sox with a career batting average of .207 and 8 home runs in 792 at bats. He batted .000 in the one World Series he got in. He was a scrub, a utility man, the guy who did the little things right. One year he earned $17,000. That was big money then. "Mrs. Esposito didn't raise any dummies," he said.

A couple of years back, he played an inning or so at an Old-Timers' game in Chicago and they wanted him to bat. He declined. "No point in trying to change things now," he said.

He played some third, some second, some short. He backed up Luis Aparicio. "In those days, as soon as you made the club, you'd sign with Spalding. That's what you signed for: two pairs of spikes and two gloves. Aparicio used my model. In fact, he let me break 'em in. He'd get a ton of his model. I got two, and he'd always be stealing mine.

"I remember seeing the Sam Esposito model in a couple of Chicago department stores. But I can't say as I remember many kids wearing them. They did try to imitate your model, Spalding did. But as far as the construction of it, it was very cheap."

"Yeah, I know. I broke my thumb twice trying to catch with it. There was no pocket, no padding. Just your name."

I could feel my hand sliding inside it again, trying to get comfortable. I could see the unyielding yellow leather of the thumb and the heel, which were too thick, and the fold that no amount of oil could soften, and the pocket that stung no matter how gently Dad threw me the ball. "Your grandma probably just picked out the first one she saw," Sammy said.

"Well, actually, it was the only one they had."

"You're kidding," Sammy said.

"My grandma didn't know any better than to go looking for a baseball glove in a ladies' department store. She lived a block from Yankee Stadium for twenty years and never set foot in it."

"But she loved you," Sammy said.

"Yeah. And when she died all I had left was the New York Yankees, which sort of explains things. Why I'm doing this, I mean."

"Which is what?"

"Covering the Senators for the Washington *Tribune.*"

"Unbe-fucking-lievable," he said.

It turns out Sammy played with Monk one season way back in '52 in Waterloo, Iowa, when they were both starting out.

"Right," I said. "Monk isn't talking to me because I'm a girl. And everyone else isn't talking to me because of Monk."

"It's a long season," Sammy said. "You never know. In baseball, you just never know."

"Yeah, like the other night. We were winning, 6–0, in the middle of the fourth when it starts to rain. Larry Barnett was behind the plate. He tried real hard to be nice. He waited three whole hours to call the game."

"Poor dumb bastards," he said.

"Baseball," I said.

"Well now, don't go feeling *too* sorry for them," Sammy said. "They're still getting paid long money. And they're still up there in the Show."

His voice echoed over the line and somehow the bad connection reminded me of the way things used to be when my love for baseball was new and I oiled my glove nightly and slept with the scent of Speed-EE Mitt and Glove Dressing infiltrating my dreams.

"I quit coaching last year," he said. "I'm assistant athletic director now."

"Sammy, you hung 'em up!"

I think he detected the disappointment in my tone. "Well," he replied. "I been trying to win ballgames one way or another for forty years. Don't you think that's enough?"

Maybe I was wrong. But it seemed as if neither of us really

wanted to say good-bye. I know I didn't. I liked him even better now.

"Well," Sammy said. "Call again. Call anytime. We'll talk ball or whatever. And remember, it's a long season."

"I will," I said. "I will."

Minneapolis

May 6   The Streak has acquired a life of its own. It started out one day with a loss and has grown, day by day, loss by loss, until it is no longer a finite thing, a result, or even a record, but something much larger, Loss, a thing so deep, a vortex so compelling that it is irresistible and also indescribable. Because Loss can really only be known or defined in opposition to something and the Senators haven't won yet, so they cannot really say what it is to lose and to lose and to lose again no matter how many times people like me ask.

Still, we ask and they try to explain, which is unusual. When ballplayers seek solace in words you know things are bad. Brawn, the linguist, is in Monk's doghouse because he forgot he wasn't supposed to talk to me and said after loss Number 24, "It's not whether you win or lose but the way you play the game."

"How," I said.

"How what?" Brawn said.

"How you play the game."

"Oh yeah," Brawn agreed. "That is a problem."

Demetrious has only one thing to say. "Shitpissfuck, shitpissmo'fuck" has become his mantra.

Stein, on the other hand, grows more expansive by the day. Like yesterday, after loss Number 24, he decided the Streak is an alien invasion. "It's like the blob that devoured Cleveland, or the Thing, I mean. It's this slimy, icky amoeba-like thing, oozing all over the place and sucking up everything it touches. That's what losing is."

Today the Thing sucked all the air out of the Metrodome. How else can you explain the short circuit that caused the air-conditioning to fail in the middle of the fifth inning? Not that it mattered except as a metaphor. By that time all the life had been sucked out of the Senators, too.

Lefty O'Donnell was the starter. Lefty is neither a southpaw nor an Irishman. He's called Lefty because of his politics, which are decidedly right of center (he's starting a Washington Senators chapter of the John Birch Society). He's actually Italian, but his mother remarried after his father, Gino, left and he was given his stepfather's name.

Anyway, Lefty walked in the first three runs by walking the first six batters he faced. "Give the bleepers something to hit," Monk said, patting him on the butt the way baseball managers do. So Lefty laid that baby on in there and gave up a two-run double, prompting Rump to go out to the mound for a conference. "Hey, Lefty," he said. "Some of our infielders are married. And some of them might even want to have kids." Lefty nodded and walked two more.

Later, after loss Number 25 had gone into the books, Buck, who is an optimist, said, "You've got to give accreditation where accreditation is due. It was a team effort on behalf of our athletes. If you throw out the first inning, we were in the game."

And Stein, who is getting to be a regular philosopher, said, "It isn't a monkey on our backs. It's Godzilla." At which point he began scratching his armpits and hopping around the locker room, grunting.

What else can they do? They are possessed and they know it. For others the Streak is a metaphor for the human condition or a divine plan for testing the human spirit. But the players cannot afford such lofty abstractions. They are at the mercy of the game that can shatter hearts in a million pieces the way a fastball in on the fists can shatter your best bat. Jimy Boy says it is God's will. But the players know better. They know it is baseball's eternal internal dynamic working its way through to a not yet logical conclusion. They are powerless to do anything about it.

Monk doesn't even try. All he does is mumble and spit and cross himself. His job is safe. He has called for more prayer but not for any more batting practice. I asked Rump why. "None of the coaches can throw the ball sixty feet, six inches," he said.

The team batting average is .197. With men on base, it's .146. Every fly ball is a field trip. Every ground ball requires a posse. The clubhouse is a morgue. The dugout is worse. There is nothing to be done except wait or demand to be traded. Demetrious was first on line, calling a press conference to announce, "I'd rather ride the pines on Mars than play the outfield for these mo'fuckers. Then again, playing for these fuckers is like playing on Mars." He's one to talk. He played a single into a three-run triple today and left four men in scoring position, a fine individual effort.

Whatever it is that has worked for them in the past, they have tried it or tried the opposite. They have shaved or not shaved. They have eaten grits or not eaten grits. They have crossed themselves or not crossed themselves. The entire starting lineup is either using Stick's bat or touching it before heading for the on-deck circle. Fat lot of good that's done. Stick is leading the league in home runs and strikeouts. But so far only the strikeouts have rubbed off on anyone. Today fourteen Senators went down swinging.

Yesterday Rump shaved the beard he's had for sixteen years, figuring either it would change his luck, or if it didn't, at least nobody would recognize him. Actually, I did recognize him. I was right. He does look like Robin Williams. He went 0 for 4 anyway in his first beardless game ever in the majors and was surrounded in the locker room afterward by fifty reporters looking for any new variation on a loss and almost as many photographers shoving each other out of the way in an attempt to get the best picture of his heretofore unseen chin. "I didn't shave it," he told them. "I plucked it out hair by hair. I'm into pain."

Last night he got a call from a counselor at the National Chronic Pain Outreach Association, not to mention a few from groupies with sadomasochistic fantasies. "Avoid advertising your despair," the counselor told him. "But be honest with yourself and share your pain with those close to you."

So he asked me to share his pain at breakfast this morning. At first I thought he was kidding, then I got a look at his face, which is raw and dabbed with little pieces of toilet paper where he's cut himself. His face is a metaphor for the Streak. "The thing is," he said, "you couldn't not give a damn and do this bad. But you can't give this much of a damn and do any better."

It's a paradox, all right. They try and they try and they try too much. And in trying too much, they overswing and overthrow. "You're overswinging!" "You're overthrowing!" someone will say. And then they try not to try so hard because that is the one sin baseball never forgives. You can't body-check some goon into the boards. You can't spear him with your helmet. You can't punch his nose up into his brain. All you can do is relax, and that is the one thing they just cannot do. As Rump says, "In baseball, if you suck it up too much, you just plain suck."

So they wait for the immutable laws to work in their immutable way. And they remind themselves that the best teams lose 40 percent of the time and the best hitters connect one time out of three. They are ballplayers and fatalists.

May 7 I don't think it can get any worse than today, the twenty-sixth loss of the season. Rump went for the collar again, the tenth time this season. And when he came to bat in the eighth, Tony Diaz, the Twins manager, got up on the steps of the dugout and started screaming, *"Easy out! Easy out!"*

Tony and Rump haven't gotten along ever since Rump played out his option when Tony took over the Yankees some years back. Rump never said why. He just said he'd never play for the guy.

The count went 0–1. Now everybody was on the steps of the dugout. *"Easy out! Easy out!"*

Rump swung at a pitch in the dirt for 0–2. Now the whole damned Metrodome was screaming. *"Easy out! Easy out!"* And you know how loud that place can be. It reverberated around the stadium like the wave, only aural.

Rump backed out of the box and leaned his bat against his legs and reached for some dirt. Lots of dirt. Then he stepped back in and looked at a chest-high fastball from Reardon for a called strike three.

Bench jockeying, infield chatter, the clubhouse needle, they are voices of the game and Rump has heard them all. But I don't think he's ever heard those words before, not even in Tee Ball when he was six. One thing Rump Doubleday has never been is an easy out. And he's never taken one either. In fact, the more inexorable his slump becomes, the more he talks. His postgame interviews have become a daily exegesis. One day he's opening up his shoulder too much; the next day he's going back to an upright stance; and the day after that he's resolved to back off the plate. But not today. Today he just sat facing his locker, waving us all away.

I asked Buck what happened.

"He just come in the dugout saying it over and over. 'Easy out. Easy out.' I thought sure he was gonna break his bat or something. We all did. But he just racked it and said, 'Can't get it done at home. Can't get it done at the plate. Easy out? There isn't one.'

"What he mean by that, A.B.?"

I shrugged and glanced at Rump, who was still slumped in his chair by his locker, refusing all entreaties to talk. Buck read my mind and Rump's posture. "Somebody put a hurt on him somewheres," Buck said. "And it ain't just his bat."

Kansas City

May 8 Demetrious showed up at Beanie's room at four this morning looking for me. He was wearing a trench coat and a glazed look. "Where that fucking Berkowitz at? Where that fucking Berkowitz?"

Apparently he was fairly exercised, so Beanie suggested he take off his coat and stay awhile. Demetrious accepted the invitation and threw his coat on the floor, revealing his naked self and a semiautomatic pistol.

I got this from Roy, the road secretary, who thought I ought to know even if telling me costs him his job. Roy is my new hero. He says Beanie swears it was just a water pistol. But I'm spending today in my room just in case. Apparently Demetrious didn't like something I wrote. Jesus. All I said was he plays rightfield like a fourteen-year-old punk rocker trying to follow Fred Astaire for the first time. Somebody must have told him it wasn't a compliment.

May 9 The Senators are now officially the worst team ever in the history of major league baseball. People will argue for years about who was better, Willie or Mickey or Joey Proud? Baseball is about conjecture and imagination. But no one will ever argue with this. No one *can* argue with this. This is incontrovertible.

This is what happened on the night the Washington Senators lost their twenty-seventh game in a row and eclipsed the mark set 101 years ago in Louisville, Kentucky. First they got a lead. This was extraordinary enough, being only the fifth time this season they've had one. It came on Buck's first career grand slam, a shot majestic enough to raise even the most exhausted cynic's hope that we will all soon be sent home to our loved ones. Hope is a setup.

Mr. Juanderful, whose right arm is three inches shorter than his left and bends in places other than the elbow, gave up four runs in the seventh to tie the game and was ejected when the home plate umpire went out to check the ball and a lion's tongue fell out of Juan's back pocket. An honest-to-God lion's tongue. Arroyo said it was his lucky charm, but the umpire gave him the heave anyway and confiscated the tongue to send to the commissioner after finding strange tonguelike marks between the seams of the ball. Arroyo went bonkers, saying he couldn't live, much less pitch, without his lion's tongue; that it has special, supernatural powers that no Anglo ump would understand. But the ump wouldn't budge, physically or otherwise. And that's when Arroyo slugged him. No doubt the ball and the tongue will end up in Cooperstown. No doubt Mr. Juanderful will end up on suspension.

But then Buck came to the plate in the top of the ninth with two down and Stein on first and hit his second home run of the night. The Senators led again 6–4, and we were all convinced that Jimy Boy's prayers had finally been answered. Milo, who's been out here for the last five games, figured either Buck had taken Jesus into the batter's box with him or that God was just as bored as we were.

Wrong. I think God was just laughing at us. 'Cause this is what happened in the bottom of the ninth. With one out and a man on second, Mug Shot misplayed a routine fly to center and then threw it past Rump, allowing one run to score. Rump's throw was too late to get the runner advancing to second, which did not augur well. So it was still one out with a man on second and one run in. Monk called for Big Foot Harrison, who got two quick strikes on Frank White and broke his bat with a hummer inside. But White managed to get his bat on the ball and dribbled a grounder past Mancusi at third. If the ball's hit right at him, Mancusi is fine. He only has a problem when he has to bend or move to either side. The ball rolled through his legs and all the way into the leftfield corner, allowing the tying run to score, and White to go to second. This mightily upset Big Foot, who hit the next batter and then balked the runners to second and third. Monk had seen enough. He called for the Gooch. The Royals responded by sending up a pinch hitter with a .198 batting average, who bounced sharply to Stein at first. Stein made a head's-up play, getting the sure out at first. Unfortunately, he then proceeded to hold the ball and have a friendly chat with the first base umpire about the balk call. It was during this prolonged exchange that the winning run scored from third.

Monk closed the locker room after the game for a moment of silence. According to Rump, when it was over, Big Foot shrugged and said, "My bad, fellas, my bad." And Mancusi shrugged and said, "My back, fellas, my back," which is the first time anyone has heard him say anything other than "Yo" all season. By the time they opened the doors, the clubhouse was empty. The entire twenty-four-man roster, including the Gaijin, who is a quick learner, was hiding in the trainer's room. The only exception was Rump, who was immediately engulfed by a swarm of sweaty, jostling, pissed-off bodies known collectively as the working press, a monster with voice-activated tape recorders for ears, microphones for arms, TV cables for veins, and thirteen minicams where the heart should have been.

The monster was in a feeding frenzy: it needed air bites and quick quotes. It needed to know the mood of the team. It needed to know how Rump felt. It needed to know the obvious.

Rump sat calmly at his locker, regarding the surging behemoth. "Over here, Rump! Over here! In the back! Rump!"

Rump scratched his chin, which is raw, and began quietly and calmly to soothe the beast. "You know, my first year in the minors, at Aberdeen, we had a ten-game losing streak. The manager, Peaches O'Meara, called a team meeting after the tenth game. He said, 'Boys, what we've got to do tomorrow is go out there with all our todays and not our yesterdays.' So we went out there and won one for tomorrow."

"Louder! Rump! Again! Rump!"

Even with all its electronic ears, the monster couldn't hear. The monster began talking to itself, "Did you get that? I didn't get that! I can't hear a fucking word! *Shhh!*"

Rump spoke again, louder.

"It's a good thing Peaches didn't live to see this," he said, " 'cause right now I can't tell our todays from our yesterdays and I sure as hell don't want to think about tomorrow."

"Rump! Rump! Mood, Rump!"

Rump scratched his chin some more. "I'd say we're disconsolate, despairing, and depressed. I'd say the mood of the team sucks."

"Speak up, Rump! Again, Rump!"

"I said, *'We're Disconsolate, Despairing, Depressed.'* I *said, 'The Mood of the Team* Sucks.'"

I was standing on the stool in Stein's locker, looking down at Rump and the monster. The beast was quieter now, almost sated, though it is never really satisfied. "I didn't get that last bit, Rump. You say the mood of the team—"

"Sucks!" Rump said. *"It Sucks!"*

"Yeah," I said over his shoulder. "But how do you *really* feel?"

Rump laughed. But Stein, who had just emerged from the shower dripping wet, suddenly decided to get serious. "How does it feel?" he demanded. "How does it feel? It feels like jerking off with Number 3 sandpaper."

May 10   If you want to know about America, study the coffee shop. Other countries have pubs and bistros and cafés with red-checked tablecloths and Amstel umbrellas. America is a coffee shop culture. America is white Formica etched with golden boomerangs. America is plastic containers with serrated edges and foil tops containing exactly one half ounce, no more, no less, of half-and-half. America is waitresses named Pennie, who put smiles in circles above the letter *i*.

Pennie had taken our order. I was tracing the boomerangs in the Formica. Rump was rolling an empty half-and-half container between his fingers, which are callused and bent with time. "I once figured out that I have spent four hours a day, seven days a week, thirty weeks a year, for the last sixteen years in places like this," Rump said, tossing the menu aside. "That's what? Ten thousand hours? Give or take a few. And that doesn't count the time I've spent in lobbies. Just sitting. I'm very good at lobby sitting. You think I've wasted my life?"

"Nah, only ten thousand hours of it."

I was trying to cheer him up. I figured it was the least I could do. I owe Rump. I'll always owe Rump. I met him last year at spring training when I was still working for Today and Rump was still the All-Star catcher for the New York Mets. I was doing that Doc Gooden piece and Doc wasn't talking to the press. So I went to Rump, which is what everybody does. I remember how nervous I was that morning before going to the park. It was my first day of spring training. And I wanted to look just right.

When I was young, little girls wore Mary Janes on the first day of school. I wore Mary Janes on the first day of spring training. I was staking my claim. It's *mine*, too. It hardly mattered if anyone but me understood the gesture.

Getting dressed for the Mets that morning, I was a little girl again, only I didn't have any Mary Janes to put on. I had no idea what to wear. No way of saying, "I belong." It took me three hours to decide, and I ended up in a clingy pseudo-silk skirt and a clingy V-necked T-shirt, which Rump later pointed out was more V than neck.

Of course, he didn't point it out until we had been sitting in the clubhouse talking for a half hour. I remember thinking what a good guy he was, what good stuff I was getting. It didn't occur to me that the good stuff was me. Anyway, we were just getting ready to go out on the field when he nodded toward my cleavage and said, "Do you always dress like this when you go to the ballpark?"

I looked down and saw the problem. "Not anymore I don't."

I think maybe that was the day I saw myself fully for the first time. You could say I had been postponing it for a while. I have a history of doing that. I remember the day I knew I needed a bra, which was two years later than I should have had one. I was in fifth grade and still playing ball at recess with the boys. I hit a bouncer to short and bounced all the way down the basepath. I was out by a mile. I left home a little girl with a Sammy Esposito glove. By the time I got to first, I was in puberty.

It wasn't so much that I was self-conscious about my body. I resented it for getting in the way. So I ignored the obvious until my mother forcibly dragged me to the foundations department at Lord & Taylor. It was your basic tape-measure job. I went straight into a 34C. Even then I didn't really come to grips with the situation until Rump called attention to it my first day of spring training.

"You can't go out there like that," he said.

He took off his Number 19 NEW YORK METS T-shirt and handed it to me. It was still sweaty from the windsprints he had run on the warning track and it clung to my clingy pseudo-silk skirt and hung to my knees. I looked like a little girl in her daddy's undershirt. I wore it to sleep every night for a week and then framed it and hung it over my bed.

Last June, when I decided to go over to Sports, I thought of

Rump and went out and bought an entirely new locker room wardrobe. This was not as easy as it sounds. Think about it. What do you wear to the locker room when everyone else is naked and thinks you ought to be? There is no locker room equivalent of the power suit. I can't wear freebie golf shirts, like MacKenzie, or the same pair of jeans every day, like Girard. I can't go prep because that would be butch and therefore provocative. And I can't do clingy pseudo-silk with plunging necklines. I need clothes that are attractive but not seductive; clothes that say, "I may be a girl but I ain't meat." I used to think getting dressed every day was the hardest part of my job until everyone but Rump stopped talking to me.

"We're going to win tonight," Rump said.

"We are?"

"Yup. It's destiny. We were meant to be the worst team ever. We were meant to have this record, and now that we do we can win. Mug Shot is going to hit the Big Fly. And Pentacost is going to pitch a three-hitter."

"And you?"

"Me? I'm going to go 0 for 3 and lower my average to .067," he said.

He was still playing with the half-and-half container, rolling it back and forth against his callused fingers. "Baseball's funny. Hitting. Sometimes you get so locked in, you can see the seams on the ball. You can see the spin. It's kind of like a time warp. Everything is real time except you and the ball. The ball comes at you, and the more it spins the slower it goes. You're just hanging over the dish, waiting on that baby. And whatever the pitcher throws, it doesn't matter. Because you're locked in."

He dropped the half-and-half container on the weird gold-flecked Formica and shrugged. "Me. I'm locked out."

Pennie arrived with eggs that weren't quite as perky as she and said, "Will there be anything more?" and stood there for two minutes after we assured her we had everything we needed, and said finally, "Uh, Mr. Doubleday, sir, could I, uh, have your autograph, please, Mr. Doubleday, sir?" Rump signed his full name on her little white apron and put a smile inside a circle over the *i* in Fitzgerald.

"JoAnne's made an appointment for me to see a Jungian analyst when we get back to Washington," Rump said when Pennie finally left. "Some guy named Funk. He says I have to stop thinking of the slump as *my* slump and start thinking of it as *our* slump, in the collective sense."

"You mean Dr. C. Hyman Funk, the radio guy?"

Rump nodded sheepishly. "JoAnne heard his call-in show one day and called up to ask whether there is a great collective unconscious slump."

"Sounds like a story to me—an exposé of baseball's collective unconscious."

"You wanna come?" he said.

"You mean you're really going to go?"

He gave me that look that married people always give single people.

"Sure I'll come," I said. "But what will the doctor say?"

"Leave him to me," Rump said glumly. "Maybe he can find an archetypal flaw in my stance."

"Don't worry, you'll hit," I said. "You always hit."

He shrugged. "I never hit at age thirty-six before. I was never . . ."

He was playing with the half-and-half again. "Never what?"

"Never . . . ?" He looked away. "Nothing," he said. "How's Michael?"

"How should I know?"

We both laughed.

"How's JoAnne?"

"She thinks it's all *your* fault. She thinks you're bad luck. She thinks women in the locker room are a violation of her marital vows."

"Great," I said. "Send her my regards, too."

Rump smiled. "Does Michael ever get jealous?"

"Nah. He trusts me. Besides, he knows none of you bastards are talking to me."

"Fucking ain't talking," Rump said.

"No, but it's professional suicide."

"True," Rump said.

"The only time Michael got really pissed was when this weight coach at the University of Southern Maryland threw me out of the locker room last fall. Son of a bitch picked me up by the scruff of my neck like a cat picking up a kitten, only not so gentle. He was this bowling ball of a guy. No hair, all steroids, no neck. I was standing in a corner talking to this little running back, Randy Hunter. I'm facing the corner and he's completely dressed. So it's not like I was in a position to be looking at anyone's private parts even if I wanted to. And this guy, this coach, picks me up and dumps me on the front step with all the drunken alumni.

"I had no quotes. I blew my deadline. I cried all the way home. And when I got back to the office, Sal really reamed me out. So I told him what happened. Then he gets all over me for not telling him what happened before."

"Why didn't you?"

"You gotta play hurt," I said.

Rump laughed. "Oh yeah, I forgot," he said.

May 11   American Airlines Flight 351 from Kansas City to Dulles International was the last regularly scheduled flight this team will take this season. The Washington Senators insulted the stewardesses, poured Salisbury steak dinners down each other's pants, and otherwise dismantled the interior of the Boeing 727 in celebration of their first win of the 1989 season.

Mug Shot hit the Big Fly, Pentacost pitched a three-hitter, and Rump went 0 for 3 just the way he said they would, and the Senators beat the K.C. Royals, 4–1.

It was a scoreless game when Mug Shot came to bat with the bases loaded in the top of the sixth. Mug Shot is not a favorite among pitchers in the American League. Mug Shot is a hot dog. Back in the seventies there was a guy named Willie Montanez who was considered a hot dog. The line on Willie was: "There isn't enough mustard in the world to cover him." But Willie never did TV commercials for Dijon mustard the way Mug Shot does, stark naked except for a mustard coating. Mug Shot says, "I am stunned the way I am."

Mug Shot is a handsome devil. If he smiled ever, we'd all be stunned about the way he is. Of all the guys on the team, he is undoubtedly the best groomed and the best dressed and the only one with his own personal manicurist. He says he promised himself when he got out of the joint that he'd never be dirty again or badly dressed again. He never wears jeans. His beard is trimmed better than most French hedges and he wears his hair in a Fade with his number, 13, shaved into the back of his head. His uniform is also perfectly tailored. And he only picks his teeth with a gold-plated toothpick.

He is equally meticulous about his pregame preparation. He eats exactly 1²/₃ cups of grits every morning, except when he can't find them, in which case he eats 1¹/₃ cups of Wheaties. He doesn't trust hotels with these measurements, so he carries a set of red measuring cups with him wherever he goes. Sometimes he wears them around his neck. He always sits in the window seat of the second row on the left side of the team bus (the one that has the hump of the wheel under your feet) and Row 9, seat A, of the plane. He also kisses his bat where it says MUG SHOT MODEL in the on-deck circle.

Mug Shot not only admires his home runs, he names them. Of course, there haven't been that many of them. None so far this season. A solo pump is a Boogie Rap; he literally dances around the bases. Sometimes he does the Cool Jerk, sometimes the Mashed Potato. Mug Shot is into old white rock 'n' roll. A two-run shot is an MX Missile, the distance of which determines whether it's a Fission, a Fusion, or a Total Meltdown Trot. Fusion he does with flaps up; Fission with flaps down. On grand slams, he improvises. Once he did a Michael Jackson Moon Walk all the way around the bases. Another time he did the whole thing backward, à la Jimmy Piersall. Then they banned it.

No one seems to mind any of this except the opposition. After watching the full performance for the first time in spring training, Demetrious told me, "I fully understand my man Mug Shot has to follow a disciplined routine to get into the right physical and mental condition to do his thing."

Mug Shot wears thirteen chains around his neck and thirteen wristbands on his arms, six on the right, seven on the left, to match the Number 13 on his back and his hair. He says he is not superstitious. But he will not step into the batter's box until all thirteen chains and all thirteen wristbands are perfectly aligned and his golden toothpick is fixed firmly between his bicuspids.

Mug Shot never goes to bat without his toothpick. He never goes out to centerfield without his toothpick. Some guys carry their own personal bat cases on the road. Mug Shot carries his own personal engraved toothpick holder. "I pick it with my pick," he says, "and sometimes when I get back to the hotel, if I need a toothpick hypotheticallywise for what it's meant for, getting meat out or something hygienical like that, I'll use it then, too."

Baseball players believe that the wood of certain bats has a precise number of hits in it. Mug Shot believes the same is true of his toothpicks. Anyway, this was a magic toothpick. He went 2 for 4 with it Tuesday. So he knew when he came to bat in the top of the sixth last night it still had some good wood in it. The count was 3–2. Bret Saberhagen, the Royals pitcher, got so sick of waiting for Mug Shot to get his chains, his wristbands, and his toothpick in the proper alignment that he just laid the ball on in there, thinking, I guess, that Mug Shot would never get ready in time. "Even I could have hit it," Rump said later.

Mug Shot timed his swing perfectly. The ball sailed into the dew and over the leftfield fence. Mug Shot walked to first, got down on his knees, and pressed his hands together in prayer, which Milo immediately said guaranteed him a new contract from Jimy Boy. He got up, walked to second, and prayed some more. And some more at third. And finally, when he got all the way to home three minutes later, he got down on his knees and kissed the plate. "Like the fucking Pope arriving in America," Stein said.

Rube opened the case of champagne that he has dragged from Washington to Milwaukee and from Milwaukee to Minneapolis and from Minneapolis to Kansas City. The players did what they always do with champagne. They poured it on each other. Some of them, like Mug Shot, even celebrated by talking to me. "The last white girl I fucked wore white Jockey shorts. Do you wear white Jockey shorts, Berkowitz, hypothetically speakingwise, that is?" It was the first thing he has said to me in three weeks. It was also off the record.

On the record, what he said was "Speaking from a historical tangent, I'd say this is probably definitely the highlight film of my life careerwise."

Rump said, "It just goes to show, you can't lose them all." And Monk said, "It's unbe-fucking-lievable. I'm as happy as if I was in my right bleeping mind."

But the best quote of the day came from Piggy, who said, "Now we can get back to the business of contending," which was fairly hilarious considering they are now 18½ games out of first place.

On the plane, Mug Shot wouldn't take the toothpick out of his mouth except occasionally to admire it. One by one, the players came by to touch it. When the dinner trays arrived, each of the Washington Senators removed a toothpick from its little white sheath and clenched it between his bicuspids in silent tribute. That's when Stick stood up on his seat, unzipped his fly, and started singing "Louie Louie." He had had a few pops by then. But so had we all. I think Stein was the one who started in with the food. Who could resist? Stick was such an easy target. Pretty soon the hash browns and the peas were flying. Only the Gaijin managed to finish his meal. The Gaijin always finishes his meal and usually three more.

We were somewhere over Tennessee when Stick sat down, fastened his seat belt, took his Louisville Slugger out of his pants, put a copy of *Sports Illustrated* on his lap, and pressed the CALL button. "Can I help you, sir?" the beleaguered stewardess said.

"I'm having a little trouble with my seat belt," Stick replied.

As she leaned over to help, *Sports Illustrated* fell to the floor and she came face-to-face with the Stick's stick. "Oooh, baby," he said. "I just want to put my luggage in your overhead rack."

"Get fucked, sir," she replied.

And all over the cabin, the cry went up, "The Stick has struck out again!"

It was right after that that the SEAT BELT sign came on and the captain said we were going to be experiencing some turbulence, though I think he meant we already had. Anyway, it worked. Everybody pretty much sat still for the rest of the flight. It was 5:00 A.M. when we got into Dulles. There were two thousand fans waiting for the Senators and one reporter wearing an 0–162 T-shirt waiting for me. Michael kissed me and handed me the early edition. "I like your stuff," he said.

"I like yours better," I replied.

When I woke up at noon, he was gone.

Home Stand

May 12 The Sports Department is on a diet. We have been ordered to lose four hundred pounds. And it's all Pincus's fault. If he hadn't gotten stuck behind the wheel of his Lincoln, this never would have happened.

Pincus covers college hoops. Rumor has it he actually once *played* college hoops. Of course, this was twenty years and 189 pounds ago. According to department lore, he quit the team one day after missing six open jumpers, explaining that his athlete's foot was killing him. Nonetheless, the experience was formative:

he hasn't taken a bath since. Guys like him are usually called gym rats. Dr. Deadline calls Pincus a gym skunk.

Anyway, the way Dr. D explained it, Pincus was on his way back to the office from some playground league game when he got stuck behind the wheel of his baby-blue Lincoln. It's one of those cars with power seats and a tilt steering wheel that locks into different positions depending on the comfort of the driver. For Pincus, this was not exactly optional. Pincus weighs at least three hundred pounds. The power seats succumbed to his girth a long time ago.

He parked as usual in Ross Mitchell's parking space and discovered that his custom-made sheepskin tilt steering wheel had no intention of letting him out. It was locked in position. Pincus was pinned. This is not a place anyone wants to be pinned, as I learned when I mistakenly accepted a ride home from him one day last fall. I called Dr. D as soon as I got out of the shower. "Why didn't you tell me, you son of a bitch?"

"Rite of passage," he replied.

Pincus is not only a gym rat. He is also a pack rat. His Lincoln is his office. Pincus has every stat sheet from every University of Maryland basketball game for the last twelve seasons in the back of that car. Not to mention a few hundred college media guides and the wrappers to one hundred granola bars and the desiccated peels of several many bananas (one of which I had the pleasure of discovering the day he drove me home). Pincus says they keep him regular.

Anyway, Pincus was stuck. Sal sent Vito and the Doctor down to help. To hear the Doctor tell it, they tugged and pulled on him for at least two hours, which was truly an act of charity considering Pincus's liberal definition of personal grooming. His idea of a shower is dousing himself with the Dry Look, a case of which he keeps in a box under his desk. On a good day, he smells like an old sweater that just went through the dry cleaner for the one hundredth time. And this being one of those unusually hot days in May, it was not a good day to be in Pincus's immediate vicinity, though the rescue did attract quite a crowd.

The more Vito and the Doctor pulled, the more Pincus yelled, "Watch the merchandise!" Finally Sal said to call the Fire Department, that they had special equipment for pulling people out of wrecks.

Ross Mitchell was just coming back from seeing his pal Tommy Jacomo at The Palm when Engine Company Number 9 pulled into the parking lot with the Jaws of Life. Ross is a fitness fanatic. He runs marathons and keeps gravity boots in his office, and whenever you go up to talk to him, he's either hanging upside down or sucking in his stomach and daring you to give him your best shot. Ross is very proud of his body fat percentage, which he keeps track of with his own engraved set of fat calipers. "Ten-point-one percent," he says. "Same as the day I graduated from Princeton."

Ross did not like the sight of Pincus pinned in Ross's very own parking spot by his custom-made sheepskin tilt steering wheel. And his mood did not improve when the Fire Department had to saw through the steering wheel to extricate Pincus from his own car and then handed him a ticket condemning his car as a fire hazard. "I'm going to have to brainstorm this one," Ross said. Ross likes to turn nouns into verbs. He's very big on interfacing.

The next day the meat scale was installed outside Sal's office. Ross and his public relations men had interfaced and brainstormed and decided that, it being "Corporate Fitness Week," it might make a very nice promotional tie-in to dare the Sports Department to lose four hundred pounds by the end of the baseball season. As of this coming Sunday, *Trib* newspaper boxes all over the city will be carrying the legend: TAKE A LOAD OFF WITH SPORTS!

I arrived just as Sal was convening the first weekly Sports Department weigh-in. Irene, his administrative assistant, was handing out 1000-calorie diets prepared by the nurse and explaining the chart on the wall outside Sal's office where all of us are expected to record our weekly weight loss. "Every Friday we're going to publish the weekly total," Sal said. "And at the end of the season we'll publish the department standings."

"With names or without?" Pincus said morosely.

"I think to begin with, we'll just go for mass," Sal said.

Pincus looked relieved. Until Sal said, "Henceforth, there will be no more press box crab cakes. No more Popeyes. No more chili dogs. No more corn chips. And no more beer. Fritos and Cheez Doodles are also banned from the Sports Department."

"What's left?" Rocky moaned.

"What are we supposed to eat at the ballpark?" Vito demanded.

"It says here you should brown-bag it," Sal said. "The nurse suggests hard-boiled eggs."

"What if you're not fat?" asked the Doctor, who is allergic to everything with calories.

"Get a note from your doctor," Sal said. "Anyone else?"

Roth shrugged. Pincus wheezed. Vito bit into a pretzel.

"All right, then, in alphabetical order. Berkowitz, you're first."

There were a serious number of catcalls as I slipped off my shoes. I wasn't taking any chances. The press boxes haven't been particularly kind to me either. "Go for it, Berkowitz!" "Shake it, Berkowitz!" Just as I was about to step on the scale, Ruth arrived to tell me the latest gossip from the Business section and Vito began to hum the music to "The Stripper." I hesitated for a moment as I caught her eye.

"C'mon, Berkowitz!" Sal said.

I stepped on the meat scale, not at all happy with the metaphorical implications, and caught a glimpse of myself in Sal's office window. Dad's right: I am cute. Why couldn't I be willowy instead? I hate cute. Ruth shook her head and walked away. "Do we get the other measurements, too?" Rocky wanted to know.

"Only if I get yours," I said.

"Last one into Berkowitz's pants is a rotten egg," Vito said.

"I don't sleep with men who sweat through their sports jackets," I said.

There was a lot of hooting and hollering at that as well as the rest of the proceedings. Still, Sal managed to get through most of the section. "Deadline: one hundred forty-five. Vito: one ninety-five. Zeke: two ten. Zeke's running to fat. Rocky . . ."

I have never seen Rocky without his orange plaid sports jacket on and I've never seen his orange plaid sports jacket without the *Racing Form* poking out of all its pockets. Rocky wasn't going anywhere without the *Racing Form*. "I'm not taking off the *Form*," he said.

"Okay, okay," Sal said. "*With* the *Racing Form*."

Rocky stepped forward. "One ninety-three with the *Form*. Milo: one sixty-three. Marcus: one eighty, you handsome devil. Pincus . . ."

It's an astonishing fact but true that despite Pincus's estimable girth, he can't find pants that stay up around his waist. He wears only polyester and only shades of olive green. The pants all hang low in the saddle, revealing more than just a crack of his hairy behind, and they're all beaded around the crotch from his thighs rubbing together as he walks. Pincus waddled to the scale, thighs rubbing, and said, "Can I take off my shirt?"

"*Nooooo!*" came the answer from twenty-five voices.

Pincus got on the scale, which fortunately can hold up to one thousand pounds. "Pincus," Sal said. "Three hundred and four big ones. On the nose!"

"You mean on the hoof," Rocky said.

Sal was last. Most sports editors are chesty little guys who go in hard when they slide. Salvatore Aiello is an exception to the rule. He is the only concave sports editor in America. He'd actually be kind of cute if he wasn't so bony and tall. He told me once he was six-four in sixth grade. So coaches were always recruiting him for basketball, or volleyball, or badminton.

Sal couldn't play a lick. But he ended up a three-letter man at the University of Maryland, having been the manager of all three varsity teams and sports editor of the student paper as well. He wrote a column called "Foul Tips" with lots of juicy inside stuff. Milo saw it a lot while he was out there covering Terps games and signed Sal up as a stringer, which is how he ended up at the *Trib*.

Now that he's sports editor, he comes to work every day wearing a Turnbull & Asser shirt, the shoulders of which invariably reach his elbows, and carrying a brown bag lunch, faithfully prepared by his wife, containing two creamed cheese and jelly sandwiches on raisin pumpernickel (without the crusts), which he eats with two vitamin-enriched double chocolate shakes. He spends all day pulling up the pants of his expensive Italian suits, which are always falling down no matter how much they are tailored, and sucking his thumb, which he always calls everyone's attention to by claiming to have a hangnail. By the time he goes home to his lovely wife Merrill every night, he's got blue ink all over his white collar and Chee-tos crumbs and Pepsi stains all over his suit.

Because of his imposing physique, Sal is always trying to sound a lot gruffer than he is. So he yells a lot and calls everybody by their last names. But his voice isn't exactly mellifluous or deep and when he shouts he sounds like a terrier left behind by its mistress. In Sal's case, his bark *is* lots worse than his bite.

I was nominated to weigh him in. "All right, Berkowitz," he yapped. "Can we get this over with? Quietly?"

Vito was humming "The Stripper" again. Everyone else was yelling, *"Go! Go! Go!"* Sal stepped on the scale and frowned.

"One thirty-nine and a half," I said loud enough so everyone could hear and stuck a dollar bill in the waistband of his low-riding Italian suit. But the loot wouldn't stick. Not at the waist anyway. It traveled down his thigh and caught at his knee and Sal shook his leg until the bill fell at his feet in full view of the entire staff.

"In my office, Berkowitz," he said.

I closed the door, winking at the guys, and turned to find Sal with his head in his hands, whimpering. "One thirty-nine and a fucking half. My playing weight. How am I supposed to enforce this fucking thing?"

May 13 Today Rump and I went to see Dr. C. Hyman Funk. I have to say I felt a little awkward intruding upon Rump's session, but it was soon apparent that I was the only one who did. Rump and Funk had hashed out the ground rules over the phone. Rump said he wasn't coming without me. Funk said okay.

Funk is what we in the trade like to call a "media shrink." He's always available for your basic psychobabble quote in the event of a mass murder or an attempted suicide by a noted government official. In fact, Funk is quite proud of the fact that he is the host of the only Jungian radio call-in show in America, "The Daily Archetype." So even though he huffed and puffed about confidentiality and the sanctity of the doctor-patient relationship, he immediately agreed that everything was on the record and said I should feel free to clean up his quotes if I wished. "You know what to say," he said.

Funk was clearly agog over the fact that all of Washington would know tomorrow morning that he had Rump Doubleday in his waiting room on Saturday, May 13, at 11:10 A.M. Rump was equally excited about the possibility of never having to come to another session if my story makes Funk look stupid enough.

"Johnny! Ms. Berkowitz!" Funk greeted us effusively at the door and showed us to two matching leather-and-chrome easy chairs that were easy only in the sense of getting into them. Actually, they resembled medieval torture racks more than chairs. They were chairs that said to whoever sat in them, "You're not here to get comfortable." They defied you to sit up or relax or leave. The seat was a taut leather slab slung on an incline. I kept sliding backward into the abyss.

The room was as white and as bare as a squash court. There were a couple of plants dangling from bookshelves and framed degrees on the walls but no couch and no modern art lithographs open to phallic interpretations. It was hot as hell in there and so bright you had to squint to get a good look at the good doctor, who sat facing us in an olive-green La-Z-Boy recliner, his thirteen chins cascading down his shirt, his half-bifocals perched upon his hairy Roman nose.

"So, Johnny," he began, "have you given any thought to the archetypal dimensions of your slump?"

"You mean the great collective unconscious slump?" Rump said.

"Yes, Johnny," Funk said, smiling tightly. "*That* slump. As we discussed over the phone, this is, after all, a universal slump. It is not just *your* slump or *a* slump. It is Slump."

"Uh-huh," Rump said.

"So," Funk said.

It was your basic analytic opening. But Rump wasn't your basic analytic candidate. He had never been to a shrink before—only the First Lady's hypnotist. Funk waited in vain. I slid back in my leather-and-chrome chair, abandoning all hope of sitting up.

"So," Funk said again, clearing his throat. "Any significant dreams of late?"

I figured either Rump was going to bash him in the face for calling him Johnny or tell him about the sunflower seeds. He did neither, which surprised me. Rump has been dreaming about sunflower seeds for weeks, the same dream every night since Opening Day. He's sitting in the dugout stuffing sunflower seeds in his mouth, the way ballplayers do, only he forgets to spit them out. So his mouth gets fuller and fuller until his cheeks bulge and he starts to gag and somebody, he's not sure who, comes up behind him and performs the Heimlich Maneuver and he coughs up a clump of seeds, which have begun to sprout like the first buds of spring. But by the time they hit the ground, the sprouts have turned brown and begun to die. He's been telling everyone about the dream. But he did not tell Funk.

"No dreams at all, Johnny?" Funk said again.

"Nope," Rump said.

He squirmed in his chair, which, given its unforgiving construction, was no easy feat. "Jesus, it's hot in here," Rump said, wiping his brow and putting his hand up to his eyes to shield the glare.

"Ah yes, my grow lights," Funk said. "Don't you like them?"

Funk was in fact sitting under a blazing arcade of track lighting. It wasn't just any track lighting. You could have taken a family portrait in a cave in all that light. It was a revolutionary idea in psychiatric treatment: sweat the son of a bitch.

Funk dabbed the perspiration from his upper lip and explained. "Everyone's doing it out at NIH. They were conducting some research on Seasonal Affective Disorder Syndrome, SADS we call it, which, as you know, is why there is such an enormous suicide rate in winter, especially in Sweden. Dark, depression, it's obvious. But they also found quite by surprise that light therapy positively regenerates the immune system. I don't need to tell you how important that is in this day and age. We've got to look out for those T-cells, each and every one of us."

"The great collective unconscious T-cells," Rump said.

I started fantasizing about all those eggheads baking themselves under grow lights and sprouting little green buds from their bald spots. I grinned at Rump, but he only looked at his watch. He was dripping. I was schvitzing. Funk was oblivious. "You ought to look into that, my dear," he said to me. "It might make a nice little story. Call NIH. Tell them Funk sent you."

It was only eleven-twenty. Rump sighed and started doodling on a prescription pad. He kept drawing the same thing over and over: a circle with a square inside it. "May I see that, Johnny?" Funk asked.

Rump pushed the pad across the end table toward him.

"Hmmmm," Funk said.

It was a practiced "Hmmmm," a patient "Hmmmm," an expectant "Hmmmm." "Hmmmm," he said again. "What occurs to you in connection with that, Johnny?"

Rump shrugged.

Funk tried again. "Tell me, Johnny, have you ever flown over a baseball stadium?"

Rump shook his head. "Well then, have you ever seen one of those aerial shots from the Goodyear Blimp?"

"Yeah, sure, why?" Rump said.

"Well, does it *remind* you of anything?"

Rump looked at him blankly. Funk pushed the pad back

across the table. "Think, Johnny, think! Don't you want to get into your quaternity?"

Rump glanced at the pad. "I guess it looks a little like a stadium," he said cautiously.

"Exactly!" Funk said. "The baseball stadium is a very basic thing. An archetype! If you look down at it from the sky, you see a circle and within that circle a square, a diamond, if you will. This gives us a kind of mandala, does it not?"

"Mandala?" Rump said.

"Yes! Yes! Mandala." Funk turned his head toward me. "*M-a-n-d-a-l-a*. Get this down, my dear. It's key." Then to Rump again, "The mandala is the most ancient symbol of the universe and, I might add, one of the most powerful archetypes, the four within the three!"

"Listen," Rump said, "the only thing I know about three and four is that if you go 3 for 4 you've had a pretty good day and I haven't had any of those lately."

"Yes, yes, yes," Funk said. "And that's why we're here, Johnny. To work on your 3 for 4s."

Rump sighed. Funk kicked his La-Z-Boy into an upright position and leaned forward. Evidently he had come to a decision that required some serious body language. "Johnny," he said. "Our time together is short. And we have a lot of work to do. A lot. This is quite out of the norm what I'm about to do. But I fail to see how I have any choice. I'm going to have to educate you as well as treat you."

Rump rolled his eyes. Funk wanted to know if I was getting enough stuff. I nodded. "Take this down," he said. "Jung said that when a patient dreams of a shape that combines the circle and the square, there is usually a problem of integration of the personality. We call it squaring the circle. It is a symbol of the self.

"Squaring the circle. Did you get that? You want me to repeat it?"

I shook my head. Rump started doodling again. It's amazing how long fifty minutes can be. I looked over his shoulder. It was the circle with the square again. "What does that suggest to you, my dear?"

"Me?" I said.

"You."

"I dunno. It's not my doodle."

Funk threw his hands up in exasperation. "It's *everyone's* doodle," he said. "It is the *universal* doodle. The circle with the square is an ancient symbol of the sun. And you, Johnny, are the sun of your universe. You are drawing yourself."

Funk kicked back the La-Z-Boy in exclamation. Rump handed me the pad. "A self-portrait," he said.

"Nice," I said.

Funk was losing control of the session. He lowered his many chins and growled. "Where in this configuration would you place the catcher?"

Rump pointed to the bottom of the circle.

"And the pitcher?"

Rump pointed to the center of the square.

"Et voilà!" Funk said. His shirt was soaked with sweat. Perspiration ringed his underarms. He didn't notice. His T-cells could have been boiling for all he cared. Funk was building to a crescendo of insight and analysis so compelling that only a fool couldn't see it, unless, of course, he was blinded by the grow lights. "The mound is in the middle of things, is it not?" he said.

Rump and I nodded involuntarily.

"Thus the catcher is waiting, passive, is he not?"

We nodded again.

"The catcher is outside the self trying to receive from the middle!"

Funk paused for effect. "The catcher," he said portentously, "is *decentered.*"

"Oh God, not that," I said and wished I hadn't.

"I guess that's why they call me Rump," Rump said and started to laugh. "Listen, Doc, let me educate you. You've got it all wrong. The catcher *calls* the game. It radiates from him. He *is* the center."

But the doctor wouldn't hear of it. He was flushed with his own exquisite powers of perception and deduction. All this from a doodle! The session was a triumph! The session was also over.

Funk stood, his eyes and upper lip glistening. "I think we have really gotten somewhere today," he said. "You are having trouble with your otherness, Johnny. Catching is feminine, receptive. You must integrate this into your maleness. You must come to terms with the choice you have made. When you accept the otherness of your position, you will find your stroke again!"

"And just exactly what is the bat an archetype of?" Rump said merrily.

Funk frowned. "If there is one thing Jungians and Freudians agree on, Johnny, it's bats. Also bananas."

The doctor clapped Rump's shoulder affectionately and opened the door. "By the way, Johnny, do you have any children? JoAnne didn't say."

"No, why?" Rump said, quickly and a bit more sharply than necessary.

"Oh nothing," Funk said. "Just wondering."

And frankly so was I. Not so much at what Rump said but at his tone. He changed the subject immediately, and as the door slammed behind us, he said, "Now I know the problem. I'm a fucking wuss. Do me a favor. Trash the fucker." For a change, he wasn't laughing.

May 14 I have come to the conclusion that if you study a ballplayer's locker long enough you'll never need to ask him anything, which is a relief considering the quality of conversation around here. What the Washington Senators don't say, their lockers do. It's almost as if the locker is an external projection of a player's psyche, all jumbled and messy yet distinct, separated from its neighbor by idiosyncrasy and red, white, and blue chain-link fence.

Being ballplayers, their lockers have more similarities than eccentricities. They are built like altars, shrines to their unvarnished selves. They all have a bat rack and twelve pairs of spikes and six boxes of sneakers, gratis from some sporting goods company eager to curry favor. One of the sneaker boxes is invariably crammed with unanswered fan mail and maybe a few snapshots from groupies with advanced marketing strategies. Everybody has at least three gloves, one of which is probably in the process of being worked in. And of course, there are caps and pressed uniform shirts; batting gloves in an array of different colors; and lots of dirty underwear, bikini mostly. Wristbands are big, especially colorful ones, though more so among the brothers. Every locker has a box of baseballs waiting to be signed for children waiting to be acknowledged by distant heroes. Jocks and cups dangle from hooks screwed into the sidewalls. There are family portraits and backgammon games in almost equal proportions. And everybody has a stash of either Red Man plug or Copenhagen chewing tobacco or packets of sunflower seeds or Double Bubble chewing gum or some combination of the three. Tobacco chewers tend not to be seed spitters, though they may also be bubble blowers, a talent and a taste that eludes me.

But if you look long enough and hard enough at a guy's locker, eventually you'll find the one thing that differentiates him, that makes him more than just another ballplayer. Like Stein, he's got a Haggadah next to his October 1988 *Playboy* pinup. Also, the borders of his locker are lined with cocktail napkins inscribed with the names of ambitious girls. Buck has a jar of Tony Chachere's famous Creole Seasoning, which he puts on everything from tacos to baloney, a sample jar of Growth Plus Scalp Cleanser & Conditioner, and a butterfly net. He collects butterflies. He says they remind him of home.

Mancusi has a set of golf clubs, which he can't use because of his back. Lefty O'Donnell, who wears a SOLDIER OF FORTUNE T-shirt under his uniform, has thirteen back issues of the magazine and a semiautomatic water gun that looks like an Uzi. Mug Shot has a jewelry box in which he keeps his forty-seven gold chains, including one with a diamond Number 13 pendant, and a makeup kit. The Gaijin has twenty-three takeout menus. The Stick has a two-headed dildo and a package containing two hazelnuts. The label says: "Crack these nuts and you're 95 percent sure of preventing AIDS." And Brawn has all his personal belongings. That's because he lives in the clubhouse. He has two girlfriends, and on nights when neither of them is available, he sleeps on the training room rub-down table.

Rump is reading Erik Erikson and *When Bad Things Happen to Good People*. Lawson has a rack of brochures advertising God and a sign that says: TAKE ONE. Fennis Tubbs, Rump's backup, hides his Grecian Formula inside the right shoe of his old pair of spikes. Mr. Juanderful massages his rubber snake every time he pitches.

Benito Jones, the reserve infielder, is the most anal man on the team. His locker is pristine. Of course, that's partly because he never plays. Every T-shirt is perfectly folded and ironed. Every sneaker box is stacked perfectly on the one beneath it. He has a tray full of nail brushes and facial soap and scented powder. Benito has a problem with bodily fluids.

It doesn't take long for such things to get around in a locker room. And Stein, who is not above exploiting such vulnerabilities, has been known to blow his nose on Benito's game shirt. Stein is also a master of flatulence. He not only *is* flatulent, he is flatulent on cue. He times his farts and, occasionally, lights them.

Today, before the game, he walked up to Benito's locker, mooned him, and lit a match. Then he let go a really good one. The match flamed up, and *poof!* Then another and another! It was a regular symphony of flatulence! *Poof! Poof! Poof!*

I thought Benito was going to pass out. Then Monk stalked through the locker room on his way to the dugout and all the laughter stopped. "Just keeping 'em loose, Skip," Stein said, failing to keep a straight face.

"Unbe-fucking-lievable," Monk replied. For once I couldn't have said it better myself.

May 15 Last night Milo came to dinner. It was not exactly what people have in mind when they talk about your basic Washington power party. In fact, it wasn't like any dinner I've ever been to.

I live in a building called the Cairo near Dupont Circle, which is sort of a halfway house for singles on their way to a commitment or on their way out of town. All the apartments in the Cairo are the same. They all have hardwood floors and one exposed brick wall and a living room that is also the dining room. In the old days, they called it the vestibule. The kitchen is the size of a microwave. It has every conceivable convenience except counters. Then again, I never worried about counters until I decided to have a dinner party in Milo's honor.

I was standing in the living room chopping dill on my standard-issue singles round oak table, talking to Ruth over the phone about how to poach salmon steaks, when Michael arrived with the vodka and the wine. Ruth is a terrific cook, but she doesn't like to admit it because she thinks somehow it will compromise her feminist credentials. For me she made an exception.

Anyway, I had the receiver under my chin, and the cord barely reached to the kitchen where the cream sauce for the fettucini was being prematurely overcooked. The last time I cooked pasta it was called spaghetti and cream sauces were still trendy. Well, in order to reach the buzzer to let Michael in, I had to stretch across the salad bowl, which was on the other side of the dill. As it turned out, this was a mistake. I guess I pulled the cord too far because the receiver slipped from under my chin and boomeranged across the table, dumping the dill on the hardwood floor and splattering the salad dressing all over the exposed brick wall.

It was too late for takeout. People were due in fifteen minutes.

I have cooked dinner from scratch as opposed to from the freezer twice in my life, once for my mother and once for Michael. I was nervous both times and burned the Hamburger Helper both times. This was much worse. It's one thing to cook for your mother or your lover. It's another thing to cook for the best sportswriter in America.

"And he said I could play," I said.

"I guess he spoke too soon," Michael said.

Milo turned fifty a year ago. He's a little man with a sportswriter's paunch who keeps his baseball glove on a pedestal in his office. When he has trouble writing, he goes and puts his hand inside the glove, and the feel of the leather, old and cracked as it is, soothes the spirit and puts him back in touch with the words. Somewhere deep inside that pocket, he always finds the muse, but not necessarily happiness. His wife of twenty-six years left him last winter. She got tired of playing second fiddle to the Masters Golf Tournament and the World Series and the Super Bowl and that damned baseball glove. It was quite an office scandal. She showed up at the annual Sports Department Christmas party with Milo and left with the editor of the Business section, telling Milo in a loud voice that "some men know where to put their hands and some don't."

Milo has been in something of a slump ever since. He's writing lots of sad little stories about paralyzed jockeys with aborted dreams. He's also running around with lots of women half his age, groupies rejected by ballplayers. Vito set him up with this girl named Bette a couple of months ago, and Milo's been writing happier stories recently. Bette's a piece of work. Dr. D says Sal told Milo first time he met her, "Some women are too dumb to fuck." But apparently Milo is not looking for intellectual stimulation at this point in his life. When he asked if it was okay to bring Bette to dinner, I said sure, why not. Unfortunately, this was after I had already also invited Sal and his wife and before Dr. D told me Sal's opinion of Bette.

So aside from the dill in my hair, I had reason to be nervous.

Sal and his wife, the Turnbull & Asser queen, were the first to arrive.

"Berkowitz," he said. "You know my wife, Merrill."

Even in my living room, the guy was still calling me Berkowitz.

"What a lovely, uh, place you have," Merrill said.

This was gracious, considering that with four of us in the living room all the available floor space had already been occupied. We were close enough that we could have been playing "Duck, Duck, Goose." It occurred to me that I had never had four people in my living room before. Then the doorbell rang.

"Oh hi, Salsie!" Bette squeaked, buzzing him on the cheek. No doubt about it, Bette can fill a room, and there wasn't much room to fill.

Merrill held out her hand limply. Michael passed the goat cheese. Milo grinned. Milo had had a few cocktails. Michael handed him another.

Everyone in the newsroom knows Milo drinks vodka gimlets, which is why a lot of young sportswriters in America who would otherwise be smoking dope now also drink vodka gimlets. Milo had three of Michael's gimlets. Sal had one. Merrill had seltzer. Bette had a runny nose.

We assumed the standard cocktail party positions on the couch, which was made just a tad more awkward by the fact that Michael had persuaded me to put the dinner table where the coffee table usually is so we wouldn't have to set it up while everyone was there. This meant that in order to converse, you had to look either under the table or over it to see whomever you wanted to talk to. This might explain the silence that had descended on my first Washington dinner party, but I think there was more to it. Bette excused herself to go to the bathroom for the third time in half an hour.

Merrill sat primly with her cocktail napkin balanced perfectly on her knee, refusing any cheese because of her diet. Sal stared into his drink and Milo smiled at the bathroom door and said, "Quite a girl, isn't she, A.B.?"

Bette returned more animated than before and sniffling more than before. In the kitchen, Michael put his forefinger to his nostril and inhaled. Bette saw this, apparently, and misconstrued his intention. "I'm sorry, Mikey," she said. "Anybody want a little toot? How 'bout a line, Salsie?"

Sal started to choke. Merrill delicately crushed her cocktail napkin between her perfectly manicured fingers. Michael changed the subject. But Bette would not be deterred. "C'mon, y'all. It's really great stuff. I got it from some guy at the *Trib*."

It was at this juncture that Merrill allowed how she really wasn't feeling very well and made her apologies and got herself and Sal out the door before anyone had a chance to say good-bye. "Too bad," Bette said as the door shut behind them. "She's such a nice gal."

"Let's eat," Michael said.

So we sat down to congealed fettucini, which looked about the way I felt. Ruth had neglected to mention that cream sauces should not be made a month in advance. I don't think Milo noticed. I don't think he noticed much of anything. He was beaming. All of him was beaming. His nose was as bright as a lighthouse beacon. His head began to bob and weave. "Did I ever tell you 'bout the time Ray Leonard and I went fishing, A.B.?" As a matter of fact, he had told the story twice already during cocktails. Michael shrugged. I shrugged. "Oooh, tell that one, I love that one," Bette said.

The evening was clearly a disaster. But I still wanted to impress Milo. I wanted him to think I'd been around. So I ignored the bobbing and the weaving and started telling him about the time I met Joe Frazier at his gym by the railroad trestle in North Philadelphia. Sal had sent me up there to do a piece on a little featherweight guy. I forget his name. Big Joe is standing by the heavy bag, giving it a workout. I figure it's Joe's gym. Joe's a fighter. I'll ask him about the little guy. "Well, miss," Joe says, very serious-like. "Bigs mens what makes the world go round. If you know what I mean, miss."

Michael laughed. Bette laughed. I laughed.

Milo did not laugh. Milo was in his fettucini, cold-cocked by God knows how many vodka gimlets. After a few seconds, when it was clear he was not getting up by the bell, I truly began to regret the cream sauce.

Michael got to him first. Milo doesn't have much hair, but what he's got is long and curly in the back. Michael grabbed a fistful of it and pulled him out of the sauce, so to speak. Milo came up smiling. "Bigs mens what makes the world go round," he said.

Bette kissed the cream from his cheeks. Michael went to the bathroom to get towels. I went to the kitchen to make coffee. By the time we returned, Milo's pants were down around his knees, his blue Oxford shirt was unbuttoned, and Bette was going to work on his boxer shorts. We headed for the bedroom fast, grabbing the platter of fettucini on the way. We sat in bed and slurped pasta and argued over how strong Michael had made the gimlets. He still swears he wasn't pouring heavy.

In sportswriting, getting drunk is no sin. But getting so sloshed you can't remember a good line is. Milo McHenry has made a career of never getting beat while drunk or otherwise. When we got up in the morning, he and Bette were gone. But I found a note scribbled in pencil on Merrill's crumpled cocktail napkin. It said: "Bigs mens what makes the world go round. Little ones just watch it from their fettucini."

When I called the office, Irene said Milo had taken a 7:00 A.M. flight to Vegas to cover some heavyweight fight. So I left a message for him in case he called in: "Tell him he can play."

May 30   As it turned out, the winning streak that began with a toothpick in Kansas City ended with a triple play the next time the Senators took the field. It felt normal losing again. Still, everyone on the team was very glad when they won the next game and realized that no precedents had been set. Suddenly the Washington Senators faced the prospect of being disappointingly mediocre. That would be a *real* letdown.

Except for a weekend series in Cleveland and a quick trip to Chicago, we've been home the whole time. And so has Michael. So I haven't had much time to get this stuff down.

It's a funny thing about our relationship—and I still can't quite figure it out. When I'm on the road, I never think about him except on deadline or late at night when I'm alone in my room and then I always think about him. When we're together, which is about as often as Charles and Di, I *assume* us. Which is not the same as taking us for granted. When Michael's here, I never sit around wondering, "Is this right?" or "Will it last?" or "Why don't I think about him with two gone in the bottom of the seventh?" When he's here, we just are.

He asked me last night, "What do you see in me anyway, other than a flash lede?"

"Well, for one thing," I said, "you make me laugh."

"C'mon. I'm serious."

"Okay. Seriously. You do things I would never do and then get me to do them."

Like riding around in his Triumph with the top down, eating McDonald's and listening to the police radio until three in the morning, which is what we did last night after the doubleheader. Or taking tap-dancing lessons, which is something I swore I'd never do ever since I was six, and that stupid ballet teacher told me I was the worst snowflake he'd ever seen.

"Police radio and tap dancing are not the basis for a lasting relationship," he said. "C'mon. I want to know. What is it? My legs?"

(He does have great legs.)

Conversations like these always make me nervous unless I'm having them with myself. And even then I'm likely to avoid them. But Michael wasn't going to let me blow him off.

"Stability," I said finally.

"Oh great, thanks."

"I mean you make stability charming. Seductive. Possible."

"That's even better," he said.

But it's true. And after Mom and Dad, it's no small feat either. Michael's parents were high school sweethearts. He says they never slept with anyone other than each other. He always thought that was the way it was supposed to be. After his father died, he told his mother he was sad his life hadn't been that way. He wanted his dad to meet the woman of his dreams. His mother told him, "It's all right, Mikey." She calls him Mikey. "You probably had more fun than us." But Michael says she was just being nice. Michael also says his dad would have liked me a lot.

I guess what it comes down to is: Michael has this way of reading me; usually when I'm most angry at him for *not* reading me, for not asking what's wrong when it's obvious something is, for not saying what are you thinking when it's clearly something important. That's when the specter of Mom and Dad hangs low and foreboding and he says, the way he did last night, "You know just because we're playing house doesn't mean you have to act like your mother. And I'm sure as hell not going to be your father. I'd never just let you run off with some old ballplayer."

"Fat chance," I said, and pinched his cheek and went back to getting this all down. Like I told him: history must be served and I've got two weeks to catch up on. But the truth is, I didn't want to have another conversation about giving up my apartment.

So here goes.

Right after we got back, Mr. Juanderful was suspended for a month. Monk got so desperate for pitching he decided to give Stretch his first start. Piggy was all excited. Everyone knew Stretch could throw the hell out of the ball. It was just that no one ever knew where it was going. Stretch was wild all right.

People said if he ever got it under control, he could be a great one.

Stretch is the closest thing we have to a natural. He was born knowing how to throw. It's *a priori* in him, though I like the way he says it better. "It comes natural, is all."

Stretch is a big old white boy from Newnan, Georgia, who is known as Stretch pretty much for the same reason that Stick is known as Stick. The guys have been teasing him about the road trip when a hooker knocked on Stretch's door and said she was looking for Mr. McCarthy. Stretch pointed to his father's room down the hall and said, "You got the wrong one." Stretch said it was the only honorable thing to do. Of course, he only sent her away because he already had a girl in his room. Stick pointed out that that was not a good enough reason.

The first time I met him, Stretch told me he didn't talk to no woman in no locker room, that we was all there just to look at his particulars, and he for one wasn't gonna be a party to it.

"Put on your pants, Stretch," I said.

"Whah?"

"Put on your pants. I'll wait."

This was in spring training, when there's always time to wait as well as to make a point. I turned my back and waited while Stretch ransacked his duffel bag for something clean, which took a while. "I thought you just wanted to, well, you know, *look*," he said, tapping me on the shoulder when he was suitably draped.

"Look, I'm twenty-nine years old," I said. "I've seen 'em before, and frankly, yours isn't any prettier than anyone else's. I really would prefer it, I mean I would really appreciate it, if you'd just keep on your pants.

"I'm a reporter, you know, not a voyeur."

I'd been practicing this speech for months, waiting for the right opportunity. Unfortunately, my big punch line fell a bit flat, since Stretch had no idea what a voyeur is. But I think he got the general idea and we were buddies after that until Monk laid down the law. Stretch being Piggy's son and Piggy being Monk's pal, there wasn't much Stretch could do. But he apologized for not talking to me anymore and puts his pants on whenever I'm around.

In addition to his ample particulars, Stretch has a gut that hangs over his belt and arms as wide as many thighs. And when he goes into his windup, the arms and the legs and the gut all get going in different directions. Rump says he's not sure which is scarier to the batter, the speed of the ball and its apparent lack of direction or the sight of Stretch unraveling on the mound.

Like most pitchers, Stretch regards his arm as an honored guest that dropped in for a cup of coffee and stayed. He never talks about "my arm." It's always "the arm," as if it belongs to someone else. Like most naturals, Stretch knows intuitively that this arm is a gift, a loan from some higher authority that can be taken away as surely as it was given. He is forever circling the arm over his head to make sure it's still there. You'd be amazed at the number of pitchers who wreck careers this way.

Stretch reminds me a little of Ryne Duren, the Yankees' ace reliever in the late fifties, except that Ryne was thin and angular and Stretch is wide and soft. I read in Ryne Duren's book once how he used to throw his last warmup pitch over Yogi's head just to send the batter a message. In my early days, before I decided I was going to be Joey Proud, I thought maybe I would like to be Ryne Duren. Ryne Duren was very fast and very wild. So I practiced throwing one over Yogi's head just to give the batter a message. Later it occurred to me that this was my first literary endeavor.

Stretch is that kind of wild.

No one was quite sure what to expect of him in his first major league start, but everyone in the dugout was wearing a batting helmet. So was everyone in the stadium. It was Sunday, May 21, Batting Helmet Day. As it happened, Stick farted just as the Senators were about to take the field. It didn't seem consequential at the time. Stick often farts. But it became one of those things that happen in baseball, like Wade Boggs eating only chicken and Mug Shot eating only grits, where almost anything, including farting, can become invested with religious significance if it happens to coincide with winning. In the first inning of his first major league start, Stretch struck out the side on nine pitches. Piggy, who was sitting in the dugout instead of the bullpen for the occasion, remembered that Stick farted.

He also remembered that Monk was sitting on his hands by the water cooler with his legs crossed, left leg over the right knee, looking as if he had to pee, when Buck hit the Big Fly that won Stretch's first major league game and ended a four-game losing streak. Piggy is a baseball man. Baseball men remember everything.

So on Tuesday, just before the Senators took the field, Piggy reminded Stick that he had farted and Monk that he had sat on his hands with his legs crossed, left leg over the right knee. Stick is as accomplished a farter as there is in the league, right up there with Stein. He didn't need any encouragement. And Monk is as superstitious as he is religious, the two things being not entirely dissimilar. So he didn't need any encouragement either. When the Senators won their second game in a row, no one needed to be reminded what to do when the next game began.

It was after that third win that Monk called a clubhouse meeting and told his boys not to bathe until the Senators lost. No one, not even Rump, objected, probably because no one thought it would last as long as it did. And also because in sports there is a long though somewhat dubious relationship between the lack of personal hygiene and victory. Back in the forties, there was a football coach named Pete Cawthorn who refused to let his players bathe for the entire season. "Goat it, boys," he said. Seems that he didn't want them associating with any sweet-smelling women.

So for the last ten days, Stick has farted, Monk has sat like a man who had to pee, refusing to move for the duration of the game even when he really did have to pee, no one has bathed, and the Washington Senators have won ten games in a row.

Spring comes with a vengeance to the nation's capital. One day it's gray and just this side of raw. The next day seven hundred thousand lawyers in yellow ties are eating hoagies in Lafayette Park. It's the same thing with pennant fever. It's an all-of-a-sudden kind of thing. The last time the Senators were in the World Series, it was 1933. So I suppose the city can be forgiven for this sudden and absurdly premature fever inflicted by the national pastime. Even supposedly rational, which is to say cynical, sports editors are not immune. Sal ran a story yesterday about the night sixty-five years ago the Senators won their first and last World Series, when white ribbons with the words I TOLD YOU SO magically appeared all over the city and a funeral procession in honor of the late John J. McGraw, manager of the losing New York Giants, made its way down Pennsylvania Avenue.

We are in thrall. One radio station has been giving away IOUs for play-off tickets. The first pair went to the first caller who could name Ossie Bluege's second wife: Wilor. The second pair went to anyone who could identify Ossie Bluege (the Senators' third baseman from 1922 to 1939).

Scalpers have been charging $100 over face value for box

seats along the first base line. Sutton Place Gourmet had a run on sauerkraut. Jimy Boy praised God and the 6–4–3 double play on a special Sunday service broadcast nationally to an estimated audience of four hundred thousand sinners. Ross Mitchell hosted a party for the entire squad. Twenty congressmen showed up in NATS T-shirts to eat Ballpark franks served by waiters in tuxedos and ball caps. "What a bunch of ass-licking geeks," Stein said later.

For the last ten days, the Senators have been the talk of the town. Talk shows are talking baseball. Cabbies are talking baseball. Georgetown hostesses are talking baseball. Will Buck maintain his .300 average and be the Senators' first Rookie of the Year since Bobby Allison in 1959? Will Mourning get the green light to steal on his own? Will Rump ever come out of his slump? And think how good the Senators will be when he does!

Stretch and I went on a late-night radio show together after his second win. It's hosted by a guy named the Fanatic, and the conversation went something like this: "Well, Big Guy, the guys are really playing heads-up ball."

Stretch, who is no rocket scientist, thanked him and replied, "Rarely will I do anything unstupid, especially when we're going good."

Then the Fanatic started taking calls. A guy from Gaithersburg said I was the luckiest person in the city because I had gotten to see every game. I asked him for his definition of luck. A woman from Frederick sighed and asked Stretch if he was married. A teenager from Rockville asked me if I thought the Senators were too good to be true. I didn't flinch. I'm not sure I even thought. I blurted out the truth. "Nothing about the Senators is too good to be true. In baseball, you're never as good as you seem when you're going good and never as bad as you seem when you're going bad, unless, of course, you're the Senators, who really are *that* bad."

The next day I was *persona non grata* all over town. The Fanatic's telephone lines lit up with people calling me an ornery bitch and worse. The office calls ran 5–1 against me. The letter writers, anonymously, of course, called me a know-nothing motherfucking kike Hebe slut. Even Sal thought I was too tough on "the boys." They win a few games and suddenly they're his "boys." But then again, as I told him, he hasn't seen every game.

For the last ten days the Senators have been impersonating the '61 Yankees, including the attitude. I guess they're entitled. I

don't know how else they're going to get through the rest of the
season. And it has had some professional advantages for me.
I haven't had to write "zapped," "thrashed," "whipped,"
"rocked," or "shelled" once. Also, Stick has forgiven me for the
item in the Schnoz and is back to asking if I'm getting enough.
Every day when I get to the clubhouse, he assumes another position out of the Kama Sutra and asks if I've done it like this.
"Absolutely," I say. I think he believes me.

Why shouldn't he be in a good mood? He's a career .259
hitter who's batting .280 and leading the league in home runs (15)
and strikeouts (55). His agent, Marv Cox, who also represents
Stein and Brawn and Tubbs and Mourning, just got him a major
endorsement contract ("six figs, Big Guy!") with Johnson &
Johnson for a new Stick deodorant. They've been spending a lot
of time at Stick's locker discussing the prototype. Marv's a former player who became an agent mostly so he can still hang
around the locker room. He's always swatting guys on the ass
and bragging about the megadeal for five hundred thou per he
got the number one guy in the 1981 baseball draft. Of course, it
was all Marv's doing. The guy's .379 batting average had nothing
to do with it.

I got an unsigned postcard from Nashville with a picture of
Elvis on the front and the lyrics to a Dead Milkmen's song on the
back: "When my time comes, that's how I want to go, stoned and
fat and wealthy and sitting on the bowl." I was glad to know
Billy's doing okay. I saw in the paper he's hitting .289 and playing every day. I miss him.

This weekend we went to Cleveland for a three-game weekend series. All the way there on the plane, Stretch and Stein
debated whether it was safer to cross the ocean in a rowboat or
walk across the desert without water. Rump pretended to be
asleep and told me about it later. Stretch, who gets prickly heat,
argued fiercely for the ocean. Stein, who can't swim, argued for
the desert. Finally they took a poll. The twenty-four-man roster
was split down the middle, except for Brother John, who said he
walks and swims with Jesus. Brother John gives goodness a bad
name.

Milo says Lawson reminds him of this guy Pat Kelly, who
played for the Orioles some years back before going into the
ministry. Earl Weaver was still managing then. Pat kept telling
him, "Earl, I walk with God." Finally Earl told him, "I'd rather
you walk with the bases loaded."

Lawson accepted Jesus as his personal Savior one afternoon seven years ago after bouncing out with the bases loaded for the third time in the same game. The manager pinch-hit for him in the ninth and Lawson went to the showers, where, and I am quoting from his personal testimony on the back of his Christian baseball card, "I got down on my hands and knees and asked Jesus Christ to come into my life. And He did. I was slain in the Lord in the shower. I mean, I really got zapped by the Holy Spirit. And let me tell you, it was exciting. I am excited still. I am excited every day I walk with the Lord."

Brother John was with the Brewers when he got saved and had a few rocky months where he wasn't sure whether his calling was pitching God or playing ball. His pastor told him God had called him to minister to the unwashed and unsaved. So Lawson accepted the entire Brewers middle infield as his flock and went to work saving them. The Brewers management wasn't too keen on his priorities and traded him to the Indians, where he formed another Bible study group and went to work on their infield. He got traded three more times before he ended up here. For sure Lawson is the first guy in the majors to be traded six times for refusing to sin. And he's the only guy on the Senators who was thrilled to be made available to Jimy Boy in the expansion draft. He told me in spring training that he has personally led five starting pitchers, three second basemen, four catchers, and two relief pitchers to the Lord. Pentacost is his latest convert; now he goes out to play with little crosses on his spikes just like Lawson does, and thinks he's looking at a crucifix every time his foot bisects the pitching rubber.

The day I met Lawson at spring training, I introduced myself, saying the obvious. "Hi, I'm A. B. Berkowitz."

"Hi," Lawson replied. "I'm a sinner."

Stein, of course, knew Brother John in the old days with the Brewers when Lawson really was a sinner and very accomplished at "keeping it wet," as Stein puts it. Brother John turns pale every time Stein puts on his JEWISH JOCKS FOR JESUS T-shirt and asks about his ex. "Yep, I remember John before he got so brotherly," Stein said in the locker room our first day in Cleveland. "You run into a lot of old settlers you used to know, Brother John?"

"Old settlers?" I asked Rump.

"Trim," he explained. "Girls."

Brother John pursed his lips. Stein would not be denied. "I

wonder what all those old settlers think of the new Brother
John?"

Lawson zipped his fly, reached for his Bible, and said,
"They're grateful."

Later that night, I guess it was about one in the morning
actually, the phone rang in Rump's room. It was Stein. "Some
guy down here in the lobby wants you to poke his wife," Stein
said. "He's a big fan of yours."

"Nah," Rump said. "But I'll watch."

So he went down to the lobby, where Stick and Stein and
Mancusi were waiting for him. Just about that time, Lawson
wandered by. "C'mon, brother, how 'bout witnessing some
skank for old times' sake?" Stein said. No one knows what got
into Lawson, but he went along. Rump says maybe he thought he
could save them all. But he couldn't even save himself. I think
Rump only told me all this 'cause he can't stand Lawson. Anyway, Rump and the husband watched as the Senators had their
way with the missus. Lawson went last. And when he was done,
he kneeled at the foot of the bed and prayed for forgiveness. The
husband took offense at this derogation of his wife's honor.
"Whaddya mean?" he said, putting his hands around Lawson's
throat. "That's the best you've ever had."

Rump was telling me this story by the batting cage yesterday before the doubleheader. And quite naturally, I started to
laugh. "No, wait," he said. "That's not the funny part."

"It's not?"

"Nope," he said. "The funny part is, I saw Stick and Stein
and Mancusi and Brother John standing outside the trainer's
room waiting on Rube this morning. Turns out 'the best they
ever had' had the clap. I asked Stick about it. He shrugged and
said, 'You gotta play hurt.' "

Today is the last day of the home stand. There was a birthday party for Stein in the locker room after BP. When I came in,
Stick, Mancusi, Mourning, Mug Shot, and Stretch were standing
there naked, with birthday hats on their heads and hot dog rolls
on their peckers. Mug Shot's idea. "Shush," Stretch said. "It's a
surprise."

On the table in the middle of the locker room there's always
a box of balls waiting for guys to sign and tins of chocolate chip
cookies shaped like bats and balls from little old ladies in Annan-
dale. Stein's birthday required something special. And it *was* special. There in the middle of the table was a chocolate cake deco-

rated with a life-size marzipan penis. Fully erect, I might add. "Was this your idea?" I said to Stick.

"Nah," he said. "But I posed for it."

Then the Senators went out and won their tenth straight ballgame. Buck hit a two-run home run, Stick added a solo shot, Pentacost got his third win of May, and Demetrious Mourning flipped off the crowd for booing him when he struck out with the bases loaded in the sixth. I have to say I thought he was over-reacting. But the truth is nobody thought much about it because, after all, the Senators won.

Kansas City

May 31   Demetrious Mourning missed the flight to K.C. this morning. He didn't check into the hotel. He didn't show up for batting practice. And when he didn't show up by game time, everyone knew what that meant. Stick forgot to fart before the team took the field. Stretch hit the first four batters he faced and was sent to the showers. Monk uncrossed his legs in the middle of the fifth inning. And by the end of the seventh, the Senators were behind, 10–0. Our headline tomorrow is going to read: SENS IN MOURNING; LOSE 10–1. OUTFIELDER IN DETOX. The winning streak is over. Everyone can take a bath.

Kansas City

June 1 The way Rump tells it, what happened is Buck was in his room watching the adult cable channel when Stick got the binoculars on him. And Buck was *involved,* if you know what I mean. We're staying in one of those horseshoe-shaped hotels with rooms built around a courtyard and an outdoor pool. So it really isn't hard to get a look across into someone else's window, especially if you've had a lot of practice. Stick and Stein have been developing this particular skill for the last ten years. So Stick handed the glasses over to Stein, his roomie, and says, "Tell me when."

Stein watched and watched, narrating the whole way with body language and sound effects—" 'Yes! Yes! Oh my God, yes!' Now! Stick! Now!" So Stick picked up the phone and dialed the poor dumb son of a bitch, who answered, which was definitely a rookie mistake. "Hello," said Buck. "Hello," said Stick. "This is God. Stop it!"

Buck didn't say a word all the way to the ballpark. When he got to the clubhouse, Stein gave him this long, knowing look and said so everyone could hear, "Anybody get any post?" Post is postgame, as in trim, skank, dome, and skull. Post is what you get when you hound the beef successfully.

This was about twenty minutes after I found out Buck had

been named the American League Player of the Month for May and ten minutes after Sal told me he wants a major takeout on the guy and to go find him quick. Buck's had practically the best first two months ever, certainly for a rookie: .327, with 9 home runs and 30 RBIs. That's better than Joey Proud's first season back in '68. MacKenzie was saying just the other day how much Buck reminds him of Joey; same uppercut lefty swing. Funny, I hadn't noticed the similarity before. I've been after Sal to do this piece for weeks. Of course, he wasn't interested until everybody else said it was a good story. Oh well.

By the time I got to the park, it was pouring. The forecast was terrible. Batting practice was history. I figured I'd get the interview and still get back to the hotel in time to have a real dinner.

But I couldn't find Buck. He wasn't in the players' lounge or the locker room or the shower. Finally Rump gestured toward the dugout and said, "He's got his game face on."

Usually Buck wears his cap back on his head the way I remember Willie Mays. It makes him look boyish that way, and also he thinks it hides his bald spot better. But today he had the bill pulled down to his nose so I couldn't see his eyes, which are as brown as the infield dirt. He was staring straight ahead, just watching the rain. It was falling on the tarp, splashing against the canvas, running in rivulets down from the pitcher's mound. The rain came harder. And the streams became rivers and the rivers became puddles like the ones you jumped in as a kid.

Buck's teeth began to chatter. The only noise was the hiss of the rain on the roof and the *k-k-k-k-k* of Buck's teeth. The dugout started to leak. Water dripped from the roof onto the bill of his cap and from the bill of his cap onto the front of his blue satin warmup jacket. *K-k-k-k-k.* His teeth chattered louder now. His face was wet. I couldn't tell if it was from the rain or something else.

"I guess you noticed I stutter," Buck said finally.

It occurred to me then that I had never heard him use the first-person singular before. It's always "Buck this" and "Buck that" and "Buck stops here." It also occurred to me that I had never heard him stutter.

The rain came harder, beating a syncopation on the roof, a drummer's rain. I couldn't see the outfield wall. I couldn't see the scoreboard. Minutes passed. Maybe even twenty. The harder it

rained, the slower Buck talked. "I guess you notice I be kind of
shy," he said. "Insecure-like."

He was still staring straight ahead at a wall he couldn't see.
He wouldn't look at me at all. I nodded anyway. "One reason is
because of my momma. My daddy never did marry my momma.
She wasn't but a kid herself when Buck was born. Fourteen, I
think my grandma says. She hung on him fierce and ran off when
he wouldn't do the right thing by her. I guess I was two then."

I wondered how long it took him to form this sentence, how
many years of hiding the fact behind a stammer no one but him
notices. I waited and I wondered and I listened to the rain.
"Coming up, I lived with my daddy. But he was in the Navy, see.
So his momma raised me up. He sent postcards from wherever
he was. I got 'em still. I lived with my grandma in my daddy's
house on one side of town. My momma lived all the way on the
other. She got herself married when she was seventeen. Had a
whole mess of kids. Sunday mornings, I'd go to my granddaddy's
church and pray she would come for Buck. Sunday afternoons, I
went over and had dinner with her new family. But she always
sent me home after. I loved my daddy. But I wanted my momma.
I guess everybody wants his momma. It created some conflicts in
my mind, so to speak."

The puddles became floods. Steam hissed and rose from the
infield. Rain splashed on my notebook, blurring the words as fast
as I wrote them.

I'm always astonished when people talk to me this way. I'm
astonished when they talk to anyone this way, divulging themselves without any warning. I still do not expect it. But I do not
question it either. The one question deadline reporters never ask
and probably always should is: "Why are you telling *me* this?"
You just keep writing, hoping they don't stop, hoping you get it
all right.

"In school, the kids was always teasing me. Kids, they cruel,
you know? 'Where's your momma at, Buck Buchanan?' 'Buck
ain't got no momma.' Some days I'd be walking down the road,
just walking, you know. And I'd see a car coming and I'd think,
'There's my momma. Buck's momma's in that car.' But it just
kept on going.

"Then one day when I was getting ready to get on home
from school, my momma showed up at the gate. I run to her.
'Momma. Momma.' But she ain't looking for Buck, see. She
wasn't waiting on Buck. She's waiting on DeWayne. DeWayne

was her oldest 'cept for me. DeWayne was her boy. So I start running. Like I ain't seen her or nothing. I kept running till I seen my grandma setting on the porch. I ain't seen my momma since. And I been stuttering since."

Buck pushed the cap up on his head and I could see now that the wetness was the residue of tears. There were fault lines on his cheeks where tears had come and gone. "Wandette was the only one that didn't tease me. She kinda shy too. I guess old Buck suaved her off her feet. Leastwise, for a while he did. We got a little girl now. She's four in September. Her name is Sherron. She's my little lady."

He reached into his pocket and pulled out a packet of sunflower seeds and a crinkled picture of a little girl with ribbons in her hair and spaces between her teeth. "See?" he said.

He cradled that picture in his hands, protecting it from the drip drip drip that was falling onto the bill of his cap and from the bill of his cap onto his warmup jacket. He hugged that picture as if he was as little as she was.

"Wandette left last month. Just up and quit me. Left a note saying she didn't want to be hitched to no man that was always gone and to take care of her baby. Now, how is Buck going to 'splain that to that child? I sure don't know."

He sighed and wiped away a tear. "Sherron, she's living in my daddy's house with my grandma now. I send her postcards. I called last night. My grandma, she put Sherron on the phone. Sherron says, 'Daddy, Daddy, I love you, Daddy.' And you know what? She was stuttering. She couldn't hardly say hello to her daddy."

I thought about telling him about Mom then, about the divorce when I was thirteen, about her running off with a former ballplayer who owns a paint store now. I wanted to tell him I understood. I wanted to tell him it was okay to tell me these things. I wanted to make it even between us. But I didn't want to interrupt him. I didn't want him to change his mind and say, "Oh, by the way that's off the record." I certainly didn't want to ask him how he felt about being named American League Player of the Month, but I did, and I think maybe he was a little relieved to change the subject. What he said was "Once I step on the baseball field, I feel free. You can have but so many problems in life and then you're out there and the sun is shining and I feel like it just eliminates everything. It just blocks it out of your head. And I feel free."

The squall had stopped by then. The mist in the outfield was lifting. A batboy came down the tunnel pushing a shopping cart filled with bats. I could hear his spikes scraping against the concrete and the percussion of colliding lumber. We were going to play ball after all.

Buck excused himself to go get dressed. So I sat there with my soggy notes, crying a little for him and a little for me. The deep rumble of male voices grew closer. It was Lefty and Rump, getting ready to go down to the bullpen. Lefty took a gulp of water from the fountain and spat it at my feet. Rump nodded at a sign on the dugout wall: DUGOUT MUST BE CLEARED 45 MINUTES BEFORE GAME.

I had made another dumb rookie mistake.

"Why didn't you tell me?"

"Buck," he said.

Arlington

June 2   I spent the day in my room with the curtains closed and the blackout shades drawn, sitting on my bed writing Buck's story in my underwear. I always write best in my underwear, which is why in the press box I never wear shoes. I have wondered about the relationship between words and underwear and I have come to the conclusion that it's best not to think about it. I took the phone off the hook and put the DO NOT DISTURB sign on the door and sat in my underwear and thought lofty thoughts. My Radio Shack was humming. My fingers were flying. I was writing and reading aloud to myself, thrilled with the sound of my own words in my own voice. Usually I hate the sound of my own voice, which is one of many reasons I rarely tape interviews. But I liked my voice today. It sounded rich and full and good. Nothing quite like a reporter who knows she's got good stuff. That's what we call it when someone spills his guts, good stuff. Personal pathos is always good stuff. Personal tragedy is better. Tragedy is great stuff and the person to whom it happened is a spiller. A spiller is always a great guy.

Buck had spilled his guts. I'd like to tell you I thought twice about writing it. But I didn't. I just wrote it, is all. And I told myself it was okay because it would have come out anyway and besides he didn't say it was off the record and what's more the words I was reading aloud to myself in my underwear were so exquisitely compassionate and so finely crafted that Buck wouldn't even know he had spilled his guts to a reporter whose mother ran off with another man when her daughter was thirteen. That's what I told myself. Even though it was a lie.

So I was in a great mood when I got to the ballpark and feeling more than just a little bit smug. I knew what I had that Girard and MacKenzie didn't have. I had a scoop. I had Buck. I had hit that sucker out of the ballpark. Like Sal says: I was all over it.

In the press box, the AP machine was coughing up last night's results and this morning's write-throughs. It's a comforting sound, that *chooka chooka chooka* of words and paper spitting out the news. The fact that thousands of machines in newsrooms and press boxes all over the country are spitting out the same words at the same time with the same *chooka chooka chooka* makes me feel connected. It makes me feel relevant. *Chooka chooka chooka.* It is the sound of a wired person. It is the sound of belonging. So I always look at the wire machines first thing. This time I noticed a Washington dateline.

> Jimy Boy Collins, owner of the Washington Senators, has ordered mandatory drug testing of the entire major league roster in light of the recent admission by outfielder Demetrious Mourning that he snorted cocaine between innings of Senators games.
>
> The first round of testing began late last night after the Senators' loss to the Kansas City Royals, the *Washington Post* reported. Of the players reached last night for comment, only catcher Rump Doubleday said he would refuse to comply with the owner's order. "This is a free country," Doubleday said. "I am an American citizen. This is an invasion of my privacy. I won't do it."
>
> Doubleday, the perennial All-Star catcher, is mired in the worst slump of his 16-year career, batting .188 with one home run and five RBIs. A club spokesman said this morning, "What's he afraid of anyway? If he's clean, he shouldn't have any problem. We expect him to set an example. This is not what Reverend Collins means by 'Just say no.' "

Girard was reading over my shoulder. I could smell his pants and feel his breath on my neck. It was coming out in short, staccato gusts. He was laughing to himself. "Way Rump's going, probably scared he won't be able to hit the bottle," he said.

MacKenzie joined him. "Yeah, did you hear Stein needling him last night? 'Hell no, Rump won't go.' Jesus, it was something. I've never seen Rump so steamed. I mean, he was *pissed.*"

"Me neither," Girard said. "Not even at me. Hey, Berkowitz, where were you? Your boy was looking for you."

They all had it. They all knew. I was fucked. And they all knew that, too.

"Yeah, where were you, anyway, Berkowitz?" MacKenzie said.

Where was I? I was up in the press box congratulating myself on my great interview with Buck. I went down to the locker room, all right. I listened to Monk say, "No bleeping comment. I ain't got horseshit to say with Berkowitz around," and I got pissed and left for the plane. I got pissed and I got beat.

"Hey, Berkowitz, your office called."

It was Leon, the press box attendant. He handed me one of those little pink message slips with all the little boxes: RETURNED YOUR CALL, URGENT, PLEASE CALL. But there was no little box for the message on my little pink slip. It said: "Sal says, 'Where the fuck have you been?'"

Irene put me on hold. Must have been at least ten minutes before Sal picked up. So I sat there watching the grounds crew water the basepaths. I always love it when they water the basepaths. I love it when the dusty dirt turns chocolate brown. I love those funny brooms they pull around the infield that swirl the dirt like icing. I love it when they lay down the baselines that look so white, so straight, the borders of the game.

"Where the fuck have you been?" Sal said.

Somehow I don't think he wanted to hear about Buck, and what great stuff I had, and I certainly didn't want to tell him about sitting in my room in my underwear listening to my own words roll off my own tongue. In newspapering, either you're out front on a story, which means you beat everyone's ass, or you're playing catch-up, which means they beat yours. I definitely wasn't out front on this one.

"I fucked up," I said.

"Goddamn right you fucked up," Sal said. "How many times do I gotta tell you. You gotta go down to the locker room."

There didn't seem any point in telling him that I did go down to the locker room and how nobody is talking to me anyway because of Jimy Boy and Monk and 1-800-U-LOSERS and Ross Mitchell threatening to sue the club on my behalf. Sal hasn't made a deadline since 1976, but he didn't want to hear about that either. I read once where Red Smith, who was only the best sports columnist ever, said the reason he liked writing a daily column was if he served up turkey on Thursday, there was always a chance he could come up with veal for Friday. I figured maybe once Sal read the piece on Buck, he would feel better. But a tearjerker can't hold a candle to breaking news.

"You better get your boy Rump. And you better get him now."

I had maybe twenty minutes before they closed the locker room. I ran all the way, skidding down the ramps, elbowing the elderly, spilling beer, and generally giving the working press a very bad name. He was surrounded when I got there. I couldn't even see him. I stood on my tippy-toes. I looked through Mac-Kenzie's legs. I could only hear half-sentences and fragments of obscenities. I didn't know if I had heard what I thought I heard. I wrote it down anyway. In a pinch, even half a quote will do. There were three minutes left by the time it was just him and me.

Rump was on autopilot. I could tell by his voice how many times he had given the same interview. But rote Rump was better than no Rump. He nodded. He knew. He's been repeating himself like this for sixteen years. "I told them Jimy Boy could go piss in a pot," he said. "I said, 'I'm not afraid of anything, including him.' I may be hitting only .188, but I will not pee on command for Jimy Boy Collins or God. And if Jimy Boy doesn't like it, he can shove it up his righteous ass. Does that help you any?"

I had my foot up on Rump's chair and my steno pad on my knee and I was writing as fast as I could. It's times like this I understand baseball best and why it is Rump says if you press too hard, you squeeze the bat too tight and you're not quick enough to get around on the fastball. If I had squeezed my pen any harder all the ink would have come out. My fingers were turning red, cramping. My handwriting was illegible. I knew I wouldn't be able to read my notes in twenty minutes.

I started to laugh.

"What's so funny?" he said.

"I'm standing here taking notes I can't read about grown

men pissing in a pot for a religious fanatic who believes God is
going to put them in first place by September 14, and I just
noticed you have the hairiest toes I've ever seen."

He wiggled his toes and started to laugh too. "You want the
rest of it?" he said.

He knew I did. He was nice enough not to make me ask.
"No, I'm not doing coke. I don't smoke dope. I haven't smoked
any dope for years. That's off the record. It just gets me depressed, though I don't know what could be more depressing
than this shit. I couldn't be doing any worse if I was doing lines
between innings, could I?"

I closed my notebook. He put on his sanitary hose. "Meet me
for a drink later?" he said.

June 3   Pretty much everyone was down at the bar by the
time I got there. Stein was looking down some girl's shirt and she
wasn't objecting. Stretch was drinking a pitcher of beer from the
pitcher. Guttierrez was shimmying by himself in a corner to
music that was unidentifiable except by the vibrations it sent up
your legs. The noise was intense, the light predictable. It was a
still life of a bar. You know the place: wooden glass-racks above
the bartender's head, a couple of fake Tiffany lamp shades and
stained-glass windows, bentwood chairs, and fried zucchini
sticks. Sometimes I wonder if all these bars aren't really one bar,
a hologram of a bar projected into every airport hotel in every
city in America, and if all the people—the salesmen, the stews,
the ballplayers, the writers—who inhabit this mobile everywhere
aren't really the same people in the same place, drinking the
same drinks and ordering the same rounds.

Rump was waiting for me in a blond-wood booth, eating
fried zucchini and drinking B and B. I'd never seen Rump drink
anything but beer before. Then again, this was a season of a lot of
firsts.

"There's been something I've been wanting to ask you for a
long time," he said. He leaned forward, past the music. I braced
myself. Not him too.

"Why'd they name you Ariadne?"

"Why'd they name you Rump?"

"I think you know the answer to that," he said.

I ordered a beer from a waitress who named twelve different
brews before I got a chance to tell her I wanted a Miller Lite.

"How'd you know? I never tell anybody about Ariadne."

"I checked you out," he said. "I have my sources, too, you know."

I didn't know whether to feel flattered or invaded. He was smiling, so I decided to feel flattered.

"Anyway. Why Ariadne?"

"My mother was in labor for seventy-three hours. When it was over, she was in a very good mood. She thought it was funny, Ariadne. She also thought it sort of balanced out the Berkowitz."

"Ariadne, daughter of Minos, who gives Theseus the thread that leads him from the labyrinth."

"Jesus, Rump, what'd you do, go to the library?"

"Webster's English Dictionary," he said, ordering another drink. "So you going to take me by the hand and lead me out of my labyrinth, Ariadne?"

There were two possible interpretations and I chose the more benign. I told him he'd find his way out of his slump. "That's some name, Ariadne Berkowitz," he responded.

"Don't forget the Bloom. Ariadne Bloom Berkowitz. You try going through high school with the name Ariadne Berkowitz. It guaranteed me a sense of humor."

"Try playing baseball with the name John Fitzgerald Doubleday."

I decided not to worry about him. "Your parents are liberals, I take it?"

"My mother went to the theater one time and Kennedy was there. At intermission, he touched her shoulder while bending over to tie his shoe. Monk would have liked her. She didn't wash for two weeks, the shoulder anyway, and she never wore the dress again. When she found out she was pregnant, she announced it was going to be a boy and that she was going to name him John Fitzgerald Doubleday. Later, she told me it was a good thing I was her third, 'cause if I had been the first, I would have been an only."

"It's a great baseball name, John Fitzgerald Doubleday. Right up there with Mookie and Bobo and Choo Choo and Moose. My personal all-time favorite is Calvin Coolidge Julius Caesar Tuskahoma (Buster) McLish. Too bad they didn't name you Abner. Too bad you're not related to him."

Rump swizzled his B and B and smiled.

"Who said I'm not?"

"You did. A million times. In a million stories. I even asked you in spring training, just to make sure."

"I lied," he said. "You are talking to the great-great-nephew of Abner Doubleday. I was born to play ball."

"You're kidding."

He shook his head. "My mother did the family tree just before she got leaned on by Jack Kennedy."

"Can I write it?"

"Nope," he said. "Not until I hit."

"My God, Rump. You *are* baseball."

"I know," he said.

"Of course, you do know your great-great-uncle is a fraud. You know they made him up."

"I know," Rump said.

"I did a story on it last fall. They had this commission in 1903 to determine the origin of the game. Albert Spalding was the chairman. He wanted to debunk the myth that baseball descended from the British. It had to be the all-American game if he was going to sell his all-American sporting goods. So he put together this commission to find the inventor of baseball. When they couldn't find one, they invented one. Might as well make him a Civil War hero while you're at it. After three years of correspondence and testimony, they came to the conclusion that the best evidence was that Abner Doubleday invented the game of baseball in Cooperstown, New York, in 1839."

"I know," Rump said.

"I talked to this guy at the Hall of Fame. He said, 'It was the age of invention. They needed an inventor. They couldn't accept the idea that baseball had just evolved.' They based their conclusion on the testimony of this guy Abner Graves, who said he went to school with Doubleday. I mean, your uncle. But Graves was five when your uncle was nineteen. And he was in West Point the year he was supposed to invent baseball. So he couldn't have been in Cooperstown unless he was AWOL."

Rump just sat there while I went on telling him what he already knew.

"The guy said probably baseball was developed in some small town pretty much like Cooperstown, probably around the time Doubleday was supposed to invent it. So there was no sense in debunking the myth. But there's no history in it either."

"I know," Rump said.

"So why didn't you tell anyone?"

"There's all kinds of myths, Ariadne Berkowitz. Baseball is what we want it to be. I didn't want to be part of mythology. I just wanted to play ball."

Some one put the Temptations on the jukebox. Rump smiled at the choice. "C'mon," he said. "Let's dance."

June 4   Last night I dreamed I met Joey Proud. I was sitting in the press box at Arlington Stadium when he came up to pinch-hit for Rump. It was weird. Everyone in the press box acted as if it was no big deal except me. I was jumping up and down yelling, "It's Joey Proud! He's come out of retirement to save the Washington Senators!" But no one seemed to notice or care. They just kept eating their hot dogs and filling in their scorecards as if this happened every day. Me, I was leaning out of the press box, shouting his name, trying to get his attention while he rubbed his hands in the dirt. But of course he didn't hear me. He stepped up to the plate and hit the first pitch over the centerfield wall. The ball flew out of the park and I flew to him. I do not know how. It was a dream. Joey was galloping around the bases without any trace of a limp and I'm trailing behind like an angel over his shoulder, trying to ask, "Where was the pitch?" But he didn't stop and he didn't hear me. As we rounded third, the catcher, who's a Christian but a very hard-nosed guy, set himself in front of me as if he was waiting for a throw and knocked me out of the stadium. It was a Disney-type collision, a cartoon disaster. I bounced off his chest protector. *B-o-i-n-g! B-o-i-n-g!* And over the centerfield wall. *B-o-i-n-g!*

This time it was the phone ringing, waking me up.

"Get up, Berkowitz!" the voice said.

It was a few minutes before I was sure where I was and I have no particular recollection what I said in the interim. "Berkowitz, Berkowitz," Sal said. "Wake up, Berkowitz."

"Huh?" I said.

"Listen, Berkowitz, it's important. Tiger Battle just called."

"What time is it?"

"It's eight-thirty," Sal said.

"*Your* time," I said.

"He called a half hour ago," Sal said. "I could have called you a half hour ago. You gotta call him. Now. He says he won't talk to anyone but you. It's your account, Berkowitz!"

When Sal says something is your account, it's his way of saying, "Do it or die." I took the number and went back to sleep.

I woke up three hours later with the phone ringing again. "Did you get him?" Sal said.

Even half-asleep I can lie. "The line was busy," I said. "I'll try again now."

"Call me," Sal said.

Tiger Battle, the pride of the Crimson Tide, has been the All-Pro defensive end of the Washington Redskins for the last six years. In those years, the 'Skins have won the Super Bowl twice and gone to the NFC Championship four times. Each time Tiger made the interception or forced the turnover that led to the go-ahead score. As John Riggins, the bon vivant running back, once said, "Ronald Reagan may be President but I'm king."

Tiger Battle is king. He is also six-nine, 270 pounds, runs the forty-yard dash in less than five seconds, and wears size thirty-six Jockey shorts. In this case, when people say he is larger than life, they are not being metaphorical.

If Tiger Battle takes a leak, the *Washington Post* strips it above the banner. Sal is not one to be outdone in this regard. He once led the page with a headline that said: BATTLE HAS CRAMP. And it wasn't even the regular season. So if Tiger Battle calls the Sports Department asking to speak to someone, that person is likely to get a 7:30 A.M. wakeup call from Sal.

Last fall I did a major takeout on Tiger. He wasn't talking to the press at the time except at once-a-week team press conferences, which is the trendy thing to do. So when he agreed to an interview, his first with a local scribe in over a year, Sal was practically apoplectic. Michael said, "You'll dine out off this for a year." And I have. I think it's what got me the Senators beat.

Tiger said to meet him for breakfast at his favorite watering hole in Georgetown at 9:00 A.M. Breakfast turned out to be purely liquid. Tiger drank ale with apricot brandy chasers. I drank bloody Marys. It was a Monday, the Redskins' off-day, and Tiger was supposed to make an appearance at Children's Hospital at four. At five-thirty we were still sitting there drinking when his wife called for the sixth time and Tiger told the bartender for the sixth time to tell her he had left already. Tiger was seriously shit-faced. Giggling Georgetown coeds kept coming by and asking for autographs. And Tiger kept saying, "Sure, I'll give you an autograph. Right after you give me a blow job." Also, he called Vernon Marks, the Cowboys' wide receiver, "a little nigger picker."

I staggered back to the office at seven-thirty, wrote 3,000 words, maybe 250 of which detailed Tiger's drunkenness, profanity, and racism (in a nice way, of course). Sal killed all 250 of them, ignoring my protests that he was sanitizing reality and that all those people in the bar were going to think I was some kind of fool. Sal told me to go home and get some sleep.

I went to Kramerbooks, a Dupont Circle hangout, to meet Michael instead. All I remember of that episode is that I got up to go to the john and passed out on my feet on the steps to the indoor café. I was very hot-shit and very hung-over the next morning.

Tiger let it be known through the Redskins' PR people that he liked the story, and it was no wonder. He came off like the all-American boy, which surely he is not, except by the most liberal interpretation. Athletes never personally tell you they like something. They only personally tell you if they think it's a piece of shit. So this was a big fucking deal. When he announced after the next game that he wasn't talking to "no reporters no way no how except Berkowitz," it was a *major* fucking deal. That's how Tiger became my account.

In the final game of the regular season, Tiger shattered his ankle while being ground into the turf of RFK by the Refrigerator, who was sent into the Bears' lineup with the express purpose of blocking for Neal Anderson and sitting on Tiger Battle. You could see the bone sticking through Tiger's sock. It was one of those football injuries that TV likes to show over and over again in slower and slower motion. Maybe one day they'll be able to mike the bones so we can hear them snap too.

Tiger said it hurt like hell but what he was really afraid of was being asphyxiated. "I've never been a lawn chair for a three-hundred-and-fifty-pound refrigerator before," he said as they carried him off the field.

Tiger was operated on that night and I had my interview request in the next morning. I got his wife, Linda, on the phone and she took my number and sniffed. I didn't like the way she sniffed, but she was very proper and said he would call when he had something to say. Sal made me call every day for a week and then every other day for a month and then once a week until I left for spring training. Each time Linda Battle took the message and each time she sniffed and finally I didn't blame her. But still

Tiger did not call. And he did not show up at minicamp either.
That was a month ago.

The Redskins report to training camp in Carlisle in about
four weeks, and every one in the whole city is holding their
breath waiting to find out whether he's going to gut it out or
retire. That's why Sal woke me up at seven-thirty in the morning.

Linda recognized my voice. "Oh, it's you," she sniffed.

"I got a message Tiger called," I told her.

"He's gone fishing," she replied. "I can't say when he'll be
back."

"Fishing?"

"Fishing. When he's not fishing, he's hunting. And when he
isn't hunting, he's chasing women. He's a man's man. Isn't that
what you people call him? Of course, some women don't need
chasing. Some women chase him. Some women ask for interviews."

It occurred to me at that moment that she really did think I
was sleeping with her husband or had had the pleasure at least
once. Nine times out of ten her hunches are probably right. Lots
of wives think this about me. Rump's, for instance. I always
shrug it off. But suddenly it was very important to make Linda
Battle believe she was wrong where I was concerned. It wasn't so
much a case of ethics or professional pride, though I certainly
invoked those totems. It was more that she sounded so awfully
alone. I wanted her to know I wouldn't do that to her.

"Are you married?" she said.

"No," I said, "but I'm living with somebody."

"Hmmmm," she said.

"Look, there's nothing I can say to make you believe me. I
know that. But I don't sleep with athletes. This is my job. I'm a
professional. I'm not that dumb. Besides, you know how quick
that would get around? You think these guys would be discreet? I
know one woman who went to bed with a hockey player one
night and the next day there was a sign up in the locker room
giving her a five on the skank scale. She never went back to the
locker room again.

"Besides, there's this guy, Michael. I can't lie to him, and if I
did he would know. And believe it or not, I don't want anyone
but him. Bigger isn't necessarily better, you know."

That got a chortle out of her at least. And then silence.

Sometimes people tell you things over the telephone that

they would never say to your face. I think it has something to do with the illusion of anonymity. Maybe Linda Battle fantasized she was talking to one of her girlfriends. Or maybe I had said the right thing. But when she started to talk, there was no stopping her.

"Everybody says, 'But he always comes home to you, Linda.' Yeah, right. He always comes home to me drunk. Do you know what it's like to be married to someone who never comes home unless he's drunk or zonked on those pills the doctor gives him after the game? Then they put it in the paper. Tiger says, 'Just give me a Pearl and a Percocet and I'm ready to play.' Very funny. I'm worried for him. I don't think he's addicted or anything like that. But all you people laugh and love it when he moons everybody from the Lincoln Memorial at two o'clock in the morning. 'Oh, there's Tiger. Tiger's at it again.' Do you know what it's like to be married to that?"

"No, I don't," I said.

"No, you don't. You don't know him at all. But you'll write an article about what a good ole boy he is after nine hours in a bar."

"It's my job," I said.

"I know," she said. "I'll tell him you called."

Tiger didn't call back, though I left another ten messages over the next two days. Each time Linda was a little friendlier. By the tenth call she just started laughing when she heard my voice. Before she hung up she said, "By the way, I believe you, A.B."

Home Stand

June 5   We are home for a week before heading out for a long West Coast swing. Michael is on his way back from Miami. Ruth is in a snit about another guy who called her "dear" during an interview. And I am in deep shit with Sal. All I have to say is thank God for Rocky, which is not something I say very often.

Rocky owns horses, trains horses, handicaps horses, writes about horses, and gambles on horses. He says there is no conflict of interest because the one thing he does not do is like horses. In fact, he's never been on one as far as anybody knows, and the mere thought of petting one or giving one a lump of sugar gives him hives. As far as Rocky is concerned, horses are a very unreliable and somewhat distasteful variable in his mathematical crusade to beat the odds.

Anyway, there was a bad spill the other day on the backstretch at Pimlico and a young jock was thrown from his mount and paralyzed. He was riding one of Rocky's horses, which had to be destroyed. Rocky was pretty distraught when he called in his story. "That was a twenty-thousand-dollar animal," he said.

Rocky dictated his story about the young jock to Raoul, the copy aide, and announced he was "taking an early slide." Rocky always takes an early slide, which means he's going out to swap lies, which is what old sportswriters say when they are about to get very drunk. His lede read: "Young Juan Gomez doesn't know it yet, but he'll never walk again."

Captain Fuck-up read it and passed it on to Harvey, the copy editor, who read it and sent it down to the composing room. It wasn't until ten minutes before the presses started to roll that Sal took a look at the page and went batshit. Dr. Deadline said he hadn't seen Sal so mad since some stringer devoted an entire lede to a two-hundred-foot-long urinal at the start of the New York Marathon.

So they had to tear up the page at the last minute and the whole section was thirty minutes late getting off the floor. Sal was still screaming bloody murder at Rocky when I arrived. I headed straight for the meat scale outside his office, from which vantage point I could hear Rocky saying, "Whaddya mean, tasteless? It's a great fucking lede."

Sal's office is one of these glass cubicles with venetian blinds that haven't moved or been dusted in the last thirty years. They are hell on his Turnbull & Asser shirts but great for Sal-watching. Davis and Dr. Deadline decided it would be a good time to get weighed, too. Together we watched Rocky get reamed and tipped the scale at 460 pounds.

"What's *wrong* with it?" Sal said. "What's *wrong* with it? Nothing's *wrong* with it. So what if Juan Gomez and 235,000 of his closest friends find out he'll never walk again from the Washington *Tribune*?"

Sal's veins were popping. His eyes were popping. His suspenders, which he had pushed a foot past his chest, popped against his ribs.

"I'd give it a nine," said Davis.

The Doctor demurred. "Nah," he said. "His left eye isn't twitching. He's gotta twitch to be a nine."

Sal's left eye started to twitch. "A nine," the Doctor said.

I have noticed since coming over to work for Sal that the only time you really have to worry is when he starts sucking his thumb. It always starts innocently, like his cheek itches or something. Then pretty soon he's chewing on his thumb as if he's biting his nails. But the thumb stays there and stays there until he knows that you know that what he's really doing is sucking his thumb. Then he mutters, "Goddamned hangnail." I have noticed Sal sucks his thumb a lot when I'm around. I think he has a problem with women.

Rocky was just closing the door when Sal started sucking his thumb.

"A ten," the Doctor said. "No question. A definite ten."

"Excellent," Davis said. "Just excellent."

I figured there were two ways this could go. Either I was going to get off easy, thanks to Rocky, or it was going to be much worse than I ever imagined.

"Berkowitz! In here now!"

When Sal summons you through a plate-glass window, you know you're in trouble. But all he said was "Once more and I'm going to the bullpen for long relief. Weigh in before you leave. And get Tiger Battle on the goddamn phone." Then he put his head in his hands and sucked his thumb and didn't even pretend it was a hangnail.

"I have weighed in," I said.

"Yeah? How much?" he said.

"I've dropped four pounds since the beginning of the season."

"Good," he said. "That means I can eat some Chee-tos. I'm starving."

June 6 I came in early this morning to call Tiger Battle. It seemed the politic thing to do. I can't think of anything else to get Sal off my back. As it is, every time I dial his number, Sal is literally breathing down my neck, sucking his thumb and scribbling questions in wax pencil on the desk: "Ask re: ankle!" "Run yet!" "Hurt!?!"

I don't know what the hell Sal thinks I'm going to ask him if not how is the ankle, have you run yet, and does it hurt?

It was 9:30 A.M. when Sal took up his position on the corner of the desk as I punched up the number again. It rang maybe twenty times before someone answered. I was about to hang up when I heard Tiger say, "Battle."

"Berkowitz," I replied.

Sal's eyes were blazing with the kill. "You got him? You got him? She's got him!" he yelled, though the office was empty except for us.

"Speak up, Tiger, I can't hear you," I said, shaking my fist at Sal, who went back to sucking his thumb.

"So, how's the ankle? Uh-huh. Uh-huh. I see. You run any yet? Mmmm. Right. That makes sense. Does it hurt? Really? You're kidding. That much, huh?"

"What!?! What!?!" Sal said. He looked like he was about to implode.

I cupped the phone and put a finger to my mouth. Sal would not be shushed. "What about training camp!" he cried. I thought for a minute he was actually going to grab the receiver.

"What about training camp?" I said. "Right. Gotcha. I understand. Okay, well, keep in touch. Let me know. I'll see ya round the block."

I hung up. Sal was frothing at the mouth. *"Well,"* he panted.

"He says he hasn't run yet, on the advice of his doctors, that he's expecting to be in training camp as usual, though who knows, that the ankle is good enough to kick the shit out of you, and that you should leave me alone. That's a direct quote."

Sal was pulling his hair.

"What else did he say? Why did he call?"

"He said he called because he'd been out all night and had a few pops and he thought maybe it was time for us to get naughty."

"That's *it?*" Sal said.

"That's it."

"Goddamned son of a bitch," Sal said, stomping his feet. "He can't treat my reporters this way. I'll—"

"You'll what, Sal?"

This had a calming effect on him. Sal sucked his thumb and considered his options, which were few. Sal's personal prudishness is one of the things I really like about him. It's so cute and so opposite his editorial style. Like the time he wanted to turn the women's room into a men's room, which would have meant I'd have to walk down two flights in order to go to the bathroom. Sal was adamant. I offered a compromise. "Make it coed," I said. "There are stalls."

Sal was aghast. He started coughing and turning pink. "But, Sal," I said. "You're the man who sends me into locker rooms full of naked men I do not know. And you won't share a bathroom with me?"

Sal stomped into his office then, which is what he did this morning after finding out once again about the baseness of man. I wrote a thirty-inch story about Tiger before going out to the ballpark. It said absolutely nothing new except that Tiger was expecting to go to training camp, which we treated as a major scoop even though he had never said previously that he wasn't going to training camp and even though expecting to go doesn't say a hell of a lot. But Sal was happy, and for a day I wasn't in deep shit with anyone.

June 7 Michael came to the park with me tonight and suffice it to say it's the first and last game we will be attending together for a very long time. It was my idea so I have no one to blame but myself. I thought maybe if I took him with me one time, he'd stop telling me how easy I've got it in the fun and games department and how I ought to hang out at 3-D cops someday if I really want to see some animals.

So Roy got him a press pass with field and clubhouse privileges and I took Michael downstairs for batting practice, warning him all the way not to expect idylls or anything. Of course, the Washington Senators have never been on such good behavior. A couple of them even doffed their caps and inquired after my family. For a while I was sure I had been set up until Roy reminded me that the commissioner's special assistant in charge of media relations was attending the game.

Michael leaned against the batting cage and watched the guys hit. It was a gorgeous day. Lilting voices carried on lilting clouds. "Yup," he said, his nose pressed against the screen, "I can see just how bad you've got it. Maybe I'll just have to come on over to Sports."

Red Smith once said: "Never complain to the reader about

your job because all he knows is you've got free seats on the fifty-yard line."

A. B. Berkowitz says: "Never complain to your lover either."

It's amazing how the most hard-boiled reporters get all gaga around ballplayers. I introduced Michael to Buck and Rump, both of whom he insisted upon calling Big Guy.

"Big Guy?" I said as we made our way back upstairs.

Michael hates it when I call people Big Guy. He especially hates it when I call him Big Guy.

"They're bigger than I thought," he replied and went off to get some dinner while I read the pregame notes.

He returned a few minutes later with crab cakes and beer. "I don't drink on deadline," I said.

"Oh," he said. "I thought you said you were a sportswriter." He was feeling very merry.

The game was close and unusually well played, tense even. And I was starting to get tense when it was still scoreless at the end of six and Zeke started yelling for copy. Then with two down in the bottom of the eighth, Mug Shot tripled, his first hit since replacing Demetrious as leadoff man, and Guttierrez walked.

Now that Demetrious is gone, Guttierrez represents our sole threat to steal. He's a threat, all right: he's been thrown out in each of his ten attempts so far this season. And this was no exception. What he was doing taking off for second with two down and the count 2–2 on Buck, I don't know. Even Monk isn't stupid enough to have given him the green light. The replay showed he was out. Close but definitely out. Michael disagreed. He jumped up and down screaming, "He was safe, damn it! He was safe!"

"Shut up," MacKenzie yelled.

"No cheering in the press box!" Girard growled.

I yanked Michael's arm. "People are on deadline," I said.

So he sat down and began reading over my shoulder. Reading *aloud* over my shoulder. Nobody should ever read running copy aloud over your shoulder. It's the journalistic equivalent of your mother showing naked baby pictures to your boyfriend on your first date.

Michael read: "The Senators squandered scoring opportunities in the first and the fourth, stranding Buchanan, who twice doubled off the centerfield wall. Meanwhile, Pentacost, who came into the game with a respectable 3.42 ERA and a 3–8 record, which would surely be 8–3 for any other team, scattered seven hits, all but two of them singles. So the score remained 0–0 through six.

"Then with two down in the bottom of the eighth and runners at the corners, Guttierrez inexplicably took off for second, where he was cut down for the tenth time this season, taking the bat out of Buchanan's hands and the Senators out of the inning.

"Manager Monk McGuire stormed onto the field, moving considerably faster than Guttierrez had. At first it appeared he was going out to argue the call. But when he got to second, it was apparent that his argument was with his shortstop, not the umpire. McGuire chased Guttierrez all the way back to the dugout and then sent Benito Jones out to play short in the top of the ninth."

"How can you say that?" Michael said. "You don't know what Monk said. Maybe Guttierrez was hurt. This isn't reporting. This is bullshit."

I bit my lip and kept writing. By the time Michael stopped lecturing me, the game was over, thanks to a solo homer by Phoenix's leadoff man, and it was time to go downstairs.

A word is in order here about the eating habits of the Washington Senators. To them, food is a matter of either superstition or guzzling. There is no in-between. Watching them inhale their postgame meals is an extraordinary culinary experience. They snarf, they slurp, they drool, especially some of the older players, who invariably look like they ought to be wearing bibs. There are a few exceptions to this rule: Rump, Buck, and, of course, Benito. But for the most part, as Milo says cheerfully, "They look like pigs at a trough."

Also, you can always gauge the mood of the team by the way the players eat. And they were eating angry. Stein chomped on a hoagie like he was biting off its head. Pentacost spat watermelon pits at Guttierrez's feet. Rump took one bite of his ham and swiss sub and fired the entire thing into a garbage can ten feet away.

And Stick . . .

Stick likes to eat in the raw. So do I, actually. It's kind of the last frontier of freedom, sitting there in your wherewithal drinking a beer and picking your teeth. Stick is good at that. So I wasn't surprised to see him approach the buffet table in the buff. It's his way. But this time he didn't see anything that appealed to him. So he took his schlong and spread it across the cold cut platter kind of the way you'd spread mustard on rye.

His famished teammates were awestruck; astonished not so much at what he did but at the thought they might actually have to buy a meal.

"Oh my God," Michael said.

"It ain't 3-D," I said. "But it's home."

June 10 Riley O'Ryan got hit in the nose trying to field a comebacker yesterday, which was the only thing that distinguished our fortieth loss of the season from all the others. Today Riley showed up in the clubhouse wearing a pair of glassless black horn-rims with a splint at the nose. Whenever he felt like grossing someone out, he would stick his finger through the place where the lens was supposed to be, rub his eye, and stick his finger in his mouth. Stein immediately renamed him Eson, which of course is "nose" backward.

Anyway, Rump and I were standing by the batting cage when Eson came up and stuck his finger in his eye. Rump was waiting to hit. I was waiting for Rump to tell me about this bioenergeticist his wife sent him to yesterday. And we were both waiting for Eson to get lost. It's hard enough to have a conversation between rounds of batting practice without someone coming up every two seconds and sticking his finger in his eye and saying, "Umm umm, love that eye gook."

"Her name is Maya and JoAnne swears by her," Rump said. "Stein's wife took her a couple of weeks ago. Maya asked where it hurts and JoAnne points to her chest. So Maya pounds on her rib cage for ten minutes and massages her chest until JoAnne starts to scream. JoAnne says it was a good scream, the silent scream of all the things she had repressed since she was a girl. When Maya asked what she was thinking about, JoAnne said, 'All the men who have felt me up since I was ten.' JoAnne is very committed to Maya."

Rump was staring through the screen at Buck, who was taking his cuts. His eyes followed the parabola of the ball into the gold ribbon of seats that rings the upper deck.

"Rump! You're up!"

"How many?" he said.

"Five," Stick replied.

Eson stuck his finger in his mouth. Rump stood in. He

fouled back the first three pitches. The fourth dribbled down the first base line. The last hit the screen that protected Piggy, who was throwing BP.

"Ah shit," Rump said.

"That's the name of my golf game, 'Ah shit,' " Eson said.

Rump resumed his stance behind the cage. It is an ancient posture and we all do it reflexively, foot up on the metal bar, feeling the vibrations of the ball as it clanks into the metal skeleton of the cage. It is a reassuring sound to everyone but a hitter.

"Maya said I should bring my favorite bat. So I brought my bat, and when I got there she made me lie down on a pile of mattresses and kick my feet like a three-year-old. She told me I needed to get in touch with my tantrum. So I kicked my feet and then she said I was carrying a lot of tension in my neck. Then she started to strangle me and I started to scream, which she thought was a very positive sign. I told her I thought it was very predictable under the circumstances."

"Rump! Three!"

He excused himself and took his hacks: fouling back two more that rattled the cage and vibrated up my leg. He swung and missed the last pitch completely. Eson offered him his glasses. Everyone else looked away. Rump returned to my side and blew a bubble. He is a very accomplished bubble blower, an artist of a bubble blower, a metaphorical bubble blower. He blew the bubble to its fullest dimension and waited, letting it collapse of its own weight, before gathering it back on his tongue.

"Maya told me to take my bat and hit this other pile of mattresses. So I hit the pile of mattresses for fifteen minutes, which she said would help resolve my conflicts about hitting. I told her it's the only thing I've hit for three months."

"Rump! Two! Rump! One!"

They were hustling in and out of the cage now, taking their final swings. With each swing, they followed the arc of the ball and listened for the tenor of the contact and hooted or hollered appropriately. Rump swung at Piggy's final pitch and hit a loud foul, four rows deep in the leftfield stands. It had a good sound, but still it went awry.

"Listen, I need to talk," he said, leaning on his bat. "Would that be okay? I mean, would you mind?"

We agreed to have dinner on the road.

Batting practice was over.

West Coast Swing

June 20   I am sitting by the pool at the Disneyland Motor Lodge drinking a beer from a Mickey Mouse mug that was served to me by a waitress in a Minnie Mouse costume who used to be a computer technician in Olney, Maryland. You sure do meet a lot of interesting people on the road. The main advantage of a West Coast trip is that instead of lobby sitting, you can do pool sitting and hot tub sitting. Like this morning, I'm in the hot tub minding my own business when a fifty-year-old guy with a seriously terrible rug drawls, "You stew?"

"Nope," I say.

"You're Continental," he says. "I can tell Continental a mile away."

"Nope."

"American, then. You're American."

"Not Continental. Not American. Not anything."

"United!" he says.

Which is why I'm no longer in the hot tub but sitting here by the deep end watching MacKenzie, who is typing furiously into his computer. He's been doing this for almost two hours now. MacKenzie never types anything furiously. A little while ago, Stein told Girard to go ask what he is working on. Girard comes back and says, "He's typing, 'My wife's name is Susan. My wife's name is Susan,' over and over again."

This is the longest road trip so far this year, two full weeks. The American League schedule maker has gone batshit, what with these two expansion teams this year. We've got another two-week trip to the Coast coming up in July. Maybe they'll get it straightened out by next year. But this season is a bitch.

We've been gone nine days now. Seattle was wet and uneventful except for my thirtieth birthday, which I spent watching our forty-fifth loss of the season and eating boiled Ballpark franks with a single candle stuck in each of them, courtesy of Roy, the road secretary, who is still the only member of the front office talking to me. Phoenix was dry and depressing. Monk had high hopes for the series, Phoenix being the other expansion team in the American League. But we managed to lose two of three there, too. Monk immediately announced that for the rest of the season there will be no hard alcohol on the team plane. Regularly scheduled or chartered.

This set Stick off so much he called a press conference to denounce Monk and demand that the Washington Senators be treated like men. While he was at it, he denounced the franchise as bush league because the players have to carry their own baggage on road trips. "What ever happened to perks?" he said. "No wonder we can't get the job done. In Detroit, they got guys who go out and start your car after the game. That's class."

I mentioned this to Lefty O'Donnell later, thinking somehow he'd share my incredulity. "Oh yeah," he said. "You gotta have that."

Anyway, Piggy got wind of this, and it got him going again about the Modern Ballplayer. Piggy doesn't much like the Modern Ballplayer, except his son, who is the only reason that Piggy is still wearing a major league uniform. In spring training I asked him to define the Modern Ballplayer. He thought for a second and said, "The Modern Ballplayer has lots of equipment. He's got bats and he's got balls. He's got it easy. He rides in cars." Then, as if on cue, the bus taking us back to West Palm appeared on the field and made its way all the way around the warning track until it got to the Senators' dugout. God forbid the Washington Senators would have to walk fifty feet from the clubhouse to the bus.

Anyway, we start a three-game series against the Angels tonight. I did the math a few minutes ago: we are now on pace to lose 123 games, which would make us the worst team ever, worse even than the 1962 Mets, who tortured Casey Stengel's syntax by losing 120 games. It's getting hard to think of new ways to say we lost. I haven't used "rocked" in a while. I think maybe we'll get rocked tonight.

I just noticed I used the word "we" four times in the last paragraph. What is this "we" stuff? Milo says "we" is terminal sportswriter disease. And he's right. I didn't know I had it. Either I am a very sick individual or I want to be one of the guys more than I ever realized.

Windy, the erstwhile general manager, has shuffled the roster a little, sending down Charlie Bold III, the relief pitcher whose grandfather, Charlie Bold, had one major league at bat in 1914. He has been replaced by another young reliever named

Boom Boom DeForest, who gives up a lot of home runs and who
has decided in the interest of team unity not to speak to me.

In other news of interest, the Gaijin has gained twenty
pounds. When Rube demanded an explanation, the Gaijin said,
through his interpreter, "I like airplane food." He is also batting
.200 and wearing a TRY GOD button. "Very nice Lord," he says.
"Very nice."

Buck is getting to be something of a national story, thanks to
me. I have to admit I was a little nervous the first time I saw him
after he read my piece, which was, I guess, about two weeks ago
already. I was coming in the clubhouse just as he was walking
out, and as we passed he whispered, "Thank you." Later, after
the game, I told him about Mom and how she ran off with a bush
leaguer when I was thirteen and how I stayed with my dad and
was raised by a maid named Lolita Nurse. I told him how I was
just now trying to figure out love and how I'm not sure I've got it
right, though maybe Michael is the answer. Buck nodded and
said, "I fully underestimate you."

Rump has been watching videotapes of his swing from 1985,
when he hit .312. He hasn't said anything more about what he
wants to talk about and I haven't asked. Lawson wants him to try
Jesus. Jesus is the only subject Lawson will discuss with me,
probably because he knows I won't quote him.

I guess the biggest development of the trip is that Stick has
resumed his daily training room exercises. The other night in
Phoenix, he emerged from the shower at full mast, got down on
his knees in front of me, and said, "How 'bout one little kiss for
the Stick?"

I said, "Sure, Stick. You can kiss my ass."

Ruth will love that one.

I've been calling Michael every night from the press box to
read him my lede. Every night I wake him up and every night he
says the same thing: "It's fine. It's nice. Send it. I love you."

On Thursday night, when Fast Eddie Hernandez actually
pitched a five-hitter and the Gaijin ran into the leftfield wall to
make a game-saving catch in the bottom of the ninth, I was so
stunned I couldn't write. I mean, I was really blocked. And when
I'm really blocked, I start to get dry heaves. So I called Michael,
though I had sworn I was going to let him sleep. "Why don't you
just say they won; that's amazing enough. You're going to leave
the English language dead on the press box floor and you along
with it."

"Okay," I said.

Ten minutes later, all I had was a scorecard full of hair. On deadline, first I get dry heaves, then I pull my hair. I think I'm going bald. I called Michael again. For sure, it's the first time he's written a baseball story on deadline while sound asleep. "How 'bout 'The Gaijin hit the fence and for a while it looked like they might have to send the wall to the hospital for X rays,'" Michael said. "'But the wall, the Gaijin, and the Senators survived, winning . . .' What was the score?"

"Two to one," I said.

"'Winning their first game in a week, 2–1.'"

"I'll give you the byline," I said.

"Just let me get a good night's sleep," he said.

"Good lede," the Captain said when I phoned in. I made the team charter by three minutes.

Somewhere Over California

June 22   Stein's in love.

It happened two nights ago at a local joint known as the Jell-O Bar. This is no ordinary Jell-O bar. This Jell-O bar features Orange County's only regulation-size Jell-O ring. It's a tank really, twelve feet square, and filled knee-high with Jell-O. The whole thing is on rollers, and every night at the end of competition, they roll it into this room-size refrigerator and change the color. The reigning doyenne of the Jell-O Bar is one Ms. Charlene Merryweather, a former body builder and mud wrestler who wanted to get into something cleaner and is now (according to the marquee outside) the World Champion Diva Jell-O Wrestler of Orange County. She takes on any comers six nights a week, though the bar has a roster of ready opponents, all of them chesty and all of them as unclad as Charlene herself. They're kind of like what the Washington Generals are to the Harlem Globetrotters, permanent foils, buxom losers. At the Jell-O Bar, Charlene reigns supreme. In lime, she is undefeated. Her last loss came three years ago one April evening, on orange night. Orange always gives Charlene trouble. You figure it out.

Anyway, Stein heard about the place from some of the Angels and organized an expedition. Stick invited Brawn, who invited Mug Shot, who invited Rump, who invited me. I don't turn down invitations these days from anybody.

By the time I got there, it was past midnight and Stein was stripped down to his Calvin's and knee-deep in Jell-O. It was lime night. Stein was in trouble even with his batting gloves on. Charlene was one slick customer.

It was quite a sight watching them go at it pec to pec, quad to quad, two perfectly defined American bodies, oozing unsweetened lime slime (Charlene will not perform in the sugared stuff) and panting with exertion and lust. "Oooohh, Momma," Stick said. "I want to eat the green from your eyes!"

Mancusi had to restrain the Stick from going into the tank.

"Go for it, Dickhead!" Mug Shot said.

Mug Shot was taking action on the side. The price against Stein was climbing. "Come on, man!" Mug Shot said. He had laid some serious dollars down on Stein.

Stein lunged, an error in judgment, and did a header into the gook. Charlene, who clearly had the home-field advantage, reached down, grabbed him by the nape of the neck, and pulled him to his feet. Stein came up snorting and gasping. Charlene ignored his distress. With a practiced *je ne sais quoi*, she jerked his left arm behind his back, turned him 180 degrees, stuck a slimy knee in his groin, and flipped him over, headfirst. It was quite a move. She calls it her Jell-O Roll.

With that, the bartender sounded the gong, ending the third and final round. Stein stumbled out of the ring murmuring her name. "I think Mrs. Stein is about to have company for breakfast, lunch, and dinner," Rump said.

A half hour later, Stein was standing at the bar when Charlene emerged from her dressing room in a lime-green halter and shorts, which it turned out matched her hair. She changes her hair nightly, too, in order to be color-coordinated with the Jell-O of the evening. Green hair or not, Charlene is quite a looker and an aficionada of pecs. Stein spends a lot of time on his pecs. Charlene liked what she saw.

There are some women who know how to turn the most banal gesture into a mating call. Charlene is one of these women. I am not. When I climb on a barstool, I clamber. Not Charlene. She mounted that stool, wrapped her legs around its red vinyl seat, leaned her upper body strength into Stein's airspace, and sucked an ounce of lime Jell-O from his inner ear. Thus romance was born.

Stein was too moved to speak. All he could do was moan. "Any of you boys want to give Charlene a ride home?" she said.

Stick, a thoughtful roomie if ever there was one, spent the night on the floor in Brawn's room. The DO NOT DISTURB sign was still on Stein's door at 1:00 P.M. the next day when Stick started banging on it, demanding his toothbrush. No answer was forthcoming. So Stick got out a dentist's mirror, which he saves for just such occasions, and stuck it in the space between the carpet and the door and enjoyed Stein's conquest vicariously.

Charlene reluctantly returned to the ring last night wearing a batting glove on each hand and Stein's diamond NUMBER 16 pendant around her sixteen-inch neck. He must have taken something out of her, though, because Charlene lost her first match in three years, and it wasn't even orange night.

Stein couldn't make it out there to see her tonight, since it was getaway day. But Charlene showed up at the airport to bid her man farewell in a red halter top, red shorts, red hair, and very red eyes. They kissed deeply and parted with many keenings.

Oakland

June 23 When we got to the hotel an hour ago, Charlene was waiting in the lobby. I think Stein just added some new muscle to the roster, which is a lot more than Windy has done lately.

June 25 Sometimes after work we all go down to this bar called The Pit and play this game, "Wake-up Call." Basically, what we do is go around the table comparing our most embarrassing awakenings. My favorite until this morning was Michael's story about going home with a woman and waking up not knowing where he was or who she was. So he sneaked into the bathroom and went through the medicine cabinet until he found her name on a prescription for Valium.

I think I win the next round of "Wake-up Call."

I came to this morning in a double bed attached to a twenty-five-cent massage machine in a room with a view of a garbage dump in a motel somewhere in America. I was fully clothed. Even so, the implications were unsettling.

In the last five months, I have slept in thirty-six different beds. I have slept in singles, doubles, queens, and kings; I have slept North, South, East, and West. I have slept in four different time zones, Standard and Daylight Saving. I have slept uphill and downhill, on the right side and on the left. I have woken up in the middle of the night and walked into walls where the bathroom was supposed to be, where it was when I last knew where I was. On nights like that, I wake up feeling as if I'm levitating somewhere over America.

This was not one of those nights. This time I really didn't know where I was. And I really didn't know how I'd gotten there. The room, which looked like thirty-six other rooms I have slept in since the first day of spring training, offered no clues. And there wasn't anyone I could think of to call who might know the answer to some of these questions except maybe the front desk. And that was a little embarrassing.

I called Michael instead. "Hi, it's me. I don't know where I am."

"What do you mean, you don't know where you are?"

"I mean, I don't know where I am. I'm in a motel room in a double bed attached to a twenty-five-cent massage machine. I was in Oakland last I checked."

"Doing what?"

"Drinking martinis in the locker room with Stick and Stein and Mancusi."

The awful truth was out of my mouth before my consciousness could process it. Suddenly I remembered I had a headache. Also, my stomach didn't feel so good. "I thought you didn't drink on deadline," Michael said.

"I don't. I mean, I didn't. I mean, Michael, how do I find out where I am?"

"Try calling the front desk?" he said.

"What am I supposed to say? 'Hi, I'm a guest in your hotel. Could you tell me where I am?'"

"Sounds about right," Michael said.

"Oh, Michael, would you do it?"

"Do what?"

"Call the front desk."

"You wake me up at five-thirty in the morning to call the front desk of the motel you're sleeping in to find out where you are?"

"Please," I said. I sure know how to sound helpless when I want to.

"Give me the phone number," he said.

Michael called back in three minutes to inform me that I was a guest in a Best Western Motel along a freeway three blocks from Oakland Alameda County Stadium. By that time I had opened the front door to find the morning paper. Even with a hangover, a sportswriter reaches reflexively for last night's scores. For some reason, Northern California Sports sections are all peach or green or rose or chartreuse. This Sports section was tangerine.

There on the section page in a sickening profusion of tangerine was a picture of myself curled up in a fetal position on the floor of the Oakland Alameda County Stadium visitors' locker room. It was a nice picture. It had good composition. At the bottom, you could see Stick's feet and me snuggled up against his big toe. The picture was worth a thousand words, all right. The caption was bitchy but superfluous: "Washington *Trib* reporter A. B. Berkowitz at work in the Senators' locker room after yesterday's 4–2 Oakland win. Story on D5."

It wasn't much of a story. But it didn't have to be. There, squeezed between the transition box and the late box scores was a two-paragraph story by an unnamed staff writer detailing my fall from grace.

"Michael, I passed out at Stick's feet on the floor of the locker room."

"How do you know?"

"It says so, right here on page D5 of the Oakland *Daily Mail.*"

"That's my girl," Michael said.

"Michael."

"What?"

"What do I do?"

"Take a shower. Have a laugh. You're fucked."

Yesterday was one of those rare early games, an 11:00 A.M. start, to accommodate TV executives and "The Saturday Game of the

Week." Why they would want to show the Senators rolling over for Mark McGwire and company beats me, but they did. I wrote fast and went down to the locker room, fully expecting there would be nothing new to write. It was a pro forma visit. Why should they have anything different to say after the forty-eighth loss of the season? I mean, how many ways are there to tell me to fuck off?

So when Stick and Stein and Mancusi said, "Yo, Berkowitz!" "C'mere, Berkowitz!" I was surprised and curious. When you've got as few sources as I've got and someone says, "C'mere," you c'mere. I should have known something was up: Stick wasn't erect.

Stein had a brew in each hand and offered me one. "C'mon," he said. "Let's make nice."

I don't know what I was thinking. Maybe I wasn't thinking. God knows I wasn't thinking what they were thinking. I took the beer.

"Look," Stick said. "Me and Stein and Mancusi, we've been talking and we think this Monk shit has gone on long enough. Right, Stein?"

Stein nodded. Mancusi said, "Yo."

"I mean, it's a long season for all of us. Why make it harder? Right, Stein?"

Stein nodded. Mancusi said, "Yo."

Stick stuck out his hand. "Peace?" he said.

Should I tell you I was dubious? Should I tell you I hadn't eaten breakfast and all I was worried about was their hearing my stomach growl? Should I tell you I only had four hours' sleep and my judgment was impaired? I'll tell you what I told them: "Life's a bitch and then you die." Witty, huh?

"Get this girl another beer," Stein said.

"I got a better idea," Stick said.

Stein nodded. Mancusi said, "Yo," and Stick disappeared into the trainer's room, which should have told me something, but I was into major league denial. The locker room was pretty much empty except for Rube and a couple of Bay Area reporters and photogs, doing a feature on the Gaijin. The Gaijin is big wherever he goes.

Stick was back in a few minutes, carrying a tray of martinis. He handed me one and bowed. "I want to propose a toast to the beginning of a wonderful new relationship," Stick said.

Stein began singing "Auld Lang Syne." Mancusi said, "Yo."

I stood there holding the martini, admiring the condensation beading on the glass, knowing my judgment was clouded, knowing this drink was dangerous, knowing I would drink it anyway. Let me tell you what was going through my mind. I knew I had no business sitting there swigging martinis in the locker room. I knew it was dumb. I could hear Sal's voice saying, "What are you, stupid?" I also knew that baseball players have their own code, their own initiation rites, ways of testing each other and the outside world. I had talked to other reporters about these initiations. Often large, fake rubber bugs are involved.

I thought this was my test. I raised the glass to my lips. "Peace," I said.

The visitors' locker room in the Oakland Alameda County Stadium is all white and green, like the A's uniforms. It didn't take long before the colors were running together, swirling, making a palette of my head. My brain vibrated like one of those machines they've got down at my stepfather's paint store, a Red Devil Shaker they call it. No doubt about it, I was sloshed.

We drank to Monk and we drank to God. We drank to Buck's bald spot and Stretch's stretch, to Rump's slump and the Gaijin's diet. We drank to the Sports Department of the Washington *Tribune*, which at last count had lost exactly twenty-three pounds, and to Jimy Boy's bypass surgery a year ago. "Heard it took seven hours," Stein said. "Six and a half just to find his heart."

He was being so nice I didn't even bother to point out he had stolen the line.

That's the last thing I remember. That and Stick's laughter. He was cackling. The room was spinning. I was on the floor. I was at his feet. Just like in the picture in this morning's Oakland *Daily Mail*.

I found a note taped to the mirror in the bathroom of my room at the Best Western Motel by a freeway three blocks from Oakland Alameda County Stadium. It said: "Call me, Jimmy T." Jimmy T is the PR guy for the A's. He worked for the Brewers when Dusty Barnes was the manager there. Barnes's nickname around the league was the Breathalyzer. One year his team gave him a uniform with the Wisconsin legal limit on the back instead of his regular number. Jimmy T took care of Dusty. And Jimmy T took care of me.

I took a shower and walked to the stadium, counting the number of fast-food restaurants along the way, which sort of helped keep the horizon straight and my mind off the inevitable.

I counted one Denny's, one Bob's Big Boy, one McDonald's, one Gino's, one Burger King, one Wendy's, one Taco Bell, one Shakey's, and one Chucky Cheese between the Best Western and the stadium.

I also tried to calculate the odds that Sal didn't know. The Oakland *Daily Mail* is a small-circulation daily with under fifty thousand readers. It isn't part of any syndicate as far as I know. Maybe, just maybe, the story hadn't gotten picked up. Maybe the wires wouldn't get the photo and Sal wouldn't get the picture.

"*Sure,* babe," Jimmy T said when I got to his office.

"What happened?" I said.

"You don't know?"

"C'mon, Jimmy."

"I found you in the tunnel outside the visitors' locker room," he said. "You were calling Stick's name."

This sounded vaguely familiar, but only in the way that you remember something that happened to somebody else who told you about it three years ago.

"Do you remember him out there rolling around in the grass cackling? What an asshole!"

I saw him then: lying in the dirt of the coaching box along the third base line. He was rolling back and forth cackling, hugging himself, while some guy took his picture for the cover of *GQ*. It was one of those fancy studio guys with a photographic umbrella. He was standing over Stick, who was lying in the dirt, rolling back and forth in a halo of artificial light, hugging himself and cackling.

That cackle was in my ear. It was in my head. It was everywhere.

"Son of a bitch," I said.

Twelve hours ago I was talking turkey to Jimmy T. Now I am sitting in the departure lounge at San Francisco International Airport waiting for the red-eye flight to reportorial damnation and trying to understand.

What is this need I have to confess? Why is it I feel compelled to reveal, to apologize, to own up to everything? When I was three years old and I stole the pink plastic pocketbook from Wendy White's Barbie doll—a one-inch square of pressed plastic —I confessed. When Rachel Summers took the Flexible Flyer down the hill next to the duck pond where the ice was thin, I apologized.

Boys don't do this. Milo didn't apologize for taking a dive into my fettucini. Dr. Deadline didn't own up to getting locked in the press box in Tiger Stadium. Stick didn't confess to propositioning a transvestite in the lobby of the New York Sheraton.

So why did I feel I had to call Sal? It wasn't like a preemptive strike was going to help. "Oh, by the way, in case you didn't know, I passed out dead drunk in the locker room and it was on the front page of the local Sports section, but don't worry, I won't do it again."

Not a good idea. So I sat by the phone in the press box all day, waiting for it to ring, resisting the impulse to tell all. I wrote my American League notebook and I threw up. I heard people laughing behind my back and threw up again. I picked up the phone to call Sal at home and hung up. I dialed his number and let it ring until he answered and hung up again.

In the press room, Girard said, "Get this woman a martini." I fled with a bowl of chili I couldn't possibly eat. By the time I got back to my seat, I had to throw up again, which meant going to the press room again. Girard said, "This round's on me."

What did I drink, one martini? One beer? You don't get this sick from one martini and one beer. That's when I decided for sure that Stick had spiked my drink. Why else would he go to the trainer's room to mix a martini?

I staggered out of the bathroom. The phone at my desk was ringing. My head was ringing. My feet pounded against the concrete floor. Why was I running for it? I let it ring. Once, twice, fifteen times. "Answer your fucking phone, Berkowitz," MacKenzie said.

I answered the fucking phone. Michael said, "It hasn't come across the wires yet. How's your hangover?"

"Better now," I said.

I took a chance. I called the office. Raoul answered. Raoul said nothing. Captain Fuck-up got on. Captain Fuck-up said nothing. "Just calling to check in," I said.

"Give me sixteen inches," he said.

I was safe! I turned my attention to the Stick. What would I say? What could I say? "You put something in the drink I shouldn't have been drinking, you son of a bitch!" I waited and plotted. The phone did not ring. I did not call. I would not confess. I would not act like a girl.

After the game I went down to the locker room with Girard and MacKenzie, determined to act like I belonged. Stick saw me before I saw him. "Sleep well?" he said. "Sweet dreams?"

Stein giggled and slapped his thigh. Mancusi laughed so hard he couldn't even say, "Yo." Stick fondled his bat and cackled. *That* cackle. "Oooh, baby, you were hot. You were good. You were too much for most men. But the Stick isn't most men. The Stick is the Stick. The Stick is the Louisville Slugger. Come to me, baby. I'm as hard as Chinese arithmetic."

"You son of a bitch," I said.

When I got upstairs to the press box, the phone was ringing. I picked it up and snarled. "What?"

"Get your ass back here," Sal said. "Get your ass back here now."

Home

June 26, A.M. There were three hundred followers of Jimy Boy Collins waiting for me outside the entrance to the Washington *Tribune*. They were picketing and praying and not, I might add, for my soul. They wanted my ass.

"One, two, three, four—we don't want your dirty whore! *One, two, three, four—we don't want your dirty whore!*"

They were chanting as one, raising their voices to heaven and Ross Mitchell. *"Berkowitz must go!"*

Ross had called in the cops to help with crowd control, though I guess when you march for God you tend to stay in line. They were the neatest picket lines I've ever seen. Two beefy motorcycle patrolmen stood by the barricades watching, laughing, cracking their gum.

I sat in the cab with my luggage on my lap reading their signs: A WOMAN'S PLACE IS NOT IN THE LOCKER ROOM! LET OUR SENATORS GO! GO FORTH AND COVER WOMEN'S BASKETBALL! WINE IS A MOCKER, PROVERBS 20:1. There were also lots of signs with blow-ups of me dead drunk on the floor of the Oakland Alameda County Stadium and the words: BASEBALL, APPLE PIE, AND THIS?

"Hey, lady," the cab driver said. "That look like you."

"No shit," I said.

One by one, the protesters peeled off from the picket line and climbed the front steps, dumping one, two, three, four, as many copies of the *Trib* Sports section as they could carry, in a pile in front of the bronze bust of Ross Mitchell's grandfather, Ross I, the founder and patriarch of the disgraced Washington *Tribune*. There were children in SENATORS T-shirts and mothers with babies at their breasts and white-haired grandfathers with canes. One old blue-hair even struggled up the steps with her walker. And as each of them came forth, the others chanted, *"Take it back! Take it back! Take her back!"*

Jimy Boy stood above it all on the top step. He looked pleased. Very pleased indeed. The more pleased he looked, the deeper he thrust his hands in his pockets, the more his eyes shone, the more he raised his cleft chin to heaven. "Jesus loves you," he said to each of them. "This is God's work." And when the pile reached Ross I's chin, Jimy Boy raised his hands like Moses about to part the Red Sea and said, "Let us pray."

Heads bowed and I thought about making a break for it. Maybe they wouldn't notice me while they were busy praising Jesus and each other. But I couldn't move. I was having an out-of-body experience. I wanted to find out what was going to happen.

Jimy Boy quieted the crowd in an instant. All he had to do was raise his bushy eyebrows and one fat finger to heaven.

"My friends, baseball is a sacred trust. Baseball is God's game. We, His humble servants, must not let this trust be defiled. We must not let this transgression pass."

"Take it back!" "Take her back!" "Berkowitz must go!"

Jimy Boy nodded. Yes! Yes! He was with them! "As you know, my good friends, in a few moments I am going to venture forth into the lions' den to demand our voices be heard, to demand the Word of our Lord Jesus Christ be heard."

I was transfixed. The cabbie was losing interest as well as money. "Hey, lady, what's it gonna be?"

There were as many reporters leaning out of windows as there were in the crowd. Monday is always a slow news day. Just my luck. I saw guys from the *Post* and the Washington *Times;* from Channels 4, 5, 8, and 9. I saw everybody but Michael.

"What's it gonna be?" the cabbie said again.

"My ass," I replied.

I told myself to walk slowly so I wouldn't be noticed. Not that I had any choice. I was carrying a briefcase, a computer, and two weeks of dirty laundry in my luggage. Somehow that seemed symbolic. "Excuse me," I said. "Coming through," I said.

I was maybe three steps from the front door when the shoulder strap on my dress bag broke and laundry started falling out of the unzipped pocket where I had stuffed it. It's not as if I had a lot of time to pack. I bent down to get my bra and dropped my panties. I picked up my panties and dropped my stockings. I was down on all fours collecting my undies under the watchful eye of Ross I, Jimy Boy Collins, fifteen reporters, and three hundred born-again baseball ideologues. Then someone yelled, *"It's her!"* The camera crews from Channels 4, 5, 8, and 9 converged on me and my shorts. That's when I decided to run for it.

All the way up in the elevator, I rehearsed my lines. *It was a setup. They spiked my drink. They slipped me a Mickey.*

I never realized before just how long a walk it is to the Sports section from the elevator. You go through Business, turn right at National, go past City side, Obits, Health and Food, around the morgue to the oldest part of the building, where air-conditioning has not yet been invented and where on any given day over eighty degrees you'll find five ancient rusted fans blowing ancient wire copy across the assignment desk.

"Way to go, Berkowitz!"

"Bottoms up, Berkowitz!"

"Really drinking 'em under the table, huh, Berkowitz!"

It was one of those ninety-degree days you get in June in Washington when the decision to locate the nation's capital in a swamp seems a particularly cruel joke. The windows were open, the fans were blowing, and all the reporters were screaming "cocksucker" into the telephone except Dr. Deadline, who was making the rounds with the first Pincus petition of the season. Dr. D has been the proprietor of the Pincus Meter for nine years now. The Doctor claims he is allergic to Pincus. He has also been exposed to him longer than anyone but Zeke and Milo and Sal. After their first summer together, the Doctor unveiled the Pincus Meter, which is to say the Doctor's nose. On any day when the temperature goes above fifty, the Doctor will assign a given number of Pincus Points on the Pincus Meter to the smell emanating from Pincus. A 50 is foul. A 60 is odoriferous. A 70 is rank. An 80 calls for a petition. A 100, and the Doctor demands a recall.

Milo told me the Doctor got eighty signatures on the first

petition he circulated. It stated: "We, the undersigned, demand that Pincus take a bath."

Sal wasn't sports editor yet. He was still layout editor then. His name was first on the dotted line. He has had what you call your basic personnel problem with the petitions ever since. "What am I supposed to do, fire him because he stinks?" he said to the Doctor last time this happened. "*You* run him a bath."

Sal has settled on a new strategy of posting the petitions on the door to his office with a big red arrow in wax pencil saying: READ THIS. There is considerable sentiment around the department that Pincus doesn't know how.

The Doctor greeted me with his clipboard and his Bic when I arrived at Marcus's desk, which used to be my desk until Sal gave it away during spring training. "Hey, Berkowitz, sign. It's an 80!" the Doctor said. I can honestly say that for the first time in my life I was overjoyed to see him. When the Pincus Meter is running, the Doctor doesn't know from anything else.

"An 80?"

The Doctor sniffed the air.

"Maybe even an 85." He smiled. "By the way, saw your picture in the paper," he said. "*Everybody* saw your picture in the paper."

It was hard to miss. There on the department bulletin board, where the Senators schedule and the Jim Palmer Jockey shorts pinup used to be, was my picture surrounded by black crepe paper and inscribed RIP. In my mailbox there was a brochure from the Minnesota detox program at Hazelden, a JUST SAY NO T-shirt, and an airplane barf bag from Pincus.

I put on the T-shirt. What the hell.

That's when I heard Sal. Through the plate-glass window. He was sitting at his desk sucking his thumb when I knocked. "Jimy Boy and Beanie are on their way up. Whatever you do, don't say a fucking word. And take off that goddamned T-shirt."

Sal and Milo and I waited by the door as Jimy Boy wafted through the office, parading down the aisles with his hands out waiting for someone to kiss them. His chest was swelled up like a watermelon and his teeth looked kind of like the little white pits. Actually, I had never quite noticed before how much he has in common with a watermelon. He's greasy on the outside and his skin has a mushy pink watermelon quality to it. Also, it's pitted.

As usual, Jimy Boy's scent preceded him.

"What's that smell?" Sal said.

"Clubhouse cologne," I replied. "It's so he can smell like one of the guys."

Milo held his nose. "One of the guys, my ass. He smells like a French poodle just home from the groomer."

"Uh-uh," Sal said. "He smells like Pincus."

Finally we agreed Jimy Boy smelled like what Pincus would smell like if he had gone to the dog groomer.

Jimy Boy had been waylaid by the Doctor at Zeke's desk. He had the clipboard out and his spiel ready. "It's a petition to get Pincus here to take a bath. Pincus hasn't taken a bath since the 1961 World Series. You see, Reverend, despite whatever else you might have read, we here in the Sports Department of the *Tribune* are really a clean-living bunch of God-fearing Americans. Most of us, anyway. We just want the laws of common decency upheld."

"So do I, son, so do I," Jimy Boy said, signing.

Phones were ringing off the hook, and as usual no one was answering them. Once in a while Raoul, or one of the other copy aides, will pick up the receiver, bellow, *"Sports!"* and then someone's name. *"Berkowitz, fifty-nine! Milo, fifty-one!"* This happens maybe once a day. The rest of the time, the lights on the telephone consoles just blink until they stop.

For some reason, Zeke was in early. And for some reason—maybe he was just showing off—he decided to answer the phone ringing in his ear. Maybe he wanted Jimy Boy to see what a responsive news organization we really are.

"Sports!" he bellowed.

Then: "Anybody know if Tommy Thomas bought the Big One?"

At least fourteen voices responded: *"DOA!"*

Zeke nodded. *"He's outta here!"* he barked and slammed down the phone.

It was at precisely this juncture that Sal showed Jimy Boy and Beanie and me into his office. Jimy Boy looked at Beanie, Beanie looked at the chair. Beanie wiped the chair with Beanie's handkerchief. Beanie was wearing a TRY GOD button in his lapel. Already Sal was pissed, which was good.

"Reverend," he said. "Beanie. How can I help?"

Jimy Boy's fat little perfectly manicured fingers were pressed together as if he was going to pray again. I noticed for the first time how the flesh of his ring finger folded over his wedding band. He sighed deeply. It was the deepest sigh I'd ever heard. It was a sigh that said the world is fallen and he had seen too much of it. It was a sigh of disappointment, of resignation, of despair at the wickedness of man and especially A. B. Berkowitz. It was a sigh that threatened to engulf us all.

"So?" Sal said.

"So," Jimy Boy said, pressing his fingertips together until they whitened.

"So," Beanie wrote. Beanie writes down everything Jimy Boy says.

"Sal," Jimy Boy said. "I can call you Sal, can't I?" Sal squirmed and nodded. "Sal, I can tell just by looking at you that you are a God-fearing man. Am I right, Sal?"

Sal was starting to gag. I wasn't sure whether it was the Clubhouse cologne or the content.

"Sal, I know you are a God-fearing man and I know that a God-fearing man would not willingly and knowingly transgress one of God's laws. Am I right, Sal?"

Jimy Boy is not big on waiting for answers unless they are coming from upstairs. "Of course I'm right, Sal. So, being a God-fearing man, I know you will now do the upright thing, the moral thing, the only thing. You will free yourself from this moral quagmire. You will let your spirit soar. You will let this woman go."

Jimy Boy has not uttered my name since April.

"And you will do it because you are a God-fearing man. Because baseball belongs to the family. Because drunkenness is a sin. Because a woman in the locker room is an abomination unto God."

Sal finally got a word in edgewise. "Since when do they have 'Thou shalt not assign a woman to cover the Senators' in the Ten Commandments?"

"God's word is law," Jimy Boy said. "God has spoken. God has spoken to me, His humble servant, on many occasions."

"God has told you Berkowitz here should not cover the Senators?"

"He has," Jimy Boy said. "A woman in the locker room is a blasphemy. It is a violation of everything good and right and true. It is a disgrace to the national pastime. It is an insult to God. It is a sin."

"Is that all?" Sal said.

But Jimy Boy misunderstood him. "No, I have a few more things to say," Jimy Boy said.

In fact, he was just getting started. Jimy Boy was primed to lay on some words. He stood, he kneeled, he beseeched, he prayed. He allowed how the least Sal could do was cover the second annual Super Stars Ministry banquet coming up in August, at which three fourths of the starting rotation would be giving testimony about their one-on-one relationship with Jesus. It was a righteous performance. Even Beanie couldn't get it all down. Jimy Boy keened, he moaned, he cried unto heaven, while everyone in the office peeked through the venetian blinds that have not been dusted for thirty years. Sal sat back in his chair, folded his arms across his Turnbull & Asser shirt, and rolled his eyes, which was the first hint I got that I might survive.

When he was finished, Jimy Boy was kneeling at Sal's feet. "You done?" Sal said.

Jimy Boy returned to his seat. "I'll tell you what I'm going to do, Jimy Boy. I can call you Jimy Boy, can't I?"

Jimy Boy shrugged.

"Here's what I'm going to do, Jimy Boy. I'm going to have Ms. Berkowitz here take some time off from the team. It's a long season. It's already been a long season. And I think Ms. Berkowitz could use some perspective. Then, when she's gotten some perspective through her thick skull, I'm going to send her back to the team. And you know why, Jimy Boy? Because I believe in that Christian mercy you're always talking about. I'm going to forgive Ms. Berkowitz her sin just the way you would forgive one of your flock. Yep. I'm going to send her back to the Senators, which, come to think of it, should be punishment enough. And before I do, you know what I'm gonna tell her? I'm gonna tell her one more strike and she's out."

Jimy Boy started to protest. Sal raised his hands. It was his turn to play Pope. Jimy Boy stood and sighed and turned at the door. "One more thing, Sal," he said. "Jesus loves you, Sal."

When he and Beanie had made the turn past the morgue into Food, Sal looked at me and said, "*You* are saved. *You* are born again. *You* better get down on your hands and knees and thank God for him. Because Jimy Boy Collins just saved your ass."

June 26, P.M. "Come on, kid, let's eat," Milo said after Sal got done with me. "I'm buying."

At that particular moment, I would have followed him anywhere except maybe the visitors' locker room at the Oakland

Alameda County Stadium. He picked up my bags and hailed a cab and I was halfway through my second bloody Mary at the Garden Terrace of the Four Seasons Hotel before I realized how long it had been since I had eaten or slept. Of course by then I didn't care.

Milo reminded me of Wells Twombly's law, which is, "If there is an open bar anywhere in the world, within thirty minutes a Chicago sportswriter will be there." And he consoled me with tales of his own debaucheries. Like the time he got so drunk in an airport bar on his way home from the World Series that he took the wrong plane and ended up in New York with a Jamaican janitor mopping his shoes at 2:00 A.M. and saying over and over, "Ain't no Parking Lot One here, mon, only A, B, and C, mon."

I knew I was laughing too loud. Nothing at the Garden Terrace of the Four Seasons is loud. Not the color scheme, not the cocktail piano, not the waiters who arrive at your table as if on tip-toe, bringing another round. I accepted without thinking. A moment later my head was in my plate. I had gotten sick all over the floral oriental china of the Four Seasons Hotel. When I looked up from my disgrace, the second in as many days, Milo was beaming. "We're even, kid," he said.

June 27   "You've been assaulted," Ruth said.

We were sitting at our usual table at The Pit, eating the usual burgers, drinking the usual beer, having the usual conversation. "Really," she said. "It's an assault. It's an assault on your childhood, your memories, on your illusions. It's an assault on everything you've held dear since your grandmother took you to Saks Fifth Avenue and bought you that stupid mitt."

"Glove," I said.

"Mitt. Glove. I think you should sue."

"For what, Ruthie? For being themselves?"

"What they are is gross and offensive and they have made it impossible for you to do your job," she said. "I don't get it. It's not like you don't have grounds. I don't get why you're not grossed and offended and pissed."

"I don't get it either," I said.

I was smiling. But Ruthie was pissed on my behalf and even more pissed that I wasn't. "You come back here and you tell me stories about men who look you up and down and say, 'Go away.

Fuck you. I hate you.' And you laugh. And you want me to laugh. But I can't laugh at that. I just can't. And I don't see how you can. I mean, my God, they set you up."

"You're right," I said glumly. "Intellectually, I know you're right. I should be offended. I should be angry. There must be something wrong with me because I'm not."

Ruthie shuddered. The bartender sent over a round of martinis on the house. "I don't understand. Why do sportswriters put up with this? Would David Broder put up with this? Would Breslin? I mean, my God, Milo had a column the other day about some baseball player pouring a bucket of ice water over his head. And he wasn't angry, either."

"Yeah, Spike Miller of the Indians. And when he apologized he said, 'Everyone makes mistakes. Some people make better mistakes than others. I made a good mistake.' Isn't that terrific?"

"No, it isn't terrific. I'm tired of boys just being boys. I thought at least you'd know better."

"Maybe I'm just another jock sniffer at heart," I said.

Ruth groaned.

Someone told me the other day that I always sit forward when I interview, which is a very aggressive posture. I've been very conscious of how I sit ever since. So I stopped bebopping in my seat to Anita Baker and slumped back in my chair, giving in to Ruth's need to take this seriously. Maybe she is right. Maybe I need to take this seriously, too, at least my part of it.

"All the time I was growing up, I wanted to be a ballplayer. I wanted to be Ryne Duren. I wanted to be Joey Proud. Maybe I wanted it so much that I can't bring myself to see it for what it is now that I'm really there. Maybe it's Freudian. Maybe I'm reliving my presexual infatuation with my father through the Washington Senators."

Ruth rolled her eyes.

"I dunno. Maybe it's because of Grandma, because once she died the only thing I had left was baseball, the New York Yankees. Your shrink would probably say I'm projecting my love for her onto them. And maybe I am. You want me to hate these guys. And I can't even if I hate some of the things they do. I can't hate Buck. I can't hate Rump. I can't even hate the Stick. I can't hate baseball."

"Oh, right, I forgot," Ruthie said. "Baseball is inviolable."

"Unassailable," I said, grinning.

Ruthie still wasn't smiling.

"Shit, Ruth. What do you want me to say? You spend all day long going on about being a journalist, a woman in a man's world. If I remember right, you were all in favor of me getting off the women's page, where I had to describe the color and texture of everything anybody ever wore to an interview.

"So now I'm a woman in a man's world. I go in there every day and they belch and they fart and walk around naked scratching themselves and saying, 'Shitpissfuck.' You're very big on being a woman in a man's world as long as they wear suspenders and deal in junk bonds.

"Well, these guys don't wear suspenders. They're all stripped down. They crap, they fuck, they pee, they eat. They're guys. Maybe I envy how comfortable they are with themselves. Maybe I like them because they put me in touch with my own baseness."

Ruth hissed. "C'mon, Ruthie. You tell me. I come back from every road trip and all everybody wants to know is 'What's it *really* like in the locker room?' So I tell them and they laugh and they say, 'Yeah, *really*, tell me more.'

"I can't tell you why I'm sitting here with a shit-eating grin on my face. I can't tell you why I smile every time I think of Lawson praying for forgiveness in a hotel in Cleveland after the first gang bang of the season. Maybe it's just too much fun. Maybe it's because I can't go to work and scratch when it itches."

Ruth didn't look happy. Maybe Ruth doesn't itch.

"C'mon," I said. "Have a martini."

"No thanks," she said.

June 29 I've spent the last three days sitting at my desk answering hate mail and following the Senators in the Washington *Tribune.* They've lost four straight without any help from me. Stick is batting fifteen points over his career average and is still leading the league in home runs and strikeouts. Buck is still everybody's early choice for Rookie of the Year. Rump is still hitting under .200. And I'm still in deep shit with the entire Christian community. Every morning the pile of Sports sections under Ross I's chin grows a little higher. And every day the crowd grows a little thinner and a little more vocal. So Ross and Sal have agreed to go on Jimy Boy's Christian Fellowship Entertainment Network talk show in exchange for an end to the daily protests. We tuned in yesterday to get an idea what they're in for. His cohost, Lola Lord, wears a gold name necklace with JESUS on it and says "Praise be" a lot. You think maybe it's a stage name?

Maggie Blum, vice chairman of the Society of Women in Sports Journalism, called to say my colleagues have decided to issue a statement on my behalf deploring the conduct of the ballplayers involved as well as Jimy Boy Collins. Maggie's an original, I mean a pioneer. She's a hockey writer in Philadelphia and she's lasted a lot longer than a lot of players have. For some reason, a whole bunch of the first women sportswriters were hockey writers. Maybe it was a coincidence. Or maybe, as Maggie says, the editors figured those farm boys from Canada would be more polite. The first time she covered a Flyers game, one of the French-speaking players came up to her, handed her a puck, said, "Hey, Ma-ggie, I check heem good for you. *Boom!*" And elbowed her in the ribs.

I really like Maggie. She's one of the people who fought all the early fights so that people like me could get jobs like this and then screw them up completely. I was very glad to hear from her until she said, "Off the record, A.B., that was really dumb. Don't do it again, huh?"

Michael called from Miami to tell me I had been knocked off the front page down there by a pregnant drug dealer who shot off a cop's face and gave birth two hours later. I was hoping he'd be back this weekend but he promised his mom he'd stick around for a couple of days. He says she is the only non-Jewish pinochle player in Dade County. "Come on down," he said. "She'll teach you." He's been wanting me to meet his mom for months now. I've never met anybody's mom. I'm almost ready for The Visit. But not now. Not like this. Besides, Sal said he wants me in every morning at ten-thirty sharp, including Saturday and Sunday, to read the wires while Zeke is on vacation.

And today Sammy Esposito called to tell me these things happen. "Yeah," I said. "But why do they all happen to me?"

"You're in the Show, aren't ya?"

"I *am* the Show."

Sammy laughed. "How'd you get started in ball anyway?" he said.

"I tell people it's 'cause my father needed someone to play catch with. And probably that's true. But also I think I needed a way to be close to him and a way to be different from my sisters.

I mean, I'm a middle child, after all. My older sister, Celia, was born knowing how to window-shop. She could put on her own nail polish by the time she was four. No way I was going to *outgirl* her. And Emma, she's the baby, which is all she had to be. So I needed a way to get some minutes."

"Playing time," Sammy said.

"Mom always hated sports until she ran off with Bill."

"Bill?"

"My stepfather. He played some second base for the Indians' Double A team back in the fifties. I couldn't believe she ran off with a ballplayer. Of course, he was long since retired when she met him. But it didn't seem fair. I don't know, maybe I was just jealous 'cause she got to hang out with a ballplayer. Bill was nice enough. He was always offering to have a catch. He still had soft hands. But I never really took him up on it. It would have been a betrayal. I only played catch with Dad.

"Mom always gave him such a hard time when he as much as put the ballgame on the tube. She said, 'He always makes time for you girls and the New York Giants.' He'd turn it on to get the score and she'd put on the opera louder. So finally he just started driving around listening to games on the radio. He carried water for the Giants once, which I guess wasn't much compared to Bill. Anyway, he loved the New York football Giants. On Sundays in the fall we used to go out and listen to Al DeRogatis broadcasting the games. Mostly, I remember his voice filtering through the static. 'Tittle calls the signals at the twenty.' For some reason the signal on the radio was always bad when the Giants had the ball. By the time we tuned in again, Charlie Conerly was at quarterback. We never knew what happened.

"Sports made us allies, Dad and me. It was like this secret we shared. It's funny. When I think about it now, what I remember is the static and Al DeRogatis's voice floating in and out like when you're in and out of consciousness. Sometimes louder. Sometimes faraway. Sometimes just out of reach. Then the season was over."

Sammy's voice was like that, coming into range suddenly, loud and clear. "Well, anyway," he said. "It's a long season. Baseball is a funny game. You never know.

"And, Ari. Don't be so hard on your mom."

I'll have to remember to tell Ruth to add him to the list of reasons I can't hate baseball.

June 30 Today I got a press release from the Colonnade
Hotel in the Catskills announcing that Joey Proud has signed on
as director of special events/sports and will be hosting the Joey
Proud/Miller Lite Invitational Heart Foundation Golf Classic in
September. It was one of those computer-generated Mailgrams
that go to maybe five thousand writers all over the country (not
to mention at least three at the Washington *Tribune*), all with the
words IMPORTANT. FOR YOUR EYES ONLY written in mechanical
hand on the front. Usually it's the kind of thing I throw away.
Or never see. This time I knew it really was meant for my eyes
only.

It was just a year ago that Joey Proud stood at home plate at
Yankee Stadium, as Ruth, Gehrig, DiMaggio, and Mantle had
done before him, squinting at the afternoon sun and accepting
his final moment of approbation. It was his day, Joey Proud Day,
his last day as a Yankee. The Stadium was packed and draped
with red, white, and blue bunting. The mayor, the governor,
Joey's mother, wife, two daughters, and only son were there.
Even his hero Mickey Mantle came, though he wasn't scheduled
to broadcast the game. Joey's cap was perched back on his head.
You could see the lines etched in his face from a lifetime squinting into the sun. Joey squinted once more and gulped and scuffed
his feet in the dirt at home plate the way retiring heroes do and
said, "I don't know what to say. All the best lines have been took.
But a guy gets real tired of scuffing his feet in the dirt and saying,
'Aw, gee.'"

I was watching on TV in the office, sitting on Pincus's desk
and remembering *Pride of the Yankees*. It was my first week in
Sports.

Laughter echoed off the façade in left and caromed back
again in an undifferentiated roar. It crashed against itself like
waves against a shore. Joey nodded over his shoulder toward the
monuments beyond the fence in centerfield, a cemetery of sorts
to fallen idols. Ruth, Gehrig, DiMaggio, Mantle, and now Proud.
"When they told me they were putting another plaque out there,
I told 'em, 'The way I been playing, they might just as well
bronze me.'"

In the roar that followed, no one heard the scream coming
from the field box just beside the Yankees' dugout. No one *could*
have heard it. In fact, no one noticed a thing until a line of blue-

jacketed New York cops streamed down the aisle with a stretcher and an oxygen tank. It wasn't until a half hour later, until well after Number 11 had received the key to the city and the commendation of the state and the certificate announcing Joey Proud Day in the borough of Brooklyn, as well as a year's supply of frozen fish sticks, a portable elevator for the staircase in his home in New Jersey (a gift from his teammates), and a Dreamland four-sleeper camper, that anyone bothered to tell him that his son's heart had stopped, that Joey Proud, Jr., was unconscious and had been taken to the hospital.

So Joey never played his last game as a Yankee. He never had his day. He went to Lincoln Hospital instead, where Grandma died, where one September day surgeons had pieced together his Achilles heel, and paced outside the ICU in his uniform and his spikes while a team of twelve doctors tried to save his son's life. Reporters who were there say Joey never said a thing. He just kept pacing and digging holes with his spikes in the linoleum floor.

And then he disappeared.

A couple of weeks later, the Yankees' PR people issued a brief statement saying that Joey Proud, Jr., had been transferred to a facility in western Pennsylvania. No further details were released at the request of the family.

Reporters all over the country tried to find Joey's son. Joey told them all to get fucked when he bothered to answer the phone. Finally they gave up trying. No one had heard a word about him until the press release from the Colonnade Hotel showed up on my desk today. IMPORTANT. FOR YOUR EYES ONLY.

I called a guy I know in the commissioner's office who used to do PR for the Yankees. Everyone used to do PR for the Yankees. We went out a couple of times. "Listen, off the record," he said. "Joey Jr. is in a facility in Pennsylvania for people in a persistent vegetative state. Joey took the job in the Catskills to pay his kid's medical bills. But you didn't hear it from me."

He also said, "I think maybe Joey's ready to talk. Why don't you give him a call."

Reporters never expect anyone to return their calls, especially Joey Proud. I was just sitting here filing my nails when the phone rang. "Hi, it's Joey Schwartz," he said.

"I didn't know you were Jewish," I replied.

"Let me tell you something I learned a long time ago. When

you're going good, you're Jewish. When you're going bad, you're Italian."

"So you're going good, huh?"

He laughed and said he'd see me in the Borscht Belt in two weeks.

I told Sal, who raised his eyebrows and said if I go to the All-Star Game, make my deadlines, show my face, and stay sober, I can meet Joey Proud at the Colonnade.

My God. How do I ask him about his son?

The All-Star Break

July 10 The Grand Ballroom of the Bond Court Hotel can seat eight hundred in a pinch. And in baseball, any freebie qualifies as a pinch. The annual All-Star Game banquet is the best baseball has to offer in the way of snarfing until the play-offs, when beat writers refine the art of stuffing their faces to new heights. Major league baseball isn't as imaginative about the care and feeding of the fourth estate as the National Football League, which understands that the best way to a sportswriter's heart is through what is commonly known as a good spread. A good spread is any spread that is free. Which is to say, anything from turkey dogs to instant onion dip. A *really* good spread is what Pete Rozelle always put on at the Super Bowl when he was commissioner. Milo was reminiscing just the other day about the five-hundred-pound Caesar salad at Super Bowl XXII. He devoted a whole column to the recipe and got fifty hate letters because the NFL left out the anchovies.

> 840 heads romaine
> 840 coddled eggs
> 1,400 ounces garlic oil
> Juice of 175 lemons

980 ounces Parmesan cheese
350 cups croutons

Baseball hasn't even heard of Caesar salad. Baseball relies on its ancient claim to the allegiance of all Americans, as well as red meat and scotch, to attract reporters to what would otherwise objectively be just another boring made-for-television event. Even so, the feeding frenzy in the Grand Ballroom of the Bond Court Hotel was extraordinary. Who knows? Maybe it was the heat. It was ninety-six in downtown Cleveland and not much better in the Grand Ballroom of the Bond Court Hotel. Anyway, the raw bar was under siege, held captive by grown men with oyster juice running down their chins and cocktail sauce on their fingers. The players were also under siege, held captive by grown men with oyster juice running down their chins and cocktail sauce on their fingers. It was hard to tell which made the All-Stars more self-conscious, the suits and ties they were wearing or the wives draped over their well-tailored arms. Waiters plowed through the throng, sloshing eight hundred freebie fresh fruit cocktails (with stewed grapes) on round cork trays and yelling, too often belatedly, *"Watchaback!"*

In the middle of it all, in the very center of the room, stood a platform maybe ten feet square covered with Astroturf and the perfect likeness of a baseball diamond. Over home plate squatted an ice sculpture of a catcher, cap turned backward, arm cocked in readiness behind his head. It was an enormous work, a life-size rendering, a tour de force. The likeness was astonishing, from the protective cup right down to the forearms that looked as if they were meant for a lifetime of kneading pizza dough. No doubt about it. It was Rump. And Rump's rump was melting.

In fact, he was leaking from all his private parts. Home plate was a lake. The basepaths were drowning. "My cup runneth over," I heard a voice say.

I peeked through the catcher's icy legs. A well-chiseled hamstring splashed on my head. There on the other side of the diamond were Rump and Mrs. Rump watching the dissolution of what ballplayers like to call "the groin area."

"Hell of a way to go," I said.

"I'd say it's pretty much the way things have been going," he replied.

"Oh, John," said Mrs. Rump, who is the only person in America who does not call her husband Rump.

Rump scratched his forearms, which I have noticed is something he does right before he steps into the batter's box and in other moments of stress, like at Dr. Funk's office. "JoAnne, I'd like you to meet A. B. Berkowitz from the *Trib.*"

"A pleasure," I said. "It's also nice to see your husband in his clothes for a change."

I didn't mean it the way it sounded. You know—smartass and competitive. At least, I don't think I did. I think it was just one of those things you blurt out when nothing's going right and you feel as if every time you open your mouth you're back in high school. Anyway, Mrs. Rump was not amused.

"John's told me a lot about you," she said.

"He's told me a lot about you, too."

She was pert and blond and compact the way baseball wives are; a bouncy former cheerleader who only went down on lettermen. She didn't look like a woman who would drag her husband to a hypnotist, a Jungian therapist, and a bioenergeticist named Maya. For a moment, I decided appearances are deceiving. I was wrong.

"Ari's at our table," Rump said, taking each of us by the elbow and deftly steering us out of the path of an oncoming tray of freebie fresh fruit cocktails. Rump and his party, which is to say Mrs. Rump and me, had been seated at Table Number 1, as befit his status as the only catcher ever to appear in ten straight All-Star Games. Rump is almost as embarrassed to be here as I am. These things happen when you let the fans vote. So, despite Stick's bitching (he is having a career year) and Buck's numbers, Rump is the sole representative of the Senators, who, I might add, came into the All-Star break with a record of 23–59, exactly the same as the 1962 Mets, thanks in no small part to Rump's .151 batting average. If the first half of the season is any indication, this All-Star appearance will certainly be his last, which is why the pooh-bahs have taken it upon themselves to commemorate his career in a three-hundred-pound chunk of ice, an ephemeral testimonial if I've ever seen one.

"*Ari,*" *he said.*

It didn't occur to me until later, but that was the first time he has ever called me anything but A.B. I hope JoAnne didn't notice the familiarity in the tone, the prerogative. All I know is I was grateful for being rescued from a horde of drunken colleagues who draped their fat arms around my shoulder, breathed cheap scotch in my ear, and wanted to know why I couldn't hold my fucking liquor.

The All-Star Game is a convention like any other convention, except that it is a convention of baseball men, who are recognizable from their fallen chests, their polyester wardrobes, the leathery red quality of their skin, and the smiles that derive from knowing they have the best jobs in the world. Like any other convention, the All-Star Game is a boondoggle, the whole point of which is to schmooze, to be seen, and to do as little work as humanly possible. For me, the All-Star Game is penance. Cleveland is my purgatory. Under the circumstances, there isn't anyone I particularly want to see. And Sal said if I have so much as a beer, I'm history. You know how ballplayers are always saying, "I'm just happy to be here." Well, I'm not. Especially not sober.

We were deep into the green salad with the crumbled egg, the bacon bits, and the Thousand Island dressing when I heard a cement truck voice say, "Hey, Berkowitz! You ever been hit in the kidneys, Berkowitz?"

There were fourteen of us sitting at the table, one of those large round jobs used only at weddings, conventions, and bar mitzvahs to seat people who either don't know each other or don't want to see each other. It had the predictable banquet centerpiece of three daisies, two carnations, a rose, and a tulip with a TABLE NUMBER 1 stuck in the middle of it and the predictable fresh fruit cocktail sitting in the middle of each place setting. Such a table is an invitation to enforced isolation. You really have to go to some trouble to be heard.

"I *said*, 'You ever been hit in the kidneys?' " The cement truck was churning again.

Somebody moved the centerpiece, for which I will be forever grateful, and revealed to me the pockmarked countenance of Bernie Squire. I recognized him from his shirt and tie. They matched. All Bernie's shirts and ties match, which is to say they are all made from the same inexplicable brown plaid. He's got thirty of them—thirty of the shirts and thirty of the ties. Bernie Squire is known in press boxes across America for these ensembles. Dr. D once asked about them and Bernie said, "This way I can get dressed in the dark. That okay with you, asshole?"

Squire is a columnist from Detroit and also president of the Baseball Writers Association of America, a job he takes very seriously, along with the extra dough he gets for keeping score at

Detroit Tigers games. He is the man who signed my BWAA card, which allows me into any major league stadium in America without a ticket. The day I got my card was one of the best days of my life until I read the note that accompanied it: "Over my dead body. Squire."

Bernie is your basic meat-and-potatoes guy. He started out covering boxing fifty years ago when it was still called fisticuffs, and punches everybody in the biceps all the time just to remind you of that fact. In Bernie's world, either you box or you play ball. You're a man's man or a faggot. Unless, of course, you're a broad. Broads do not belong in press boxes unless they are serving scotch and crab cakes. Bernie likes to remind me and everyone else of that fact every chance he gets.

"I *said*, 'You ever been hit in the kidneys?' "

Squire is of the opinion that if you haven't recently been hit in the kidneys, you cannot possibly cover a professional fight. It doesn't matter that he is seventy years old and the closest he has come to being hit in the kidneys was when one of Larry Holmes's bodyguards threw him out of a press conference ten years ago after the schmuck called the heavyweight champion of the world a racist son of a bitch. Bernie's a *man*. He knows what it's like to be hit in the kidneys. After all, he was in a schoolyard fight when he was eleven.

"You ever face major league pitching, Berkowitz? You ever hear any chin music?"

"No, Bernie, have you?"

"Bernie ain't hit shit since Little League," said Paul Pileggi. Pileggi bird-dogs for the Tigers. He and Squire go back a ways.

"Neither have I," I said.

"You hear that, Paul? She played Little League."

"You played Little League?" Rump said.

"Yeah, I pitched for the Blue Jays of New Rochelle, New York. I had a hell of a curve. The manager was an SOB, though. He gave me a cap but no uniform. Just to put me in my place, I guess. I mopped up."

JoAnne was not interested in my former career. It's my present circumstances that she wanted to discuss. She has this squeaky little voice, like she's still in seventh grade or something, which I would think would make it difficult to take anything she says seriously. Apparently I am in the minority on that issue. Everyone perked up as soon as she opened her perfectly pert little mouth. "Personally, I don't think women should be allowed in the locker room. Do you, John?"

Around the table, notebooks materialized from nine polyester jacket pockets. Bellies that had been comfortably slouching under the table were suddenly sucked in, alert. Squire, who brags he never takes notes, reached for a cocktail napkin. These guys know a story when it's handed to them, all right. All eyes were on Rump and the missus.

"I mean, I don't see what kind of woman would want to be in a locker room full of naked men she doesn't know, unless, of course, she just wants to look."

Mrs. Rump batted her eyelashes. Rump shot her a look, the rough translation of which was "For God sakes, stop."

"Unless she's just hard up," Squire said, prompting.

"JoAnne," Rump said.

"Bernie," I said.

But JoAnne was not to be deterred and neither was Bernie. He was into deep commiseration.

"I mean, I think it's just *disgusting*," said Mrs. Rump.

Bernie was scribbling and nodding, nodding and scribbling. "I know. I know," he said.

"And so do a lot of *other* wives."

"JoAnne."

Rump was fucked. He couldn't tell his wife to fuck off in front of nine men with open pads and microphones. He couldn't warn her everything she said was on the record without that, too, being on the record. And most of all, he couldn't get her to shut up. One thing about the working press, they never misquote anyone who's telling someone to fuck off. So Rump just sat there scratching his arms and saying *"JoAnne!"* whenever he could get a word in edgewise. I wanted to help. But opening my mouth was the one thing that was sure to make it worse. So I just sat there. Soon enough, I was scratching my forearms, too.

"I was talking to Jane Stein and Carol Lawson and some of the other wives just the other day at Bible study. And we all think something should be done. I mean, I don't want some woman"—JoAnne stared at me—"watching my husband get dressed and"—she stared at me again—"*undressed*. I didn't marry him to share him with some woman who can't hold her liquor and—"

"Hey, Bernie," Pileggi said. "I think Berkowitz just took a shot in the kidneys."

Just then the waiter arrived with a pyramid of prime ribs, the slabs stacked precariously on one another, the *au jus* cascading from one plate to the next and from the bottom plate onto the front of his starched white jacket. It was a veritable waterfall of *au jus*. The blood was on the floor.

"Prime rib *au jus*," he announced. Only it came out as "oh Jew. Prime rib oh Jew." Around the table he went, announcing each prime rib oh Jew, fourteen oh Jews in all. When he got to me, I said, "Rare, please," but there was no changing the subject. JoAnne was relentless.

"In fact, Mr. Squire, we've written a letter to the Reverend Collins expressing our feelings. In light of recent developments, that is." She paused for effect. "I have a copy right here. You might be interested in reading it, Mr. Squire."

Mrs. Rump reached for her purse, and as she did I heard the dull thud of Rump's size-ten Gucci loafer colliding with Mrs. Rump's sensible blue pump. Probably I was the only one close enough to hear it. But Mrs. Rump was in no mood to keep anything to herself.

"Don't you go kicking me under the table, John Doubleday. I'm a person with my own personal ideas. I'll say what I want. And you can quote me on that, Mr. Squire."

She was batting her eyelashes again.

"JoAnne!"

Rump was turning pale and raking his forearms, which looked about as raw as the uneaten beef congealing before him. He had to know what was coming.

Every reporter has a fuck-you voice. It's the voice you use when you know you've bagged some poor bastard and now, because you're a professional and your object is, of course, to be fair, you're going to give him a chance to tell his side of the story, which of course can't be *the* story because you've already got *that*. I've heard fuck-you voices so sweet they'd make the cherry blossoms bloom in winter. And I've heard fuck-you voices that might as well be sentencing you to thirty years to life without parole.

Which must have been what Rump felt when Bernie Squire looked across the table and said, "What about what the missus here has to say? You wanna comment on that, Rump?" Any voice asking whether you want to comment on your own demise is the ultimate fuck-you voice.

By this time reporters were standing three-deep around us, craning their necks, ties and pads askew, tape recorders thrust in the general direction of a mouth, any mouth. It's times like this that reporters remind me most of ants converging on an errant glob of Cheez Whiz, circling, nudging, trying to get theirs without even knowing what theirs is. One guy sees another guy taking notes. Maybe he's writing his shopping list, who knows? But the other guy has to find out. So he wanders over, friendly-like, and starts taking notes, too, even if he has no fucking idea what the subject of the conversation is. You write it down and hope like hell you figure out what they're talking about later. I can't tell you how many notebooks I have filled with verbatim quotes like "The guy is a pig, a scumbag," and "I don't care what he says, I think he's full of shit," where I have yet to learn who the pig is, why he is a scumbag, and what he's said that's so full of shit.

The ants were circling our table. There was no getting through.

"Hey, bub. *Hot stuff! Hot stuff! Watchaback!*"

The waiter had returned with our string beans.

"Hey, you, you want beans?"

Rump shook his head no.

"You?"

Mrs. Rump shook her head no.

"You?"

I shook my head no.

"Fuck the beans," Squire said.

"Whaddya mean, 'Fuck the beans'?" Pileggi said. "I happen to like beans."

"Fine. So have the beans." Squire took the bowl from the waiter and dumped its entire contents on Pileggi's uneaten slab of prime rib with the *au jus* lapping over the side.

Rump put his head in his hands and gazed at his reflection in the *au jus* on his plate. He didn't even bother to look up. He just started to talk. "I've been in this game sixteen years," he said. "For sixteen years I've been getting dressed and undressed with women in the locker room. I don't know what it's like *not* to have women in the locker room. Somehow I've survived. *Intact.*"

Rump looked at Mrs. Rump. "Frankly, I don't see what the big fucking deal is, JoAnne. I mean, all you've got to do is keep your fucking shorts on, JoAnne."

Then he turned his attention to Bernie. "As for being hit in the kidneys, Bernie. Last time I looked, the guys who cover the White House were never fucking elected to anything. Right?

Bernie? I mean, Bernie, whatever happened to who, what, where, when . . ."

Rump looked at me.

"And how," I said, though all I could really think of was why. Why was this happening to me? Why was Rump defending me?

"And how," Rump said. "At least when women cover baseball, they don't try to pretend they know as much as we do. At least they ask questions, Bernie, instead of telling you how it was back in high school. You played ball in high school, didn't you, Bernie? That was back in the dead-ball era, right, Bernie?"

"Hey, Bernie," Pileggi said. "I think *you* just took a shot in the kidneys."

Rump stood and stared at Mrs. Rump, who was now also staring at the *au jus* on her plate. "Now, if you'll excuse me, gentlemen, I think I'll go watch myself melt."

July 11   I guess it shouldn't have come as any surprise that I wasn't sitting in the main press box. Bernie Squire had seen to it that I was sitting as far from the main press box as it is humanly possible to sit and still be in Cleveland's Municipal Stadium. If I had been any higher up behind home plate, I could have seen not only Lake Erie but Lake Michigan, too. As it was, I could smell them both. And, as it was, I was just as happy to be there.

Believe it or not, baseball has its own etiquette, particularly where seating is concerned. By right and tradition, when the All-Star Game is played in an American League city, the beat writers covering American League teams get seats in the main press box where the half-smokes are hot, the beer is free, and the stat sheets are plentiful. Everybody else gets to sit in what is politely called the auxiliary press box, which in Cleveland consists of three rows of upper-deck seats with pine boards stretching the length of them, a couple of telephone jacks, a couple of TV monitors, and a speaker at the end of each row from which locker room quotes are piped after the game.

By all rights, I should have been downstairs with the half-smokes and the beer and the stat sheets. And Bernie. I wasn't exactly dying to see him. So sitting upstairs between the Chillicothe *Mirror* and the Ypsilanti *News* didn't seem so bad, even if I was the only reporter in the vicinity that had a deadline in the next seventy-two hours.

I spent the day taking calls and saying "No comment" to every reporter doing a folo on Bernie's column, including the Chillicothe reporter sitting next to me, the only person in all of sports who hadn't seen my face spread across the sports pages of every paper in the country. Bernie's column had been picked up by AP, UPI, and every paper on the Detroit syndicate. Sal read me the headline over the phone at 7:00 A.M.: CATCHER AND THE MISSUS IN ALL-STAR SPAT. The subhead was: IS D.C. REPORTER THE OTHER WOMAN?

"I hired you to report the news, not make the news," Sal growled.

"You told me to show my face."

"I told you to stay out of the fucking headlines. Mitchell's got a rod up his ass on this one. Jimy Boy will have his born-again pickets out front again all fucking week."

"Sal."

"Don't Sal me."

"Sal."

"What?"

"All I said was 'Rare, please.' "

Thank God I can still make Sal laugh. "So what's this shit with Rump and his wife, anyway?" he said.

"Beats me."

"It better not," he said. "Sniff around."

One thing about sitting up where I was in the auxiliary press box of Cleveland stadium, there wasn't going to be any sniffing around, though I have to confess I *am* beginning to wonder about Rump and the slump and the missus and what it is he said he wanted to talk to me about and never did.

I was still wondering when he came to bat in the twilight in the bottom of the second. On the TV monitor down the row, NBC flashed the predictable "wife in the stands" shot. Only this was no predictable wife. Usually the baseball wife is biting her nails for her man, murmuring his name, or just plain praying. Mrs. Rump did none of the above. Mrs. Rump sat there stone-faced, holding a placard that said: BASEBALL WIVES FOR PRIVACY. Rump, looking equally stone-faced, took a called strike three.

It was a beautiful night, even in Cleveland, one of those evenings when the warm air holds you in a sweet embrace and just won't let go. Everything was simple, primary, irreducibly itself: the green of the outfield, the brown of the dirt. From up-stairs in the auxiliary press box the players looked small enough to be little boys, which of course they are. I was glad of the perspective, or the "perspectus," as Buck calls it. From up there it was easy to see that Rump is in a lot more shit than me.

He struck out again in the fifth and again in the seventh, both times looking. It had to be an All-Star Game record. Caught looking three straight times. You can't look much worse than that. Nobody could figure what Tony Diaz, who was managing the American League, was doing leaving him in there. Nobody plays the entire All-Star Game, especially nobody hitting .151, unless, of course, somebody wants you to look bad. Diaz likes to make people look bad, especially Rump. Diaz is a scumbag. This is not a word I use lightly. Often, maybe, but not lightly. I think I hate him almost as much as Rump does. Last time I interviewed him, he was leaning back in this big leather chair in his office with his feet up on the desk and his arms folded behind his neck. The only problem was he was stark naked from his waist to his sanitary hose. So if I wanted to talk to Tony, I had to look him in the balls or not look at him at all.

The American League was losing as usual, 5–4, in the bottom of the ninth. The crowd was heading for the exits. All the reporters in the auxiliary press box except me had gone downstairs by the bottom of the eighth in order to get to the postgame press conference. Everybody was going to want to hear what Tony and Rump had to say, since there sure as hell wasn't anything else to write.

It was midnight. Deadline was 12:10 A.M. One thing about the auxiliary press box, nobody on deadline was ever expected to write in it. I had a phone, which was ringing (the Captain again, pleading for copy), and a TV, which was flickering, but light? No light. Forget the light. Cleveland's Municipal Stadium is lit by 920 metallic halide lamps and 398 fifteen-hundred-watt incandescent lamps, which together generate one million peak-beam candlepower. You ever try reading the LCDs on a portable computer screen in the glare of one million peak-beam candlepower? Take my word for it, you can't. Reporters are big on talking about how they can't find the words. Well, I couldn't find the words. Any words. They were disappearing before my eyes, decomposing into little gray specks. I had no idea at all what I was writing.

I put the computer in my lap. I saw nothing. Between my

legs. Nothing. I wrapped my arms around the screen. I put the machine on my seat and my butt on the pine shelf. Nothing. I held it up. I held it down. I tilted it this way and that. I saw nothing. And the phone kept ringing. (Zeke!) I let it ring. There was no point in answering the sucker. I was late. I knew I was late. And I couldn't find the fucking words.

I guess I must have looked up when Wade Boggs singled with two outs. I know I heard the crack of the bat and I know I saw him round first. Dimly it occurred to me that Rump was due up next and that perhaps I ought to watch. In fact, he was kneeling in the on-deck circle, scratching his forearms, a fact I noticed later on the replay. But I was too busy trying to find what I had written to watch what I was writing about.

Besides, I couldn't believe even Diaz would let him hit until Rump was announced and everyone left in the stadium but me began to boo. Sid Fernandez, the Mets' lefty and Rump's former battery mate, was on the mound for the National League. Rump, who bats righty, took his time getting to the plate, figuring along with everyone else that Moe Kendell would be popping out of the NL dugout any second to replace Fernandez with a right-handed pitcher. But Moe stayed put, spitting arcs of tobacco juice at the dugout steps. Talk about indignities! Rump was going so bad, Kendell wasn't even bothering to play the percentages with him.

I hit the DONE button and called the office. I sent whatever I had, and I had no idea what I had. Zeke answered. "You got eighteen inches. Rump's up. Man on first. I'll dictate a flash lede."

"No shit," he said. "We're very advanced here in the nation's capital. We actually got TV."

If Yankee Stadium is the cathedral of ballparks, Cleveland's Municipal Stadium is the mausoleum. It is a monument to architectural homeliness. Vastness is its only virtue. When it is empty, there is no greater emptiness. When it is full, it holds 74,483 people, more than any other park in the major leagues.

There were maybe thirty thousand people left when Rump took a fastball at the knees for a called strike two. And all thirty thousand were on their feet—not so much out of expectation but in resignation. Their hearts were already in the parking lot. He fouled off the next pitch and the next and the one after that. By the fifth pitch, the exodus had stopped. Fans who had been trudging to exits turned and stood together on the concrete steps.

Rump fouled off a sixth, a seventh, an eighth pitch, all of them weakly. Not a loud foul in the bunch. The ninth foul was a pop-up that landed just behind the American League dugout. The tenth was a dribbler down the third base line.

Now people were into it. A vocal minority was screaming, "*K! K! K!*" The rest were exhorting Rump to escape the lure of history. Nobody in memory had struck out four straight times in an All-Star Game, much less four straight times looking. All I kept thinking was "Please God, at least let him go down swinging."

He fouled off another and another and another until he had fouled off seventeen pitches in all. And with each successive pitch, it seemed the stadium inhaled. There was no breeze. No air at all.

Every at bat tells a story, some as simple as a child's tale. You know: three strikes and you're out. This one was different. This was a five-act drama with no intermissions. This was a thirty-six-year-old catcher in search of redemption, trying to get around on a sneaky-fast southpaw who just wanted to go home. This one would be the subject of baseball exegesis for the next fifty years.

Fernandez bent low at the hips, waiting, studying, gauging the man at the other end of the conundrum. The roar, which had abated with Rump's last swing, mounted again, a low, dull, inchoate sound that escalated toward a crescendo. Rump backed out of the batter's box and scratched his forearms. Fernandez circled the mound. The umpire whisked home plate for at least the fifth time. Then Rump stood in again and the low, dull roar began anew. Fernandez went to his belt.

What would he throw? What should he throw? What would Rump be looking for? In and out, up and down. Slow stuff. Heat. Would Fernandez cross him up or challenge him? The rhythms, the options, the patterns of the game, the choices dictated by all that came before, a lifetime of tendencies collectively called "the Book," and the imagination to do the right thing all presented themselves in the crucible of the moment.

It was 12:21 in the morning.

The receiver lay on the pine shelf beside me. Zeke was cursing on the other end of the line. "Send something! Send anything! We're off the floor in five minutes!"

Fernandez has this odd, jerky motion, like a slingshot, nothing fluid or classical. He's kind of fat, Fernandez, and when he comes across his body with the pitch, it's as if it's coming out of his uniform. This pitch was a fastball at the knees, a fastball on the inside corner. Fernandez had made his choice. He dared Rump to be what he once was: the best low-ball-hitting catcher in the major leagues. It was a choice that presumed the passage of time and reflex. It was a choice that said, "Let's see what you got left," and gambled that the answer was "Not much." Fernandez gambled wrong.

Later, at the press conference, Bernie Squire kept stomping his feet and yelling, "Where's the fucking spic? I'm on deadline!" And when Fernandez, who's Hawaiian, finally showed, Bernie growled at him like the pitch was a personal offense or something and said, "Where was the fucking pitch, Sid?"

"Over the leftfield wall," Sid replied.

I know I screamed as Rump rounded the bases because Zeke told me to knock it off. The stadium was throbbing and so was my heart and it was hard to tell where the percussion began or ended. "Gimme the fucking lede," Zeke said.

Raoul came on the line and said, "Zeke says you should give me the fucking lede."

Raoul hates taking dictation. He also hates answering the phones and sorting the mail, but he loves his job. Raoul supports a family of five on his salary as a copy aide in the Sports Department. And the only thing he hates more than taking dictation is being home with his three kids, which is why he works two shifts a day. He gets in a lot of TV time that way. He is the only man in America who has seen every episode of "The Love Boat" at least twice. He is also president of Congressman Fred (Gopher) Grandy's fan club. "You gotta love 'The Boat,'" Raoul says.

Raoul was deep into a Buddy Hackett episode when I happened to call. Raoul was not happy to hear from me. "You ready," I said.

"Buddy's in the closet in Doc's cabin," he said.

I started to dictate.

" 'Battling to regain his self-esteem, battling to stay alive in the count, battling to keep his team in the game, Rump Doubleday, Washington's beleaguered catcher, fouled off seventeen consecutive pitches, all of them weakly, before hitting a majestic two-run home run with two outs in the bottom of the ninth to win the All-Star Game for the American League and redemption for himself.' "

"Slow down," Raoul said. "What am I, Evelyn Wood?"

" 'Sid Fernandez, of the Mets, the losing pitcher and Doubleday's former teammate, was standing at home plate to greet him, a violation of baseball etiquette perhaps but the human thing to do. Doubleday was escorted down the third base line by a throng of fans who jumped the barricades to be with him.

" 'It was an at bat that lasted an eternity, or to be precise, eleven minutes. And when it was over, a thirty-six-year-old catcher was young again—if only for a moment. Pitch by pitch, the tension in Cleveland's Municipal Stadium mounted until it seemed the place was emptied of oxygen. The capacity crowd of 74,000, most of whom were on the way to the exits when Doubleday stepped into the batter's box, stood with him awaiting his fate.' "

"Whew," Raoul said.

" 'Baseball keeps records of almost everything, but not the longest at bat or the most pitches fouled off consecutively or the most dignity reclaimed in a single at bat. But if Doubleday lays claim to this title, surely no one will dispute him.

" 'Doubleday, who came into the game batting .151, was chosen as Washington's sole representative to the All-Star Game because of what he has been, not because of what he is today. The decision to honor him at this year's banquet was a clear signal that no one expects him to be around to accept the accolades a year from now.' "

"Accept the what?" Raoul said.

"Accolades."

"Acco . . ."

"*A-c-c-o-l-a-d-e-s.* Accolades."

"What's 'accolades'? A social disease?"

"Don't think, Raoul. Just type. 'In recent days, the indignity of the worst slump of his Hall of Fame career, persistent trade rumors, and a highly publicized dispute with owner Jimy Boy Collins over his refusal to comply with mandatory drug testing have been compounded by a spat with his wife about the presence of female reporters in the locker room, which became public during the banquet at which he was honored.' "

"Some fucking sentence," Zeke said, breaking in on another extension. "Pretty high-tone shit. I'd make you rewrite it if you weren't twenty minutes late already. Punch up the sub."

He hung up before I got a chance to tell him to drop dead.

I took a deep breath, inhaled the night, and resolved once and for all I am too good for this shit. Down the row, the television monitor was showing yet another replay of the home run from yet another angle. They were calling it a tape-measure job, though I knew there wasn't any number they could put on it that would measure how much it meant to Rump.

That sounded punchy. *I* sounded punchy. I had twenty minutes to punch up my sub. I started writing in the darkness, trying to remember what I'd said, trying to see what I was writing, hoping for some quick quotes from the locker room. "Already they are calling it a tape-measure job. But there isn't any number that can measure how much this awesome two-run shot meant to Rump Doubleday."

Zeke likes "awesome." I figured if I got "awesome" in the second sentence, I might be able to get away with "redemption" in the third. I was trying to decide if there was any way to use "awesome" and "redemption" in the same sentence when the squawk box at the end of the row began to vibrate. Thank God! My pipeline to the press conference was open. "Testing, one, two, three. Testing." There was a screech of feedback and then the sound of a telephone ringing.

A voice echoed through the empty stadium. It was a familiar voice. It belonged to Beanie. "Halloo," he said.

Beanie reminds me of a parakeet I once owned before Mom asphyxiated him with Mr. Clean. He chirps, which comes in handy in public relations. He also fancies himself something of a ladies' man, which just goes to show what's happened to standards in this country. All weekend he's been tripping around the lobby of the Bond Court chirping "Halloo" and nuzzling this chippie named Carmen. I kind of like Beanie, even though his whole job is never to tell me anything. He's so good at telling me nothing that he got this special trip to Cleveland as a reward. His mission here was to answer the phone in the winning locker room in the event the President of These United States should call.

No doubt about it. It was Beanie's voice echoing through the night. But for once he wasn't chirping. "Carmen, I told you not to call me here unless it was a real-life emergency," he said.

The line went dead on Carmen and I went back to work, smiling. A moment later, the phone rang again. "What the fuck! I thought I told you not to call me here," Beanie said.

"What? Oh my God. Excuse me, Mr. President. I'm sorry, Mr. President. I'll get him, Mr. President. Rump! Rump! It's for you, Rump! It's the *President*, Rump! I'm dead meat."

On the television monitor, Rump was standing in his underwear, cracking up.

July 12   I reached for my watch and it was gone. My watch —the one Grandma gave me with my name and the New York Yankees logo on the back. My watch was gone.

I had a plane to catch and bags to pack and no watch. My watch was gone.

But it couldn't be gone. I remember looking at it last thing before the Halcion kicked in and trying to figure out just how late it was without turning on the light. I remember because I couldn't make out the Roman numerals by the light of the highway filtering past the rubber blinds on my window in the West End Motor Court by the Lake.

"It's seven thirty-five," Jane Pauley said.

It was three in the morning by the time I got back to the West End Motor Court by the Lake and decided which of the equally uncomfortable double beds I would not get any sleep in. It was one of those nights when adrenaline vies with fatigue, when you can't close your eyes or keep them open either. A beer would have been nice. But everything was closed. So I got out my journal and settled for a Halcion, which is my favorite kind of sleeping pill, mostly because of the name. And that's how I know I looked at my watch because I always look at my watch when I take a Halcion because somehow it helps to know how late it is when the drug kicks in.

"It's seven fifty-five," Bryant Gumbel said.

It was right there on the night table. Well, it's not really a night table. It's a headboard that turns into a night table that turns into a headboard again, one of those Formica units that's supposed to look like wood and connects two double beds in motel rooms circa 1962. My watch was right there on the night table next to the keys and the journal and the plane ticket and the press credentials and the Gideon Bible and the Halcion.

My watch was there and now it's gone.

I put it right there, right after I decided on the bed closer to the door, and right after I took the pillows off the bed by the window and the polyfibered bedspread, too, one of those bedspreads that give only the illusion of warmth, because no matter how hot it is outside, I'm always cold when I'm alone in a motel.

Maybe I left it in the bathroom.

"It's eight o'clock here on 'Today,'" Deborah Norville said.

In the bathroom, there were three tumblers wrapped in wax paper, three unopened bars of Dial soap, and a strip of paper dangling from the toilet attesting to a standard of sanitary propriety. But there was no watch. My watch was gone.

I looked in the mirror and saw the tarnished brass chain hanging limply against the door to my room. The door to Room 113 in the West End Motor Court by the Lake was open. Not open exactly. I mean, not ajar. But not closed either. The teeth of the lock, the three brushed chrome prongs, were resting against the metal strike, and the tarnished brass chain was resting against the door, which wasn't exactly open but wasn't exactly closed either.

The door was open. My watch was gone. It was not in the bathroom and it was not on the night table where I left it at three in the morning when I took the Halcion because no place was open to get a beer. The ticket was there. The keys were there. The Halcion was there. My watch was gone.

Someone was there.

I looked around Room 113 in the West End Motor Court by the Lake, where for twenty-nine dollars anyone can get a bed and for just a little bit more get laid, too. I knew the place was trouble when I saw the cyclone fence around the parking lot. A motel surrounded by a cyclone fence is always trouble.

The door was open. My watch was gone. Someone had been there. *Someone must have been there.*

"It's eight-fourteen," Willard Scott said.

I looked in my pockets. I looked under the bed. I looked in my briefcase, my bag, my underwear.

Look in the drawers.

I did.

Look again. Call.

"West End."

"My watch is gone."

"So?"

"So. My watch is gone."

"We'll send someone down."

"It's eight thirty-five," Deborah Norville said.

Someone knocked on the door.

"It's open," I said.

The door was open.

"My watch is gone."

"Uh-huh."

"I *said*, 'My watch is gone.' "

He had a vacuum cleaner the size of a fire hydrant and an ass to match. "Can't we just *look* under the beds? I want to find my watch. Not eat it."

Down on all fours, we pawed through the brown shag carpet and the dustballs for a small, square watch with a white face and black Roman numerals and my name and the NEW YORK YANKEES logo engraved on the back and for something far more elusive and far more valuable: corroboration. That what had happened had really happened. That I had left my watch on a Formica night table by one of the two double beds in Room 113 of the West End Motor Court by the Lake at three in the morning. That the Halcion kicked in. That the door was open. That my watch was gone. That someone had been there.

"Ain't nothing here but this," the guy said, handing me a bobby pin and an unopened condom.

"Flip the mattress."

"Flip the mattress?"

"Flip the fucking mattress!"

We flipped the fucking mattress. We tore the fucking sheets off the beds. We tore the fucking room apart. It was 9:00 A.M. My watch was gone. Jane Pauley was gone. The guy with an ass the size of a fire hydrant was gone. Joey Proud was waiting in the Catskills.

My watch was gone.

The door was open.

The Halcion kicked in.

At the airport, I called Mom collect. "My watch is gone. My plane is gone."

"Half the season's gone," she said optimistically.

I wanted to tell her about the miles, the beds, the deadlines, the airplanes, the time zones crossed and crisscrossed until you no longer know where you are or who you are other than a byline or even what time it is except that you have this one thing, a watch, a gift of childhood from a grandmother who didn't care if you liked baseball better than Madame Alexander dolls, a watch that clings to your wrist and reminds you, binds you, to some objective standard of time and place.

It was a tank watch with petite Roman numerals. The year before she died, my grandmother put on her open-toed shoes and took the CC train downtown to Cartier, where she told the man, who disapproved, to engrave it with my name and the NEW YORK YANKEES logo. I wore it everywhere. I wore it until the alligator band disintegrated on my wrist. It was my first jewel, my first womanly possession, and coming as it did from someone who kept rose sachet in a porcelain heart on her dresser, it meant more than I knew. Until it was gone. She gave me that watch and with it permission to be whoever I was to become. And now that watch was gone and with it all barrier to dislocation.

In the telephone booth with my computer on my lap and my dress bag at my feet and ink stains from the game beneath my fingernails, I tried to tell Mom this. I tried to tell her about the sleeplessness and the loneliness and the grossness of it all. But all I could manage was a whimper. "My watch is gone," I said.

"I know, dear," she said. "But don't worry. I'm sure you'll have much better luck in the mountains than I did."

The Catskills

July 14   Dad always said the Colonnade was a swanky joint. I liked that word, "swanky," I guess mostly because it was his word and also because he always snapped his fingers when he used it which at the time I could not do. Whenever he used it in conjunction with the Colonnade, Mom rolled her eyes and said, "Come on, Howard, it was a dump in 1956 and it's a dump now. They should have dynamited the place years ago."

For a while in the thirties, forties, and early fifties, the Colonnade was *the* place to be in the mountains. And not just for its privileged guests—"schvingers," my grandmother called them— but for all those pimply-faced kids from Bayside who bussed tables for the summer. The Colonnade, it was said, had all the best people, the best tippers, and the best gimmick of any place in the Catskills. Where else could Jews from the Bronx pass a weekend in a neo-antebellum plantation with a white-columned portico where black waiters served mint juleps and kosher corn fritters to everyone who crossed the threshold?

"*Schlockmeisters,*" my mother said.

Mom is not very romantic on the subject of her honeymoon or the Colonnade's Southern Belle bridal suite, where she and

Dad passed the first weekend of married life. It was a three-day
pass of a honeymoon, most of which was spent in a canopied bed,
where Mom first experienced the gravitational pull of the planets. I guess there must have been something good between them
once. When the honeymoon was over, she went back to selling
foundations on the Lower East Side and Dad was shipped off to
Germany to fight the Cold War.

Twenty years later, the children of the original owners, Else
and Myron Hansburg, decided Mom was right and resolved to
dynamite the place. But then the landmarks people got all hot
and bothered and started circulating all sorts of petitions to the
citizens of Sullivan County and former Colonnade guests to pre-
serve this relic of the Old South on old Route 17 between Living-
ston Manor and Roscoe, New York.

The landmarks people argued, in essence, that the place was
just too funny to destroy. And it was hard to quarrel with their
logic. So the Colonnade was preserved with the stipulation that
the portico, then puce, would be returned to the original antique
white.

A couple of months before the final decision was handed
down, Dad decided a family pilgrimage was in order. Mom
rolled her eyes and muttered something about stale corn fritters
on her pillow. They were not getting along at all by then. The
stars were long gone from their relationship. It was February
and as raw as it had been during that three-day pass in 1956. It
was also a raw, awkward time for me. I was twelve.

Mostly, I remember the halls. They were blue. Blue walls,
blue doors, blue floor. The blue carpet had this weird gold and
silver design in it. I thought it looked kind of like snakes tangled
up together. But then I decided, no, it really looked like a chandelier had fallen from the ceiling and had been smashed flat into the
floor. I have since become an expert on hotel carpet. My friend
Bob, the architect, says the whole point of hotel carpet is to hide
spills and other accidents of pleasure. But I am not convinced. I
think the psychology of loneliness is at work in these halls. I
think the tangled snakes and the smashed chandeliers are intended to forestall boredom and solitude as you make your way
down lonely corridors trying to figure out what the carpet looks
like and who the hell would have thought of it.

The Colonnade's halls were my first hotel halls. They reminded me of the streets behind Yankee Stadium in the years

before the city got around to putting in vapor lights. So dark. So empty. They were halls you could get mugged in.

I also remember the corn fritters, which were stale, and the chlorine fumes from the pool in the basement, which wafted through the lobby into the ventilator shafts and up to our rooms on the thirteenth floor. It was there, on the second day of our thirty-two-dollar-a-night weekend special, that I got my period for the first time and realized I was not going to play for the New York Yankees. It was there that Dad got the call saying Grandma was dying. And it was there this morning that I met Joey Proud.

Joey's secretary said to meet him at 8:00 A.M. in the Wagon Train Coffee Shop, which was The Tara in the old days. There is also a Giddap Bar and Grill, which has lots of tubular furniture and lassos on the menu, and a Hoedown Aerobic Studio and Juice Bar. Somehow over the years, the plantation ethos has transmogrified into cowpoke metaphor. "That's progress," the PR bunny told me.

The Colonnade is under new management these days—some Western outfit that runs mountain chalets took it over with the idea of turning it into a Yuppie getaway. So they installed a minibar in every suite, a Jacuzzi in every bathroom, and fennel in every dish, except of course the boiled beef. Still, the Yuppies did not come. So now, in a final effort to stave off foreclosure, the Colonnade has once again become a family resort with baby-sitting available twenty-four hours a day, diet blintzes on the menu, and Joey Proud, the new director of special events/sports, conducting daily baseball clinics and nightly bingo games.

The chances of Joey Proud being anywhere by 8:00 A.M., especially a buffet breakfast honoring the winners of the Over 35 Men's Softball Tournament, were zero considering his insomnia and his penchant for rye. But I was there at 7:59 A.M. I know because the hostess told me so. She also told me when it was 8:11 and 8:22 and 8:25. She smiled the first three times I asked.

The last time I was late for a breakfast interview, I stood up a coach at Maryland Tech who spent the first half hour telling me he had problems with Jews as a group. "How 'bout as individuals?" I replied.

I haven't been late to an interview since.

At 7:59 A.M., the Hoedown Aerobic Studio and Juice Bar was empty except for one particularly effusive blond aerobics instructor in clingy black sweats cut off at the knees and four overweight matrons in bulging spangled warmups bought specially for the occasion. It was low-impact hour at the Hoedown Aerobic Studio. "Come on, now, girls," the effusive blond pleaded, cranking up Madonna to top volume. "Let's get energetic!"

The Wagon Train was also empty except for me and one equally effusive PR bunny with a stack of press packets commemorating the first annual Joey Proud/Miller Lite Invitational Heart Foundation Golf Classic press day, who was energetically explaining to me that Mr. Proud would be unavoidably detained.

"By rye?" I said. But she was gone.

I read the glossy four-color press packet, which was like every other press packet: one history of the Colonnade, one Joey Proud fact sheet, one Joey Proud YOU GOTTA HAVE HEART bumper sticker, one Colonnade ball-point, one Colonnade room rate card, and a recipe for kosher corn fritters. I reread the clips that I stole from the morgue, though there wasn't anything in them I didn't already know. I skimmed the copy of *Proud of the Yankees* that Dad sent me from my room at home. I ate scrambled eggs that had been incubating under infrared grow lights since Mom saw stars. I thought about what I wanted to ask him. I always write my questions on the inside flap of my notebook so I can find them when things go dry. I read them again. "Who's better, Willie or Mickey or Joey Proud? Hero growing up? Shill? The injury. Dreams. Rumors re: son."

The truth was, I didn't really want to ask him anything. What I wanted was to tell him about Sam Esposito and my grandmother and wearing my Mary Janes to school on Opening Day of the baseball season. I wanted to tell him about my career throwing out base runners against the garage door on Eldridge Court. I wanted him to acknowledge our common ground, that sweet spot inside where motion becomes memory and memory becomes love. But most of all, I wanted to like him.

"Hi, I'm Joey Proud," he said.

"Hi, I'm nervous," I replied.

"Why?" he said. "Scared I was gonna pull on your titty?"

We were standing by the potatoes, those pregrated hotel hash browns that always come with a twist of orange and a rotten strawberry. There was a whole chafing dish of them. I kept telling myself, "Just look at the potatoes," "Remember the potatoes," "Hang on to the potatoes." I looked at those potatoes as I had never looked at potatoes before. They were white potatoes sitting in a stainless-steel chafing dish of orange grease between seventeen pounds of microwaved knishes and fifty links of microwaved sausage; all of it incubating under infrared grow lights. I studied the white of the potatoes and the orange of the grease and the red of the lights and the glint of the stainless steel. The potatoes looked as if they belonged in a hospital morgue. They looked embalmed. They looked the way I felt.

When I looked up, the Wagon Train was filled with overweight, overaged softball players in lime-green JOEY PROUD golf shirts and white patent-leather shoes, saying things like "Yo, Joe!" and "Fucking A, Joe," and "My man, Joe." Fifty-year-old white guys should never say "My man" to anyone, much less Joey Proud. One guy named Mitch from Jersey wrapped his arm around Joey's shoulder and said, "Yo, Joe, I saw you strike out four times against Catfish Hunter at the Stadium in September 1968."

"Yo," Joey replied, clapping Mitch on the back with a little too much enthusiasm. "*Cretino*," he said when the guy disappeared. "I was on the DL in September 1968. Fucking ankle. Fucking Hunter."

Joey looked around for the PR bunny. "Can't anybody get a cup of fucking coffee around here?"

He was holding a stack of oversized JOEY PROUD baseball cards. On the back they have his stats, his height, weight, marital status. On the front there is a portrait of the slugger in his pinstripes and his youth. It is a watercolor. And in the painting, his visage hovers over the façade of Yankee Stadium, the one Jake Ruppert built. Joey is gazing off in the distance, across the Harlem River, past 158th Street where the Polo Grounds used to be. Toward what? I made a note to remember to ask him. The future, maybe?

Standing there in the Wagon Train Coffee Shop, he could see only as far as his next cup of coffee or maybe his next cocktail. His eyes were bloodshot. His lips were cracked. In a way, his vision was as limited as it was when he was young and a presence hovering over the Bronx. Joey couldn't see then that the future was what I was looking at now. Bad legs. Bad eggs. Bad nights. The future's always the same. But they can't see it. They are too busy racing their bodies in a losing battle against sinew and time. It's a battle we all lose. But athletes lose it sooner and they lose it harder, too, because they think they never will. It's a setup, all right. All their lives, their bodies tell them lies. They say hard things are easy, that problems are solved with the crack of the bat or a perfect peg to home. It is the lie at the center of sport. And

they believe it because they are naturals. Because we fix their
parking tickets and their girlfriends and anything else that cannot be fixed by a line shot into the gap. *"Sure, Joe, no problem, Joe.
We'll take care of it, Joe."* And then one day, hard things are no
longer easy. The reflexes go and along with them the forbearance
and the adulation. Then it's *"Hey! Slow down, motherfucker, you're
doing ninety-five mph in a fifty-five-mph zone."* And the hardest
thing of all is accepting that it was all a lie. They are old before
they are forty, washed up before they begin to be adults. And
everybody wants to know why they are such fucking assholes.
You can't grow up if you spend your whole life perfecting the
rhythms of childhood.

"Coffee," Joey said. "Can't anyone get me a cup of *fucking*
coffee?"

The PR bunny returned with a silver-haired lothario in tow.
He had a name chain around his neck that kept getting caught in
his chest hair. His shirt was open to his "pupik," as Grandma
used to say. "Mr. Proud, this is Irv Pollack," she said. "He'll be
your playing partner today."

"Fucking A, Joe," Irv said.

"Fucking A," Joey replied. "How 'bout we grab a cup of
coffee, Irv-boy?"

"No thanks, really, Joe," Irv said, patting his stomach. "I've
had too much already."

"Tee-off time is 10:00 A.M., Mr. Proud," the PR bunny said,
taking Joey by the arm. "Your limousine is waiting."

"A-fan-culo," Joey said.

It was a stretch white with lots of fake mahogany paneling
and fake cut-glass decanters filled with rye. There were four of
us, Irv and Joey and me and the PR bunny, sliding all over each
other in the fake leather interior, trying to avoid bumping into
Joey's ankle, which was propped up on the seat between me and
Irv.

A couple of years ago, Else and Myron Hansburg's children
sold off the Colonnade's back nine to developers who are busy
dotting the mountain landscape with town houses. So the Joey
Proud/Miller Lite Invitational Heart Foundation Golf Classic
has been relegated to a public course a half hour away in Liberty.
The ride there was not exactly a happy one. For ten minutes, no
one said a word except "Excuse me." Everyone was waiting for
Joey to be Joey, to do what was expected of him.

What do you do when the dream ends and you wake up one

day with a family to feed and time and pain to kill? You make a living being Joey Proud.

He reached for the rye.

"You hear the one about St. Peter and the pussy?" Joey said. "God calls St. Peter over and he says, 'Hey, Pete, I was down on Earth and I made this man and this woman and I forgot to put their sexual organs on them. You take this pecker and this pussy down there and put them on Adam and Eve. Okay?' St. Peter says sure and he's getting ready to leave and God says, 'Wait a minute! Come back! Be sure to put the pussy on the short dumb one.' "

The PR bunny laughed and Irv laughed. And they both said that sure was a good one. I myself was feeling nauseous. I told myself I always feel nauseous while trying to take notes in the backseat of stretch white limousines. Joey belched and grew silent again. The PR bunny said she was new on the job, that she had worked at the Sands in Vegas until May. "They had quite a few celebrity golf tournaments at the Sands," she said.

Which reminded Irv of Barbi Benton's bazongas. Turns out he once went snorkeling with her in St. Bart's and she was topless and he kept diving just to see her tits float up in the water.

"She's a very dynamic person," the PR bunny agreed.

"*Queste e-culo*," Joey said.

Only the chauffeur understood the reference. "It means 'some piece of ass,' " he told me later. But Irv and the PR bunny laughed anyway.

"Hey, Joe," Irv said. "We got a Heart thing coming up in Wilmington. Nice tournament. Ashburn always plays."

"They got good crabs in Wilmington," Joey said. "I led the league in the crabs. Six straight years. Major league record."

"Still hold it?" Irv said.

"Still hold it," Joey said. "And my wife was second four straight times."

A cortège of golf carts waited by the clubhouse door: one for each of the networks, two for local TV, two for local print media, and three more for the PR bunny, the club pro, and the bartender. We were all assembled so we could watch Joey Proud play a round of golf exclusively for our benefit. That's what press day is all about, shaping reality to the needs of the news biz. Joey wouldn't be playing this round of golf if we weren't there. And we wouldn't be there if he wasn't playing the round of golf. The usual rules of cause and effect get a little blurry on such occasions. But it is part of the equation of press day to make believe that none of this is true, especially on camera or in print. Press day is the modern definition of the willing suspension of disbelief.

Joey did nine three-minute one-on-ones. The ground rules were: no one asks about his son. Nobody did. Nine times, Joey smiled the same smile and delivered the same lines. *Q: "How's it feel to be out of uniform, Big Guy?" A: "My wife says I was* always *better out of uniform."* Smile. Wink. Next. *Q: "What do you miss most about the game, Joe?" A: "Answering all these original questions."* Smile. Wink. Heh. Heh. Heh. And when everybody had their shot, when everybody had everything they needed, which is public relations talk for all they're going to get, Joey looked at the PR bunny and said, "Do we really gotta play *all* eighteen holes?"

Joey lives in one of those exclusive condo resorts built on a golf course designed by Jack Nicklaus somewhere in New Jersey. The seventeenth fairway is his backyard. Now here he was standing outside a clubhouse that looked like a Quonset hut on a public course with dying greens and crabgrass fairways and a PR bunny who couldn't understand why he didn't want to play the whole round. How could we all pretend this was for real if Joey didn't play all eighteen? Joey rolled his eyes and said, "You want eighteen. You'll get eighteen."

Joey reached for his driver and stepped up to the first tee. Nikons clicked. Minicams whirred. Pens noted the time. Joey turned and winked and hooked his shot two hundred and seventy yards into the rough. "You should put this shit in *Modern Maturity*," he said.

And still, as he stood there with the club in his hands, you could see the power of the stroke, so similar, so familiar, the ineffable coordination of eye and hand and muscle that made him what he was. Joey was whole again with the club in his hands. Until he tried to walk, that is. His knee locked and his leg balked and the Nikons and the minicams and the poised pens all recorded that, too. Aging athlete pathos is always good stuff. Joey threw his driver at the caddy and limped to the cart, using both hands to drag his right leg into his seat.

"Want me to drive?" I said.

Joey looked at me for a second, gauging whether I was trying to humiliate him, and looked away just as quickly. The course was unkempt; littered with divots and dandelions. The sun darted behind a cloud and stayed there. The mountain air went suddenly chill; a fine cold mist began to fall. It was not a great day for photo ops or for an aging hero with an aching Achilles heel. "It's fucking freezing out here," he said, rubbing his ankle.

I was shivering. I had been shivering since breakfast. But it hadn't occurred to me that it had anything to do with the weather. I turned on my tape and started to ask a question. My teeth started to chatter instead. "Cold-hearted bitch," he said, but he was smiling.

Then he reached into his JOEY PROUD/MILLER LITE INVITATIONAL HEART FOUNDATION GOLF CLASSIC golf bag and handed me his extra-large JOEY PROUD/MILLER LITE INVITATIONAL HEART FOUNDATION GOLF CLASSIC sweater. "Here, wear this. Go on. I'm not gonna wear it. It's like wearing your jockstrap to '21.' "

The sweater is as huge as Joey and as green as centerfield at Yankee Stadium at four in the afternoon. It's got a baseball embossed over the heart, two-dimensional but life-size. The seams are stitched with darker thread, and between them it says: JOEY PROUD, YOU GOTTA HAVE HEART. It felt like cashmere on my skin. The label said: 100% VIRGIN ORLON ACRYLIC. You could look it up.

"Hold on," Joey said, finding the ignition.

He floored that baby and careened down the fairway in pursuit of his ball. Joey drove like a maniac. He did wheelies. He did 360s. He zigged. He zagged, never coming to what you'd call a full stop unless absolutely necessary. At each succeeding tee, he'd hobble out of the cart, whack his ball two hundred and seventy yards, and take off again before anybody could get close to us. On the fifth hole, he knocked his ball forty yards out of bounds, detoured across the parking lot, swooped down upon his prey, and grabbed that sucker without taking his foot off the accelerator. On the ninth hole, he stopped to pee in a sand trap.

Behind us, twelve golf carts with three network crews, two local TV crews, two local media types, one playing partner, one caddie, one golf pro, one PR bunny, and one bartender were flooring those babies in mad pursuit. Joey never slowed down enough to allow anyone with a Nikon, a minicam, or a pen to get close enough to him to record any of this. Which isn't to say they didn't try. If Joey zigged, they zigged. If Joey zagged, they zagged. Soon everyone was doing wheelies and 360s. The cameramen clutched their cameras. The photogs clutched their film canisters. I clutched Joey's arm. All the time he was whooping and hollering and smiling into the wind. Every once in a while Joey would look over his shoulder and shout, "Poor dumb bastards," but a gust swallowed the words. The wind picked up and bellowed in my ear until I realized that the roar was not the gale at all but me. I couldn't stop laughing.

Recklessness was always part of his charm: sitting along the third base line cradling my Sam Esposito glove, I admired it from afar. But this was different: clutching it by the arm, holding on to it for dear life. After the fifteenth hole, I stopped worrying about not asking him any questions. What's to ask? I knew what it's like to be Joey Proud.

On the seventeenth hole, the tee stood atop an enormous hill overlooking a craggy ravine and a mountain brook. Joey hit his shot and zoomed down the path, heading straight for the water. Closer and closer we came until we were maybe ten yards away. No way he makes that turn.

But Joey did. Unfortunately, the network guys behind us did not. Their accelerator stuck. The driver jumped out. But the on-air talent in his brand-new JOEY PROUD/MILLER LITE INVITATIONAL HEART FOUNDATION GOLF CLASSIC sweater and his Gucci loafers went down with his ship. So much for the dry look.

"Think they got enough?" Joey said.

Someday people are going to look back at the eighties and remember the mousing of America. I can't prove this, of course. But empirically speaking, I've been in enough hotel bars, fitness parlors, and twenty-dollar hair salons in the last year to feel entirely comfortable with the generalization.

I was thinking about this while waiting for Joey in the Giddap Bar and Grill. He said he'd meet me after boiled beef and bingo. He swore he'd be there by 11:00 P.M. The guy at the next table winked when I asked the hour for the third time, and thought I was looking for action. No doubt about it, hanging around Joey was expanding my horizons as well as my sense of time. I was operating on three hours' sleep. I'd been with him practically all day and I hadn't even gotten to ask a question yet. My notebook was empty. My mind was blank. I didn't know whether to hate him or pity him or laugh at him or, at midnight, when he still hadn't shown up, give up on him.

It was a strange kind of disorientation. I came to the Colonnade to confront what I had been and what he had been to me. But you can't confront the past if it keeps standing you up.

So I sat there, curled up in a dove-gray love seat on a mauve carpet looking at happy foursomes sitting at dove-gray tables in knock-off Marcel Breuer chairs, imagining that's where I sat when I was twelve and Joey was my hero and the Giddap Bar and Grill was called The Plantation. Of course, there was no way to know. There was no hint of what went before in the place, none of its colors or geometry. And yet, even though none of it was as I remembered, it was completely familiar. My past had become the ubiquitous present. I had been in this place before, all right. But not *here*. I had been there everywhere. That's when it hit me.

Gray! Pink! The mousing of America!

It's a design statement, all right. Probably it was even an original idea once. But now it's just a trickle-down interior. It's as if the great tan middle class decided all at once to get cool, to get single. Tan is families. Tan is station wagons. Tan is a relationship. Gray is bloodless, uncommitted, chickenshit. Gray is the eighties before AIDS. Gray is mouse.

"What's so funny?" Joey said, plopping himself down in a dove-gray love seat next to mine. He was looking a little dove-gray himself.

"Nothing," I said.

I had my tape recorder and notebook out on the table. This, too, was a statement. Joey ordered a rye and a Sambuca, which was another, and put his bum leg up on the table next to the pretzels and the tape recorder and the notebook filled with unasked questions.

"Saw your picture in the paper the other day," he said.

"Oh shit."

"Stick got ya, huh?"

He said it so matter-of-factly, as if everyone knew, when in fact everyone who knew didn't believe me. "He does it with tranquilizers. Keeps a bottle of that shit in his locker. He did it to me once."

"You?"

"Yeah, me. Our last year together on the Yankees. Right before he got traded. He got bored with dildos and rubber snakes and started zapping guys. Funny guy, Stick. Me and him used to do all kinds of shit. One time, in Cleveland, he had these animal squirt guns. There was like a window in the clubhouse under WILL CALL. The ticket line ran right over the grill in the pave-

ment. Me and Stick used to squirt girls' pussies. Shit. None of
'em ever knew what happened. Just suddenly they were wet."

Joey laughed and laughed at the thought of all that wet
pussy. "Stick got traded the next year for being a bad influence.
And, of course, an asshole."

I ordered a beer and another round for Joey Proud.

The tape recorder was turning now. Joey ignored it. "Feel
this," he said, taking my hand and placing it on his ankle. The
tendon was tight, lumpy. Joey frowned. "Doc says I need another operation. Hip replacement or some such shit. What's that
song? 'The hip bone's connected to the thigh bone'? Doc says the
ankle screwed up the knee. And the knee screwed up the hip. All
those games. Now this. I'm dreading to do it. I don't want no
more operations. I thought I'd be dead by now."

He talked about his pop, who never played any ball but boc-
cie 'cause he had a hole in his heart, and how they took him home
to Brooklyn to be buried, and how the doctors said these things
are often congenital, which, in addition to the rye, is why he
figured he'd be dead by now. I had my chance right then to ask
about his son, but I didn't. There's always a question you don't
want to ask, which is the question they don't want to answer,
which is why guys like Sal always tell you to ask that question
last. That's good advice, but my heart doesn't stop racing until I
ask it. I figure it's not really fair. I know what's coming and they
don't. I asked Joey about the game instead. "Do you remember
the moment? Do you remember running down to first?"

"Sure," he said. "It was like my life snapped in half."

"I was there. I was nine."

"Yeah?" he said.

Joey looked at me different for just a moment, as if I existed.
Or at least I thought he did. Anyway, it was just enough to make
me go on. It all came out in a rush of memory and hoped-for
connection. "My grandmother lived behind the Stadium on Wal-
ton Avenue. I could see centerfield from her window. Or I
thought I could. I mean, I wanted to. Her building was called the
Yankee Arms. It had a coat of arms in the lobby, a white glass
background with two blue bats crossing like swords."

"What's her name?" he said.

"Delia. Her name was Delia. She's dead."

"Oh," he said. "I never knew my grandma."

"She bought me my first glove. Helped me sneak it into

Temple on the High Holy Days. I watched the Yankees from the window."

"What's that building up on the hill?"

"Which one? There's two. The Concourse Plaza, where we went to Temple, and the Bronx County Courthouse."

"The courthouse. Yeah. Some cocksucker used to stand up there on the step with a mirror and shine it in the visiting teams' eyes. Hell, it was like looking at lightning. You couldn't see the fucking ball. Hell, you couldn't hit it out in centerfield anyway."

He ordered another rye, another Sambuca.

"You did. You hit it out of the Stadium."

"That's right," he said. "I did. Once."

He reached for his ankle. "It snapped," he said. "And Pop died. And nothing was the same ever since."

I asked about the dreams. Mantle had them, too. Recurring dreams. Of failure. Of banishment. Dreams about falling out of the sky. "I read once where Mickey had this dream that he's late for the game and he can hear Bob Sheppard announcing him," Joey said. "You know that voice. 'Now batting, Number 7, Mickey Mantle.' But he can't get in the Stadium. The door's locked. And the fences and the gates, too. And he can see Casey and Whitey and Billy all looking around, waiting for him. And he hears Bob Sheppard again. 'Now batting, Number 7, Mickey Mantle.' But he can't do nothing about it. He can't get in the game.

"After I read that magazine article, I started dreaming it, too. Every night. Every fucking night."

He shook his head at the irony. Mantle's heir. Mantle's fate. Mantle's dream. Even Joey's nightmares aren't his own.

A fat guy stuffed in a baby blue tux thrust a menu in Joey's face. "Just write: 'To Herb, one of the best, from one of the best.'"

Joey smiled and signed. "It's my job. Boiled beef and bingo. Joey Provenzano does the Borscht Belt."

"You farted when I asked you for an autograph."

"I did?"

"Yep," I said.

"Well, shit. I'll give you one now," he said. "And I won't even charge you. I get paid to be a mensch."

The waitress brought another round. She was dressed in black. Black lace stockings. Black halter. Black cowboy hat to signify she worked the Giddap Bar and Grill. She had a Bic in her holster, which was longer than her skirt.

"C'mon back," Joey said, reaching for her as she walked away.

She waved over her shoulder and he shrugged. He was slurring his words. It was late. I told myself, "You can ask about his son tomorrow." I closed my notebook and started to collect my things. "Stay," Joey said.

And then his hand, his thick slugger's hand, was on my knee. Not my knee really. My thigh. There's a world of difference between a knee and a thigh. A knee can be interpreted. A thigh means business. Especially that tender, vulnerable inside part where Joey Proud's hand was holding on for dear life.

I tried to look at this hand objectively, like any other hand trespassing upon my person. It was a large hand; thick, that is. It had rivers of veins and gullies between the knuckles. It was an American landscape, this hand. And it was moving north, toward trouble.

"Scared I was gonna pull on your titty?"

That's what he said, wasn't it? And I *was* scared. Scared that he'd say what he did; scared that he'd do exactly what he was doing.

"Please," I said, meaning "Don't."

He didn't hear. He wouldn't have heard Bob Sheppard announcing his name. The man whose career statistics I had engraved upon my heart, the man for whom I wore Mary Janes on Opening Day, the man who farted when I asked him for an autograph outside Yankee Stadium, was passed out dead drunk in my lap.

The Giddap Bar and Grill was empty now except for the cocktail cowgirl, who was sitting on a stool watching Charlie Rose interview Charles Manson. It was a little bit hard to get her attention, given that I was pinned in a dove-gray love seat beneath two hundred and ten pounds of Americana. On the one hand, it was pretty funny being pinned under an idol. On the other hand, I couldn't move. So I sat there with Joey Proud in my lap, waiting for someone to notice.

Luckily, Manson quit yammering at Rose and the cocktail cowgirl was a responsible waitress. "Another round," she said, before sizing up the situation.

"Coffee," I said.

"Squeeze play," she replied.

Apparently she knew both baseball and Joey. She pursed her lips and pulled Joey out of my lap and loosened his tie. "I'm all right," he kept saying. "I'm okay."

"*He's* all right," she muttered as if I wasn't there. "He passes out in her lap and tells her *he's* all right. Well, thank you very much, Mr. Joey Proud."

We poured four cups of coffee down Joey's throat and I gave the cocktail cowgirl a twenty-dollar tip. I think both of us were wondering why we were taking care of him. She told me that when Joey's in the hotel they keep the bar open specially for him. The waitresses draw straws to see who gets Joey duty.

"He's my hero," I said. "He hit on me."

She nodded. "That's what they all say, dearie. That's what they all say."

We got him to the hall, and Joey propped himself up against the mirror between the elevators. The mirror was smudged with fingerprints, guests who had left a trace of themselves there in the glass. Joey bowed his head against the ephemeral graffiti. His cracked lips caressed the cool surface. I watched his breath cloud the mirror with moisture and I watched him suck it in again: in and out, in and out. Each time he inhaled, his image came clear in the glass and I was sure of everything. *The bastard jumped my bones and I hate him.* Then he breathed again and I was confused.

They were old-fashioned elevators with a semicircle of a clock above the doors and a big ornate black hand marking the whereabouts of the cars. All but one were resting resolutely in the lobby. Car Number 4 was parked two floors below us in the basement.

I reached under Joey's arm and pushed the button. Minutes passed: two, three, four. I wasn't about to walk to the eleventh floor, and Joey couldn't. I pushed the button again. Finally the green light above car Number 4 blinked on and the black hand began to move. Joey looked up and smiled at both of us in the mirror. "Oh well," he said. "You know Stick always called me Mouse. Said I was hung like one."

He was laughing when the elevator door slid open. There before us stood a man and a woman in an ancient embrace, which in high school we used to call a hand job.

Joey looked at me as if to say, "See." But all I could see was the headline as Jimy Boy Collins fell to his knees, pecker in hand, and raised his voice to heaven. "Sweet Jesus, I have sinned."

"Sweet Jesus, what's that smell?" Joey said.

Once, a long time ago, my parents sent me away to summer camp, a place not too far from here. It was the summer Mom left. So I was not exactly a happy camper. The girls were all nice Jewish girls and the counselors were all nice Southern Baptists. I returned home to Richmond eight weeks later, saying, "I beg your pardon" and knowing how to spell "masturbation." I learned then and there you could get away with murder if you were polite about it. Manners are a definite plus when you've got Jimy Boy Collins groveling at your feet and a voice-activated microcassette tape recorder in your pocket.

"Reverend Collins, I'd like you to meet Joey Proud."

"Oh my God," Jimy Boy said. "Oh my sweet Jesus."

"A pleasure," said Joey, who actually sounded sober, though, of course, it *was* a sobering sight.

"A. B. Berkowitz, the Washington *Tribune*," I said, extending my hand to Jimy Boy's companion, which was a little bit bitchy considering that she was busy stuffing her boob back under her red-sequined spaghetti strap.

"Jimy Boy just calls me Lola," she purred. "He always says, 'Whatever Lola wants, Lola gets.'"

"Oh my God," Jimy Boy said.

"*Queste e-culo,*" Joey said.

Sal always says there are some stories that write themselves. This was one of those. I sat on my bed in my underwear and wrote:

The Rev. Jimy Boy Collins, owner of the Christian Fellowship Entertainment Network, Super Stars Ministry, and the Washington Senators, fell to his knees seeking divine forgiveness, as an elevator carried him and a female companion to their penthouse love nest for what was to be an evening of illicit passion.

Collins and his companion, who identified herself only as Lola, were caught in flagrante delicto when the elevator door of this once posh Catskill resort hotel opened, revealing their compromising and impassioned embrace. "Get your hand out of my pants," Collins was heard to say.

Joey Proud, the former Yankee centerfielder, was waiting for the elevator when the door opened. "I guess Jimy Boy got the shaft," Proud said.

Proud, Director of Special Events/Sports at the Colonnade Hotel, added, "I am appalled and disappointed. Reverend Collins is a man of God, as well as a baseball man. Baseball was a family game in my day, which is to say last year."

Collins remained on his knees in the elevator, begging forgiveness and pleading with this reporter not to disclose what he called "thy servant's humble failing," despite Proud's exhortation to "get up and act like a man."

"I'll give you anything you want," Collins told this reporter. "I'll call Monk. I'll give you complete access. I'll call off the pickets. *Anything.*"

At Collins's direction, the Senators have refused to speak with this reporter on the grounds that women in the locker room are, in the words of manager Monk McGuire, "an abomination." In recent weeks, supporters of Collins have picketed outside the offices of the Washington *Tribune* demanding that this reporter be fired.

Told that the reporter could not promise to withhold the information, Collins responded, "You little bitch. I'll get you for this."

"Down, boy," Proud said.

"Jimy Boy!" Lola said.

"I'm ruined," Collins said.

Jimy Boy Collins is known as a crusader for moral purity. He has long campaigned against what he has called "the malignancy, the cancer, the lesion, and the pus of sin." He came to prominence in 1981 as the lead singer of the Christian rock band the True Believers, best known for the hit song "Jump Back, Jesus." In the mid-1980s, Collins founded the Super Stars Ministry, a Christian athletes outreach program, whose stated goal is to "go to bat for the heroes who go to bat for the Lord."

This is the second major crisis of the season for the troubled franchise and its beleaguered owner. On Opening Day, outfielder Stick Fuller exposed himself in the locker room in front of the President of the United States. Collins pronounced Fuller a "social malignancy" and fined him $10,000. Fuller promised never to do it again.

I don't know how late it was when I finished writing. Late enough, anyway. All I needed was a couple of quotes from Stick and the commissioner and I could hit the DONE button. I was too wound up to sleep and too sleepy to do anything else. There was no one in good conscience I could call except maybe the desk clerk at the West End Motor Court by the Lake. I dialed the number and asked what time it was.

The desk clerk was not amused.

"It's the least you can do, unless of course you've found my watch," I said.

"What you say, lady?"

"My watch. I checked out yesterday. Room 113. Did you find a watch?"

"You crazy, lady? You know what time it is?"

"No, of course not, I don't have a watch."

"Shit, lady, it's three-thirty in the morning. You gotta call back tomorrow. I don't know nothing about no watch."

At least I knew what time it was. But that just made it harder to sleep. I wasn't eager to take any more Halcion. But I didn't want to be alone either. I dialed Michael and remembered he is in Boston, taking his mother to visit his father's grave. His father died ten years ago today. Went at his typewriter just the way he said he would—only twenty years too soon. The paper ran the unfinished column as it was. God: I should be there with him. I should have at least sent flowers. I wonder if you can send flowers at three-thirty in the morning.

I called Ruth and woke her up. "They stole my watch, Ruthie, and then he jumped my bones."

"Joey stole your watch?"

"No, he only jumped my bones."

"You have a moral hangover. Go to sleep. I love you," she said.

I sat by the window and looked at the mountains, their peaks shrouded in darkness, and started to write this all down. It's not too often you go one-on-one with the illusions of childhood. I want to get this right.

The night is clear now; the air is so fresh it almost hurts to breathe. The wind has driven off the clouds and the moon is a sliver of illumination, hanging there against the sky.

217

It's a crescent moon. So bright: like a dagger of light, daring me to look away. I can't. But I can't focus, either. I am looking too hard. But for what?

Wait a minute. I've seen this before, the summer Mom left. It's weird, eerie. Lurking there in the moon's radiant glow is a faint intimation of the whole. Astronomers call it "earthshine," an earthshine moon. I looked it up once. It isn't what it seems. It's indirect illumination from the sun to the earth to the moon. Earthshine. Much-traveled light. It's always there, the astronomers say. The truth of things always is. Just sometimes we don't notice or bother to look or know what it is we're looking at.

There's earthshine on my pillow. I should sleep, I know. But who can sleep with earthshine in their eyes? Not me. So I'm sitting here instead thinking about what I have seen, or was supposed to see or just plain didn't notice in the banal light of day.

Ugh. I'm sounding like an English major again. So much for keeping it light, tight, and bright, huh?

When I get tired like this, I want things to mean something, just like when I was little and I wanted coincidences to mean something. Earthshine has to mean something. It's trying to tell me something. Not to settle for a sliver of gaudy illumination when the whole is waiting there in the darkness to be found? Sounds like a crock of shit to me.

And yet. There's an arrow of light cutting across the blanket, pointing the way to a heap of clothes at the foot of my empty double bed. My 100 percent virgin Orlon acrylic JOEY PROUD/ MILLER LITE INVITATIONAL HEART FOUNDATION GOLF CLASSIC tournament sweater is bathed in earthshine. In this light, the baseball over the heart almost looks real. It looks like it's about to fly out of the Stadium and into the night. It is spinning. Or maybe that's just me.

So this is it, huh?: 100 percent virgin Orlon acrylic idols in 100 percent virgin Orlon acrylic clothes. Maybe that's all there ever was, synthetic heroes who jump your bones and promise more than anyone can deliver. Then again, he did give me the sweater, which was the only one he had.

I'm pooped. I do not know which light to trust. In the morning I'm going to have to ask him about his son.

July 15, A.M.   In retrospect, it was the sound of the empty tape that told me everything I needed to know about Joey

Proud's son. Sometimes you listen so hard for the words, you forget about the sounds. *Whoosh! Thwack! Thwack! Whoosh! Thwack! Thwack! Whoosh!* It is the sound of a rented stretch white limousine with rye sloshing in fake crystal decanters doing eighty down the highway; the sound of rubber pressing hard against the joints in the road. *Whoosh! Thwack! Thwack! Whoosh!* It is the sound of the fast lane, the sound of life on cruise control. It has its own rhythm, its own hum. It is the hum of recycled air, of motel rooms with windows that do not open, of ballparks that banish the sun. It is the hum of insulation. *Whoosh! Thwack! Thwack! Whoosh!* I listened to that tape, waiting for the answer that I now know by heart, and watched the numbers on the counter. *Whoosh! Thwack! Thwack!* And I decided finally that it is the sound of life passing you by, though nestled in the backseat of a rented limo doing eighty down Route 17, you might be forgiven for thinking you were passing it.

I asked him about his son. Six minutes and 32$\frac{1}{2}$ seconds later, Joey said, "Leave him out of this, you hear?"

Whoosh! Thwack! Thwack! Whoosh!

All the time his fingers were dancing in the air, reaching for an unseen bat, trying to get a grip on what he remembered of safety. His thick slugger's hands, which had reached for me the night before, now reached for the safety of the bat and the soothing rhythm of a swing.

Whoosh! Thwack! Thwack! Whoosh!

A single tear made its way down his cheek and splashed onto his lime-green JOEY PROUD/MILLER LITE INVITATIONAL HEART FOUNDATION GOLF CLASSIC pants. Joey Proud reached for the rye and grew silent again.

Whoosh! Thwack! Thwack! Whoosh!

It was five-thirty in the afternoon. I had been awake since seven, when I sat bolt upright in bed, scared once again I had overslept, roused by anxiety. I called Sal and told him what I had on Jimy Boy.

"Do you know what time it is?" he said.

"As a matter of fact I don't, but just listen anyway," I said. And he did. "Holy shit," he said. "Write the sucker."

"I already have."

"You got notes?"

"I got tape."

"Holy shit."

Sal said to hang with Lola and Jimy Boy until I heard from

him. Dr. D would get quotes from the locker room. Milo would columnize. The entire City side staff would stake out Jimy Boy's office and I would be back on the beat when the team returned home on Monday. "If you're gonna write that thumbsucker on Proud, you better do it this weekend," he said.

I sat outside Jimy Boy's door on the thirteenth floor of the Colonnade Hotel, studying the royal-blue carpet with the gold and silver design that still looked as if a chandelier had been smashed into it, and waited for Lola and Jim. I sat there all morning and didn't move except to call room service or the front desk to ask the time. At 1:00 P.M. Jimy Boy emerged, took one look at me, and said, "Jesus Christ," in a tone that was less than holy.

Lola appeared a half hour later carrying a stack of eight-by-ten glossies and pulling one of those collapsible baggage carts stewardesses use. "Actually, I'm an actress," she said, handing me a stack of pix. She said she met Jimy Boy two years ago at an Athletes in God banquet in Richmond, where she was part of the general entertainment, greeting guys, looking pretty. She had been seeing him ever since, usually once a week, and never in Washington.

Of late, the Colonnade had become their home away from home. Jimy Boy told her no one would ever look for him here. At first she had doubts about their relationship, but Jimy Boy assured her "there was nothing wrong with giving succor to the Lord's messenger." He told her the Lord whispers sweet nothings in his ear and he would whisper them in hers. Also, he promised her a job as the emcee's sidekick on the Christian Fellowship Entertainment Network talk show, "Bible Banter." Of course! I knew I had seen her somewhere before. Lola Lord! The born-again Vanna White.

"Anyway," she said. "Look at the bright side." Lola is one of those people who only look at the bright side. "He may be a fornicator, but he likes girls and he isn't even kinky." Seems Jimy Boy prefers the missionary position.

I called in the quotes, faxed the glossy, and dictated an insert. Sal got on the phone and said, "You bagged the fucker. Grab the limo."

So there I was sitting in the backseat of a rented stretch white limousine making another grown man cry.

Whoosh! Thwack! Thwack! Whoosh!

"It was supposed to be *me*," Joey said. "It *shoulda* been me."

All his life Joey played as if his heart was sure to break. And it did. He just didn't know it could break this way. "Jesus," he said. He was whispering now. "It was *supposed* to be *me*."

He reached into his pocket for his wallet and pulled a snapshot from the billfold. It was a picture of a little boy in a YANKEES shirt that reached all the way to the floor and his father's YANKEES cap. Just barely you could see the toothy grin under the bill of the cap. Just barely you could see his ribs through the cloth. "He was always such a skinny little fucker," Joey said. "Tall but thin. You know. Didn't weigh more'n thirty-five pounds when he was six. I remember 'cause that's the year he said he was gonna play ball. I laughed. 'Yeah, sure, Big Guy.' But, you know, what the fuck?

"So I took him to spring training and he hung around with me, which his mother didn't like one bit, and looked after my bats. He was the worst bat boy ever. He kept bringing everybody the wrong wood. Finally he brought Andrews, the shortstop, one of Blake's corked bats. So Andrews hits this mammoth home run. I mean, he hit the ball small. And so all spring the little cocksucker walks around like Charles Atlas or something. Thinks it's 'cause he bulked up over the winter. I think he hit .400 that spring with that bat. Finally somebody told him when we were breaking camp that it was corked, and he went 0 for 24 to start the season. Never came out of that slump. Got traded the day after the season ended. Joey was crushed.

"Anyway, we came north, and my first off-day I took him out for Little League. He was a tough little mother. All these kids are all over me, asking for autographs, pulling on my arm. Joey's out there trying to catch fly balls. He dropped six in a row, if I remember right. The manager says, 'No problem. No problem. We're glad to have Joey Proud's son on our squad.'

"It was the third game of the season when Joey got sick. Just passed out cold sitting on the bench. They took him to the hospital in his uniform and called my wife. The doctor said, 'Come quick, it's his heart.' Said he was born with it. Some kind of congenital anomaly, he called it. Just like Pop. My wife stayed with him the whole time in the hospital. I was on the road.

"Anyway, that ended his ballplaying days, which was just as well. Doc said probably he would be okay, but you never know. That's what he told my wife anyway. When I talked to him, he just shook his head. Joey was happier after that. I guess being sick meant he could be himself instead of Joey Proud's son. He

221

was president of his math club and on the chess team too. My girls, they play ball."

For an instant, a smile flickered across his face.

"Last year, him and me took Momma back home to Italy. She said she wanted to see Bari again before she died. She's been saying the same damn thing for twenty years. 'Take me to Bari, Joey. Take me to Bari.'

" 'Momma, Momma,' I said, 'you're strong as an ox, you're not going anywhere yet, Momma.'

"Joey, he says, 'C'mon, Pop, let's go. I want to see the old country.'

"So we go and I'm like some major fucking deal hero, even though I never been there before. They had this Joey Proud Day in the town square. Joey did the introduction. In Italian. Been studying the whole goddamned year so he could introduce his pop in his grandma's hometown in Italian. And I didn't know nothing about it.

"He's a smart little fucker, all right. It's just there wasn't nothing I could show him. Hell, he showed me."

Whoosh! Thwack! Thwack!

"Now they got him hooked up to all these machines. My wife's there all the time. The girls too. I can't barely look at him. He won't die. And the doctor says he can't live."

"I'm sorry," I said.

"Everybody is. I don't like to talk about it 'cause I don't like to act like a faggot. It really—"

Joey flexed his fingers again, grabbing for the air. His thoughts, whatever they were, lodged in his throat. For a minute I thought he might gag on the guilt and the sadness and the symmetry of his pain. He ran his fingers along that imaginary bat and closed his eyes to whatever demons he saw, losing himself once again in the pure, sweet solace of sport.

Three minutes and thirteen seconds later, he said, "Mickey called."

"Mantle?"

Joey gave me this look like: "Of course Mantle, who else?"

"Yeah, Mantle," he said softly. "He offered to come up here and play in my tournament. Help raise some dough. Says he knows what it is to have a sick kid. Mickey had a sick kid, you know."

I nodded.

"Great guy, Mick," Joey said. "He was my hero, you know.

When I was a kid, I wanted a cowlick just like his. I wanted everything just like his. Now I got everything 'cept the restaurant on Central Park South. Pretty funny, huh?"

Whoosh! Thwack! Thwack! Whoosh!

Joey let a few cars and a few minutes go by. And when he spoke again, it was of safer, greener things. "Did you see the paper today? Where are the Yankees? They got beat by somebody. Milwaukee. That's right. They're in Milwaukee."

He reached for my glass. We were at the Harriman Interchange by then, going south on the New York State Thruway. In the glare of the headlights, Joey looked seventy years old. "You're slowing down," he said.

"I'm not supposed to drink. Remember?"

"Me neither. But I'll die of something else first. When you've led the league in the crabs six straight years . . ."

The chauffeur, who hadn't heard that one before, began to laugh. "Hey, Joe, *che si dice,* Joe?"

"Not much," Joey replied. "Just sitting around waiting for the last rites."

We cruised down the Thruway onto the Major Deegan heading for midtown. I caught a glimpse of Yankee Stadium and imagined, for just an instant, that I could see the Concourse Plaza Hotel where from the second-floor ballroom I had prayed for Joey Proud. But the Stadium was dark. The Yankees were in Milwaukee. And as quickly as it came, the vision was gone.

In an hour, my story on Jimy Boy will hit the streets in D.C. Six hours ago, Joey was escorting a twelve-year-old girl to her birthday party. Her grandma had called. Said she was dying. And the one thing she wanted most in the world was to meet Joey Proud. He was bringing her a painting of himself; a reproduction of the watercolor on his baseball card.

"Maybe I can fuck her," he said cheerfully.

"Maybe you can," I said. "And I'm sure that's exactly why you're going."

Joey laughed—caught red-handed doing something nice.

"*Queste e culo,*" he said.

"*Queste e culo,*" I replied.

He got out at Mamma Leone's and told the chauffeur to take me anywhere I wanted to go. He gave me a picture and the autograph I had waited for since I was six years old. It said, "Sorry I farted. Your friend, Joey Proud."

D.C.

August 1   Well, I'm a hero.

All I had to do was catch Jimy Boy Collins with his righteous Christian dick in the wrong place and suddenly everyone's calling me Scoop and Ace and picking up the check. It's been this way since I woke up, which was about two weeks ago, if I remember right. Actually, I don't remember much between Joey getting out at Mamma Leone's and me waking up at Michael's two days later.

I always wondered what it would be like to wake up an overnight success. I guess everybody wonders about this, the way you wonder who's going to show up for your funeral. Well, anyway, I wonder about it, and let me tell you it's sweet. Also, it's exhausting. In the last two weeks, I've done every major morning show, except Geraldo, one three-hour sit-down with somebody from the *Washington Post* Style section, and twelve telephone interviews, the first of which woke me that morning at Michael's. Otherwise I probably would have slept another thirty-two hours. All I remember is this manic drive-time voice saying, "We're back live with *Trib* reporter A. B. Berkowitz, who this week exposed, heh, heh, heh, Senators owner Jimy Boy Collins. Good morning, A.B.!" I haven't got the faintest idea what I said.

Since then I've been wined, dined, and schmoozed. I've done

lunch with five agents, all of whom swear they can do me a deal unlike any other deal that's ever been done. And I've been invited to Ross Mitchell's country estate for a dinner honoring the nonvoting congressperson from Guam, which is why I am sitting in the backseat of another stretch white limousine, stuck in traffic on I-66 listening to René de Georges tell me I'm hot.

"You're hot, A.B. I'm telling you, you're hot. I'm talking book. I'm talking movies. I'm talking cassettes. I'm talking novelization. I'm talking Books on Tape. We'll have you and the preacher man in every frigging car in America!"

René de Georges is a five-foot-one albino literary agent in black horn-rims and elevator shoes. He called yesterday while I was trying to finish the piece on Joey and said he absolutely positively had to see me. I told him I didn't have any time, what with Ross's dinner tonight and going back on the beat tomorrow. This produced a panic in his voice which was particularly grating and made me wonder if I sound that bad when I'm desperate. René suggested we ride out to Middleburg together, and I figured what could it hurt. I told him to pick me up at the office at 4:00 P.M. I had some last-minute stuff to do and I was running a little behind. So about four-twenty, I come bouncing down the front steps in this strapless number with my Radio Shack on my shoulder and my strapless bra sagging and a brand-new pair of rhinestone fuck-me shoes wobbling under me. I'm looking up and down the block for this albino person, who is nowhere to be found, and sweating bullets and cursing the albino for being late and myself for agreeing to meet him, when this old black guy opens the door to the stretch with a flourish and a bow and says, "Miss Berkowitz, ma'am?" René was waiting in the backseat with outstretched arms and a crystal tumbler filled with Stoli on ice.

You want to know what it is to be hot: two weeks ago I'm riding shotgun in a limo with Joey Proud's favorite rye sloshing in the decanters. Today the decanters slosh for me. René de Georges may be a dweeb, but he sure does do his homework.

So here we are stuck in traffic on I-66. René couldn't be happier inasmuch as he's got a captive audience. I'll say this for the guy, he talks a good game. "We're talking bucks here, A.B. We're talking Big Bucks. I guarantee we'll do six figures. I'm not even talking mass market."

Suddenly René was digging into his Mark Cross wallet, and for a minute I'm thinking he's gonna start laying fifties on me.

But he whipped out his business card instead and his Mark Cross pen and scribbled some numbers and stuck it back in his breast pocket and put his sweaty little palm over his heart and said he's never done this before but if I don't get at least that much hardback he'll buy me lunch anywhere in the United States.

"Write this book and you'll never have to worry about working for a newspaper again. Your career will be set. Magazines will pay a fortune for your frigging byline. You'll be the first female columnist in *SI*. Of course, I'm going to need a manuscript by November. We have to get this shit out by spring. I know it's quick. But you can do it. All I want to do is see your name on the cover of the book. Baby, you're such a star."

Then he stopped and this look came over his face and for a second I thought maybe he was having a heart attack. Uh-uh. He was having a vision. "I got it!" he said. "We'll do a musical. That's it! A musical! We'll get Sondheim to do the music and Michael Bennett to direct. No, wait, he's dead. Anyway, it'll be a smash! We'll have a chorus line of guys in jockstraps and tap shoes, genuflecting and singing Jimy Boy's praises."

René waved his arm across some unseen panorama just the way they do in the movies when you're about to get your name up in lights. "We'll call it *Fastballs*."

For a second I could almost see it too, which was scary. René sank back in his seat as if he'd just had a major orgasm and pulled a pack of Gauloises from his pocket. "Mind?" he said. "Yes," I replied. Success has made me brave.

Anyway, René finally shut up about fifteen minutes ago after I told him I had to think about all this and I would get back to him as soon as I had things sorted out. I have to say the book idea appeals to me. Maybe these guys are right: maybe I can turn this diary into something, in which case I better get this all down now because once I get back to the beat the shit will undoubtedly hit the fan. So here I am again sitting in the backseat of a stretch white and trying to write without throwing up.

It's funny. I've written this story so many times I know the lines by heart. Only this time it's about me. *Q: "Are you pinching yourself to see if this is real?" A: "Yeah, well, Andy Warhol said we'd all have fifteen minutes and this is mine."* Of course, if the interview subject is a ballplayer the answer is a little different: *"No way I'm gonna get the big head. I put my pants on one leg at a time just like everybody else. I'm a regular fucking individual."*

I always kind of hoped my fifteen minutes would be occasioned by some serious civic-minded story, the kind that earns public affairs awards, like uncovering roaches in baby food. Something Ruth would have written. No such luck: Jimy Boy's degradation is my ticket to fame and fortune. Ruth keeps giving me shit about the wages of sin as if it's my fault or something. I guess I'm supposed to feel ambivalent about this. I don't. I've been waiting a hell of a long time to hear my story quoted on the morning news and have Sal say, "You really hit that sucker out of the ballpark," as opposed to "In my office, now, Berkowitz!" Besides, it's not as if the cocksucker doesn't deserve it. Why else would he be off on an "indefinite retreat"? Jimy Boy sure as hell isn't consulting the Almighty about his stock portfolio.

Ruth says I'm acting defensive. You bet your sweet ass I am. I'm going to ride this sucker as long and as hard as I can, even if it does mean listening to René de Georges yammer for three hours. Michael's been terrific, or he was until he started getting heat from the higher-ups about that stupid drug story he's been working on. You know what he did? This was the morning I got back from seeing Joey, the morning I woke up, that is. He left this jewelry box under my pillow with a ring from a Cracker Jack box and four real silver quarters. In honor of my scoop, he had put my story in the windows of both *New York Times* boxes.

I guess these days for a newspaper stiff there isn't any sweeter sound than the soft metallic slurp of change sliding down the gullet of a newspaper box. It's not quite *"Extra! Extra! Read all about it!"* but it is still a heady *quid pro quo*. Ego gratification is rarely so immediate or so fleeting as it is in newspapering, which is how editors get writers to produce. Sometimes, and this is embarrassing, I watch people standing in front of the *Trib* box at the corner skimming the morning paper and read over their shoulders, hoping they'll notice or tell me to get lost so I can engage them in conversation and see whether they've read my story. Pretty screwed up, huh? That's one reason why most times I don't even read my stuff in the morning paper. Also, I can't take my own words on an empty stomach. I read my stories later in private, where I can pretend I'm Harold Brodkey giving a reading at the 92nd Street Y.

But not this time. This time I leaned out of bed and saw Jimy Boy's plaintive puss staring at me and a headline in 150-point type: JIMY BOY SINS! My name was almost as big. I plunked a real silver quarter in the slot and spent the morning reading my own purple prose aloud and contemplating just how to go about

Working the Room. Working the Room is not something one does often or lightly. One does not Work the Room after a day hit, for example, or even after a front-page piece if said piece was a mortal lock to get on the front, like for instance on Opening Day of the baseball season when a star slugger jerks off in front of the President of the United States. The truth is: I had never Worked the Room before. Not consciously anyway.

There are two basic ways to go about it. There is the subtle get-there-before-everyone-else-and-sit-at-your-desk-pretending-to-write-expense-accounts approach, which has the appearance of comely humility. It is low-key but effective. Michael specializes in this. Then there is your basic noblesse-oblige-grande-dame entrance. This means waiting until everyone else has arrived and sweeping boldly through the newsroom, the way Bette Davis would, accepting the accolades as your due.

I chose the middle ground, somewhere between unbecoming modesty and all-out chutzpah. I wandered into the office about 2:30 P.M., just after everyone got back from lunch, and headed straight for the meat scale. A nice touch, I thought. A just-one-of-the-guys gesture. Rocky was the first to notice. "Yo, look who's back, Miss Borscht Belt herself."

"Bags one dickhead and goes to sleep for a week," Vito growled.

It is axiomatic that the amount of shit you take is in direct proportion to the size of the scoop. Nobody ever says anything nice in the Sports Department except in private. "What'd she have to give Proud for the quotes, that's what I wanna know?" Zeke said as if I wasn't standing there.

"Big fucking deal," Vito said, grabbing his crotch. "I wanna hear about Jimy Boy. Man's got small hands, don't he?"

Dr. Deadline, the departmental arbiter of taste, told Vito to crawl back under his rock. Milo hugged me where I stood on the scale. Sal shook my hand and said he liked my outfit, a pair of three-year-old stonewashed jeans and a TRIB T-shirt. This from a man who once sent me home for wearing a $150 Fiorucci denim dress to an interview. Unbe-fucking-lievable. Sucker didn't call me "Berkowitz" all day. It was all sweetness and light and "A.B. this" and "A.B. that." Son of a bitch gave me a twenty-five-buck-a-week raise—a nice little nest egg, he called it—and said I should sit my ass down and write the hell out of Joey Proud 'cause when I'm finished I'm going back on the beat.

I've been milking this sucker ever since. Yesterday Sal came by Marcus's desk, where I was hunched over the lede, and said, "What are you, Thoreau? This is a goddamned newspaper. Hit the fucking DONE button already. You're back on the beat. Now." So of course I ended up writing all two thousand words yesterday. Nice piece, if I do say so myself. It runs Sunday.

I guess you could say everything was just about perfect until the shit hit the fan with Michael. He got beat on this drug story last week. It really wasn't such a big deal, just some street punks gunning each other down at 3 A.M. on the Mall over a vial of crack. He's been playing catch-up ever since. Understand: the editors of the *Tribune* consider crack their own personal domain along with killer caddies (as in KILLER CADDY RAMS K MART, yesterday's headline) and killer bees and just plain killers. Michael's second-day story had nothing new, but it had the nice understated head: TOURIST TERROR GRIPS MALL.

Anyway, three days after the story first broke, a cop down at 3-D told Michael that one of the punks who got away wasn't really a punk after all but an honors student at Wilson High School, a national merit scholar. Seems the kid was just trying to keep big brother out of trouble. Cain and Abel stuff. A nice story, but so what? Michael made a stupid mistake. He told Rosenthal, the city editor. Rule number one is never tell an editor something you can't write. Rosenthal spent six hours trying to persuade Michael to use the stuff as a blind quote. He even typeset the headline: HIS BROTHER'S KEEPER. Michael threatened to quit if they put it under his byline. Ten minutes before deadline, Samuels, the managing editor, finally decided not to go with it, but only after reaming Michael out for being gutless and allowing himself to get trapped by a source.

Michael's been in a bad mood ever since. I keep telling him he'll be all right just the way he always tells me. Last time I said it, he told me to knock off the holier-than-thou shit and go give another interview to *GQ*. Ruth thinks he's jealous. But then she always thinks the worst. She's been predicting disaster ever since we got together. "Won't work. Competition. Screw a consultant," she said.

I can't believe he'd be jealous of anything I did. He's the only Pulitzer Prize winner on the staff other than Milo, who doesn't count because he's just a sportswriter. And still the editors are all over him about a stupid-assed honors student. Newspapers: What have you done for me lately?

So last night Michael went drinking with some cops he

knows in P.G. County, hoping to come up with something on the "Mall Massacre," as we now call it. He called at 10 P.M. all excited because he got some majordomo in the department to say on the record that one of the other kids who got away is the son of a Maryland congressman who was scoring some toot for Dad. This is a whole different ball of wax than some tearjerker about a straight-A student. Michael said he had to make some calls and file and not to wait up.

This morning the clock radio woke us with the 8:00 A.M. news. The lede was a denial of Michael's story by the same guy who had sourced it. Michael was ripshit. Samuels was on the phone two minutes later telling him to get his ass on down to the paper pronto. Michael promised he'd meet me at Ross's by 7:00 P.M. I hope like hell he gets there on time. I hope like hell we get there in time. We haven't gone a mile in the last fifteen minutes and I'm beginning to sag all over. Jesus, this bra is killing me.

August 2   Michael didn't show. The son of a bitch stood me up at Ross Mitchell's fucking Middleburg estate. I can't fucking believe it. He never even called. Ruth's right. He is jealous.

Ross's place is one of those former plantations with a driveway as long as the street I grew up on and little brass horses on painted brick pedestals and a butler with white gloves who actually announced the guests as they were ushered into the front hall. "Miss Ariadne Berkowitz and Mr. Michael Holliday," he intoned. Except of course, there was no Mr. Holliday, just a social-climbing albino in black horn-rims and elevator shoes waiting in the limo. It took René about ten seconds to figure out the look on my face and to get his ass on out of the backseat and to my side, where he gallantly presented himself as my savior and escort. Before I knew it, the butler was announcing, "Mr. René de Georges," and the albino had his arm around Dolly Mitchell, Ross's wife, and was calling her Dolly-Baby and encouraging her to write her memoirs. I've seen that socialite smile before. It looked like a frozen daiquiri.

The whole thing was a nightmare. The main course was liver wrapped in veal, my bra kept falling down, Ross took me aside and told me I shouldn't curse so much trying to be one of the guys, and René got drunk and kept introducing himself as my "great, good friend." I couldn't wait to get out of there. It was close to 1:00 A.M. by the time I got home. I don't know what

233

hurt worse, my feet, my side where the bra had dug a trough a quarter-inch deep, or my pride. I hate that word "pride."

I was limping down the hallway when I noticed Michael propped up outside my door with an empty six-pack and a bag of Cheez Doodles. It was our night at my apartment. We always stay at my place the night before I leave for a big road trip. "Lost my key," he said.

"And your voice? What about your voice?"

"Huh?"

"You could have at least called."

"Called? My whole fucking career is going down the toilet and all you can think of is 'You could have called.' Since when did you get to be Miss Manners?"

He followed me around the apartment ducking as I threw various items of my wardrobe in his general direction. "Ross was expecting you."

"So now it's Ross, huh?"

"C'mon, Michael. Grow up. They invited you to dinner. You come. You laugh it off. You kick ass the next day."

"Thanks for the show of sympathy," he said. "I *really* appreciate your support."

Michael was tearing his clothes off too now. I threw down my bra. He pulled off his pants. And so on until we were both stark naked, bellowing at each other. Maybe in the movies we would have ended up in bed. But any chance of a romantic conclusion to this particular episode vanished when I said, "It's not the end of the world. I mean, it's not like you're being picketed by Jimy Boy's Holy Rollers or something."

One of the first things I noticed about Michael was the way his veins pop out of his head. He's got this one that cuts across his right temple and throbs whenever he's on deadline. Call me weird, but I'm a sucker for a man with throbbing veins.

Suddenly the vein on Michael's right temple was beating triple time. "Fuck you, Ari. You're really an asshole, you know that?"

When Michael gets really ripshit pissed, I have the uncontrollable urge to laugh. It's a reflex learned in families where anger is urgent and belated and fierce. Michael was ripshit. I started to laugh.

"Jesus Christ. You bitch. Remind me to write you a lede on deadline again sometime soon, will you?"

He had a point. I could have conceded as much and ended

the whole thing. I could have held his hand, kissed his vein, been his friend. But I didn't. I blew him off. I said, "Listen, Ace, is it possible that what's going on here is that you're just a little pissed that for once I don't need your help, that old A.B. finally got on the front all by herself? Is that why you decided to rain on my parade?"

Michael's vein stopped throbbing. "I don't need this shit," he said. "I'm going home."

"In case you forgot, I'm leaving for two weeks in the morning."

"I didn't forget," he said over his shoulder.

He marched out of my apartment stark naked under his nine-year-old London Fog raincoat, leaving his clothes all over my floor.

Baltimore

August 3 The security guard outside the visitors' locker room at Memorial Stadium has a nose approximately as wide and as shiny as the patent-leather beak on his official eight-pointed Pinkerton cap. He is also six feet seven and maybe 150 pounds. His name is Gump Jablonski and he works very hard at looking imperious, which is hard to do when you've got his physique and a name like Gump. I've actually seen the guy salute some of the players on their way into the locker room. The man is a fool. But he takes his job seriously. It's an awesome task standing sentry to America's heroes.

So there I was first day back on the beat, bopping down the hallway toward the clubhouse, when Gump stepped in front of the door, his bony hand raised like a traffic cop, and said, "Ladies' Day today?"

Trouble *inside* the locker room is something I have come to expect. Trouble getting *into* the locker room is something I am no longer prepared for. "Huh?" I said.

Gump gazed down that nose of his and wheezed. I could see the little hairs inside his nostrils quiver at the exercise of his full powers.

Either he didn't recognize me or Ross and Sal are right—

Jimy Boy is going to make my life miserable as long as I cover the Washington Senators. All week they have been prepping me for my return, warning me about lousy tips on stories and spiked cocktails. They've been like a couple of high school football coaches psyching me up for the big game against county. "Next thing you'll be eating live frogs and chewing glass," I told them. Now suddenly they didn't seem so ridiculous.

Gump demanded to see my credentials. I demanded to see his superior. He held my BWAA press card up to the light, all forty watts of it, feeling its texture, reading the fine print, looking for telltale signs of forgery. His nostrils flared again. "Which paper did you say you was from, missy?"

"Which planet did you say you were from, asshole?"

This was definitely the wrong tack to take and added at least twenty minutes to the inquisition, which proceeded through channels while he called upstairs to verify my existence and otherwise kept me cooling my heels in the hall. A half hour passed. My colleagues waltzed by without bothering to acknowledge me except under their breath. MacKenzie murmured hello. Girard grunted, I think, but it might just have been a belch. I kept hoping one of the players would come by and tell me to get fucked so that I could prove who I was. But they were all out on the field or jerking off in the shower.

In the distance, I could hear the clank of bats and the banter of batting practice: "Yo, fuckface!" Baseball was just down the tunnel in the sun. I decided to make a break for it. But Gump caught my elbow with a bony claw. "You ain't going nowhere, missy."

I told him to take his goddamned hands off me, and put my head against the wall. First Michael. Now this. *God!*

The halls of Memorial Stadium have a unique dinginess to them. They are beige or once were and are lighted by bare bulbs in steel cages that look sort of like catchers' masks. The walls have been painted and repainted so many times that every blip of paint that began as an errant drop twenty-five years ago has been magnified into a high-gloss growth. The walls look as if they've metastasized.

When drops of paint start looking like tumors, you know you're in trouble. Damn Gump. Damn Michael. And damn the Washington Senators. God, I had no idea how much I was dreading this.

When you stop to think about it, going into a locker room

full of naked men you do not know is not really a very normal thing to do. Which is why you should never stop to think about it. And I wouldn't have if Gump hadn't stopped me and given me time to think about the weirdness and the grossness and the timed farts and the hairy balls. If you do this for a living and you do it every day, you repress the weirdness and the grossness and act as if you belong. You have to act as if you belong because baseball players are real sensitive when it comes to prudishness, which is to say they won't tolerate it. They have an unerring instinct for uncovering propriety and abusing it. Berkowitz's first rule of baseball reporting is: she who hesitates gets sick to her stomach. The corollary is: she who hesitates gets whomped.

It hadn't occurred to me that I would hesitate. It hadn't occurred to me that after more than a month away from the team I was no longer inured to this assault on my sensibilities. And not just my sensibilities. How about my person? The last time I saw these assholes I was dead drunk at their feet. My God, I could feel the dry heaves all over again.

I braced myself against the metastasized wall. I was sober, too sober, but suddenly dizzy. It was the vertigo of an "ace" reporter falling from an unaccustomed height. All my assumptions had been turned upside down. I steadied myself, one leg tucked behind me like a townie, and considered the possibility that I no longer wanted to watch them spit on each other's post-game meals or piss in each other's Lavoris or hang buggers from each other's name plates. For the first time ever, I understood why Ruth keeps asking why I put up with all this shit.

Just when I was coming to grips with the notion that maybe it was okay to be an outsider, that I didn't have to be one of the guys, Gump handed me back my press card and said, "Okay, missy, you're in."

I took a deep breath, stumbled over the threshold, and looked for the first friendly face.

"Yo! A.B! Dudical!"

Billy Blessing, called up from Triple A in my absence, got down on his hands and knees and laid a carpet of smelly white towels at my feet to welcome me back to the Show. I plopped myself down in his chair, normally a significant breach of locker room etiquette, and sucked wind, as football players say.

"You look like shit," he said.

"Good to see you, too," I replied, though he couldn't have

known how much I meant it. I was buying time, trying to regain my equilibrium. "How's it feel to be back in the bigs?"

"I'm just happy to be here," Billy said. "I'm just gonna take things one game at a time, and with the Good Lord's help everything will turn out okay. Like my hair?"

I was only half listening, trying to settle my stomach and get acclimated to that alluring scent of day-old sweat and liniment. I hadn't even noticed his new hairdo: a flattop circa 1958 in honor of Bill Mazeroski. But Billy got my attention when he started talking about his roommate in the minors, who was into butt fucking and went and got himself laid between games of a doubleheader while everybody else went to McDonald's. "Guy didn't even take a shower. He just comes back in the dugout and we're all going, 'What's that smell?' But that wasn't nothing compared to the day he got this girl to give him some skull while he was taking a shit.

"That's when I bought the Caddy. The transmission was shot, so I had it towed over to the stadium and moved in. It was nice and roomy and it smelled a lot better than he did. Bought a couple of rolls of Reynolds Wrap heavy-duty aluminum foil and draped the windows. The seats were that nice plush velour and went all the way back, so I slept good and I was never late for practice."

If ever there was a moment of divine intervention, this was it. Clearly, God wanted me to laugh. And soon enough I did. By the time batting practice was over, I almost felt back to normal.

Players straggled in, and except for an occasional raised eyebrow no one acknowledged my presence except Stretch. "Look see what the cat drug in," he said.

I think he was actually glad to see me until he remembered that he wasn't supposed to be. Piggy shot him a look and Stretch got all tangled up trying to figure out who to apologize to. "Gee, sorry, Dad. I mean, sorry, A.B. Good to see ya. Gotta go. Ya know."

It was just like old times: no one was talking to me.

I knew I could count on Billy to bring me up to date. "Well, let's see," Billy said, surveying the room. Buck's locker was empty. "He's in the shower," Billy said. "He's always in the shower, staring in the mirror counting his follicles. He's getting this hair transplant and he won't even take off his cap for the National Anthem 'cause he's got all these weird corn rows. Monk takes him aside last week and says, 'Son, if you're gonna play for Monk you're gonna bare your head for the goddamned stars-and-bars. I don't care if you are Rookie of the Year, boy. I want that fucking cap across your fucking heart. And I want to hear all the fucking words, too.' Buck was too polite to point out that the stars-and-bars belonged to the Confederacy. Anyway, the next day Monk comes out of the dugout before the anthem and stands with Buck out in leftfield to make sure he sings. Buck hummed."

"Unbe-fucking-lievable."

"Buck's lady put him up to it, the hair, I mean."

"Lady?"

"Yeah, you know that speech therapist you interviewed. She called Buck up offering help. They've been doing it ever since."

"No shit."

"No shit," Billy said. "Now the Stick, on the other hand, he's sleeping pretty much full time with his gamer. He got a new shipment of bats in last month engraved with PUSSY POWER on the barrel. Lawson got a petition together declaring the bats un-American and demanding that Stick disassociate himself from them. Stick says, 'No fucking way. There's a lot of hits in that wood.' Lawson told him he'd burn in hell if he didn't burn the bats. Stick says he doesn't give a shit as long as he's still hitting dingers, which of course he is."

As if on cue, Stick emerged from the john—flaccid. "Guess he wasn't expecting me," I said.

"Nobody was. They had a pool going whether you'd show. Me and Rump was the only two who said you'd be back."

"How is he?"

"Batting .200 and doing impersonations of Robin Williams pretending to be Abdul-Jabbar."

Sure enough, a few minutes later Rump emerged from the trainer's room wearing a catcher's mask rigged with bifocal goggles inside. Billy sighed.

"Guttierrez still hasn't stolen a base. Mancusi still can't bend over. Bobby Damn Jenkins still says 'Damn' every time he gives up a walk or a dinger, which is often. Lawson still can't hit Uncle Charlie. And Henry Aaron Poussaint still can't figure out why God made him a pitcher."

"What about Stein?" I asked.

"Still in love. Jell-O Goddess got some moves. She even bought him one of them cellular phones so he can phone in his bets from the dugout. But I don't think it's gonna last. Seems

Mrs. Stein, the *ex*-Mrs. Lawson, heard about the romance from the *ex*-Mrs. Stein, who as we all know is Mrs. Lawson. So the two got together and trashed Stein's little love nest in the hotel one day on our last road trip. Smeared the walls with Jell-O, as I hear it. Rump says Brother John put them up to it."

"Jesus."

"You can say that again. And oh, by the way, Brother John is providing spiritual counseling to his ex."

I was about to inquire after Ricky Himeshi when the Gaijin himself waddled through the door, bowing and smiling and looking like a baby Buddha swathed in double-knits with a thirty-six-ounce bat sticking out of his back pocket. "Oh my God," I said. "What is that, ballast?"

"Yup," Billy said. "And it's the closest he's come to an at bat in a month, too. Pound for pound, he's the fattest benchwarmer in the history of major league baseball. Jimy Boy's going to have to eat his contract."

"Providing Ricky doesn't eat it first," I said.

"And providing Jimy Boy ever comes out of hiding," Billy said. "You sure did put the fear of God in him, A.B."

"Yeah, and the commissioner, too."

The commissioner's office finally announced today that he was beginning his own personal inquiry into the Jimy Boy Collins affair and he would have no further comment on the "uh, matter" until the investigation is complete. I guess I can stop calling him every day.

"So what else is new?" It was beginning to be fun again.

"Of course, you've heard about the first ever official Washington Senators intelligence test?"

"Can't say as I have."

Billy reached into his duffel bag and dug out an iridescent orange folder that had a stencil of a javelin thrower on the cover and the words GET TOUGH THROUGH UNDERSTANDING, which it turns out is the motto of the Foundation for Competitive Perfection. "We gotta get tested to see why we're such big fucking losers. I'm supposed to have this shit done by game time. I gotta shower and tape. Hey, you wanna take the test for me?"

It seemed like a lark, not to mention a good story. Billy said I could write it if I didn't name the player who gave me the test. So I sat down and gave the answers I figured a jock would give. There were eighty questions in all. Billy had done the first thirty or so. It was kind of like the SATs, but for jocks. Multiple-choice and all that. Some of the questions were just plain stupid, like: *"I have never had an off-day on the field. A. True B. False C. Unclear."* Some of them were there to find out just how stupid you are: *"I participate in sports because I hate them."* My personal favorite was *"I know a few athletes who are a little weird even though they don't know it. A. True. B. False. C. Can't remember."* I chose C.

By the time I got through all fifty questions, the locker room was about to close. Girard, MacKenzie, and Brenner left, trading quotes and ignoring me. I glanced around the room. Guttierrez winked. Rump nodded. Mancusi said, "Yo."

Monk arrived, striding through the locker room, clapping his hands. "C'mon men, let's get our heads out of our assholes! We have a goddamned ballgame to play."

Billy pulled on his cup, his jock, his clean sanitary hose. So what if the team is 22–77 and on pace to lose 120 games? So what if the Vegas boys are taking over-under bets on the Senators chances of being the worst team ever?

Billy pounded his glove and grabbed his crotch. "Play ball!" he said.

Milwaukee

August 4 Occasionally, like maybe once a season, they still play baseball on a weekday afternoon. This way, they don't have to throw the word "hooky" out of the dictionary and baseball can still call itself family entertainment. These always seem to be the most beautiful days of summer, maybe because they are so rare, with soft clouds and softer voices that carry on a perfect breeze. *"Hey! Peanuts!"* *"Beer here!"* *"D.C. sucks!"*

These are days of loosened ties and high-pitched cries. *"We want a hit! We want a hit!"* Pitchers doze in the bullpen sun, taking in some rays. You can see them out there through the chain-link fence, cleats up, caps perched precariously on heads, seeking the perfect angle to the sun. Ballplayers are very serious about their tans. In the old days, they didn't have to work so hard at them. Night games have put a crimp in their style. Now it requires some thought and diligence to acquire that deep leathery hue like the pocket of a well-oiled glove. Milo says you can always tell a ballplayer by the color of his neck. It's the color of a sunset with deep white crevices that darken inning by inning as they fill with the dirt of the game.

Day games. These are the days consecrated to remembering our better, slower selves. Or so I thought until today.

Game time was 1:05 P.M. By twelve-thirty, Stretch was sunbathing by the bullpen fence in deep leftfield with Rump sprawled beside him. They made a forlorn couple. Stretch has been banished to the pen after giving up sixteen runs in his last two starts. Rump has been benched against righties. No one's even talking about his playing his way out of his slump anymore. Also, there is some hope that by baby-sitting Stretch in the bullpen, Rump can somehow talk the wildness out of him and thereby be of some use even though he's only hitting .189.

By the bottom of the first inning, Stretch was seemingly sound asleep, eyes raised toward heaven behind his reflector shades. He had positioned himself not just at the perfect angle for the midday sun but at the perfect angle for what used to be called beaver shooting. Beaver shooting is catching snatch. Snatch is pussy. Pussy is wool. Stretch is a leading member of the Washington Senators' wool patrol.

There are precious few places left in the major leagues that allow for beaver shooting. Along with unobstructed seats, this is one of the truly dreary improvements made by the spacious modern ballpark. Relief pitchers now warm up in pristine sanctity far removed from distraction. Except, of course, here in Milwaukee, where the stands hover over the bullpen and eye contact is still possible.

By a ballplayer's standard, this was truly a propitious occasion: sun, beaver, and a whole night off to hound the beef. No wonder Stretch was smiling.

It was the bottom of the third when he awoke with a start and gazed up at a vocal young baseball fan with a forty-inch bust, give or take a few feet. She was wearing a Spandex BREWERS T-shirt. "Oh my Lord, will ya get a look-see at that," Stretch said, nudging Rump with his million-dollar arm. "I think I like to died and went to heaven."

"It's Milwaukee and the bottom of the third," Rump replied.

"Son, you got no imagination. That slump is going to your pecker."

Stretch waved. Ms. Milwaukee grinned. The Brewers scored three off Arroyo.

By the bottom of the fourth, Stretch had decided this was the real thing. Being a chivalrous sort, he declared his love by scribbling an impassioned plea in red ink between the seams of an official American League baseball and heaving it into the stands, six rows and fourteen seats to the right of his intended. Like I said, Stretch is mighty wild.

But it was one of those perfect days and the romantic citizens of Milwaukee generously and decorously handed the ball from row to row and seat to seat, each reading its heated message of love and desire until finally Ms. Right clutched it to her ample bosom and murmured the word "Yes" loud enough for the entire bullpen and most of the leftfield bleachers to hear. What the ball said was "Relievers are *always* ready. Be my honey now. Stretch."

So it was that Big Foot Harrison and Pete King and the rest of the horny Washington Senators bullpen corps helped Ms. Milwaukee out of the stands and into Stretch's valuable arms. She was flushed and giggling. Stretch was debonair. "I think we should be alone," he said and escorted her to the bullpen bathroom for privacy. The door slammed shut. The Senators tied the score in the top of the sixth. No one in the bullpen seemed to notice.

Ballplayers being ballplayers, there was some hooting and hollering and banging on the urinal door. But then the bullpen phone rang in the bottom of the sixth and Monk told Big Foot to get loose and he and Rump had to go to work. So Stretch and his lovely were pretty much left in peace until the bottom of the eighth.

It had been a pretty good game up to that point, which is to say it wasn't a blow-out. Any game the Washington Senators are in after the eighth inning is already a moral victory. It is also very unusual, which explains why they're leading the league in complete games and fewest saves. Normally, the bullpen phone rings early and often or not at all. In all fairness, Stretch was entitled to presume he had the afternoon off.

He was wrong.

Buck hit his second home run of the day, his eighteenth of the year, in the top of the ninth to break the 3–3 tie. Of course, Big Foot had to make things interesting. He walked the leadoff batter in the bottom of the ninth and Monk got on the horn and told Piggy to get Stretch warm fast.

This presented Piggy with a true moral dilemma. He

couldn't very well tell Monk that his son, the star reliever, was banging some girl in the urinal. On the other hand, knocking on the door and telling his son to come out with his pants up and his arm loose wasn't something he particularly wanted to do either.

"'Scuse me, son," Piggy began politely, knocking timidly. "There's a man on first and Skip wants you to get loose just in case."

There was no reply, unless you count squealing as a response. Piggy knocked louder. The count went to two balls and a strike on the second batter of the inning. The bullpen phone rang again. "I say, son, c'mon on outta there. Skip says Big Foot walks this guy and you're in the game."

Piggy pressed his ear against the urinal door and blanched. Rump says Stretch groaned loud enough that they would have heard it at home plate except for the fact it coincided with ball four.

Monk shuffled to the mound, carefully spitting on either side of the baseline as he always does when truly pissed, and took the ball from Big Foot, and the public address announcer said, "Now pitching for the Washington Senators, Number 29, Stretch McCarthy." In the bullpen Piggy screamed, "Get your talleywanger in your pants, son, you're in the game!"

"Talleywanger?" said Pete King.

"Talleywanger?" said Rump.

"Talleywanger," said Piggy.

At which point the urinal door banged open. Stretch's double-knits were still down around his knees. "Don't worry, Pop," he said. "I'm warm."

Of course, I didn't know any of this at the time, but it did seem odd to see Stretch sprinting to the mound, considering he never moves faster than a country lope. Rump told me later that Stretch took off right quick 'cause it looked as if Piggy might chase him all the way to the rubber. Stretch took his warmups, a couple of which sailed ominously over Fennis's head, and immediately called time. You know how it seems as if the first thing a ballplayer does when he gets in the game is grab his crotch, usually right on camera as the color guy is announcing his stats? Well, Stretch calls time, signals Fennis he wants a conference at the mound, turns toward the bullpen, and reaches down, ostensibly for the resin bag. Stein comes in from first and Mancusi from third. Not wanting to be left out, Mini-Doc and Guttierrez join the conference at the mound, most of which they cannot understand. So Stretch makes it easy for them, gesturing broadly to his groin, prompting speculation in the press box that he had pulled something warming up. Monk actually ran out from the dugout. There was lots of gesturing and stomping of feet. Stein was holding his side as if he had a hernia. Through my binoculars, it was easy enough to read the umpire's lips: "Play ball, you fuck." In his haste, Stretch had forgotten to put on his jock and he was feeling just a little bit vulnerable.

Robin Yount stepped in. Stretch's pitch sailed all the way to the screen. The second and third sailed behind Yount's head. Ball four bounced between his legs.

Bases loaded, no men out. Somehow, maybe simply in self-defense, Stretch induced the next batter, Greg Brock, to swing at the first pitch. It was swing or be castrated, I guess. Anyway, the guy hit a come-backer right at Stretch. He had what baseball announcers like to call all the time in the world. Stretch considered his options. Fennis stood at the plate screaming, "Here, you cocksucker. Throw it here!" Stretch nodded and heaved the ball into the Milwaukee dugout, scattering the victorious Brewers like duckpins.

Stretch's only postgame quote was "Well, fellas, I guess I just got all balled up today."

Later, Rump and I had dinner at this old German place downtown. We ate sauerkraut and drank dark beer and he told me the whole story and I almost choked on my bratwurst, which seemed somehow appropriate. I couldn't wait to get back to the hotel to call Michael. This is the kind of stuff he loves.

There was no answer at home. So I called the office at 11:00 P.M.

"It's me," I said.

"Can't talk," he said. "I'm on deadline."

He hung up before I could even say hello. I guess he's madder than I thought. And maybe he has a right to be. But shit: Isn't he the one who's been telling me for a year that it's okay to get mad, that we don't have to be Mom and Dad, that he isn't going to melt if I tell him to go to hell? Finally, I trust someone enough to get angry and look what happens. He hangs up on me. So much for the perfect summer day.

August 6 Monk pinch-hit for Rump yesterday with the winning run in scoring position. Today he sat Rump down for both ends of a doubleheader. Against two lefties! Rump owned these guys—until today that is. Sal says there are rumors all over town that Rump will be released by the end of the week, when Jimy Boy is supposed to come out of hiding for the Second Annual Super Stars Ministry banquet. Sal's sources say he's going to announce Rump's retirement at the banquet as your basic red herring. They swear there's some kind of buyout provision in Rump's contract. Rump swears he's got three years guaranteed. Guess who I believe?

Sal's source is probably one of his poker-playing buddies. Sal's real famous for putting their words under our bylines. So I asked him, "Who says?" He gets all uppity on me and says, "I've got to protect my sources." Yeah, right.

He wants a piece saying Rump is through. He wants it yesterday. Everybody else in town has already written it. Hell, Girard wrote it in June. We're late and I know why. I don't want to write it. Even if his sources are full of shit, I can't put Sal off much longer. I'll get Rump tomorrow in Detroit, or maybe tonight on the plane after he's had a beer.

Detroit

August 8   *"Et tu?"* Rump said.

He was sitting at his locker icing his knees. He wasn't in the starting lineup yesterday. He wasn't in the starting lineup today, and he won't be in it tomorrow. But still he was icing his knees because he always ices his knees. For sixteen years he has been icing his knees and not to ice his knees would mean accepting something he isn't prepared to accept. The ice told me everything I needed to know.

There was a bag taped to the elbow of his throwing arm and one taped to his shoulder and another strapped to each knee. And they were leaking. They were *all* leaking. Every once in a while, Rump would take the bags off his knees to inspect the damage. They were red and icy except for the scars, which were white and raised and endless. The surgeons had given Rump's knees a whole new topography, a landscape of pain.

"You're late on it, you know, Berkowitz. Everybody else wrote me off a month ago."

"Yeah, well." I stared at the fissures in the speckled linoleum, cracked and chipped from generations of cleats. It was easier than confronting the truth.

"Yeah, well, nothing, you let your personal feelings get in the way of a good story. You fucked up, Berkowitz."

"What are you, my editor? And what's with this 'Berkowitz' stuff, anyway?"

Rump yanked the ice pack off his elbow and heaved it into the garbage can across the room. Stein cheered. "Best throw all year. Way to go, John-Boy."

Rump ground his molars and threw another pack at Stein's back. It missed.

"Well, here's a scoop for you, Berkowitz. Get it all down 'cause I'm not saying it twice. I'm not quitting until Jimy Boy does. And that cocksucker can't buy me out no matter what he's telling the *Washington Post*. The contract is ironclad."

He unraveled the Ace bandage from his shoulder. "What else?"

I guess they all get asked this question sooner or later, and I felt foolish for being the only asshole to agonize about asking it. Shit, guys have been asking him, guys have been telling him he's through for months. And he isn't one of those who don't read the papers: RUMP'S A GONER! DOUBLEDAY HISTORY!

So why was I standing there studying the ripples in the linoleum and trying to think of a way not to hurt his feelings? I'll tell you why: because I let my personal feelings get in the way of a good story, which almost pissed me off enough to ask it hard and direct, but not quite.

"I remember one time in spring training you said only utility guys know when to quit 'cause they're the only ones who know how hard it is to get here. I mean, you said the great ones never do. Isn't it possible—"

"Of course it's possible," he snapped. He was naked now except for the towel across his waist and the ice on his knees. "But I come from the Do Not Go Gently school of catchers. Jimy Boy personally is going to have to peel this uniform off of me."

Rump and I have been doing these lit-crit riffs for a while now. He started it one day in early April after I made the mistake of asking Stein if he thought losing was endemic to the

Washington Senators. "Yo, Stick, she says losing gives you enemas" was Stein's translation.

"Ooh, baby, sounds good to me," Stick replied.

Rump overheard this enlightened exchange and has been giving me shit about it ever since. "*Endemic?* You think anything's *endemic* to Stein? The only thing *endemic* to Stein is flatulence."

Now when we talk on the record, Rump tries to quote every book he ever read and I try to stump him with what he likes to call my college words. It's sophomoric but it's ours, and it's a helluva lot better than "We gotta keep our heads up and play 'em one game at a time."

Interviewing is a funny thing. Sometimes it's Twenty Questions. Sometimes it's free-association. With Rump, I do a whole lot of free-association. Still, I was surprised to find myself standing there quoting *Macbeth* to him. It's the only Shakespeare I know by heart. I had to memorize it in order to graduate from high school.

" 'Tomorrow, and tomorrow, and tomorrow, / Creeps in this petty pace from day to day, / To the last syllable of recorded time; / And all our yesterdays have lighted fools / The way to dusty death.' "

Rump spat sunflower seeds at my feet. "What are you—Lady Macbeth? 'Yet do I fear thy nature.' If you have a question, just ask it."

My cheeks flushed. Ballplayers talk to reporters like this all the time. But not Rump. Not to me. He turned away and began rummaging through his locker for tape. Rump always tapes. Sixteen years of taping before games have left his shins hairless and raw. It's a ritual, like icing, and like icing, he wasn't ready to do without it. "Where's the fucking tape?"

He was swearing too much. Rump never swears. There was something he wasn't saying, something he'd been keeping to himself too long, and I was just pissed enough to ask. "Something else is going on. You know what the reason is, for the slump, I mean, don't you?"

Rump wrapped the tape around his ankle tighter and tighter. Circulation was an impossibility and an afterthought. His voice was choked, too. "You're good, Ari, and you're right," he said finally, quietly. "But not now. Okay? Please."

"But."

"Drop it. Drop it now. Can't you people ever leave me alone?"

You people. "You people" is what ballplayers call reporters when they mean the opposite. "You people" means "you scum." Rump was the one guy who always treated me like a person. Now suddenly I was "you people." Maybe I deserved to be.

I thanked him for his time, which is what reporters say when they mean the opposite. What else could I do? Worse, what could I write? I could hear Sal's voice all the way up to the press box. The voice of daily journalism: "Whaddya got, Berkowitz?" "Write what you know, Berkowitz." "I thought Doubleday was your boy, Berkowitz."

All I had was a sick feeling in the pit of my stomach. All I knew is that I didn't have the slightest idea what was going on.

We were scheduled to play two, a twinight doubleheader. I told myself not to worry, I had lots of time. But lots of time is a terrible thing to have. I remember reading this interview with Red Smith once. The guy asked him how long it took to write his daily column. "As long as I have," Red said. He also said writing is easy: "You just open up a vein and let it out drop by drop."

Red Smith was a bleeder. I'm a twirler. I twirl my hair around and around my index finger like a baby getting ready for a nap. I literally get tied up in knots. I didn't know I did this until one time I was covering the National Spelling Bee and they had the press room set up in a banquet hall with beveled mirrors. I looked up after "eustomachic" and noticed I was going bald.

By the bottom of the fifth inning of the second game, I had written two paragraphs. Two paragraphs! My right index finger was numb and I had a pile of hair on my scorecard. I was hopelessly blocked. Upon reflection, and it has to be upon reflection because deadlines don't allow for anything but reflex, I have noticed that I usually get blocked after two paragraphs. For two paragraphs, you dazzle them. Then you've got to get to the point. Getting to the point can be a real problem, especially when you don't know what it is. Sal doesn't like "I don't know." Sal likes definitive. RUMP IN THE DUMPER is his idea of definitive.

By ten-thirty, I had given up twirling and I was pulling my hair instead. I read and reread those two graphs. I read them to myself. I read them aloud. I even read them to the press box attendant, which is truly low. I critiqued every comma and nuance.

"Rump Doubleday will not go gently when it is his time to

go." I knew Zeke would hate that. But tough shit. "And it appears that the All-Star catcher's time with the Senators is growing perilously short. Sources close to the team say that owner Jimy Boy Collins, who has been in seclusion and incommunicado since mid-July, will announce Doubleday's release from his three-year pact this week." A nod to Sal. "But Doubleday, who defiantly taped himself for a doubleheader he knew he would not play, refuses to capitulate to either Collins or time.

" 'I'm not quitting until he does,' Doubleday said. 'And that bleeper can't buy me out no matter what he tells the *Washington Post*. The contract is ironclad.' "

Not bad for two graphs.

At midnight, I looked up from my screen. The press box was empty. I was alone, talking to myself, pulling my hair, twitching but otherwise immobilized. It's hard to explain how this feels. It's panic for sure. All the time you're thinking, *"You're a scribe. Scribes produce. Scribes do not stare at the same two paragraphs for eight hours."* And you keep looking at the clock and the numerals bulge and quiver as deadline grows near. Pretty soon, it looks as if the twelve is going to explode or maybe it's just you. Your chest contracts. Your fingers stiffen. You do things that later you don't remember, like chewing off all the nails you just grew. You do things that later you regret.

At 12:03, I called Michael.

"Holliday!" he said, which is how he answers the phone when he's really right on it. I started to blabber or blubber, I'm not sure which.

His voice was dangerous, quiet. "Look," he said, "I'm your lover, not your editor. And right now I'm not much interested in being either one."

I swear to God it couldn't have been more than a second after he hung up that I realized what day it was. I grabbed the paper to make sure. August 8, 1989. Michael's thirty-third birthday.

When I called back thirty seconds later, the phone rang and rang until finally a news aide grabbed it. "City desk! Holliday! For you on thirty-five!"

There was a pause and some muffled conversation. "He's on deadline," the aide said. "Try back in an hour."

I don't know what I wrote. Reflex. I wrote reflex. "Make the deadline. Get something in. Get *anything* in." I sent Zeke sixteen inches at 12:23 A.M. and had him transfer me to Michael. It rang and rang and rang until the same exasperated voice came on the line. "Holliday's gone," he said. He did not wait for a message.

I still had a game story to sub out and a notes column to send. It took another hour. The good news is that I didn't get locked in the press box again. They don't lock the press box anymore in Detroit, the legacy of my night with Dr. Deadline. I took the stairs behind home plate and turned to see the vast expanse of Tiger Stadium illuminated by a single bank of lights. It looked as if a UFO was about to land in centerfield. The concourse was damp and empty except for red-and-white-striped popcorn carts still half-full and hot dog stands that still smelled of boiled water and kielbasa. My shoulders ached and my fingers were cramped, the residue of writer's block. I was too tired even to bother to try to evade the puddles of mustard and beer. I zigged and zagged my way down the ramp. It didn't occur to me to think about how I was going to get back to the hotel until I faced the parking lot littered with broken glass and peanut shells and yesterday's scorecards. The only sign of life was the weeds growing through the cracks in the concrete. A sign said: NOT RESPONSIBLE FOR ANY COLLISION OR DAMAGE OR THEFT OR FIRE TO YOUR CAR.

The security guard's box was empty. He was either making his rounds or sleeping on a couch somewhere. In any case, there was no point in yelling for help. So I stood there with my junk at my feet squinting into the fluorescent light of the guard's bulletproof box and wondering what to do. There was a phone inside and an open bag of Fritos. Maybe he'd get hungry and come back. A half hour passed; he did not get hungry. I pressed my nose against the bulletproof glass and looked through the window onto Trumbull Avenue on the other side. There was a line of cabs at the Checker Cab Company a block long, all of them empty. Trumbull Avenue looked as desolate as I felt.

Tiger Stadium is in a part of Detroit that has lately been given the name Corktown so that everybody will stop calling it a slum. This is in a city where they shoot people on freeways. And I wasn't even a moving target. Two people were killed downtown after the 1984 World Series. I remember Milo telling me about standing on the roof of the stadium and seeing an overturned taxi cab in flames. Things got so bad the owner of the club had to helicopter pizzas into the stadium for everyone trapped inside.

Tiger Stadium is the kind of ballpark that makes people

spend $100 million to build some spanking-new facility—new arenas and ballparks are always called "facilities"—in places with names like Richfield and Landover, which are places only because someone thought to put a facility there. I hate facilities. Or I did until tonight.

I don't think I've ever been so alone. No one knew where I was and everybody else wasn't talking to me. I told myself the guard would be back soon. I told myself a cab would happen by. I tried to guess who would be assigned to write my obit and killed time writing headlines announcing my own demise: REPORTER DISMEMBERED AT WILL CALL!

I sat down on the curb and my foot fell asleep. I stood up and hopped in place, which probably would have looked pretty funny if anybody had been watching. I stamped my foot and peered through the guard's shack again. It was two in the morning. I saw a cab cruising down Trumbull Avenue. It was no ordinary cab. It had a lime-green skull spray-painted on the fender and the driver's name in iridescent orange on the door. CAR FOR HIRE. RASHID B, PROPRIETOR.

There are moments in life that require nothing less than a leap of faith. My choices were clear. Either I could sit on the curb all night dreaming of dismemberment or I could take my chances on Rashid B.

"*Taxi!*"

Rashid B reached over his shoulder and threw open the door. "Rashid's my name, rap's my game. Where to?"

Like some other teams scared off by the inner city, the Senators stay out in Dearborn. The hotel was twenty-five minutes away by freeway. I told myself: "Either you'll be in bed in a half hour or they'll have to tear up the front page."

I sat back, closed my eyes, and hugged my computer. I heard Michael telling me to get fucked. I heard Rump telling me to get fucked. I heard . . . "e-e-e-e-e-i-i-i-a-a-a-a-a-a-a-o-o-o-w-w-w!" It was the aural equivalent of a chainsaw massacre. Feedback pierced the night. Guitars wailed. Or was it a distant siren? My feet vibrated against the floor. Chalk on a thousand blackboards would have been more sweet. Finally the dissonant howl subsided and a leering bass took its place. It was an emphatic beat like a percolator coffeepot gone apeshit. Rashid B began to growl.

"I wear *black* and I always will 'cause I'm dressin' for your *fu-ner-al*. I wear BLACK and I always will 'cause I'm dressing for

your FU-NER-AL! *I* WEAR black AND I ALWAYS WILL
'CAUSE I'M DRESSING FOR YOUR fu-ner-al!"

I peered out the window. The freeway was nowhere in
sight. The bass pumped but no louder than my heart.

"I WEAR *black* AND I . . ."

It figured to be a slow death. Rashid B did not appear to be
in any hurry. In fact, if anything we were lurching toward my
fu-ner-al. Rashid B was keeping time with the accelerator.

Michael will write the obit, I decided. For a moment I savored his guilt and lost myself in his remorse.

Then: I heard a siren and a trumpet's fanfare. I came to. I
had no fucking idea where I was, but I knew I had spent a lifetime avoiding it. Trumpets blared again. "Don't be sad! Don't be
smarmy! We all party in the Devil's army! Sound off! *Funk-y!*
Sound off! *Sweet* thang! Sound off! Sound off! *You* all!" Suddenly
Rashid B was doing a cappella Marine rap. "It's Judgment Day
and I'm feeling fine, / I'm checking out the fella with the Satan
sign / *down* / By the river Styx / *Get down* / wherethe *funk-y* mix
/ Movin' down slowly / *Waitin'* for the heat / Devil's got to
boogie / He's got hot feet! / *Oooowwww!*"

This was hell, all right. The street was bleak and pockmarked, the macadam long ago replaced by old railroad ties that
had been tarred over one hundred times along with the municipal promises to fix whatever had been the problem. And empty.
So empty. "Lift your heads and hold them high, *Rashid B* is passing by!"

We were doing maybe twenty mph. I read the graffiti on
boarded-up windows by the glare of flickering neon: "If voting
changed anything, it would be illegal." I saw pawnshops with
rusted iron accordion grates pulled tight against the night and
old brick buildings painted pink with arrows pointing to en-
trances that no longer existed. "Sound off! *Funk-y!*" I noticed a
sign for Rosa Parks Boulevard. I decided against martyrdom.

" 'Scuse me," I said.

Rashid B wasn't listening and he couldn't have heard even if
he was. I poked him in the shoulder. "I *said, 'Excuse me!'* "

He glanced in the rearview mirror, his shoulders shimmying
still. "Huh?"

"Isn't the Hyatt a straight shot down Michigan Avenue?" I
was screaming.

Rashid B turned down the sound somewhere before the end
of my sentence and the piercing yelp of my voice against the

253

sudden silence was awful. "Aren't we going just a little bit out of our way?"

"Miss more lights this way," Rashid B replied. "Where you live at anyways?"

"Washington. I'm a sportswriter for the Washington *Tribune* in Washington, D.C."

Somehow I thought if I said "Washington" often enough and slow enough he would see narcs and headlines and let me live.

"You shitting me, white? You go in the locker room?"

Him, too. "Yeah," I said. "I go in the locker room."

"You cold, white. You do rap?"

I nodded. It was sort of true. I had written at least ten stories about kids killed at city-sponsored rap concerts.

"Maybe you know my cous', Eric B?"

I shrugged. "Afrika Bambaataa?"

I shook my head. "Afrika's what you call the godfather of hip hop, see. Eric's more what you call an intellectual. Eric's the Truth. Eric's def. We related, you know. His daddy and mine have the same granddaddy. I was hoping he might help me get some 'sposure. They call me the Grim Rapper."

Rashid B pulled an album from underneath the seat and handed it back to me. There he was on the cover in red satin and pointed ears. "I call it *death rap*," he said. "You know, like death metal and rap. Death rap. It's real. It's true. Maybe you can help get me some 'sposure, white."

I assured him I would be glad to help in any way I could and would be delighted to pass on his album to our music critic with my highest recommendation. He grinned in the rearview mirror and stuck a toothpick between his teeth. "How you like that 'smarmy' part, white? I looked it up. Sure is hard to find something that rhymes with 'army.'"

I told him it was def and asked if he might step on it a little, and he said absolutely, no problem. But he still wasn't making much time. "You know, I been picking up fares most nights by the stadium and drivin' 'em around while I play my music. I tell 'em it's shortcut, if you get my meaning. But you the first girl and you the first one a 'em that likes my music. You cold, white."

It was three by the time we got to the hotel. Schmuck that I am, I offered him a tip, but Rashid B wouldn't hear of it. He gave me his new album, *Satan Eats Grapes*, and his business card.

"By the way, what does the *B* stand for?" I said.

"Brown. Rashid Brown."

"A. B. Berkowitz," I said, shaking his hand.

"You the Truth, Berkowitz," Rashid said.

The TV in my room was on, tuned to the in-house channel. A red glow suffused the space and the soothing sound of Henry Mancini met my ears. "Welcome," the screen said; "we're glad you're here!"

The message light was blinking. I dialed Michael without bothering to check with the front desk. "Hi, it's me," I said. "You wouldn't believe what just happened."

"Ari, it's three in the morning."

"But, Michael, we have to talk. I'm so sorry, Michael."

"It's late. I can't. Not now."

"But—"

"I've got somebody here, Ari. I've got to go."

"Happy birthday," I said. But he had already hung up.

The phone went dead; the anger clicked in. His and mine. I held the receiver to my cheek and listened to the buzz of disconnection. Okay, maybe I didn't understand how hurt he was. Okay, maybe I was a bitch. But this? "It's over, I've got somebody here"—*click? Just like Mom and Dad.*

The buzz in my ear became a numbness in my chest. I called the message desk, a reporter's reflex. Or maybe I just needed to know somebody still wanted me. "You have two messages: Sammy Esposito called at nine. 'Just checking in.' And one from, uh, Ramp."

"Rump," I said.

"Rump at two-thirty this morning. It says, 'I need to see you. Meet me at room 1411 at nine.'"

August 9 I was late. And so when there was no answer at the door, I figured Rump had gone down to breakfast. But then I noticed the aqua plastic room service tray at my feet and the half-eaten sausage sticking out of the plastic thermal dome and knocked again, harder this time. Still there was no sound except the sigh of reluctant hinges capitulating to my knock.

Rump was sitting cross-legged in the middle of the bed, wearing track shorts and his bright red GO DEEP T-shirt. He was watching "Jeopardy" with the sound off. And he was crying.

He must have been crying for a while. His nose was bright red and his face was splotched. I stood there watching his chest rise and fall and thinking how we have even that in common,

Rump and me, rotten sinuses and the wrong skin for tears. He didn't look up. So finally I looked away. The category on the screen was "Great Romance" for $50.

Rump went on crying. Soon the sniffle became a sob and the sob became a howl. Christ, I had made a grown man cry and for what? A horseshit story. God, I hate this business. "I'm sorry," I said. "I had no choice," I said. "Sal," I said.

Rump shook his head and swallowed his words. "Not it" was all I heard.

He cried harder then. I don't know what Sal would have said or what the ombudsman would have recommended. But I didn't see where I had any choice. I went and sat beside him on the edge of the bed, on the precipice of professional disgrace, my left leg curled beneath me, my right leg planted firmly on the floor, and put my arm around him. Isn't that what "Dear Abby" would have advised?

Rump put his head against my chest and his arms around my neck and bawled. I was glad I had slammed the door. We sat there like that, I don't know how long. "Jeopardy" ended and "Wheel of Fortune" came on. The inner tube's shadows flickered across the room. I thought about Sal and the ombudsman and the weight of this man. I did not think about Michael.

I knew I couldn't hold him forever. My left leg was beginning to ache and my right leg, which was supporting us both, went to sleep. It's funny, but I had never really thought about how big Rump was before. In bios and bad wire stories, he was always "the six-foot-one 220-pound All-Star." But I never gave that any weight. And as many times as I had seen him, in uniform and out, I had never touched him except maybe in passing. Rump had been my friend, my source, maybe even my hero. But he had never been tangible before.

It sounds stupid, I know, but sitting there, holding him, I couldn't imagine how I had ever written about him *without* touching him. I couldn't imagine how I had never noticed the attraction. I had seen him naked every day for the last six months, but I had never seen him as a man until now.

Isn't denial amazing? And I learned to deny from the best of them: Mom, who repressed her disinterest and dissatisfaction with Dad for sixteen years until one day she met Bill and it all melted and she was gone.

"It's okay, Rump. Whatever it is, it's okay."

He nodded and sniffled and slurped. We were both sopping

wet. Tears cascaded down his cheeks and seeped inside my collar and trickled down my neck. My cleavage became a waterfall, my navel a reservoir. He had saved up a lot of tears.

"You've got to talk about it. You can tell me. I know how to protect a source."

He laughed at that, I think, though it was hard to tell because his face was still pressed against me and wet silk will dampen any smile.

My left biceps began to shake. My right leg began to dance involuntarily. Oxygen debt had set in. I wondered if he could feel me twitching, but the moment of contemplation was short. Strengthwise, I had reached the end of my rope. All resistance was gone.

In an instant we were prone. His face was still pressed against my chest, but now he was kissing the wetness, licking his tears away. He sucked my neck dry and my breasts and my tear-streaked belly. My toes were curling, always a bad sign. Where was the ombudsman when I needed him?

I gazed at the fake stucco swirls on the ceiling. It was a fair approximation of the chaos I was contemplating. I shuddered. I sighed. I made a decision.

This will not go down in the annals of romance as seduction's greatest moment, I know. But the words popped into my head and this is what I said: "Show me your machine, Rump. Show me your machine."

He raised his chin from my belly and smiled. At least I made him smile. He remembered that April day, too, and Stick's dare. I guess for once he knew something we didn't. "You know I'm not the Stick," he said.

"I know," I said. "Show me your machine. Show me your machine *now!*"

I'd like to tell you that the consummation of all this repressed heat, this belated passion, was perfect. I'd like to tell you that the planets moved, that at least one of us saw stars. I mean, if you're going to throw away your career, your self-esteem, and your principles for a quick lay, at least it ought to be good. But the truth is I've had better. Lots better. I'm sure so has Rump— though based on the evidence of this manic, hurried coupling, my guess is he hasn't had much of anything lately. The best thing I can say about our lovemaking was at least it was quick. The worst I can say about it is it was quick. Rump made love to me like a man trying to atone. I made love to him like a woman who had just screwed herself good. So much for fucking your brains out.

Afterward we lay there in silence, not out of exhaustion or depletion and certainly not out of satisfaction but out of mortification and, I think, good manners. Neither of us wanted to inflict our disappointment on the other—though maybe I'm just projecting here. Rump closed his eyes. Mine were just opening. I stared at the ceiling and thought about Michael, who certainly measures up, and *whoever she was who was there,* and about Sal and about the haughty sneers of every Neanderthal voyeur who ever looked me up and down and said, "I know what *she's* doing in the locker room." I thought about them and thought, "They're right."

My teeth began to chatter and Rump took my hand. "Don't worry," he said. For an instant I thought he was reading my mind and I imagined we were in sync again. "You don't have to worry about getting pregnant or anything."

His voice was taut, as if he'd caught a foul tip in the Adam's apple. I looked at him and he gulped. "I'm shooting blanks," he said.

He saw the confusion in my eyes. "Blanks," he said impatiently. "I'm shooting blanks. I'm sterile."

"Jesus, Rump."

"Yeah, I know. It sucks."

"The slump," I said and he nodded. "How long?"

"May. I've known for sure since May. I decided to get a physical between quacks. It was just before we went to see that shrink, Hyman whatever."

I remembered the look on Rump's face when Dr. C. Hyman Funk asked him about his dreams and whether he had any kids. I remember thinking his face was a death mask.

He sighed. "I went to see the team doctor at the end of April. Pretty fucking stupid, huh? Guy sticks his finger up my ass and then he gives me this November '86 *Playboy* and tells me to go in the bathroom and jerk off in a bottle. God knows how many poor slobs have gotten off on Miss November. Two days later, he calls back and tells JoAnne my count is like three million and the motility isn't much to write home about either.

"That's how good the little fuckers swim. Four is Hall of Fame. One is Palookaville. Mine were a one plus. Anyway, he tells me to see this fertility specialist, a guy named Ball—can you believe that? Ball? Guy squeezes my balls and tells us we have to go home and have marital relations at exactly eight-thirty in the morning and come to his office by nine for something called a postcoital test. A postcoital test is your basic fuck-and-run.

"We were leaving for Milwaukee and Minnesota and K.C. the next day. You remember. So we made the appointment for the day we got back. We came in late. I got to bed at 5:30 A.M. JoAnne woke me at 8:00 A.M. We screwed at 8:30 A.M. and we were sitting in the guy's reception area by 8:59 A.M.

"He puts on these gloves and scrapes some stuff out of Jo-Anne and puts it on this slide and sticks it under his microscope and begins to cluck. I mean *cluck*. 'What?' JoAnne says. 'What?'

"The guy shakes his head and says, 'They're dead. They're *all* dead.' "

" 'You're saying John's sperm are dead?' JoAnne says.

" 'Yup,' he says. *'DOA.'*

"The guy actually smiled. 'Just a little gynecologist humor,' he says. 'It's really very common. It can happen to *anyone*. Even the all-American boy. Hah hah hah.'

"I thought maybe I'd kill the guy right then and there. But JoAnne's an optimist. 'What can I do?' she says. Ball shrugs. 'Get a new husband, I guess.' "

I touched Rump's cheek. His eyes were bloodshot. His lip quivered. "I'm sorry," I said.

"Don't apologize. You didn't do anything except sleep with a horny catcher who comes too soon. God! I can't believe I went to the team doctor. I never go to the team doctor. I wonder how many people that cocksucker's told?"

I started to make a halfhearted speech about doctor-patient confidentiality, but one look from Rump told me I wasn't going to get away with it. "You know, I remember the first time somebody called me immortal. It was Milo, my rookie season, and I was zoned. Man, I could see that ball forever. I was hitting .333 and I could throw. Milo wrote this column saying if I kept this up I was sure to be one of baseball's great immortals.

"For a while I thought I was, you know, immortal. Then I met JoAnne." He bit his lip and laughed. "That's what happens when you're zoned. You do these things and they're easy and you think you're going to keep right on doing them forever. You're young and nothing aches, not even your legs after a double-header. It's like being weightless. Nothing can hold you down."

He shrugged and stretched. "We got married seven years ago. We agreed we wouldn't have children until I was ready to quit. She was young. She's only twenty-eight now. There wasn't any hurry. She wanted to travel with me. She wanted to take aerobics classes. I wanted a son. Every ballplayer wants a son. A namesake for when the cheering dies and the legs go. Mickey Mantle, Jr. Kyle Rote, Jr. Pete Rose, Jr. Cal Ripken, Jr. Even Mug Shot has a Mug Shot, Jr. I guess I'm not so different from them after all."

He cleared his throat. "We started trying two years ago. Jo-Anne was bored. She got shin splints from high-impact. I said okay even though I was feeling bored, too. I mean with her. Nothing happened. Being away all the time didn't help. The doctor said there was no reason to worry. This spring JoAnne said, 'Get tested.' "

He bit his lip again and rubbed his eyes. "My knees are bad. My shoulder's bad. My elbow's bad. My sperm are bad. *'DOA,'* the cocksucker said. I got no mobility and no motility. So much for being immortal, huh?"

I started to argue with him. But he cut me off. "Baseball's almost over. I know that. And the funny thing is, I haven't got the faintest fucking idea what comes next. I thought I'd be a father. Now what? *Who* am I going to be?"

"Don't you mean *what?*"

He shook his head. "Can't go on being Rump Doubleday forever. Charity golf. 'Game of the Week.' It's like eating yourself alive. And I'm no cannibal."

Rump reached for his watch. It was 1:45 and getaway day. The bus left for the park at 3:00 P.M. "C'mon," he said. "We gotta go put our game faces on."

Somewhere Over Ohio

August 10, A.M. It's 2:00 A.M. Everyone's asleep but me. I've had too much coffee and my hands are jiggling as I write. The Senators lost another, their fifth straight, and I've lost my best friend. I could barely look at Rump at the park. To look at him is to confront my own shame and his pain, and I don't know what to do with either.

So I did what Rump did. I put my game face on and watched

the Senators score four runs on four walks and four wild pitches
and manage to lose the game anyway.

No game today. Tonight is Jimy Boy's Super Stars Ministry
banquet, where he is expected to praise Jesus and deliver his *mea
culpa*. Sal's taking me off the beat for a couple of days. I don't
have to see Rump until Monday. God, I hope I don't have to see
Michael tonight.

Home Stand

August 10, P.M. The banquet hall was in some
godforsaken town north of Fredericksburg, a two-hour drive
from everywhere. It's hard to imagine what possessed anyone to
put it there, except, of course, that the land was cheap and surely
there was nothing else like it for miles. I take that back: there is
nothing else like it anywhere. The closest I have ever seen is
some of those bar mitzvah mills on Long Island where my cous-
ins had their parties. They all had red satin matchbooks and
chopped liver molds shaped like Menorahs.

I think it would be fair to say that there has never been a bar
mitzvah in the banquet room at the Plantation Oaks Christian
Resort and Conference Centre. This is God's country, after all,
and Jimy Boy owns the joint.

The room was immense, as long as a football field and almost
as wide. The walls were painted with vast rust and peach murals
depicting the fall of Greece. There were crazed animals rearing
up over frightened nubile girls, deranged-looking homosexuals
holding hands, and old Socrates himself looking stoned out on
hemlock.

Sin was everywhere on these walls and it was magnified by
three gigantic octagonal ceiling mirrors that hovered over the
room. Over the dais hung a huge pastel Jesus, His chin uplifted,
His arms embracing the multitudes, forgiving their transgres-
sions. Western civilization was being saved all over again at Plantation Oaks.

I guess what made it especially surreal was what my mother
always used to call "the help." They were all black and all
dressed in the livery of slavery: puffy white sleeves and green

vests and pantaloons and powdered white wigs pulled back in ponytails and buns, relics of Ye Olde South. "Chicken or fish" was all they said.

The banquet was scheduled to begin at 7 P.M. Ruth and I were there by 6:10 P.M. The place was empty except for a gigantic fake marble statue of the Madonna and baby Jesus perched in the middle of a fake marble fountain filled with honest-to-God water, where, I have heard it said, Jimy Boy has been known to dip a penitent or two. At precisely 6:15 P.M. water began spewing out of the Virgin's delicately upturned mouth. "Looks like she's gargling," Ruth said.

The paper went all-out on this one. Sports sent me and the Doctor and Milo. Just as I feared, City side sent Michael. Thank God Business sent Ruth. They were writing Jimy Boy's legal situation. Milo was writing live. Dr. D was running quotes and writing color. And I was writing the denouement of the Jimy Boy Collins affair, a front-page story if ever I heard one. It was supposed to be the apotheosis of my career. I was dreading it.

The organizers had put us at Table Number 147, the last of 147 tables, and the one farthest from Jimy Boy's sight. "At least you can't smell him from here," I told Ruth.

We were almost fifty yards from the dais. I only wished I could be that far away from Michael. I found our table and immediately switched his name card, which was next to mine, with Ruth's, thereby separating us by a centerpiece of plastic flowers, a pitcher of iced tea, and a pot of decaffeinated coffee. "Christians," Milo muttered. "What ever happened to sacramental wine?"

The place began to fill up by 6:30 P.M. The Second Annual Super Stars Ministry banquet promised to be quite an event: a fundraiser, church service, and breaking news story all in one. It was strictly a black-tie affair. The room was jammed with true believers, all decked-out, and all carrying Bibles: black women in azure chiffon gowns, white businessmen in black wingtips, Piggy and Monk in cummerbunds, and a whole dais-full of oversized men stuffed in rented tuxedos whose faces were familiar but whom I couldn't place out of uniform. All of them and all of us were waiting with hushed expectation for Jimy Boy to explain.

Michael arrived at two minutes to seven. I guess he wasn't in any hurry to see me either. He nodded and ducked away, mumbling something about legwork. "Easy," Ruth said to me. "Easy."

The program began with an enthusiastic rendition of Jimy

Boy's greatest hit, "Jump Back, Jesus!" sung by Jimy Boy's son, Jimy Boy Jr. Brother John Lawson came forward to give his testimony, which he read word for word from his Christian baseball card, departing from the text only to thank Jimy Boy and Jesus for making him the man he is today. The room swelled with piety. *"Amen, Brother! Awwright!"*

The entree came and went. The dessert carts made the rounds. Jimy Boy Jr., who was doubling as emcee, told a joke about a pitcher who went to his preacher to find out if there is baseball in heaven. "I have good news and bad news," the preacher told him. "The good news is yes, there is baseball in heaven. The bad news is, you're starting tomorrow."

Jimy Boy Jr. accepted the applause as his due, a family trait, apparently, and said, "Let's hear it for good clean fun." Everyone cheered and the lights dimmed and a prerecorded chorus began to sing "Arise, O Lord." It was 9 P.M. sharp. Jimy Boy Collins walked into the glare of a single spotlight in the shadow of the gargling Madonna and got down on his hands and knees and prayed. He rose on the wings of applause and made his way through the crowd, nodding and bowing and kissing the outstretched hands of the true believers. I made a note: "Used to be he waited for them to kiss *his* hand."

The chorus reached a crescendo. A red carpet was unfurled at Jimy Boy's feet. He mounted the stairs and kissed everyone on the dais, including Piggy, Monk, and his wife. Jimy Boy Jr. he bussed full on the lips.

The spotlight narrowed on his face and he raised his pudgy pink hands to heaven. "O Lord," he said. "Good, sweet Lord."

Ruth kicked me under the table. "He's changed his part."

I looked at Jimy Boy through my binoculars. Mine was the only unbowed head in sight. Sure enough, Jimy Boy was now combing right to left. He looked seriously unbalanced.

Like most accomplished preachers, Jimy Boy is a master of practiced sincerity. His voice is a finely tuned instrument of derision, despair. It can soar with the angels or descend nine rungs to the fiery pit of hell faster than a BMW goes from zero to sixty. It pours honey on salted wounds. It summons the wrath of God.

"I kneel before you tonight, my friends. I kneel before you in judgment and in pain."

He was in his stage-whisper mode, that hushed, husky voice of repentance that begins deep in the chest and struggles against emotion to be set free. "Amen! Tell it, brother! Umm mmmm!"

"In my absence from you, my friends, I have . . ." Jimy Boy even choked up on cue. "In my absence from you, my friends, I asked the Lord for guidance." He was getting right to the point. "I asked the Lord whether to quit the game of baseball."

"*NOOooooo,*" shouted the faithful. "*Don't do it,*" they cried.

"Only You, Lord, can tell me to get out of baseball. For You are the Supreme Authority. You are the Commissioner of all. Well, let me tell you, friends, I sat in my cabin in the woods—I didn't even check the box score. And I waited and I waited for His reply. I told myself that if He asked me to make this sacrifice, to sell the Washington Senators, I gladly would; that I would accept it as part of His divine game plan."

"*NOOOooooo! NOOooooo!*"

Jimy Boy paused. "Well, my friends, let me tell you what He said."

"*Tell it, Jimy Boy! Tell it!*"

"He said, '. . . *Play ball!*' "

"Unbe-fucking-lievable," Dr. Deadline said. "You've got your lede," Ruth said.

The place went bonkers. Jimy Boy gripped the lectern, his knuckles turning white, and allowed the ovation to run its course while summoning up a tear. When he spoke again, the bravado was gone and he was back to humility. The faithful sat down.

"My friends, I am a fool for God. Yes! I am a fool in His eyes. God knows this. He expects this. He made me this way. He made me weak. He made me err."

Milo snorted.

"He made me err so He could raise me up in the searing glare of sin and say, '*You* are a sinner, Jimy Boy Collins!' "

"*NOOooooooooo!*"

"Yesssss," Jimy Boy said. "Yes. It's true. I am a sinner. And Lola Lord—"

The true believers gasped as one at the mention of the wanton name. And as they did, two spotlights converged on a forlorn figure in black cowering at a lonely table. She was trapped in an intersection of blinding wattage. Jimy Boy raised his hands to calm their fears and repeated her name. "Lola Lord. Lola *Lord. Lola Lord!*" His voice grew deeper and more emphatic. "My friends, we cannot be afraid to speak the name of temptation! Lola Lord was my temptation. She was sent by Jesus to humble your humble servant as I was sent to humble her."

"Oh my God," said Ruth.

"What a fucking zoo," said Dr. Deadline.

"Come here, my child!" said Jimy Boy. "Yes! You! Lola! Come to us. For who among us is not a sinner today?"

Jimy Boy stood there at the podium doing his God bit with a mighty hand and an outstretched arm. You gotta hand it to the guy, he knows how to choreograph emotion. Lola climbed the stairs, accepted his arm, and staggered to the lectern, where Mrs. Jimy Boy awaited them. Bathed in the purifying light of six spots, they raised their hands in victory over sin and venality and jealousy.

"Jesus Christ, it's the Holy fucking Trinity."

Michael had returned. I buried my head in my notebook and pretended to take notes.

Jimy Boy was whispering into the microphone again. "My friends, I want to tell you what happened in that elevator." He inhaled deeply and waited for the titillation factor to die down. "It's important that I share this with you. God was exercising His moral authority in that elevator. He was saying, 'Jimy Boy, you are a sinner. You must believe, as I know you do, even if we all need a little reminding now and then, that I, Jesus Christ, died on the cross for your sin. *Yours!* Sin is the chasm between us. *Please* don't let it come between us, son. Cast off your vices! Get off your knees! Come to me.' "

Table Number 147 was in an uproar. "Outstanding," the Doctor said. "Absolutely outstanding. A ten."

"Amazing how much Jesus sounds just like Jimy Boy," Ruth said.

"Probably got the same mailing address," Milo replied.

They were slapping their thighs and holding their sides. I wanted to laugh, too. But I couldn't. My sin—*mine!*—was getting in the way. The weight of my guilt embraced me, glued me to my chair. Or maybe it was just my bare thighs sticking to the vinyl. But either way, I couldn't move. My fingers were numb. I had goose bumps up and down my arms. "Shut up, you guys, I've gotta take notes," I said.

Jimy Boy clutched his Bible to his breast. "Friends, repeat after me.

"I have sinned."

"I have sinned."

"I am a sinner!"

"I am a sinner!"

"I am the victim of pernicious flesh!"

"I am the victim of pernicious flesh!"

Everyone in the hall with the exception of those at our table was repeating after him, beating their collective breasts, expurgating their collective wickedness. Their voices were relentless, uniform, seductive. Their voices were everywhere. It sounded as if they were inside of me. *"I have sinned. I am a sinner! I am the victim of pernicious flesh!"* Ruth elbowed me in the ribs. "Knock it off, A.B.!" she hissed. I had joined the chorus. I was one of them.

Jimy Boy droned on. I stopped even pretending to take notes. I barely heard a word he said. I was listening to another righteous voice thundering inside my own wretched head.

"What a fucking hypocrite you are! Who the fuck are you to judge anyone? You're just as much of a slimeball as he is. Big fucking story! PREACHERMAN PORKS BIMBO IN ELEVATOR. *And you nail him to the cross with Joey Proud, who was dead drunk and didn't know what he was saying except he wanted to get back on your good side before you wrote something nasty about his sexual proclivities. Joey Proud jumps your bones and he's a scumbag, but you'll quote him. Jimy Boy jumps Lola's bones, and you expose him.*

"You jump Rump's bones, you commit the cardinal sin, the original sin of your profession, the one thing you swore you'd never do, and hey, who needs to know about it anyway? You're such a fucking asshole, Berkowitz."

I heard Jimy Boy again. He was deep into his apologies. He apologized to his wife, to his children, to the paying fans of Washington, D.C., to all God-fearing men and women and especially his mom.

"Mom. Maybe I did it to get even with Mom. Tit for tat. Ballplayer for ballplayer. Children who are abused become abusers. Mothers who fall for washed-up ballplayers bear daughters who fall for washed-up ballplayers. At least she did it for love. I just did it to get back at her and Michael. I think."

I heard a voice singing "Amazing Grace." It was Ruth, and she was singing and trying not to laugh. Milo began to hum and then the Doctor. I hated them and their smugness. My teeth started to chatter, a nervous habit of late. Then everything went hot and I couldn't see. For an instant I actually thought God was coming to get me. But it wasn't Him. It was only the spotlight.

"There is one final thing I must do before we close tonight," Jimy Boy said. "I must thank the woman who is responsible for bringing us to our senses. For she, too, is an instrument of God. And we want her among us."

I rubbed my eyes. I fought off the glare. I felt like the Burning fucking Bush. "Jesus H. Christ," Milo said.

"Holy shit," Ruth said.

"Please God, no," I said.

"It would be easy, my friends, too easy, to cast this woman upon the waters, to vilify her, to shun her, to slam the door of Christian love in her face. And I admit, oh yes, I admit, I wanted to slam the door of Room 1337 at the Colonnade Hotel in Miss Ariadne Berkowitz's face when she knocked and confronted me with my sin."

"*NOOooooo!*" they howled. Jimy Boy was asking too much!

"I know what you are thinking, my friends. I know because I thought the same thing. But then I remembered that when the Lord, our Savior, was born, there was no room at the inn. But, there *is* room at our inn tonight for Miss Ariadne Berkowitz. There is room in our hearts. Your servant, Jimy Boy Collins, owes Miss Berkowitz a great debt of thanks. She may not know it and she may not like it, but Miss Ariadne Berkowitz helped God make me anew. Jesus loves you, Ariadne. Stand up and take a bow."

A room full of sinners was calling my name. I thought I was going to pass out. They stomped their feet. They whistled. They clapped.

"If you don't get up now, this will go on all night," Dr. D said.

"He's right," Ruth said. "Get up. Do it now."

They each grabbed an elbow and hoisted me to my feet. There was a horrible ripping sound as my flesh was peeled from the vinyl chair. Jimy Boy actually blew me a kiss and the applause stopped and Ruth and the Doctor let go and I went limp in my seat.

"Are you okay?" Ruth said.

"I'm a sinner," I said. "I have sinned."

"We gotta talk," Ruthie replied.

August 11   Ruth was right. We had to talk. But first we had to write. I don't mind saying right up front that of all the things I have written in my career none means as much to me as the piece of shit I wrote last night. Twenty-four inches saying Jimy Boy was not about to quit baseball because God had told him to keep the faith and play ball! I hit the DONE button, hung up on Zeke, and called room service. "Scotch," I said for the first time in my life.

Ruth and I are sharing a room in the "You Are the Light" wing of the Plantation Oaks Christian Resort and Conference Centre. There's a Bible on the night table and a standing lamp whose pedestal is a statue of our Savior on the cross. I filed in its glow. Then I lay down on the bed, opened my journal, and scribbled while Ruth finished. She was writing the Berkowitz sidebar, her second story of the night, which she had volunteered to do mostly so I didn't have to talk to Michael.

"Thank you," I said.

"Piece of cake," she said. "A tap dance."

A tap dance is any story that's a lot of fancy footwork and very little else. Ruth hates tap dances. This was a true act of friendship.

I drank some more and dozed. She filed and popped open a beer. "So," she said, "how was he?"

I opened my eyes and tried to focus. "Well?"

Ruthie is a good nuts-and-bolts reporter, but I had never given her real high marks for intuition before. "How'd you know?"

"I didn't," she said. "You just fell for the oldest trick in the book."

I closed my eyes again and saw myself in another bed, in another city, staring at another stucco ceiling. *"How was he?"*

The words "lay like a lox" popped into my head. This is what we said about girls in college who were not supposed to be good in bed. They don't have expressions for guys who lay like a lox.

"So," Ruth said.

"C'mon, Ruthie."

"C'mon, my ass. Tell me. You know you always feel better when you tell me."

"I ain't falling for that one too."

"Seems to me you've *already* fallen. In more ways than one. I don't need to remind you about your shabby journalistic ethics, now, do I? I don't need to tell you what your colleague, Maggie Blum, would say."

No, she didn't.

Discretion may be the better part of valor, but it's never particularly been my strong suit and it isn't much fun either. Nor is getting lectured by Ruth about my ethical lapses, which are notable and all too real. I knew I was going to tell her if only to keep her off her soapbox. The only question was how much would I make her beg. "Jesus, I'm not going to put it in the paper," she said.

I sighed. She was my best friend, after all, and she had just saved my ass. "Let's just say he was pressing."

"Swinging for the fences?" she said.

"Trying too hard."

"You mean he *struck out?*"

"Not quite," I said.

Ruthie beamed. "Just a regular guy, huh?"

"Yup," I said.

"Well, so much for the myth of the Great Jock Lover," she crowed. "*Read all about it!* MALE ICON TOPPLED FROM EROTIC PEDESTAL, ALL-STAR CATCHER EXPOSED AS SEXUAL KLUTZ."

This was the best news she had heard in months. I have to say vindication becomes her. It also diverted her from *my* failings. She was absolutely radiant; thrilled it had been so bad. I myself would have preferred more pleasure with my degradation. I was kicking myself for telling her. "For the record, Ms. Berkowitz, would you say this was a 'Wham, bam, thank-you-ma'am' encounter or just another eighties foray into boring, random sex?"

"No comment," I said.

"We're talking about establishing a historical record here, Ms. Berkowitz. This is for posterity. Just think: How many women can say they exposed a myth with one lousy lay? We're not just talking about sex! We're talking cultural revisionism. We're talking about laying waste to the Big Man on Campus. We're talking about the end of the all-American boy."

It hadn't occurred to me to look at my transgression exactly this way, but it was a relief at least to laugh, except, of course, Ruth wasn't entirely kidding. I told her she was giving me much too much credit and turned off the lights. That was three hours ago. I've been tossing and turning ever since. As usual, Ruth has gotten me thinking. That's why I'm now sitting in the bathroom, with my diary on my lap, trying to make sense of this all while she's inside dreaming sweet dreams.

I *am* disappointed, mostly in myself, but in Rump, too, and maybe if I'm going to be honest about it, for exactly the reason Ruth has in mind. I guess I really did expect some sexual heroics from him. I guess that's what we all expect from them. They're heroes: they run faster, throw farther, screw better. Right?

I should have known better because I know them better. But I didn't. I was a sucker for illusion. I was a fan. So I guess I had to go to bed with Rump if I ever was going to grow up. At least, that's what I keep telling myself sitting here in the john at 4:00 A.M. in the "You Are the Light" wing of the Plantation Oaks Christian Resort and Conference Centre. One thing for sure is true: the consummation of this fantasy was the end of myth for me.

Unlike Ruth, I don't exactly rejoice in this. For her, Rump is a symbol. For me, he is an ache. Maybe he represented something to me once. Baseball. But you don't go to bed with an abstraction.

I can't imagine what he must be feeling; I can't let myself. And I can't do anything about it except make everything worse. I wasn't supposed to be his lover. I wasn't even supposed to be his friend. Now, having been both, I can't be either, much less an objective reporter.

For a moment a little while ago, I considered waking her up and telling her about the infertility, just so she won't gloat quite so much. But for once I did the right thing and kept my mouth shut.

Yeah, Ruth. Just a regular guy.

August 13 I never thought I'd be relieved to get back to the team, but I am. Three days of hanging around the office avoiding Michael and taking shit from Vito and Rocky about being Jimy Boy's girl were enough to make me throw up and almost enough to make me glad to see Stick and Stein, who only give me shit about being Rump's girl. If they only knew. Given my choices, I'd rather be at the ballpark avoiding Rump.

When I got there, Stretch was stretched out in the middle of the clubhouse, naked except for his Sony Walkman, reading his test result from the Foundation for Competitive Perfection. "I flunked," he said.

Nobody else was around, so it was safe to talk to me.

"You can't flunk. It's an evaluation of your strengths and weaknesses. There is no right or wrong."

"Wanna bet?" he said.

The Foundation for Competitive Perfection had indeed

found Stretch wanting, particularly in coachability and guilt-proneness. His drive and assertiveness aren't much to write home about, either. As far as emotional control goes, he's a total loss. "Go on. Read it. Read it, out loud," Stretch said, handing me a computer printout detailing his fallibilities.

" 'Coachability: You have little, if any, respect for coaches and find it extremely difficult to value coaching as a contributor to your athletic prowess. The coach as father figure seems to be a great source of conflict for you. You regard demands placed upon you by the coach as an intrusion and rebel against them as a son rebels against parental authority. By extension, you may also be uncooperative with the team captain. This attitude could be reflected in extreme independence.' "

"Shit," Stretch said. "Daddy's gonna shit a brick."

" 'Emotional control: Your lack of emotional control is one of your major failings and it would be remiss of the Foundation for Competitive Perfection not to red-flag it. When you are overwhelmed by your feelings, your performance is greatly impeded.' "

"What's 'remiss'?" Stretch said. "What's 'impeded'?"

" 'Remiss' means, uh, irresponsible. 'Impeded' means 'You suck.' "

"Oh, right, I get it."

" 'Even the most superficial events can have an undermining effect on you.' "

"Yeah, like almost killing some boy with a high hard one."

" 'Your performances tend to be inconsistent and are highly susceptible to unpredictable, outside forces.' "

"You mean like getting laid?"

" 'Opponents sense your vulnerability and will attempt to psych you out. You must learn to gut it out and ignore them.' "

"I'm fucked," Stretch said. "I'm dead meat."

"You want me to keep going?"

Stretch nodded. " 'Emotional control pointers: This competitor is strongly advised to seek additional professional help. The Foundation for Competitive Perfection has counselors available to take your call at this toll-free number, 1-800-GET-HELP. Also please find enclosed a free sample motivational tape from our "Enhanced Performance" series. *However,* the competitor should be aware that progress in developing self-control will be extremely *slow* without *behavior modification,* and we strongly urge further *personalized* attention.' "

I tossed the report back to him. "What're you gonna do?"

Stretch was quiet a moment and then he said, "You ever hear the story about Hurricane Hilda?"

I shook my head. "Well, she was a prostitute at this truck stop back home. And this guy comes in and he's never been to a prostitute before and she says, 'Son, you want to experience a hurricane?' He says, 'I don't know about no hurricane. I just wanna get laid.' So she gets all naked and he gets all naked and she's blowing all over him. And he says, 'What's that?' She says, 'That's the warm tropical breeze coming up.' Then she straddles him and her tits are flopping across his face. And he says, 'What's that?' She says, 'Those are the coconuts falling off the tree.' Then he feels something warm and wet and she's pissing all over him. And he says, *'What's that?'* She says, 'Hurricane Hilda is bringing in the rain.' He says, 'Get offa me. I can't fuck in no storm.'

"Well, A.B., I can't pitch in no storm, neither. I think I'm gonna go home and open me a pizza parlor."

I was pretty sure he was kidding, but you never know with Stretch, so I asked for his home phone number just in case. People started arriving about then, so Stretch had to go back to ignoring me. I went out on the field to wait for Billy. I wanted to find out how we did on our test. Also, I figured it would be easier to see Rump the first time with his clothes on.

I was gone maybe an hour. When I came back through the clubhouse on my way upstairs, Stretch was still stretched out naked on the floor with his eyes shut and his Sony Walkman glued to his skull, talking to himself.

I was about to leave when Monk arrived looking like he'd had a rough all-night prayer session and saw Stretch and went batshit. Let me say right up front I had to do a whole lot of editing to get this one in a family newspaper. Monk stormed around the room, stomping his feet and fuming about the bleeping Youth of America and What's Wrong with This Country Anyway and When He Was a Boy Nobody Listened to This Bleeping Satanistic Rock 'n' Roll Bleep and Men Were Men and Ballplayers Played Ball for the Bleeping Love of the Bleeping Game. He might as well have been speaking in tongues.

Guys were wandering in from the field and out of the shower and Monk's tirade pretty much stopped everyone right where they stood. The wrath of Monk *is* daunting. He loomed over Stretch, hurling invective and tobacco juice and bellowing,

"Get that motherbleeping radio off your bleeping face, son, and do it now!"

Stretch started to protest, but quickly saw the futility of the gesture. Monk grabbed the Walkman and waved it above his head. "This, boys, is Sin. This is degradation. This is why we have lost eighty-five bleeping ballgames."

The much maligned Washington Senators were having trouble keeping a straight face. All of them, regardless of their emotional control, guilt-proneness, coachability, aggressiveness, and drive, had received the same free sample "Enhanced Performance" tape from the Foundation for Competitive Perfection that Stretch had been listening to on the locker room floor.

"From now on, boys, there will be no more of *this* in my locker room," Monk said, yanking foot after foot of brown cellophane from the cassette until he stood in a mound of brown tape that just managed to obscure the brown tobacco stains on his socks. "From now on, and for as long as I, Monk McGuire, am manager of the Washington bleeping Senators, there will be no bleeping word but the Good Word in this locker room. You want to listen to bleeping music? Listen to religious bleeping hymns."

Our headline was: MONK's 11TH COMMANDMENT: THOU SHALT NOT LISTEN TO R 'N' R.

By the way, according to the Foundation for Competitive Perfection, yours truly is "a true competitor, a model for teammates because of your ability to release aggression easily. You are an athlete who makes things happen and will rarely back down from an argument. You have the guts, the will, the drive, the ruthlessness to succeed at any level of competition."

As a result, Monk inserted Billy into the starting lineup, patted him on the ass, and told him to keep his chin up and nose down. Go figure. Billy says if I write it now, he's fucked. So much for that story. Oh well, I owe him one.

August 14   Buck's baseball card arrived today. He's been waiting for it since he was five years old. Every day for the last two weeks, he's been running to his locker first thing to see if a package from Topps had arrived.

Baseball cards, like crocuses, are one of the first signs of spring. The pictures of the veterans are taken the year before so their cards come out early. Rookies and unknowns like Buck must wait until spring training, which means their cards aren't ready until August, along with all the guys who got traded over the winter.

They shot Buck along with the other rookies the first day in West Palm. But something happened to the film. So they had to take his picture again in the beginning of June. I remember the day the photographer came. It took Buck all afternoon to get dressed, fussing with his cap so his bald spot wouldn't show and his eyes would. His grandma told him to feature his eyes.

Anyway, today the package was waiting for him on his Naugahyde throne. He ripped off the paper and there before him was a stack of a hundred Topps baseball cards with his likeness on each and every one. His hat was back on his head the way he wears it. His bat was back on his shoulder the way he holds it. His mustache was, well, straggly, the way it was back then.

Buck cradled his card against his chest, as if it was his baby's picture. His face said everything you ever needed to know about wanting to be a major league ballplayer.

He showed his card to Rump. He showed it to Billy. He showed it to me. Then Stein began to giggle and Stick joined in and then Brawn and Mancusi and Jenkins. Still, Buck didn't see anything wrong. Finally, Rump pointed it out to him. There at the butt of the bat handle was the word: FUCKFACE. And on the barrel, where it was supposed to say LOUISVILLE SLUGGER, someone had written the words LOUISVILLE STUTTER.

The light went out in Buck's eyes. He tore the card from the stack, hoping it was a fluke, a joke. It was a joke, all right. But the joke was on every single one of them. FUCKFACE. A hundred times FUCKFACE.

I've seen that look on Buck's face before. It's the one that means he's going to have a hell of a day. He did. He hit three monstrous shots, a triple and two dingers, and was named Player of the Game. If anger and sadness are a motivator, then I suspect Buck is in for a lot of awards.

Beanie was waiting for him at his locker after the game. Word of FUCKFACE traveled fast. "Look here, Buck, Jimy Boy is of the opinion that these, uh, cards must be recalled," Beanie began. "Of course, as you can imagine, recalling one million baseball cards is no easy task. So we have prepared this statement for your, uh, signature."

Beanie handed Buck a statement, of which he had made a hundred Xerox copies, repudiating the card and urging Christian baseball fans everywhere to return them to Topps forthwith. Buck said nothing.

"What's the matter, Big Guy, having trouble gettin' out those words?" Stick was standing there counting his money as usual. Buck took a step toward him and Stick stuck his chest out and Beanie had to step between them. Rump led Buck back to his locker and Beanie put a pen in his hand and he signed. Thus FUCKFACE made headlines all over America. Or BLEEPFACE, I should say. That's how it appeared in the Washington *Tribune*. And Sal reamed me out because I was the only writer in town who didn't say Buck was crying.

Chicago

August 16 Ran into the Gaijin a little while ago in the coffee shop. It was fifteen minutes before the team bus left for the stadium. He was presiding over three enormous banana boats. I mean, he had whipped cream and walnuts and hot fudge and bananas, not to mention three towering scoops each of macadamia nut, cherry vanilla, and peanut brittle ice cream.

I said, "Ricky, what are you doing? The bus leaves in fifteen minutes."

"Just a little something to tie Ricky-San over till he go stadium," he said. "Get me to park."

I have to say his English is improving. But his sense of geography still sucks. The hotel is five minutes away from Comiskey. I swear to God, he may have eaten himself out of the league by the time he gets there.

Home Stand

August 19 Things are getting ugly around here.

Today Piggy broke up a fight between Stein and Brother John, who apparently was instrumental in Mrs. Stein's decision to throw hubby out of their conjugal bed last night. Stein was waiting at his locker when Brother John arrived humming "Onward, Christian Soldiers." "Hey, asshole," Stein said. "What you doing fucking with my wife?"

Brother John got this look of wounded tolerance on his face. I think he must practice it 'cause it's just perfect, a righteous combination of innocent bewilderment and holy resignation at the failings of mere men. It's a look of intense provocation. "Repent, Dick. Repent," he said.

"Repent? You want me to fucking repent? I'll fucking repent when you keep your fucking repenting out of my fucking house!"

Brother John sighed and cast his eyes to heaven as if to say, "We got a big project here, Big Guy." It had the predictable effect. "Don't fucking roll your motherfucking eyes at me, you cocksucker!" Stein said.

"I wasn't rolling my eyes at you, Dick," Lawson said, his drawl measured and even and slow. "I was seeking counsel from above."

For once I was with Stein. If somebody talked to me like that, I'd have done what Stein did, which was grab Brother John by the lapels of his Johnny Miller collection suit and slap him upside the head. "You want counsel? I'll give you some major fucking counsel! Get your dick out of my fucking business, dickhead!"

Brother John turned the other cheek. He *actually* turned the other cheek. Talk about a strict interpretation of the Bible. Stein hit Lawson upside the head again. That's when Piggy arrived and stepped between them with a "Now, now, boys" bonhomie and "C'mon, men, we're teammates and besides we got another ballgame to play." Which of course is a big part of the problem. These guys do not want to play ball, and who can blame them? They've already lost 89 and there's another 43 to play.

And it's August. Other towns have the heat of the pennant race. We just have the heat. It's one hundred degrees and just about one hundred percent humidity. The Senators are playing dead. Even the field is dead. It hasn't rained in weeks. The groundskeepers water and water and resod and resod, but the field seems to have a mind of its own. It just won't stay green. As symbols go, this one's pretty potent.

The people who designed this place must have really hated baseball. It was a state-of-the-art facility when it was built, a

multipurpose stadium with whole sections of metal seats on railroad tracks that could be moved to accommodate baseball or football. But it's also one of the last enclosed ballparks, which means
there is no wind at all. In winter, at Redskins games, the noise of
the fans stomping on the metal stands rebounds against itself,
careening off the façade, which dips to the west so the dome of
the Capitol is always in view. It's like being inside a barrel and
having the entire Redskins secondary beating on your head.
They've never measured the decibel level for fear somebody'd
condemn the place as unsafe.

In summer, at Senators games, the stadium embraces the
heat and the humidity in a stranglehold. To say the least, the ball
doesn't carry, not off these bats anyway. In fact, sometimes it
seems nothing moves at all. To play at RFK on an August night
is to fight stasis on every pitch. To sit at RFK on an August night
and watch the Washington Senators is insane.

Of course, the crowds have never been better. As the team
edges toward baseball immortality, the fervor builds. These are
not joyous crowds like the ones who savored the ineptitude of the
'62 Mets. Washington types do not identify. They gloat. They
come to cheer their own superiority.

Today during infield practice Monk, who was a catcher, was
giving Fennis some practice on pop fouls. Fennis does not have
what you call soft hands. He dropped five straight. Finally a guy
behind the plate yelled, "Use two hands, ya bum." Well, that set
Monk off good. He charged the screen, screaming, "Lay off my
ballplayers! Who the fuck are you to tell my ballplayers anything? You couldn't catch nothing but the common fucking
cold."

Needless to say, despite Monk's stalwart defense, the players
are not thrilled by any of this. Last week, Mini-Doc flipped off
the crowd after committing his thirtieth error, the net result of
which was that I had to do twenty inches on whatever happened
to my pal Demetrious Mourning. (He's in rehab in California.)
Last night, the Phoenix pitcher threw at Stick's head. Stick
charged the mound, expecting his teammates to follow. If ever
there was an invitation to your basic bench-clearing brawl, this
was it. Nobody moved. Today Stick took himself and his 83 RBIs
out of the ballgame, pleading heat exhaustion and pissing off everyone in the dugout who hadn't thought of it first.

The only happy guy on the team is Rump. He's 20 for 32
since our little roll in the hay and swinging for the fences again.

Today he hit his fifth dinger in the last three games. We haven't talked except in large group interviews. I haven't got the faintest idea what to say to him. But he sure does smile a lot every time I see him. And every time he does, I want to crawl under the pitching rubber with Mr. Smith.

August 22 Command performance at the office today. Zeke called at the park last night to tell me I'd better get my ass in by 9:00 A.M. sharp. Something about a big staff meeting with Ross. "No bullshit, Berkowitz," the Captain said. "Be there."

I overslept and got in about 9:30. "Siddown," Sal said, taking the ham and swiss croissant from my hand. "You're late."

The entire Sports staff was sitting primly and, I might add, somnambulantly, in rows of folding metal chairs, listening impassively to the words of Dr. Elise R. Pepper, Ross Mitchell's personal nutritionist. Seems like the Sports Department has put on a considerable amount of weight since we went on our collective diet. Nobody but me, Milo, and Zeke, who'll do anything to kiss ass, has lost a pound. Rocky and Pincus have gained fifty-five big ones between them. With the end of the season fast approaching, and with it our awful day of public reckoning, Ross has decreed that we will all have emergency nutritional counseling.

He was midway through his opening remarks when I arrived. "I'll be damned if I'm gonna publish the collective, bloated girth of this department on the last day of the season in ninety-point type. You people are slobs. You people are disgusting. You're an embarrassment to your profession and to me personally. Now, goddammit, I want you people to listen up, sit straight, and lose some goddamned weight."

Lots of bellies retracted at that, though in Pincus's and Zeke's case, sucking it up is a tautological impossibility. Slouching is their natural configuration. Ross introduced Dr. Pepper, who, he said, will be conducting weekly nutritional seminars in the Sports Department before weigh-in. Attendance is mandatory unless we're on assignment, in which case Irene will provide us with a cassette recording of Dr. Pepper's lecture. Irene nodded solemnly, and with no further ado, Dr. Pepper snapped open her briefcase, extracting a sweet potato, and launched into a peroration on the virtues of the "noble tuber."

It was one of those God-awful days with a billion percent humidity and everybody was schvitzing except Dr. Pepper, who stood there cool as a cucumber (30 calories per 207 grams) in her size-six blue serge power suit with the make-believe silk bow knotted at her throat. The fans were going full blast and all these old wire photos that never get filed were waltzing in the air above her head. The air conditioner, such as it is, rattled and Zeke wheezed and ESPN droned on over Raoul's desk, none of which distracted Dr. Pepper in the least. "The sweet potato," she said, peering over her half-spectacles, "is a perfect foodstuff. Indeed, some populations, African and Asian predominantly, have been known to subsist on it almost entirely. Personally, if I was shipwrecked on a desert island and could choose one food to have with me, it would be the sweet potato."

She looked at Ross, who nodded his approval. "The sweet potato is high in vitamin A and fiber, as well as being calorie-dense. You can bake it or boil it. It is delicious mashed, with yogurt, low-fat preferably, as well as on its own merits. The traditional Thanksgiving rendition of the yam is, in fact, a desecration. Marshmallows!"

Dr. Pepper shuddered at the thought of marshmallows. Rocky said, "Ugh!" Pincus said, "Yum." Dr. Pepper ignored them. "The sweet potato is, in fact, the perfect alternative to the high-calorie saturated foodstuffs typical of the modern-day press box."

"You mean like *Dr. Pepper?*" Rocky said suddenly.

Dr. Pepper was not amused and thus neither were Ross and Sal and Zeke. She surveyed her audience for a more adult inquiry. There weren't any. "Questions, people," Sal said. No one said a word. Sal's phone began to ring.

"Very well," Dr. Pepper said and reached into her briefcase again.

"Ten-to-one, she ain't looking for Ruffles with Ridges," Marcus said.

Before you could say hot fudge, Dr. Pepper was pulling these beige links of make-believe fat out of her briefcase. "Five pounds," she said. "Ten pounds. Twenty-five pounds!" She grimaced and dropped the load at Pincus's feet. All the while Sal's phone continued to ring. Five. Ten. Twenty-five times.

"This, people, is the problem," Dr. Pepper said.

She nodded at Irene, who dimmed the lights, and the slide presentation began. Slide number one was a close-up of a fat globule. Slide number two was a bigger fat globule. Slide number three was a gigantic fat globule. "Letterman," Dr. Deadline said. "Definitely Letterman."

Sal's phone had been ringing for two minutes straight. Dr. Pepper didn't notice. She was deep into the horrors of butter and deep frying when Ross finally gave Sal permission to answer his phone and Sal gave Raoul the signal. Pretty soon Raoul was gesturing at Sal, waving and pointing to the phone. Sal ran a finger across his Adam's apple three times, but Raoul would not be deterred. Finally he just bellowed, "Yo, Sal, it's Vito. He's standing naked at some pay phone in Baltimore. He says he's gotta talk to you."

Raoul held out the receiver, which Sal regarded with approximately the same enthusiasm one might have for a desiccated head of lettuce. Ross nodded and went off to take a leak, followed closely by Dr. Pepper. Sal took the phone and Raoul took center stage. Suddenly it was kindergarten in the fun-and-games department.

Raoul relishes his role as the department gossip. And he's really quite good at it. He hears everything working the phones and forgets nothing. He'll be a good reporter someday. "Get *this*," he said, while Rocky made little birdy shadows against the screen. "Vito's up in Baltimore for some track meet or other and he's dictating his folo from some broad's bedroom when there's this knock on the door."

Raoul slipped into falsetto here. " 'Oh my God, it's my husband!' So Vito reaches for his shorts. But he's not in any hurry, see. 'Quick!' the broad says. 'Quick. He's a security guard. He's got a gun!'

"Well, Vito's out the window quick. *Without* his shorts. He's all the way down the block before he sees the first pay phone with a door. And who does he call? Dictation! He just finished filing. Now he's talking to Sal."

Understand: Vito never uses a computer. He's got this thing going with one of the girls in Dictation who, like Vito, is married. So he dictates his stories to her and then they make goo-goo sounds at each other for half an hour.

Anyway, there was considerable debate among us whether Vito was to be lauded for his professionalism in this instance or written off as a major league asshole. The Doctor, who has not a whit of respect for deadlines, made no effort to hide his disgust. "The guy's an animal," he said. "I mean, have you forgotten the time he jilted a paraplegic? Have you?"

No one who's ever heard this story is likely to forget it. God knows, I certainly won't. A watershed in tastelessness is what it is. And it's gotten me wondering all over again just what it means to be one of the guys.

The Doctor didn't need to be asked twice. He didn't need to be asked at all. The Doctor likes his historical mode, which is one of the advantages of always being in the office. He spared us none of the details.

"You know how Vito is big on answering the phones," the Doctor began. "Well, this chippie 'Skins fanatic calls in to talk football. She's chatting up Vito on Jack Pardee and John Riggins and how dumb it is not to be giving him the ball twenty-six times a game. Like I said, this was aways back. Vito listens awhile, agreeing that Riggo ought to be carrying the load and says, finally, 'So, tell me, are you a local girl or a visitor to our fair city?' which must have sounded pretty dumb considering she had the hots for Riggo, but it was Vito's line back then. He used it on all the girls. Before we know it, Vito's out the door to meet this 'local girl' at The Pit for a beer.

"Fifteen minutes later, he's back and he's looking pale. I mean *white* pale. 'That's it,' he says. 'I'm never working the phones again. I mean holy shit, she's a fucking gimp.'

"Turns out she was a paraplegic. Vito bought her one beer and left, pleading an early deadline. Anyway, here's the funny part. She starts calling the department every day asking for Vito: 'Tell him Joan called.' 'Tell him Joan sends her love.' Pretty soon, Vito breaks out in a sweat at the sight of a message slip. Finally, the calls stop. One day, two days and Vito's breathing this big sigh of relief. 'I'm a free man, gentlemen,' he says. That night, she's waiting for him in the lobby. Pretty soon, she's staking out The Pit. Then she gets season tickets to hockey games. It got pretty weird. Like *Fatal Attraction* on wheels. Vito stopped answering his phone. He stopped going out. Then one day, Ross called him in. Seems Joan had been calling talk shows all over town to proclaim her love for Vito. The talk show host called Ross on his car phone. Ross told the guy, 'I think Vito Marchese has finally met his match.' Served Vito right, of course. Not that he got the message or anything. He told the talk show host the next day: 'All I did was buy her a beer. It's not like I asked her to dance or nothing.' "

By the time the Doctor reached this point in the narrative, Milo was holding his stomach. Rocky was gripping his knees and people were literally falling out of their chairs in laughter. I don't know which was funnier, the Doctor's impassioned recitation or the sight of the newly powdered Dr. Pepper leaning against the file cabinet fanning herself with her *Cholesterol and You* handout. I thought she was gonna faint.

It's an interesting phenomenon of mass psychology, not to mention a terrible feeling, to laugh so hard at something you shouldn't be laughing at to begin with and not be able to stop because no one else can stop or wants to stop or thinks there is any reason to stop. I don't know about other papers but this happens a lot at the Washington *Tribune*, where nothing is what you'd call exactly sacred. My sister, the doctor, tells me this is common in emergency rooms, too. So you laugh till you ache and after a while you can't tell anymore whether the ache is from the laughter itself or from how rotten you feel for laughing altogether. I have to say the thought crossed my mind right then: "Is this what being a sportswriter has reduced me to?"

Ross returned from the men's room to find his entire sports staff writhing around at Dr. Pepper's feet. I have never seen him so royally pissed. He was screaming from the meat scale. "You people are slobs! You people are disgusting!"

"You already told us that," Rocky croaked and everyone started to laugh all over again.

I bit my lip so hard trying to keep a straight face it started to bleed. Ross glared at me. Dr. Pepper swooned. And the sight of this serious careerist suddenly turned fragile flower of womanhood got me started all over again. I covered my mouth and pretended to cough. In pretending to cough, I started to choke and Rocky started pounding me on the back. All the time, Dr. Pepper was standing there in the shadow of a fat globule, sucking on her cheeks and fanning herself and waiting for us to come to attention. Needless to say, it didn't happen.

Sal sputtered. Ross muttered. Finally Dr. Pepper turned off the machine. "I think we've had just about enough for today."

As soon as she and Ross were out of earshot, Rocky surfaced from beneath his desk. "Cocktail hour. Beer and Chee-tos on me!" It was 11:00 A.M. We all took an early slide.

August 23   Today the Gaijin split his pants. They ripped right down the middle while he was taking his last cut of batting practice. Rube practically tore the things off him. He's always saving stuff for Cooperstown. Rube is a man of history. He is also a major league snitch and it didn't surprise anybody when Beanie showed up a half hour later with a press release announcing that Jimy Boy has reassigned the Gaijin's personal services contract to the Born-Again Big Top, a wholly owned subsidiary of the Christian Fellowship Entertainment Network.

"From the Show to the sideshow," Billy said.

"Whaddya mean?" Stein said. "He *is* the fucking sideshow."

The Gaijin packed his bags, ate his last clubhouse meal (three triple-decker club sandwiches with Sloppy Joe sauce), and went around the room bowing before each of his teammates like a fallen samurai. At the door, he made what for him amounted to a farewell speech. "So very happy to be here," he said. "It been what you say, real? Now Ricky-San go circus."

"Funny, I thought *this* was the circus," Rump said.

August 24 It finally rained last night. And it really cleared the air. Everybody's in a good mood. There's no real reason for it except maybe that everyone's tired of feeling like shit. Or maybe because this is the last game of the home stand. Or maybe because Evonne Turner, late of the 1989 *Sports Illustrated* swimsuit issue, made a guest appearance at the batting cage.

She was wearing black Spandex pants, a black Spandex halter, black cowboy boots with spurs, and lots of black lipstick. Her PR person, a no-nonsense type in a Burberry raincoat, kept grabbing guys and asking if they wanted their picture "took." They all told her to get fucked until they saw who it was they were getting their picture took with. "Where's the wind machine? I need the wind in my hair," Stein said.

The mood was infectious. Even Monk posed with her, sitting on a bat propped against the crack of his behind. "Don't smile at me," he said, almost smiling. "My wife is in the stands. She might get mad at you."

Having tried everything else, Monk has decided to become a players' manager. A players' manager is a guy who doesn't enforce curfews, doesn't ban hard liquor from the plane, doesn't play the guys who pray the most, and doesn't ban swimsuit models from the batting cage. Monk is not a players' manager.

But Monk's a desperate man. He's the manager of a team that's won four games so far this month. So this week he's been nice, hoping maybe his guys would play for him. There he was yesterday sitting with the bat in the crack of his ass, talking to Mug Shot by the batting cage. "I have a serious and personal question to ask you, Mug Shot. Can you tell me why I love your bleeping black ass so much?"

Mug Shot was speechless.

"Can you tell me why I've put your bleeping black ass up on a pedestal with all those other great Washington Senators? Walter Johnson, Sam Rice, Ossie Bluege. Can you tell me that?"

Mug Shot grunted.

"Tell me who you played for before, Mug Shot? Any of your other managers tell you they love your black ass? Billy Martin tell you that?"

Mug Shot shook his head.

"Doc Edwards?"

Mug Shot shook his head again.

"Joe Altobelli? Anybody but me?"

Mug Shot shrugged.

"Well?" Monk said. "Well?"

"Shit, man, this the first time we conversationalated all year."

"Oh," Monk replied.

The dugout was equally merry. Rump was holding court after being named Player of the Week for last week. The only bad thing I can say about that is now I'm really going to have to talk to him. He's hitting .407 since Detroit and growing his beard again. I guess all the juices must be flowing.

Billy was sitting on the top of the bench spitting sunflower seeds and giving off rebel yells, not at anyone but just because he couldn't contain himself. He's playing every day now that Mancusi is back on the DL. "I'm the goddamned starting third baseman for the suck-ass Washington Senators!"

Buck's daughter is up for a visit from Nuba. She was the bat girl today. They were sitting together on the top step of the dugout and she was holding her daddy's bat and tracing his name on the wood with her finger as if somehow the repetition was going to make it real. She's going with us to New York tomorrow to meet her daddy's new girlfriend. I guess things must be getting serious with the speech therapist.

For Stein, too. Otherwise, Marv Cox wouldn't have shown up. Marvelous Marv Cox is Stein's agent. He represents probably half the team. He likes to hang around the locker room, giving everybody high-fives and saying, "How's it going, Big Guy?"

Marv always acts in his client's best interest, especially when it coincides with his own. He is an agent. He is a jerk.

He and Stein were sitting on the bench, just down from Buck and his daughter, having this animated conversation about Charlene, the Jell-O Goddess. Every ten seconds you'd hear one of them screech her name like a punctuation mark and then they'd go back to vehement whispering. Billy says Marv told Stein he better lose Charlene now before she gets any great ideas from the great Margo Adams, who, baseball fans will recall, sued Wade Boggs for lost wages, claiming she was his constant off-the-field/on-the-road companion.

Anyway, apparently Marv got this call this week from some guy claiming to represent Charlene, who dropped a bunch of names, including Margo's. Marv told Stein it might be prudent not to take Charlene on this trip to New York. Stein kept jumping up and down and telling Marv to get fucked. Even so, it was a cheerful fuck-you. Like I said, the mood *was* infectious.

Everyone was so loose: no one told me to eat shit and die. I was almost sorry when it was time to come inside. The sun was warm for a change instead of suffocating, and so bright that the sudden darkness of the clubhouse made shadows dance before my eyes. In the gloom, I saw Stretch stark naked on the clubhouse floor listening to his Walkman, an automatic thousand-dollar fine established before Monk decided to become a players' manager.

Stretch looked awful, almost as bad as he did on the mound yesterday when he hit three straight batters. He looked like a beached whale who'd spent one too many days onshore. His eyes were closed. His face was pasty, his lips almost blue. For a moment I considered the possibility he might be dead. Then I heard him mumble. "Remember the tingle."

I was sure he had lost it completely. But I was wrong. He was merely trying to regain his sanity and his location. He was listening to Dr. Susan M. Mooney, the voice of reason, try to teach him how to throw a major league baseball again.

"Remember the tingle in your wrist," she said.

" 'Remember the tingle in your wrist,' " he said.

Stretch opened his eyes and pulled off the earphones and blew a bubble that popped all over his face. No doubt about it, he's going bad. Nothing like a three-day growth and a wad of

Double Bubble on an unlined face. Stretch peeled the gum from his whiskers and said, "This here stuff is bullshit is what it is. This Mooney gal wants me to 'member how it feels to throw a goddamned strike. I don't know how the fuck it feels to throw a goddamned strike. I haven't thrown one in a fucking month. And besides, a strike don't feel no different than a ball 'cept better. It's like the difference between coming when you're jerking off and coming when you get laid. Shit."

"I thought head shrinkers were banished along with the Cars, the Pretenders, and Billy Idol."

"Not anymore they ain't."

Piggy had gone to Monk and Stretch had been given a special dispensation with regard to the No Tapes in the Locker Room rule. Behavior modification and hymns were now allowed. Or, in Stretch's case, required.

I asked if I could listen. Stretch shrugged, pressed the RE-WIND button, and handed me his Walkman. Dr. Susan M. Mooney, the Foundation for Competitive Perfection's psychic pitching coach, has one of those vaguely patronizing, accentless voices that could be from anywhere or nowhere. "Now we are going to work on visualization and actualization," Dr. Susan M. Mooney said. "Can you say that? Repeat after me. 'Visualization. Actualization.' Good! I knew you could do it!

"Now I want you to grip the ball. How do the seams feel? Do they feel smooth? Rough? Bumpy? Feel the ball in your hand: its weight, its width, its texture. Go ahead. Feel it. That wasn't so hard, was it?

"Let's proceed. Now that you can really feel the ball, I want you to get in touch with your windup. Are you taking a deep breath? Have you checked the runner at first base? Fine. Fine. Now let's work on feeling that strike. Don't *think* strike. *Feel* strike. Feel the tingle in your wrist . . ."

I had heard enough. "See what I mean? Bullshit, huh?" Stretch said.

I had to agree with him there. But I didn't want to discourage him either. So I told him that not all therapy is shit and how he ought to give it a chance. I mean, what does he have to lose? Stretch gave me that "yeah sure right" look and said "What the fuck" and put the earphones back on and lay there staring at Mount Rushmore. " '*Feel* strike,' " he said. " '*Feel* strike.' *Feel* the goddamned motherfucking strike."

The rest of the guys came in and I went to check something

with Buck and got to talking with him and his daughter. I kept
her company while her daddy took a shower and she told me
how she was going to meet his new lady in New York but she
didn't want to because it wasn't her momma. I said she was a nice
lady and Buck came back and said I was a nice lady too and his
little girl gave me a kiss. It was time to go upstairs. I can't remember the last time I left the clubhouse feeling so good. On my
way out, I noticed Stretch. He was still naked and still mumbling. Only this time he was talking about pizza.

New York

August 25 Stretch is AWOL.

He didn't make the team plane this morning, which in
Monk's book is a fining offense equal to listening to rock 'n' roll,
and he didn't meet us at Yankee Stadium either, which is grounds
for suspension. In fact, he would have been suspended immediately if it wasn't for Piggy, who had no idea where he was either,
but kept promising Monk he'd be there any minute.

Beanie was nowhere to be found, so us investigative types
did what we usually do when we can't get anywhere on a story.
We asked each other. Mac must have been really hard up because
he even asked me. "Whaddya suppose got into Stretch?" he said.

"Pizza," I said and headed for the phone.

It was one of those calls you don't want to make from the
press box, where guys can't help but notice you taking notes and
start accidentally-on-purpose reading over your shoulder. So I
called Stretch from a pay phone outside a men's room on the loge
level along the third base line.

This was not what you call your ideal interview situation.
There were street punks in ripped-off Nikes screaming
"Mo'fuck" in my ear and a fat man in plaid poking me on the
shoulder and telling me to get the fuck off the phone. Finally I
gave him the finger and he went off to find somewhere else to get
down on the game.

Still and all, I knew it was going to be a great interview.
Sometimes you just know these things. Telephones have a weird
effect on people, especially fragile people who don't like to talk

about themselves. I think somehow they forget they're talking to someone else. If they close their eyes and cup the receiver under their chin and just talk, they can almost believe they are talking to themselves. Then my voice, the voice of the outside world, becomes their own subconscious voice. Telephone interviews become interior monologues this way. This was one of those.

"How's the 'za?" was the first thing I said and it was the only thing I needed to say.

"Deep-dish and gooey," he said. "I'm gonna call my place 'Stretch McCarthy's Chicago-Style Pizzeria and Bullpen.' "

"First one in Newnan, Georgia," I said.

Stretch laughed and I knew we'd be okay. Of course, he didn't know that yet. "Listen, A.B., I can't talk to you. Monk'll kill me if I do and Daddy will get right on line behind him."

I reminded him that Monk, who has suddenly given up being a players' manager, had no jurisdiction over conversations between me and the proprietor of Stretch McCarthy's Chicago-Style Pizzeria and Bullpen. It took him a minute to grasp the import of that fact. After all, Stretch has been answering to one skipper or another since he was five years old. "Hot damn, you're right," he said.

After that, it didn't take much to get him going. The hard part was keeping up with him. One pen ran out of ink and I started fishing around in my bag for another. That one didn't work either, so I started scribbling with a wax pencil I poached from the office. It was so beautiful what he was saying, I wanted to get it all down right just the way he said it. I owed it to him. Probably I got most of it, but I was dying later when there was a word missing here and there and I couldn't remember what it was.

"The feeling's just not there," he said. "I think it's gone forever."

I started to disagree, but Stretch didn't want to be dissuaded. So I just shut my mouth and let the guy talk. You'd be amazed how hard that is to do, for me anyway. I'm always stepping all over my best quotes.

"These boys, these pitching coaches, they're real big on mechanics, you know? Oh man. Daddy's all over me about my point of release and coming across my body. Shit. Pitching ain't mechanics. Leastwise not for me it ain't. Pitching is feeling. That Mooney gal got that right. And the feeling, it's gone, is all."

Stretch paused to catch his breath. In the silence, I struggled to catch up. My handwriting was getting wild. Three words to a page, two, one. I was writing as fast as I could. But it's hard to keep up with a country boy who wants to unburden himself.

" 'Member that game in Milwaukee?"

Who could forget?

"Well, you know that pitch I threw behind Yount's head? That's when it left. I said, 'What the hell was that?' Fennis calls for the inside heater again. I threw it behind his head again. I said, 'What the fuck?' It ain't never been the same since. And lemme tell ya, it's a very frustrating experience and an embarrassing experience also, trying to throw a ball and you ain't got no idea where it's going. It's flat-out scary is what it is. I mean, in the bullpen and on the sideline it's pretty much right there. I have the good control. Then a right-handed batter stands in. And here come that fear. 'Where's that sucker gonna go?' You know?

"Daddy says, 'Don't you be worrying about it. It's the hitter's responsibility to get out of the way.' Monk, he wants me to see a minister. Mooney wants me to relax. And Rump wants me to think. Think? Shit! I ain't done nothing but.

"I get these letters every day. 'Try this.' 'Try that.' My momma says I should try some hypnotist guy who got her to quit smoking. I don't think a sucker could put me under. They'd have to brainwash me and take everything out of my head, and that ain't going to happen. I mean, it's *over*. Can't they see?"

Stretch gulped. I stretched my fingers. They hurt from writing so hard.

"It all come down to control. When I had the control, I was ready to deal anytime, anyplace. I loved the game of baseball. But it wasn't fun the way it was. When I had it, you didn't think about it. You just knew where it was gonna go. It was just here for you. It come natural, is all. When I lost it, there wasn't nothing to go back to."

Sometimes a guy will say something and suddenly you realize you're hearing something your own voice has been telling you for a long time, but he's saying it so much better than any hot-shit sportswriter ever could that you want to engrave it in your notebook so no one will ever bullshit you again. That's how I felt standing there listening to Stretch. Stretch was dealing the truth. He knew far better, and far earlier, than any of the rest of us what he was up against, and maybe that's why he sounded so relieved.

These guys with the live young arms, they're supposed to be

in command of their pitches. They are supposed to be in control. Bottom line: that's what we all aspire to, isn't it? But for a guy who throws ninety-five miles per hour, control is lots more than a metaphor. Maybe that's why Stretch knows better than anyone else how tenuous our grasp on control really is.

He's a natural, all right. He knows that control is an illusion or at best a temporary reprieve. Lots of guys talk about making themselves into ballplayers. Not Stretch. He was born knowing how to throw the hell out of the ball. It was a gift, or better yet a loan, and he respected it as such. He knew he was dealing on borrowed time. He knew he could not relearn what was never learned to begin with. He knew the ballgame was over.

"So, listen," he said, just before hanging up. "Would you maybe like do me a favor, A.B.? You think maybe you could get Beanie to send me some autographed balls and a team picture so I could put 'em up in my place? I don't think I'd best go ask my daddy."

I told him for sure I would and hung up thinking about my lede. "Stretch McCarthy is a natural, all right."

August 26   Ballplayers never cease to amaze me. Here it is Saturday night in New York City and the only thing they can think of to do is hang around the hotel bar. I got back from the theater and they were all just sitting there, the way they always are, the same couples in the same postures, the same foursomes ordering the same rounds. Buck and the speech therapist were huddled in a corner, their foreheads almost touching. Stick and Mancusi were knocking back shooters at the bar. Stein and Charlene and Marv Cox were giggling at a dimly lit table. And Piggy and Monk were drinking coffee alone in the center of the room. Lots of managers have rules against players drinking in the same bar as the skipper. Not Monk. Monk always sits himself down in the center of the bar so he can watch everybody else having a good time and, presumably, prevent them from having too good a time. Everyone ignores him.

Usually I avoid the hotel bar because it's an invitation to getting invited to places you don't want to be. But ever since Michael and Rump, I'm finding it harder and harder to be in my room alone. So I decided to have a nightcap. I told myself I might dig up something for a folo on Stretch. *Just part of the job.* That's what I always tell myself when I want to avoid telling myself the truth.

There was this bimbo at the bar with Stick and Mancusi and you could tell from the cut of her gown and the way her tongue kept licking her wet-look plum lip gloss that she was a serious baseball fan. I sat down two stools away from them. Stick was counting his money, trying to get her attention. It must have worked because before he had gotten halfway through his billfold she was gazing deep into his eyes and saying pretty much so everyone could hear, "How 'bout a blow job, big man?"

"*Whaa?*" Stick said.

She ran the tips of her mauve rhinestone-studded nails across his cheek and said it again, licking her lips for emphasis.

Stick was speechless. Mancusi elbowed him in the ribs. "Yo, Stick!"

The Louisville Slugger nodded at her and she nodded at the bartender, who winked at them both and said, "One blow job, coming!"

I guess they've been doing this act awhile because Joe, the bartender, was back in a flash with a shot glass rimmed with cream and brimming with some particularly viscous liqueur. The girl, Lisette I think her name was, batted her distinctly false eyelashes, kissed the air with her oh-so-wet plum lips, and licked the cream from the rim of the glass with a practiced and petulant flick.

Stick groaned. Mancusi said, "Yo." And Lisette, who clearly needed no encouragement, took the shot glass in her teeth, tilted back her head until her mane of long black hair practically reached the floor, and chugged the entire thing.

It's hard to say just how many blow jobs Lisette had already had. But clearly she had had enough. She slithered off her stool, blew a kiss in Stick's direction, and wobbled away on her five-inch heels in search of an elevator. There was great applause at her exit and much hooting about Stick's batting average with women. Once more the cheer went up: *The Stick has struck out again!*

Stick slid off his stool, loudly proclaiming Lisette to be a goddamned motherbleeping cocktease and plopped himself down at Stein's table. "A real pro," Stein said sympathetically.

"A CT, all right," said Marv, who also represents the Stick.

"Oh, I dunno 'bout that," said Charlene, who considers herself a feminist. "I kinda liked that girl."

Obviously, Stein hadn't taken Marv's advice about Charlene. So Marv had taken it upon himself to accompany them to New York, charging the whole trip to Stein and making sure Stein didn't get into any trouble.

"Shit," Charlene said, "she was just having fun, is all. Can't a girl have a little fun?"

"Fun my ass," Stein said.

"Right," Marv said.

"Why, you two are just the biggest sexist pigs I ever did meet," Charlene said. I love when Charlene gets her feminism and her fake Southern belle charm all mixed up. "I mean, if you boys do it, it's fine. But let a girl have a little fun and she's a ball-busting bitch."

As it happens, I was the only other female in the place familiar to Charlene and she decided to call for reinforcement. "What do you think, A.B.? Aren't they just the biggest sexist pigs you ever did meet?"

Of course, I had been sitting at the bar pretending not to listen. So now I had to pretend to be startled. I did my best "Who, me?" number and finally agreed they certainly were sexist and they were probably pigs, too, which made Charlene giggle and slap her rocklike thighs. She invited me to sit down. Stein glared at her. Stick glared at Stein. Marv bared his pearly white teeth.

It was midnight. I figured I could use a laugh. I sat down.

"Bartender! A blow job, please!"

At first Joe was startled by my request. Then he winked at me the way he had winked at Lisette and said, "One blow job, coming."

Right away, I was a hero in Charlene's book. She allowed how I was okay for a reporter person. Stein sucked his teeth. Stick said, "Shit." Marv flashed his pearly whites and said I had a very good reputation among the agents he talked to. Then my blow job arrived.

I hadn't really thought this through. But once the glass was in front of me, I realized there was only one way to go. Within seconds every ballplayer and bimbo in the joint was hovering over the table, cheering me on.

I tossed back my hair just the way I knew Lisette would, if she had dirty blond hair that ended in split ends just below her ears, and licked the cream from the rim of the glass with a flick that was neither practiced nor petulant.

"Go! Go! Go!"

There was no turning back. I leaned over and took the shot glass between my teeth and chugged that sucker as best I could. The applause was almost as sweet as the drink, which turned out to be peach schnapps, heavy cream, and a touch of brandy. Charlene hugged me tight and kissed both my cheeks and said, "You know, girl, we have a lot in common."

Of course, it may have been the booze but that struck me as the funniest thing I'd heard in a long time. Not wanting to be rude, I nodded and tried very hard not to laugh. "Really, we do. Honest," Charlene insisted. "Do you know one time, it was maybe like five years ago, I was doing some modeling, you know, for one of those girlie magazines? I did this spread where I was supposed to be this girl reporter in the locker room and go around sucking off all them boys. Do you do that, A.B.?"

"Not yet," Stein said.

I saw Rump across the room and thought, "If they only knew." Charlene was right. We *do* have a lot in common. I told her, "Sorry, I wouldn't even *pretend* to sleep with these assholes."

"Oh well," she said. I think she was genuinely disappointed. "I had a great time. I sent copies to everyone. Even my parents."

"I'm sure they were very proud," I said.

It was time to call it a night.

Home Stand

August 31 The phone was ringing when I got home from the ballpark last night. The game ran late. It was nearly 1:00 A.M. I dumped my stuff and let it ring. I stopped running for phones when Michael stopped calling me. I pressed the button on the answering machine instead and listened. It was Sal. As usual, he didn't bother to identify himself. "Berkowitz! In my office, 9:00 A.M. sharp."

Nine o'clock?

I tried to think what I might have done wrong and for a change I couldn't think of anything. Sal gave the story on Stretch real big play. I thought maybe he just wanted to tell me he loves my ass, but at nine in the morning?

I overslept as usual and got in at nine-thirty, which I thought was pretty good. Sal was pacing back and forth and sucking his thumb, waiting for me. There was no mistaking the signs: he had a live one. He was too excited even to ream me out for being late.

He leaned forward and started to whisper in my ear, but the excitement caught in his throat and before he was done the whisper had become a shout. "Get this, Berkowitz," he said. "Somebody saw your boy Rump coming out of this big-deal fertility center last week. Seems like your boy's got a big problem. I want you to check it out."

Gravity drove me into the nearest seat. "Oh God," I said.

Sal mistook my tone for his own. "Great, huh?" he said.

I shook my head. I shrugged. "So what?" I said.

Sal likes his reporters excited and he was beginning to realize that I definitely was not excited. "Hey, a little enthusiasm here, Berkowitz. This is great stuff! Human interest! ALL-STAR CATCHER CAN'T GET IT UP!"

"That's impotence, Sal," I said glumly.

"Oh, right, yeah, whatever. ALL-STAR CATCHER SHOOTING BLANKS."

I winced. Jocks and jock sniffers, they all speak the same language.

"It's still a helluva story," Sal said. "I want you to get on it right away. Work your sources. Then talk to your boy. I've got the goods."

I buried my head in my hands. I saw lights and shadows, comets soaring through the darkness. I saw myself irrevocably in bed with Rump.

"No," I said.

"No?" Sal said.

"No."

"Whaddya mean *no?*"

I tried to sound blasé. I tried to sound bored. I gulped. I said, "I don't think it's a story."

Talk about waving a red flag in front of a bull. Sal began to snort and paw his feet against the carpet. "Whaddya mean it's not a story? It's a fucking *coup.*"

"I don't see it."

"Oh," Sal said. "You don't see it. Well, *I* see it. And I'm the goddamned editor."

What I could see was a six-foot-six man threatening to extend his height another six inches by pulling every hair in his scalp straight up. Also, I could see my strategy wasn't going to work. I tried anyway. "Isn't anything private anymore, Sal?"

This just made things worse. "What do you think this is, the *Columbia Journalism Review*? I said, 'Check it out.'"

I checked the floor. The dustballs and I were unanimous. "I can't, Sal," I said. "I mean, I won't."

There are lots of ways reporters have of not writing stories. You can make a few calls and tell the editor, "There's nothing there." You can make one call to information and tell him, "I'm working it." You can lie completely and say, "It's in the notebook," and hope someone important will get shot and he'll forget. One thing you cannot do is flat-out refuse. This is a firing offense at most papers. At the Washington *Tribune*, where even if you're dead you may not get canned, refusing an assignment is a one-way ticket to night police.

I didn't see where I had any choice. The parameters of my indiscretion had never been so clear. I couldn't tell Sal I had slept with my best source, my boy, as he likes to call him, and that while Sal had the story right I was in no godly position to write it. And I certainly couldn't write it. How could I do that to Rump?

"*Can't!? Won't!?* It's your fucking job, Berkowitz. It's your story or your ass."

"Get somebody else," I said.

Sal slammed the door behind me and I headed for the nearest elevator, which of course took ten minutes to arrive. When the door slid open, I saw Michael standing there holding a yellow polyurethane cafeteria tray loaded with doughnuts. Shane Mallory, the new City desk copy aide, was standing at his side, giggling.

At least now I know how he spent his birthday. Snuggling up to a goddamned copy aide with legs as long as I am.

Michael nodded. I nodded. Shane giggled. "Great piece on that pitcher," she burbled. "I just love that name. Stretch, is it?"

"Stretch," I said.

"Really, a great piece," Michael said.

"Yeah," I said, "it's really been a great week."

Then they got off the elevator and Shane took Michael's arm and held a doughnut to his lips so he could eat and walk at the same time. I can't believe the son of a bitch is sleeping with a woman named Shane who holds his doughnuts for him.

I wandered around awhile looking at the windows on Connecticut Avenue with their 1950s fashions, noting all the HELP WANTED signs, ate a slice of pizza in honor of Stretch, and got to the park.

Tonight was the last of a four-game series with the Red Sox. It was supposed to be an off-day, but they rescheduled that April rain-out. For the Senators, it was just another day on the baseball diamond, which is the last thing they want, all except Rump, that is, who can't wait to get to the ballpark these days. He's hit in fourteen straight games and is batting .425 since Detroit. You don't want a day off when you've hit in fourteen straight games.

He was standing by the batting cage when I arrived. The Boss was playing to the empty stadium and Rump had one leg up on the side of the cage, stretching out his hamstring and bopping to the music. "Ba-bee we were born to ru-uh-uh-nn." God, he's got a terrible voice.

I stood there beside him, the closest I have been to him in weeks, watching the outfielders shagging flies. His eyes followed the arc of the ball. My eyes followed his. He didn't seem surprised that I was standing there after weeks of avoiding him. He just said, "Beautiful, isn't it?" like nothing had ever happened.

It is beautiful. Baseball is man's closest approximation to timelessness. It is the best we can do. And what I was about to say was the worst we can do. I was about to ruin it for him. I stared at the flag in deepest centerfield. A gentle breeze was blowing; the chalk of the baselines was dancing in the air. It isn't chalk, really, though everyone calls it that. It's pulverized Georgia marble. I can't tell you how good it made me feel to learn that baseball is defined by something that endures.

Between the lines. Baseball players always talk about how you gotta do it between the lines. Those lines are the boundaries of their world and in a way of mine, too. They separate those who can and those who can't, us and them. Maybe that's why so many managers hop over them on the way to the mound. *Between the lines.* Some lines are not supposed to be crossed and I crossed them and now they were blurring in the breeze, disintegrating before my eyes.

"Rump, they know," I said.

"Huh?" he said, following the flight of another ball.

"They know. About the infertility. Somebody saw you coming out of some clinic downtown and called Sal. Or at least that's what he says. He told me to check it out. He says it's great stuff."

Rump grasped the aluminum bar that runs around the back of the cage. I did the same. I figured the least I could do was look him in the eye. I turned and tried to measure his expression. But I was squinting into the sun and saw nothing but my shame. The words tumbled out of me without pause or even much thought. "Look, I told Sal I wouldn't do it. I told him I can't. And I won't. You've got to believe me. I won't write it. But somebody will. You know Sal. He thinks he's got a live one. I know what I've got to do. Think about what you want to do and let me know."

Rump's been around a lot longer than I have. He knows how this game is played. I didn't have to remind him that Sal would run the story with him or without him, with me or without me. Quashing it was out of the question. The only decision Rump had to make was whether to cooperate or not. It was hard to say which way he would get screwed worse.

"I'll do whatever you say," I said.

He nodded and blew a bubble and banged his bat hard against his spikes. I left him standing there watching Buck hit dinger after dinger over the rightfield fence. He was motionless: And why not? It's not as if there was anything he could do except stand there and wait for his sperm count to make headlines.

Great stuff, huh?

This is what we do: we take people's misery and call it human interest and give them this big chance to talk about it without, of course, mentioning the implicit or else. Or else we'll do it anyway, asshole, and you won't even get a chance to tell it your way. Talk about manipulation. Yours truly and the Washington *Tribune* had rendered Rump completely impotent and we hadn't even written a word yet about his infertility.

I barely watched the game. They lost, is all I know, and Stick hit another meaningless home run, his twenty-fifth of the season. I filed and left a message for Sal saying I had no story on Rump and sat back waiting for a call. But it didn't come. I kept hoping someone else would make the decision for me: fire me, suspend me, something. But no one did. My plane leaves at 7:00 A.M. in the morning. I guess I'll find out if I still have a job when I get to Cleveland.

SEPTEMBER

Cleveland

September 1 "The West End Motor Court by the Lake."

The cabbie scrunched up his nose and glanced over his shoulder through the bulletproof partition. "You sure?" he said.

"I'm sure," I replied.

I know this will sound stupid. I know it was insane. But I had to go back. Nothing's been the same since I lost my watch in Room 113 of the West End Motor Court by the Lake. I slept with Rump. I broke up with Michael. And I'm probably going to get shitcanned today. Half the time I don't know where I am or what time it is. And God knows I don't know what the hell I'm doing. Equilibrium is a thing of the past.

I am woozy. I'm always woozy in the air. And I'm always in the air. But now I feel as if I'm circling O'Hare in a thunderstorm even when I'm on the ground. So I held a barf bag all the way to Cleveland and stuck an extra in my shoulder bag just in case. I made up my mind as soon as we landed.

"All right," the cabbie said. "If you say so."

He left me in the parking lot of the West End Motor Court by the Lake with the cyclone fence and the broken glass. I have been dreaming a lot about cyclone fences and broken glass. Now I know why.

The parking lot was empty and so was the lobby except for a

pimp reading the *Racing Form* in an orange vinyl easy chair. He was cracking his gum and sucking his saliva and circling his picks. There was no one else in sight. I waited a minute, listening to him suck and crack, and thought I really might go mad if I had to listen to those sounds much longer. I banged the little chrome bell with the palm of my hand again. Still, no one appeared. Somewhere in a back room, Oprah was commiserating with a child prostitute. The audience booed. I banged again.

"Hughhh?" the desk clerk said, ducking through the door.

I asked if I could see the room. Room 113. I explained about the watch and my grandma and losing all sense of time and proportion. "Hughhh. You want to register?"

"No, I just want to look. I was a guest here. In July. I lost my watch. I'd like to try to find it. Just in case."

He pushed a registration card across the counter, the same brown Formica with the fake wooden grain that surrounded my bed in Room 113 where I put my watch at 3:00 in the morning on July 12 after Rump won the All-Star Game with a two-run home run with two outs in the bottom of the ninth inning.

"No, you don't understand. I don't want to register. I just want to *look.*"

He looked at me blankly and grunted. I asked to see the manager. The manager looked at me blankly and grunted. I explained all over again. "All I want to do is look. I've called here twenty times. Nobody returns my calls. The least you can do is let me look for myself."

The clerk shook his head. The manager shook his head. The pimp with the *Racing Form* and the masticated chewing gum shook his head. "Bitch just wants to look."

I tried again. "Room 113. Is it occupied?"

"Nope," the manager said.

"Then why can't I just look at it?"

"S'gainst policy."

"I'll pay, for God sakes!"

He shook his head again. "S'gainst policy."

"Since when?"

"Since owner don't want none that kind bidness no more."

"What kind of business?"

"Loose bidness."

The pimp snapped his gum and started to cackle. I started to scream. "I want to see the goddamned owner and I want to see him now. *Do you hear me? I am a reporter for the Washington* Tribune *and I want to see the owner now!*"

Ranting does not become me. My voice gets high and squeaky and I sound like a mouse in heat, which isn't a good way to get taken seriously. The clerk, the manager, and the pimp began to laugh and talk black talk among themselves. *"The bitch crazy. Ummm hmmm."* I took off my shoe and started banging the counter. I was in danger of becoming seriously deranged, which it turned out was quite effective. The manager picked up the phone and mumbled something into the receiver.

A minute later they were opening the door to Room 113. And a minute after that I was down on all fours pawing at the carpet, the same brown shag carpet with the same barbecue potato chips ground into the pile. I could see my watch: the square white face with the black Roman numerals and the YANKEES logo engraved on the back. But of course it wasn't there. Only the dustballs were there, the same dustballs I had pawed through once before.

I flung open the drawers. I pulled back the sheets. I flipped the fucking mattress. My watch was gone. My watch was really gone. I looked in the bathroom mirror and saw the tarnished brass chain hanging limply against the door. I started to cry.

Room 113 of the West End Motor Court by the Lake dissolved around me. Edges disappeared. Everywhere I looked—the chair, the bed, the television, the drawers—I saw little dots that kept getting farther and farther apart like a photograph blown up too big. My life was coming apart at the seams. It's been this way since I lost my watch in the West End Motor Court by the Lake. Ruth says it's just tiredness; the road. But I don't know.

The room swerved. I reached for the phone. Michael's number was reflexive still. I waited. My chest thickened anticipating his voice. The phone rang and rang. It was a hollow ring. "This call cannot be completed as dialed." I dialed again and my chest thickened some more. "Please hang up and try your call again." I slammed the receiver against the phone and lay down to regain my balance. I dreamed instead.

It was one of those dreams you are supposed to have in the heaviest sleep right before dawn. A dream as thick as a drug, a dream to write down and remember. I was walking along the service road outside the West End Motor Court by the Lake. I recognized it from the cyclone fence and the broken glass. I was carrying all my stuff and trying to hitch a ride. Every time I put up my thumb, the bags would slide off my shoulders and I'd have to stop and try to balance them all over again. It was night and there were trees suddenly sprouting in the middle of the road and the road became a forest and I reached for the cyclone fence but it was gone and I was scared. A truck, a blue Datsun pickup truck, gunned its engine and roared out of the gloaming, doing wheelies between the trees. I dropped my bags and stuck up my thumb. The windshield wipers beat hard against the glass, even though it wasn't raining. The glass shrieked. And I shrieked as the truck veered out of my path. Then everything was wet. I was crying; the wipers were scraping my face. Back and forth. Back and forth. Michael smiled from the cab of the truck and kept going. Another truck came. Again I dropped my bags and raised my thumb. Again I was almost run over. Rump smiled and kept on going. Then Sal and Milo; Buck and Billy. Even Rashid B. Down went my bags, up went my thumb, back and forth went the wipers. The trees turned into cyclone fence. I put down my bags and walked away. My shoulders didn't hurt. My eyes dried. I heard music and started to "Hitch Hike" with Marvin Gaye.

I woke in Room 113 of the West End Motor Court by the Lake and tried to will myself back to sleep. I wanted the end. But there was no going back. I was awake in the bed where the Halcion kicked in. I reached for my watch, but it was gone. I sat up and the dizziness was gone too. The room was standing still.

I had no idea what time it was. The late-afternoon sun was going down. The phone was smashed, the television disconnected. I wasn't about to ask at the front desk. What if I was late for the game? My heart stopped and started. What if I was? I washed my face. I looked in the mirror. "You're thirty years old. That's what time it is."

I left a hundred bucks of Sal's money next to the fractured phone and headed for the bus stop. The tarnished brass chain scraped against the door as I left. The pendulum swings. I promised to buy myself a watch in the morning.

September 2   Batting practice was over by the time I got to the stadium yesterday. Pretty much everybody was back in the clubhouse already. It was the same old shit: Stein screaming at his bookie over his portable telephone, Billy doing Run-D.M.C., Mini-Doc and Guttierez playing backgammon and cursing each other bilingually, Lawson reading the Bible to a group of bored born-agains, Buck staring at his baby's picture, and, of course, Stick bitching. This time it was his leg.

"It's my calf. I'm telling ya I've gotta calf."

Rube was kneeling at Stick's feet and fondling his right calf, which looked pretty much like any other calf I've ever seen. Apparently it looked like that to Rube, too. "I don't see nothing," he said.

"I'm telling ya I've gotta calf. I felt it pop when I was pulling on my sanitary hose. It's pulled. I'm telling ya, it's pulled. I can't go today."

I love the way these guys talk about their bodies. They're never just hurt, they're *hurting.* Or they're *nicked.* Or they're *banged up,* in which case they *can't go.* And they never have a shoulder injury or a knee injury. They have a *shoulder,* or a *knee,* or, in Rump's case, a *groin.* Only jocks have groins. Everyone else has genitalia.

I'll bet you anything that's how Benny Albani started his sportscast last night: "Stick Fuller is out with a calf." It's become common usage among jock sniffers, mostly so they can sound like one of the guys. Even Ross. Son of a bitch took himself to one of those fantasy baseball camps last winter, the Reds, I think. First day, he tears the cartilage in his knee. Later, Pete Rose comes by and asks how he is. "Gotta knee," Ross says and Pete nods sympathetically. Ross was thrilled. Guy publishes a major metropolitan daily and he comes back telling everybody this was the most important day of his life.

Anyway, if the injury is above the waist, the diagnosis is tightness. Tightness lasts three days, after which it immediately becomes tendinitis. If the injury is below the waist, it's a hip pointer, except in the Washington *Tribune.* Captain Fuck-up has been deleting hip pointers from the *Trib* since a guy in Milwaukee told him twelve years ago that a hip pointer is code for VD.

General soreness is also a very serious and common condition, especially on a last-place club. Too much general soreness leads to suspicion of jaking it, which makes the perpetrator a dog. Dogging it is treason.

"I'm telling you I've gotta calf," Stick said. "You telling me I don't?"

"Calf schmaff," Rube said. "Monk's gonna have a cow."

Stick put his weight on his foot and winced a little too broadly. "*You* tell him," Stick said. "I'm going to get treatment."

Stick hopped all the way to the trainer's room, where he

plunked himself in the whirlpool and soaked while Rube was left to explain to Monk why his cleanup hitter was taking the night off. "He says he pulled it putting on his socks," Rube told him.

"Unbe-fucking-lievable," Monk said and for once he was right.

Rube called upstairs and Beanie put it in the notes that the Stick was scratched from the lineup on the first day of September. *Out with a calf.*

I had to write my Sunday notes column after the game and I didn't have much considering I had missed BP while sleeping in Room 113 of the West End Motor Court by the Lake. So I did the entire thing about Stick's calf, noting that he had finished August with a .282 batting average, 25 home runs and 91 RBIs, all career highs and all with still a month to go in the season. The column was pretty funny, especially the part about the socks. I made sure to call in after Sal left. Captain Fuck-up was only too happy to pass along a message: "File Doubleday or come home."

I was late getting downstairs after the game and hustling to catch up when I ran into Rump coming out of the shower. So much for avoiding him. I asked if he had ever heard of someone pulling a muscle while putting on his socks. It's the kind of thing I used to ask him all the time before Detroit. I could always count on him for some little quote that would make a piece of shit story just a little less shitty. I haven't asked him anything since Detroit. So my copy is suffering, among other things. I miss him. Anyway, he said he hadn't heard of anybody pulling a calf while putting on his socks. "I'm just surprised he didn't pull something putting on his jock." He smiled and said, "You can write it if you meet me Saturday night for a drink." I started to decline and he shook his head. "You don't understand, Ari. I've made up my mind."

September 3 "Get out your notebook," he said.

"You sure? You don't have to do this, you know."

"I'm sure. Just take this down."

I was barely into the booth and barely out of my thoughtfully unprovocative Perry Ellis blazer. "Can't I order a drink first?"

"I already got you one."

The waitress arrived on cue with a Stoli on the rocks with a twist. I thanked her. I thanked Rump. I fiddled with my swizzle stick, rearranged my napkin, commented on the game. "Your notebook," Rump said.

He wanted to talk. I wanted to procrastinate, the reverse of the normal order of things. Sources do not usually have to beg me to quote them while I excavate a bowl of cocktail pretzels. But there was nothing normal about this interview situation, nothing usual about my feelings regarding Rump. I was pretty sure there was nothing he could say that would save my ass. It hadn't even occurred to me that he might try. There was no way that Rump was going to cooperate on the story and no way I was going to write it without him. The only question was what was going to happen to him when someone else did. So I fiddled with my swizzle stick and pretended I couldn't find a pen without realizing just how much I was trying to protect him.

The table had one of those cheap red candleholders with white plastic netting surrounding it, the kind you see in every pizzeria across America. Rump was holding it between his hands, warming himself in its glow. The candle shone in his face. His beard looked redder than ever, his eyes wildflower-blue. For a second, I let myself think how handsome he is, which was enough finally to make me start fishing for my notebook in earnest.

"C'mon, Ari," he said gently. "You can do it. Take this down."

Rump dictated the story, complete with punctuation. It was a triumph of managing the news. The White House couldn't have done any better. It went way beyond damage control. In one short paragraph, he co-opted Sal completely. Rump gave him the story, but denied him the exposé. Without the exposé, there was no glee. Without the glee, there was just a short, sweet, sad tale about human frailty, and you know how much sports editors like those. It was brilliant.

In one short sweet paragraph, Rump managed to save his ass and mine. There wasn't a hole anywhere except the one inside me that derived from the knowledge that he was doing this at least in part to protect me.

" 'My wife, JoAnne, and I have recently learned that we are unable to have children. Over the course of this season, I have learned a great deal about infertility. One of the things I have learned is the stress this puts on a marriage, not to mention your batting average. It's hard to explain how it makes you feel, not being able to have kids. It's one of those things you never think about until you can't. Then it's a kind of death. Talk about your basic slump. Who knows, maybe people won't feel so bad if they know it can happen to a major leaguer, too."

I had only one follow-up question. "What made you decide to tell this now?"

Rump leaned back against the banquette and pushed the red candleholder across the table toward me. I could feel its warmth on my neck and my chin. "I learned from a friend how much better you feel if you talk about it," he said. "After we talked, I started to hit. It's my way of saying thank you."

I flushed at his words which, thank God, were the closest we came to talking about "us." The candle's warmth spread down my fingers. Its light caught my gratitude. He noticed I had stopped writing. "Put that in," he said. "It's important."

Once again I had no idea what to say to him and Rump knew it. He glanced at his watch. "I think you have a deadline to make. It'll write itself. Don't worry. I'll get the check."

By the time the elevator reached my floor, I knew exactly what I wanted to say. It wasn't going to be hard to make Rump sound good in this one. The only question was whether I could make him sound good enough. I made the deadline with three minutes to spare and the Captain put me on hold while he read; I daydreamed about Rump and wondered whether I'm crazy for not loving him. I was still wondering when Sal called ten minutes later. The Captain had woken him; he wasn't about to take responsibility for how to play this sucker.

"Thought you said, '*I can't*,'" Sal said.

"Yeah well, that was before Rump said I could."

There was a pause. "Nice," he said finally. His tone was anything but.

I can't remember the last time Sal was so disappointed in a scoop. I was elated.

It was after 1:00 A.M. I went back downstairs hoping Rump would still be there. I wasn't about to go to his room.

He was there, all right, with his hands still wrapped around the candle. I punched up the story on my Radio Shack and pushed the machine across the table to him, breaking yet another rule. He read while I held my breath. "Nice," he said finally.

"Funny, that's exactly what Sal said."

"No shit," Rump said, grinning. "Well, that's just too damn bad."

I ordered another round. On me.

Boston

September 4 Stick went on the disabled list today. He has been examined by the team doctor, his own doctor, and a third allegedly impartial doctor. He has been X-rayed, biopsied, and, yes, even CAT-scanned. Tomorrow he's scheduled for magnetic resonance imaging. No one can find a thing wrong with him. But the more they test, the more he limps, and the more he limps, the more he retreats to the third person.

"The Stick is *hurting*," the Stick said. "And when the Stick hurts, the Stick sits. The Stick's gotta do what's in the best interest of the Stick."

As it happened, the Stick was sitting by his locker with pastel plastic clothespins attached to each of his ten little piggies and Dr. Ricardo J. Enrique-Hernandez, foot reflexologist to the stars, kneeling at his feet. Dr. Ricardo J. Enrique-Hernandez worked carefully, rubbing this little piggy, then that. Finally Girard asked if the Stick was embarrassed. "Nah," he replied. "It just tickles a little."

"I *meant* about pulling a muscle while putting on your socks," Girard said.

"The Stick is not embarrassed as long as the Stick is getting his $700,000 per," the Stick said.

Whatever else you've heard, major leaguers do not play for the love of the game, these guys in particular. They are hurt. They are tired. They are going through the motions. They are 54 games out of first place. The Washington *Tribune* is contributing to their mood by running a new daily feature called "Race to Immortality" comparing the 1962 Mets with the 1989 Senators. On September 4, 1962, the Mets were 35–106 and 57 games out of first. After losing all three in Cleveland and the opening game here tonight as well, the Senators are now 31–104. It's an abuse of baseball.

The roster is so decimated there are rumors the Gaijin will be summoned back from the circus. They called up a whole bunch of bodies from Triple A the other day when the rosters expanded. Some help they are. You know you're in trouble when the only phenom down on the farm is named Kluttz. None of them can play a lick except this kid Isakoff, who may be for real. He's got a real sweet swing.

Just to make matters worse, Fennis broke his thumb warming up Pentacost in the bullpen yesterday and Big Foot Harrison tripped over the mound, straining a muscle in his pitching arm. Now he's walking around strapped to one of those electronic TENS machines with his arm twitching involuntarily. Stein's jealous. "That thing'll get you high every time," he said. "I had one of them last year in Japan. Wore it every damn day. They even tested me for it. I had to pee on seventeen electrodes. Those things are outstanding."

Everybody's talking trade, especially since Windy Bragg, that crafty general manager, showed up today. Windy hasn't been seen a lot of late. He hasn't made a significant roster move since he imported the Gaijin way back in May. Girard says he's too chickenshit to pull the trigger on a major deal. But I'll be damned if I can figure out what his options are, especially with the franchise in limbo until the commissioner rules on Jimy Boy. He can't fire Monk 'cause he prays too much. He won't trade Buck. And he can't trade Stick now that he's disabled. So much for trade value. Nope. I think Windy's visit today was more or less a condolence call. He went around the locker room wheezing and clopping guys on the back, which didn't go over very big especially with Mancusi, who was putting on his corset, having been activated for pinch-hitting duty despite his herniated disc.

Physically, Stein is healthy but emotionwise he's a mess. Charlene is ripshit about being left home on this trip and she's been making threatening phone calls to the locker room. Today she invoked the dread name Margo Adams. Stein was too depressed even to call his bookie. He's 0 for 13 on the trip.

The only bright spot is Buck, who is hitting .310, with 22 home runs and 94 RBIs. That's 80 points higher than the team batting average. He's a lock for Rookie of the Year. Naturally he's depressed.

Seems his transplant is infected. He's got these rows of little red sores all over his scalp where they implanted the plugs of hair. His head looks like a needlepoint Afro. He has taken to wearing a bathing cap in the shower. I figured it was just the embarrassment. But Billy says Rube told Buck if he doesn't keep his scalp dry and the sores don't heal, they'll have to pull the plugs.

Today he drove in his ninety-fourth RBI with a triple in the top of the fourth. Of course, it was the only run the Senators scored and the only story anybody could write. So we all gathered around him after the game. Whenever I come over to talk, Buck puts a little white towel on his lap. It's an unspoken thing between us now. I always look to see if he's got his towel on. He's always draped and waiting for me when I need him. At first when he started this back in April, I thought he was just being modest. But then Rump told me Buck had asked whether he thought it would make me more comfortable. Apparently, he hasn't forgotten that day in spring training and my paralysis at the sight of his thighs. He's the only honest-to-God gentleman in the locker room. The guy really grows on you. Too bad his hair doesn't.

Anyway, I was standing right in front of him at his locker. Sitting there with this bathing cap on his head and this little white towel covering his privates, he looked like a Michelangelo sheathed in a paper doily.

I started to ask about the triple and how he keeps his concentration while everyone else is just playing out the season when this radio guy grabs the towel from Buck's lap and runs off laughing. Buck sighed and reached for another towel. He was so prim, the way he unfolded the towel and draped it carefully across his waist. Then he looked up at the radio guy and said, "Don't you ever do that again. I treat my womens with respect."

It's the nicest thing anyone has said to me in months. It's also the first time I have ever heard Buck use the first-person pronoun in an interview. The speech therapist is doing wonders. Like Buck says, "She makes all the differential."

I've got to get on Sal to do another piece on Buck. We can run it the day before they announce the Rookie of the Year award.

September 5 The commissioner's report on Jimy Boy was finally released today, ending all speculation about whose pocket the commissioner of baseball is in. In a prepared statement, the commissioner deplored Jimy Boy's behavior as "not being in the best interests of Major League Baseball.

"But," the statement continued, "Rev. Collins has personally expressed his regret to me at the situation and any possible damage done to the image of the game of baseball.

"As a consequence, and in light of the fact that the Commissioner of Major League Baseball lacks any enforceable jurisdiction in this matter, there will be no further action taken in this case. It is the opinion of the Commissioner that this is a matter between Rev. Collins and his conscience."

This it took the commissioner a month to figure out.

Jimy Boy's office released a statement a half hour *before* the commissioner's, praising the commissioner's foresight and praying for his soul.

What an upset. The suspense was just killing me.

September 6 Watching the Washington Senators, you forget the beauty of baseball. You forget the bare-handed grab, the elegant stretch at first, the choreography of a 6–4–3 double play. Watching the Washington Senators is like watching the human condition without the slapstick. It is an exercise in humility.

In April, these guys were funny. In September, they're just plain banal. They don't do good stuff anymore, like standing around the mound pointing fingers at each other while the winning run scores. They just bounce out to second a lot. They are not exactly spectacularly terrible. They are just terrible spectacularly often.

Which is why Pete King's perfect game today, the first in Senators history, was not just a surprise but an affirmation of life itself, a statement of hope and faith and possibility. Six months I've been watching these suckers and I thought I'd seen everything. I was wrong. Now I've really seen it all.

Truth is, I've barely been paying attention. I can't remember the last time I was really in the game except maybe Stretch's fiasco in Milwaukee. After a while on the beat, some reflex tells you when to look up. You see the instant of contact, the bobble at third. The rest you've seen a thousand times before and don't need to see again. Not to write another sixteen inches anyway.

So I'd be lying if I said I was paying attention when Mug Shot hit his first home run since May 10. You remember—the one that ended the Streak.

"Dinger," Girard said.

I had been watching the JIMMY FUND sign change out in rightfield and hadn't seen the pitch. It's a press box game we play. Whoever calls it first gets free beer on the next flight. Anyway, I looked just in time to see the ball land two rows into the rightfield seats and to watch some guy with a beer belly the size of a medicine ball run over some blue-hair in order to get to it. The blue-hair went to the hospital. The guy went to jail. Mug Shot went around the bases like a normal person, no Fission, no Fusion, nothing. I think the dry spell has chastened him.

Anyway, it was only the second inning, so no one thought too much of it. We had confidence Pete would falter. I mean, it was Fenway, after all, and Pete's a *lefty* and it was only his second start of the year. He found out about it when he got to the park and Piggy told him Arroyo's rubber arm had finally blown out after 3,485 major league innings—exactly two thirds of an inning less than the great El Tiante.

But when the Bosox were still scoreless and hitless after five, people began to notice. Pete had never even gone more than five before. Half-assed scorecards suddenly got serious. Everyone's posture improved. It was a strange feeling, this tension. It must have been strange for the players, too. You could see them leaning out of the dugout, biting their nails and punctuating each successive out with an obscenity and an arching stream of tobacco juice. By the end of the sixth, everybody not on the field was on the steps.

The guys on the field who looked like schlubs yesterday suddenly looked like, well, ballplayers. In the seventh, Billy made a diving grab of a shot down the line at third that really should have gone through. He came up spitting dirt and throwing. The guy was out by a step. It was a helluva play. Pete must have been really juiced by the idea of guys actually *playing* behind him because he humped up and threw the first pitch to the next batter into the dirt. Rump blocked the pitch and knocked it dead at his feet. I haven't seen him move that fast all year. It was as if his joints had been oiled in the Fountain of Youth or something. He fired the ball back to Pete, who collected himself and struck the guy out on a nasty slider, his "slide-piece," he calls it. The next two batters struck out looking and Pete practically galloped off the mound.

On the bench, he sat alone. I don't know if this was superstition or preference. But it was emblematic. Pete *was* alone. In fact, except for Mug Shot's solo shot, the Washington Senators also had been held hitless. The only other base runner was Guttierrez, who led off the eighth with a walk and didn't get caught stealing for a change. He was left stranded as Mini-Doc, Billy, and Brawn went down one-two-three.

The guys practically charged out of the dugout for the bottom of the eighth. Pete took his warmups, and a very deep breath between each one of them, and then Rump fired the ball down to Billy, who fired it on to Mini-Doc, who fired it on to Stein. Going around the horn, performing the ritual that connected them with Tinkers to Evers to Chance and every other meaningful infield in history, it almost seemed as if the Washington Senators were declaring themselves part of the game. There was a crispness I hadn't seen before. They looked real. They looked like it mattered.

The Bosox went meekly in the bottom of the eighth and the Senators did likewise in their last at bat. They were too drained even to lift the bats from their shoulders.

I studied Pete through my binoculars when he came out for the bottom of the ninth. I watched him grab for the resin bag. I watched him dig the dirt out of his spikes. I was looking for something: some detail that would define what was about to happen. His face betrayed nothing. He was still a pimply-faced kid who doesn't need to shave as often as he does.

The nerves were all in his chest. From a distance it looked as if he was hyperventilating. I could understand his heart pounding. But mine? I could understand him grabbing for the resin again and again. But why did I keep dropping my pen?

Rump went to the mound and rubbed Pete's back. Pete rubbed up the ball. When he turned to face the twenty-fifth batter of the game, he looked so serious. But more than anything else, he looked so young. Twenty is all he is. I wondered whether this presaged things to come or whether he'd always be looking back in sadness at a day of triumph he would never equal.

He fell behind 3–0 on Rivera, the leadoff batter in the ninth. Monk started up the dugout steps. Rump waved him off. Going out to settle Pete down now would be the worst thing he could do. What was he going to say? "Go get 'em kid? Make 'em hit the ball, kid?" Rump squatted and nodded. Pete rocked and threw a strike at the knees, then another. The payoff pitch was a beauty: a fastball on the inside corner. Rivera swung—he had no choice—and popped out to Billy at third.

Rick Cerone was sent up to pinch-hit for Rich Gedman, the eighth-place hitter. The "take" sign was on. Cerone didn't take his bat off his shoulder until the count was 2–1. He was up there to make Pete throw strikes and throw one he did, a batting practice fastball right down the middle of the plate. Cerone could have creamed it. I could have creamed it. But Cerone had decided to cross everybody up and bunted down the third base line instead.

It was the perfect bunt. And I swear to God, if Cerone had been a rookie like Billy Blessing instead of a fifteen-year vet who had lost more than a step there wouldn't have been anybody or any play that would have got him. The ball spun in the air off the wood and died in the dirt of the baseline. For a second no one moved, hoping the ball would twist foul. It didn't.

Billy came out of nowhere. God, he came fast. He was all speed and motion, a seamless blur of arms and legs and energy. He picked it up bare-handed and threw. Cerone slid in beneath Stein's elegant stretch. Dirt plumed. The crowd waited. The first base umpire paused a second before making the call.

"You're out!" he said.

Boston fans are respectful souls and they stood for the last at bat. Wade Boggs, who wasn't in the starting lineup, was sent up to pinch-hit. Pete put his hands on his hips and looked around at the colors and the banners. He wasn't looking for applause, I don't think. He was just taking it all in.

On television, Fenway always looks so small, except of course for the Green Monster looming over leftfield. The camera can't give you a sense of the geometry of the place. You don't see how the roof steps up from the Green Monster until it towers over the outfield and the triangle of seats that descends from the deepest part of center. But Pete did. He turned toward centerfield and stared and stared. Finally Rump had to go out and tell him it was time to get on with it.

For some reason, Pete went to the stretch. His huge right leg came up and his arms met at his waist, as if in prayer. Then he reared back and threw the worst fucking pitch of the day. Your basic hanging curve, right out over the middle of the plate. Boggs got all of it. I mean, *all* of it. This baby didn't sail. It catapulted toward deepest center. Mug Shot took one look and ran, his back to the plate, his cap, his toothpick, and his thirteen gold chains flying behind him. It was as if the entire season was riding on that pitch, on that ball. Whatever it was the Senators had been chasing all year—respectability, self-esteem—was heading for the gap. Mug Shot followed on the dead run.

The ball was falling now, faster and faster, its arc propelling it downward toward the warning track. Mug Shot reached. The webbing of his glove touched the ground. I had never seen anyone try to make a shoestring catch of a ball going away from him. On the other hand, Mug Shot didn't have any choice. Time stopped. It seemed that's how it would end, this chase for self-respect, with the ball forever just beyond his reach. Then it dipped, following its own internal logic, and dropped into the webbing of his glove. The momentum of the moment carried Mug Shot forward. He hit the wall and held on. When Rube finally got all the way out to him, Mug Shot was unconscious and cradling the ball against his chest. The replay showed he was smiling.

Who wasn't?

These guys can be assholes, but I'm really happy for them. And for me, too. It's nice to have baseball back again even for just one day.

Pete and Billy celebrated by pouring beer all over each other. "Fucking A!" was all Pete could say. "We cold, we cold," Billy yelled over and over. But I think Mug Shot spoke for everyone when he came to and said, "Baseballically, that was perfectionistic."

I had to agree with him. It was also, baseballically, the perfectionistic quote of the year. So for the first time since they all decided they weren't talking to me, I decided it was tough shit and quoted him anyway. Let him come get me tomorrow. Perfection is public domain.

Toronto

September 10 Charlene called collect. At first when the operator said who was placing the call, I didn't recognize the name. Then I heard Charlene say, "Tell her it's her pal from the Jell-O Bar," and I told the operator I'd take the call.

"A.B., honey, I'm going to make you famous," she said right off. "I have a story to tell and I want to sell. Get ready to listen."

At least she was right up front about it. She wanted $10,000 in exchange for the goods on Stein. "Good goods" was what my grandfather, the tailor, used to call them. But he was talking about a different trade. Charlene was talking sex and blackmail. She said when she got done she'd make Wade Boggs and Margo

Adams look like small potatoes in bad vichyssoise. You had to be impressed right there. I mean, I didn't know she knew what vichyssoise is.

But I was cool. I was, in fact, my most self-righteous self. I wouldn't even let her get started. Oh no. We don't do that at the Washington *Tribune*, I said. We don't buy information. We are a news-*gathering* organization. We report the day's events. If someone approaches us with information that is in the public interest, we will of course be glad to listen and evaluate the merits of the story. But not for money. "Responsible journalists do not practice checkbook journalism," I informed her.

"A.B., honey, how old are you anyways?" she replied.

I agreed to hear her out. "Off the record," I said.

It was just about 10:00 A.M. when she called and she was still going strong two hours later. I have to say she had gotten my attention. It must have been the names and the dates that did it. Specificity is always a grabber. Charlene's tales had the ring of truth. I started taking notes when she mentioned Stein and the videocamera set up in the closet.

As it turns out, Charlene has personally banged twelve of the American League's top starting pitchers and a few of the Junior Circuit's best relievers, too. This in and of itself is not that much of an accomplishment. Lots of groupies have done as much. What makes Charlene's story unusual is that she did it at Stein's behest and on videotape. "At first, I swear, A.B., I thought it was just sort of kinky, ya know? Lots of guys want to see me with other men. I thought he was just being sort of, well, methodical about it. He does like his porn after all, ya know."

I said I didn't.

"One day, it must have been July sometime, Dickie starts playing his tapes for me. He called them his 'insurance policy.' I remember 'cause we were in bed, and well, one thing led to another and he missed the team bus. He really got off on it. He was cackling and saying, 'We bagged 'em. Bagged the fuckers, honey.' That's when I got suspicious.

"Call me slow. I don't know. I couldn't believe it. Why would a man do such a thing? Know what I decided?"

"No, what?"

"I decided it was blackmail for real and for true," she said. "So I flat-out asked. I said, 'Dick Stein, are you blackmailing those boys?' He just pinched my ass and laughed and said he was going to see some fat pitches tonight. That's when I knew. Well, let me tell you, I was one pissed female. Charlene likes sex as much as anyone. Maybe more. But I do not like being used in no sexual sting operation. No sireee, bub. So I started making dupes of the tapes and saving the room sheets. Sheets can be very incriminating, ya know."

"Absolutely," I agreed.

"So, hon, you tell your people what Charlene's got. Tell 'em I got tapes of the Royals, the Angels, the Indians, the Brewers, and a few of the Senators, too. Stick and Lawson and that poor little man, what's his name? Beanie?"

"*Beanie?*" The thought was repulsive.

"I know. I know," Charlene said. "Dickie said it was an act of kindness."

"Indeed."

"Anyway, you tell your editors they can have it for $10,000."

I promised I would pass on the information. I also assured her in my most sanctimonious tone that they would never go along with her request for money. She laughed at me. Laughed hard. "Just tell 'em what Charlene's got," she said and hung up.

"Give her the money," Sal said immediately. "Tell her a plane ticket will be waiting for her at LAX. Tell her to get the first flight to D.C. and that if the tapes are real and we can verify them we'll give her the money once the stuff is in our possession."

I'm a hard-nosed reporter. I should have expected this, right? But I didn't. I was genuinely surprised, which means I am also genuinely a schmuck. And I told Sal what a schmuck I was going to sound like going back to Charlene and undoing everything I had said. It was a real principled stand on my part.

"You're whining, Berkowitz," he said.

He was right. I hate the way I sound when I whine. "But I told her we don't do these things," I said lamely and somewhat belatedly.

"Like hell we don't," he replied.

I called her back. Charlene picked up the phone without bothering to let it ring. She was very understanding. "I see, I see," she said. "I thought maybe they'd see things Charlene's way. It's going to be a pleasure doing business with you, hon. See ya in D.C."

I got to the ballpark in the bottom of the first and spent most of the game watching Stein through my binoculars. It felt kind of like a stake-out. A couple of times I actually caught myself feeling sorry for the poor dumb son of a bitch. Then I remembered Oakland Alameda County Coliseum and the first thing Stein ever said to me, which was, "Drop dead. Fuck you."

He sang all the way home on the plane: "My seatback and tray table are in an upright and locked position over you, babe." The song was made up by a sportswriter some years back and it's become Stein's theme ever since Charlene. Clearly he couldn't get her out of his head. Neither could I. The only question was whether I was going to get my seatback and tray table in an upright position over this story. I debated all the way home.

It's not like I haven't done worse this season, lots worse, than pay for a story. And this is a great one: blackmailing opposing pitchers in exchange for something good to hit. Also I've already refused one assignment in the last two weeks as a matter of principle and principle will only go so far, especially at the Washington *Tribune*. It doesn't matter that I ended up writing it anyway. Editors never remember that. They only remember "No."

I tried to think what Michael would do. Thinking about what he would do got me thinking about how much I miss him and thinking about how much I miss him got me thinking about how dependent on him I allowed myself to become.

No question about it. I had to decide this one alone. We were almost home. Through the clouds I could see the dome of the Capitol and the red beacons atop the Washington Monument. I looked for the *Trib* building with its stupid orange neon sign: YOU READ IT FIRST IN THE *TRIB.*

I heard Michael's voice and the landing gear lock into place. I braced myself for impact. "No fucking way," I heard Michael say.

Home Stand

September 11 I was waiting for Sal when he got to the office this morning.

I was impassioned. I was eloquent. I was prepared. I was also very silly. Sal grunted and said, "Grow up, Berkowitz. This ain't the *New York Times*. This is the real world. And tomorrow after we run our story, they'll do a second-day piece using all our quotes and attributing it to 'published reports.'

" 'The first baseman allegedly blackmailed opposing pitchers with videotapes of them banging his girl, *it is said.*' Don't kid yourself, Berkowitz. Their readers will read all about it. But their editors will tell themselves they'd never stoop to do such a thing." He grunted again. " *'Published reports'* my ass."

There was more truth in what he was saying than I cared to admit. I told him I didn't want any part of it. He shrugged and said I was naïve but would accept my decision as long as I showed up for the screening. "For the purposes of identification and verification," he said.

I agreed and asked who was going to write the story.

Sal smiled. He saw right through me. My naïveté was real enough. So was my jealousy. "Me," he said, rolling up the sleeves of his Turnbull & Asser shirt. "Me. I'm gonna write the hell out of this son of a bitch."

Two hours later, Charlene stepped out of Ross Mitchell's limo in a lime-green Spandex halter top, the skimpiest white tennis shorts you have ever seen, green tennis socks, and Reeboks. She waved to the gallery of reporters with their noses pressed against the glass of the seventh-floor windows while Vernon, Ross's chauffeur, held open the front door to the Washington *Tribune.* Vernon is a very dignified guy. Clearly, Charlene offended his sensibilities. You could tell just by the way he held the lime-green warmup bag containing three 120-minute videotapes featuring various members of the American League's pitching corps elite doing the theme and variations known as "Wham, bam, thank you ma'am." But duty called. So Vernon escorted her all the way up to Sal's office, where he doffed his cap and tried very hard not to betray his feelings when she kissed him full on the lips and pinched his cheek. "Lordy," he said under his breath.

Me, Ross, Samuels, the managing editor, and B. Wiley Wright, the *Trib*'s bespectacled attorney, were waiting in Sal's office. Everyone in the Sports Department was waiting outside. Funny: they all decided today was the day to come in and get weighed. The meat scale was Standing Room Only.

The VHS on Sal's desk was already warm. There were introductions all around and some pretty awkward handshakes. Ross was determined to be proper. "Mr. Wright, Ms. Merryweather. Ms. Merryweather, Mr. Wright." And so on and so on. At each introduction, Charlene wriggled her nose and cooed, "Just call me Charl, hon."

When everyone had met everyone and Raoul had inquired five times if anyone wanted coffee, Ross patted his stomach and cleared his throat. "Well, let's get down to business, shall we?"

"Oh yes, let's," Charlene said.

B. Wiley Wright got out his bifocals. Sal slipped a tape in the machine. Ross and Samuels crossed their legs simultaneously. Charlene was sitting between them. She giggled and patted Ross's seersuckered thigh. "Now, now, it's all right, hon. You've seen this a thousand times before."

Well, maybe not a thousand times. Ross turned red. Sal turned out the lights. The tape began to roll. Charlene provided the narration. I provided the corroboration. I fingered an Angels southpaw and the Brewers knuckleballer, the Phoenix ace and a Seattle reliever. Charlene said there were others, lots of others, but that Stein hadn't perfected his taping technique until late July and some of the film just wasn't worth watching 'cause you couldn't tell what was what anyway.

It was just as well. They all looked pretty much the same. These were quickies. There wasn't even a whole lot of heavy breathing. "Your basic ballplayer is, well, basic," Charlene explained.

Ross thanked her for her analysis and said he thought the pictures spoke for themselves. Indeed they did. Vito and Rocky and Pincus were peeking through the venetian blinds outside Sal's window and panting. I don't think Ross or Sal or Samuels noticed. But Charlene and I did. She winked at them. Rocky swooned.

The tapes kept rolling. Lawson was easy to identify because he was the only one who prayed when it was over. Charlene said she only did him because Stein wanted to fuck him over, and apologized for the poor quality. No one laughed but me. Everyone else in the room was leaning forward, squinting at the screen, trying to make head or tail out of the thrashing going on before their eyes.

"Stick," Charlene said. "It's the Stick. Dickie wanted to make sure he had something on everyone who knew about his 'insurance policy.' So I did the Stick. Or tried to."

As always, Charlene was matter of fact. "Couldn't get it up," she said. "Not so as it would do any good. You know what they say about them big ones: it's like putting marshmallows in a parking meter."

Beanie's fate was worse. All I could see was his shadow. All I could hear was Charlene's inimitable voice calling out clear as day, "But where is it, hon?" Then there was an explosion of laughter from the closet where Stein was perfecting cinematography.

Sal flipped on the lights and the gray eminences of the Washington *Tribune* sat there in stunned silence, rubbing their eyes in disbelief, and pretending they were just trying to adjust to the light. Charlene shrugged. "Screwed one, screwed 'em all," she said. "How 'bout it, gents? Do I get my dough?"

Ross cleared his throat again, but it didn't quite work and his voice cracked like a teenager's. "Give us a minute, will you, uh, Charlene?"

"Sure, hon," she said.

I started to get up and go with her, but Sal motioned me to stay. I watched through the blinds as Charlene signed autographs for Vito and Rocky and Pincus while Ross and company debated the merits of the story. Ross looked around the table for comments.

"We could be vulnerable on a right-of-privacy action for expanding the invasion," B. Wiley Wright said, cleaning his glasses.

"We'll look like shit for paying her," Samuels said.

"Print the sucker," Sal said.

Ross flexed his right triceps, which is what he always does right before he makes a big decision. "Dolly'll love it," he said finally. "Let's go with it. Give her the money. Tell her it's a gift from my wife."

Vernon drove Charlene to her hotel. Sal sat down to write. I went home. Dr. Deadline is covering for me tonight. The story won't hit the streets till the game is over. Sal told the Doctor not to bother to get any comments because that would just tip people off. Deadline is one lucky son of a bitch. "I'm just gonna play dead," he said.

As for me, this is my last day off until the end of the season. And I'm going to spend it trying to figure out what the hell to do when I have to face these assholes tomorrow.

September 12 The clubhouse was a zoo. I mean, the animals were truly out in force. There were more reporters in the locker room than there were on Opening Day. "Must be a dead animal around here. The vultures are circling," Lefty O'Donnell said.

And they all wanted one thing: Stein's ass. In his absence, they might have settled for Lawson's ass or Stick's ass. But as you might have expected, all three asses were unavailable for comment. Stein was hiding in the trainer's room. Lawson was holding chapel in the toilet. And Stick was getting treatment on his calf.

That left me. Let's just say my arrival did not go unnoticed. All fifty members of the working press descended upon me like, well, like vultures. They were elbowing each other in the ribs and tripping over each other's TV cables and telling each other to get fucked all in an effort to get to yours truly, who told each and every one of them the same thing. "No comment." After fifteen minutes of this, I felt like hiding too. But all the good places were taken.

So I went and sat down between Rump and Billy, hoping nobody would notice. For a while it worked. In the absence of a real live source, desperate reporters with a story to write and no one to quote will take anyone with a mouth who's stupid enough to open it. They tried everyone. "Whaddya got to say about Stein?" Girard hollered. "He comes to play," Brawn said. "How would you describe the atmosphere in the clubhouse?" Brenner yelled. "No speaky no English," Guttierrez said. "What will this do to team unity?" MacKenzie bellowed.

Billy smiled beatifically and nodded at me. "Why don't you ask her?"

"Son of a bitch," I said under my breath.

"Berkowitz! Berkowitz! Yo, Berkowitz! Here, Berkowitz!"

Billy lent me his stool and I stood up in front of the cameras, trying to remember what all those State Department spokesmen say when they want to say nothing very seriously. The TV lights went on. Shutters clicked. It was a piece of cake. "I have no comment on this morning's story in the Washington *Tribune*. I did not write the story. I am not part of the story. I suggest you direct any further inquiries to either the source of the story, the subjects of the story, or the author of the story . . ."

It was at this precise juncture, just as I was running out of things to say and people to blame, that I heard a familiar twang and caught a glimpse of a familiar lime-green Spandex halter.

"Come on out, you pussy, Dick Stein. Charlene is here and she wants an accounting!"

Charlene was, in fact, pressing her considerable upper body strength against the concave chest of Lionel, the clubhouse attendant, who was standing in the door doing his manly best to keep her from crossing the red, white, and blue threshold. She brandished an incriminating videocassette in her left hand and made an ominous fist with her right. "I've got the evidence, you shit. Come on out and fight like a man."

Well, let me tell you, the working press forgot about me right quick. "*Let her in!*" they crowed. "*Let her in!*"

"Nope," Lionel said. "No way, nohow, she ain't got no credentials."

"I'll show you my credentials," Charlene growled, pressing her chest forcibly against his. In an instant she was through the door and up on the buffet table conducting a full-scale briefing on the events of her summer with Stein. Lionel went for security. Mug Shot went crazy. "Wild thang," he said. "Wild thang! You nasty, girl." I think Mug Shot wishes he had a curveball.

Charlene batted her lashes at him and took another question.

With Lionel gone, no one was guarding the door and thus there was no impediment and also no warning when Mrs. Lawson and Mrs. Stein, both of whom had had the pleasure of reading about their husbands' exploits in the morning paper, arrived together and joined the throng standing at Charlene's feet. At the first lapse in questioning, Mrs. Stein put her two cents in. "You leave my husband alone, you Jell-O wrestling bitch!"

Then it was Mrs. Lawson's turn. "Home wrecker! Sinner! Prevert!"

They are both tousled blondes in the Farrah Fawcett motif and it is hard to see what Stein and Lawson got out of their wife-swapping arrangement except narcissistic confirmation of their own clean-cut—if dated—taste. Even angry, these two were perky and, well, cute. Charlene towered above them, pecs flexed, quads bulging. "Evidence," she kept saying. "Charlene's got the evidence. I got the evidence here." She brandished the tape again. "And I got the evidence here." She thrust her pelvis forward and patted a small bulge in her stomach.

There was your basic pregnant pause as the implications of her words sunk in. Then The Wives began to shriek. I don't know why, but baseball players always talk about The Wives as if they are some holding company in Delaware. Anyway, The

Wives began to shriek and the suddenly dutiful husbands came running. Stein was naked except for his JEWISH JOCKS FOR JESUS T-shirt. Lawson was worse than naked. He was unfrocked. They stood there face-to-face at Charlene's feet, two men who have nothing in common except her, first base, their respective wives, and their prospective paternity. "I'll get you for this, you cocksucking son of a bitch," Brother John said.

" 'Cocksucking son of a bitch?' " Stein replied. "My word, can this be *our* Brother John?"

Whatever shred of Christian restraint was left in Lawson's mortal soul disappeared with a right aimed squarely at Stein's chin. It was a good shot, actually. But Stein held his ground and then he did the most amazing thing. He turned the other cheek. Lawson had him by the throat when Charlene intervened. "Boys, boys," Charlene said in a tone that commanded attention. "You can step outside and settle this all later. But right now Charlene's got some pressing business to attend to, like finding out which one of you yahoos is the father of this here child. Far as I can see, neither of you's worth a damn. One of you loves Jesus too much. And the other one just loves himself."

The Wives began to protest. "No problem, honey, you can have 'em both," Charlene said. "I just wanna know who's gonna pay for *this*."

Charlene was rubbing her tummy again. The Wives started arguing among themselves about which one of them was going to raise the child. Stein started bellowing about safe sex. And Lawson started to pray.

He asked God's forgiveness, his wife's forgiveness, his ex-wife's forgiveness, Charlene's forgiveness, Stein's forgiveness, and the unborn child's forgiveness. "I'm a Christian," he said. "I'll take full responsibility."

And he promised, down on his knees stark naked before God, fifty members of the working press, and his astonished teammates, that if they all forgave him, each and every one, he'd quit baseball right here and now and join the ministry.

"Can't, son," Piggy said. "We got a ballgame to play. And you is starting."

September 13 Today Pentacost got shelled. Stein got suspended. Lawson went 0 for 4 and the Senators lost their sixth straight since Pete King's perfect game. In the Race to Immortality, the standings are now: '62 New York Mets, 35–110; '89 Washington Senators, 32–111.

Sal said, "I told you so." Raoul said René de Georges called again. Ruth said Shane was hanging all over Michael at a City side party. And Rump wants me to meet him for lunch tomorrow. Shit. What a day.

September 14   There's this new sports bar on the Hill not too far from RFK, P. J. O'Reilly's, Ltd. For some reason, all sports bars end in "Ltd." or "Saloon" or both. Rump told me to meet him there at noon. It's the kind of place you usually see in the suburbs with a jock's name on the marquee and said jock in residence at the oak bar on alternate Thursday nights. It's got your basic television the size of my apartment, lots of fake antique beer signs for FORT PITT ALE, and prefab tables that are supposed to look fresh-hewn from polyurethaned logs; and, oh yes, bowling trophies bought up from somebody's estate sale.

P. J. O'Reilly's, Ltd. used to be a disco. It is huge. It has a batting cage at one end of the room and a boxing ring at the other, both of which have reserved seating for VIPs. I was scared Rump would be sitting at one of those tables or, God forbid, by the free-throw court, where macho types throw up air balls while waiting for their next order of frozen fried zucchini. He wasn't.

He was sitting in a secluded corner surrounded only by pictures of the 1923 Washington Senators and one dying fern. He was wearing his SEPTEMBER 14 T-shirt in honor of Jimy Boy's spring training prophecy. The corner was as romantic as a sports bar gets and dark except for the luminescent EXIT sign above his head. The glow was intense, but no less so than the way he looked at me.

"Ari," he said.

Something about the way he said my name, so softly it felt like a caress, told me I was in trouble. I looked at the TV: a female weightlifter was trying to clean-and-jerk 430 pounds. I looked at the bar: two deflated footballs dangled from the nouveau Tiffany shade. I looked at the EXIT sign shimmering above Rump's head. It was glowing red, turning everything from my face to Rump's beer a dark, crimson hue, though I suspect my face would have been turning red anyway. The crisp white letters were vibrating, bending, leering like crazed beasts in a cartoon nightmare. I couldn't take my eyes off that sign.

"I had to see you," Rump said.

I shrugged as if he was saying less than he was and ordered a beer. I thought about the places we have shared: the bars, the coffee shops, the airport lounges, the carry-outs, the room service. Our relationship, such as it is, is a function of mobility. We relate in transit. "We can't go on meeting like this," I said.

"JoAnne's left," he replied.

He wouldn't accept any condolences. He wasn't looking for sympathy and I don't think he was particularly upset, either. I only wished he was.

"It wasn't working. I should have known when she joined Bible Study that it wasn't going to last. Even before the baby stuff. We were too young. I married her 'cause she was the kind of woman who married a ballplayer. She married me because I *was* a ballplayer. Now she wants out . . ."

He looked at me and started scratching his forearms. "And I want something *more.*"

I was starting to squirm. The EXIT sign shone in my eyes. I closed them against the light. The letters burned into my consciousness. EXIT. EXIT. EXIT. There was none.

He reached across the table for my hand and then decided against it and scratched his forearms again as if he hadn't really meant it at all. He was nervous; the words were spilling out of him. "Look, I know there are rules against this sort of thing. I know you're not supposed to sleep with a source and that you feel pretty bad that you did. You shouldn't. I mean, don't. I don't. I just feel bad that it was, well, you know . . ."

He cleared his throat. I was starting to scratch my forearms too.

"Look, I don't know if I'm going to play another year. Maybe it is time to quit. Then there wouldn't be any conflict of interest, right? You could go out with a *former* ballplayer, couldn't you? I need to know. It makes a difference. I think I love you, Ariadne Berkowitz."

This was just about the worst news I'd had all season. My cheeks flushed and my toes went cold and my mind raced, trying to think what to say. His words, unsettling as they were, had a certain clarifying effect on my consciousness. A declaration of love after all is a kind of Waterloo. And this one set me free.

Finally, irrevocably, I knew what I felt, which just made it harder to say it to Rump. I never meant for this to happen. I never thought it through beyond getting even with Michael because he dared to say he isn't my father and doesn't have to put up with all my bullshit. I was hurt, abandoned, like Mom leaving all over again. And Rump was there.

I looked at him and thought there is no reason not to love him, except that I don't. He's decent, kind, a friend. Just like Dad. Mom didn't have any reason not to love him, either. Except that after a while she didn't.

All these years of blaming her for leaving us, for leaving him, and now suddenly looking at Rump I understood. She really *is* in love with a ballplayer. I'm in love with the game. Not the man. Not this man. Not that way.

But I couldn't tell him that. I didn't want to hurt him. What I told him was: "The season's not over. You never know what's going to happen with you and JoAnne. Give it a chance. Why don't we talk at the winter meetings. Maybe by then we'll know who all the free agents are, okay?"

"Sure, sure," Rump said. "I understand. Fine."

I'm not sure he understood at all. But who could blame him? When I have a hard time dealing with things like consequences I take refuge in evasion or stupid jokes, which is all I offered Rump in exchange for his honesty and his feelings.

I called Ruth from the ballpark and told her what happened. She was uncommonly quiet for Ruth. "What?" I said. "What?"

"Oh, Ari, it's just that you're always looking for the easy out."

"You're supposed to go for the easy out," I reminded her.

"Yeah, but this isn't baseball. It's his life. And he has a right to know. You allowed him to care about you. Christ, you went to bed with him. Why don't you just tell him the truth? Tell him you made a mistake. And don't hide behind ethics. Unless, of course, you don't really think it was a mistake. Unless you're not being honest with yourself about how you feel. About him and Michael, I mean."

"No," I said. "It's not that. I know that now."

"Well, if it's not that and you're just waiting for the season to be over to end it for you, then you're just being a complete chickenshit."

"Is that all?"

She sighed. "What else did you say to him?"

"I said, 'Let's shoot some hoops.' He ate frozen fried zucchini and I went five for nine from the free-throw line."

"Great," she said. "Just great."

Minneapolis

September 16, A.M. MacKenzie passed out on deadline last night. The chili and the beer finally did him in. He didn't miss much; another 6–2 loss. But he looked pretty pathetic slumped over his computer. What's that line about going at your typewriter? Well, let me tell you Mac was gone, as gone as you can get without being dead.

There's this famous press box story about a guy in New York who passed out once at a ballgame and all his buddies filed for him. Milo told me about it last spring. Anyway, I was done writing early, so I figured what the hell and sent twelve inches under Mac's byline to the Washington *Times.*

So did Girard. Like I said, it's a famous press box story.

Anyway, this morning at breakfast MacKenzie found me and Danno in the coffee shop and said, "They liked yours best, Berkowitz."

It was the first time he's talked to me since April. Danno winked at me. I know what he's thinking: What do you care about these slobs anyway? I have no good answer to that question. Then again, neither does he. He filed twelve inches for MacKenzie, too.

September 16, P.M. I used to take solace in room service. It was an exquisite pleasure hiding self-indulgence behind deprivation. I would curl up in my underwear and order the most unseemly things; things none of us eat anymore. Like eighteen-ounce New York strip steaks and baked potatoes oozing with salted butter and sour cream and vodka and tonics. I always asked for Stolichnaya and they never had it, so I felt entitled to order two that way. For this pleasure, I forgave them the watery steak and the string beans with pimiento bits. I have always wanted to meet the person who decreed that string beans must

329

have pimiento bits. I'd like to know his thinking on the subject. Also, I'd like to know his favorite food.

Anyway, I would lie in bed reading back issues of magazines I never buy and flipping the channel on my remote control and wait for the forthright knock on the door and the obsequious kid with zits who always acted so grateful for the 20 percent tip. When the door shut behind him and I lifted the stainless-steel dome and saw the condensation puckering on the Saran Wrap above the New York strip, I knew all was right with the world.

Then the menu changed. Whoever it was that decreed the marriage of string beans and pimiento has now got a thing for Tex Mex. Good-bye New York strip, hello Huevos Rancheros.

So there I was curled up on a Saturday night in my polyester bed in the middle of Middle America and it's 10:30 P.M. and all I can get is a refreshing microwaved taste of the Southwest. A taco salad loaded with taco meat, whatever that is, cheese, onion, and iceberg lettuce, all served in a crisp deep-fried flour shell. Or Quesadillas loaded with Cheez Whiz and dehydrated guacamole. Do you have any idea what a microwave does to Cheez Whiz?

I put the TV on first thing as usual. It never occurs to me to actually be alone in my room. I was flipping the dial and pleading with room service for meat, any meat other than taco meat, when I saw Joey Proud. I was two channels past him by the time I realized who it was. Of course, the remote only went in one direction, so I flipped through all fifty-six channels, including ESPN, Cinemax, the weather, adult viewing, basket weaving, and the 4H club, before coming around to Joey again.

I didn't recognize the host. He was one of those squeaky-clean sincere types who nods at everything and listens to nothing. "So, Joey, you look good."

"I do," Joey agreed affably.

What he looked like actually was a ten-year-old boy with jowls and crow's feet. He had on one of those tan windbreaker jackets boys wore to elementary school in the fifties, a JOEY PROUD/MILLER LITE INVITATIONAL HEART FOUNDATION GOLF CLASSIC T-shirt, and chinos. Joey's apparel described him perfectly. He was stuck in time.

"How ya feelin'?" the host said.

Joey grinned. "Lots better than I expected."

The audience roared; the host beamed. "Ya know, Joey, and this is something I've always wanted to know, I've heard that sometimes you swung so hard you could smell the wood burning when you hit the ball."

"No way," Joey said, curling his fingers the way he always did. "Either I struck out or I hit a home run. I never did smell shit."

The audience broke up at that and so did the genial host, who, sensing he had gone about as far as he could with this line of questioning, got this stricken look on his face that signaled a change in tone. But his tone didn't change. When he spoke again, it was with that same gee-whiz upbeat delivery. It wasn't until halfway through the question that I think he or Joey realized just how big the gap was between his words and his tone. That's when the audience gasped. It reminded me of a sportscaster who once segued into a story about the rape of a player's wife by saying, "Gotta bad one for ya, folks."

"So, Big Guy," the host said, "we hear your kid's real sick. Heart, is it? Such a shame. Says here in this story out of Washington that you've been working the Borscht Belt to pay the bills. Careful now, slugger, they're gonna name you Father of the Year."

I turned up the volume. The camera zoomed in on its prey. Joey blinked at the lights and curled his fingers around an imaginary bat, or maybe a neck. He started to answer, but nothing came out. The camera never left Joey's face. Finally, Joey mumbled something about hope and prayers and lots of letters from people all over the country. Then the band began to play "Take Me Out to the Ballgame" and the host was standing behind his desk saying, "Joey Proud, everybody. Thanks for coming by, Big Guy." And Joey stumbled off the set. Nobody in his entire major league career had ever made him look that bad. In that instant, I forgave him everything.

The only question was: Would I forgive myself? You think that's stupid, right? Well, probably it is. But the way I had it figured, I was responsible. I do this interview. I get this great stuff on his son. I agonize about how to write it. And some yahoo comes along and turns Joey's pain into a thirty-second sound bite, a bit, and sends him off with a trumpet fanfare looking the way no hero is ever supposed to look. Which is why I was sitting in bed at ten-thirty on a Saturday night with cold Huevos Rancheros and a shitload of guilt on my plate.

Who could I call? Who would understand? Other than Michael, that is?

I dialed the phone and Sammy Esposito said hi. He was a hero once, mine anyway. I figured I wouldn't have to explain it to him, but when I heard his voice, suddenly I wanted to.

After all this time, I'm still amazed that people talk to me, talk to any reporter, revealing themselves to someone they do not know. Now I was doing the same thing, looking for a connection over a long-distance wire.

"He's a big boy," Sammy said. "He can take care of himself."

"Yeah, and I'm short. I'm small. And if there's one thing I've learned this season it's that big guys tell small girls things they do not tell other guys. I look harmless. I try to look harmless. And it works. Sometimes they tell me I remind them of their little sisters."

"And then you feel like you have to protect them because you're not as innocent as you look," Sammy said.

He did understand.

"Sometimes when it's time to write I can barely make it upstairs to the press box. It's like every word, every sentence, every quote is a weight I can't support. What if I'm wrong? What if it's all wrong? I can't bear the weight of my own power. I seduce them into doing this, into telling me what they don't want to say. Then I have to think of a way to do what I have to do without betraying them. It's a pact with the devil is what it is, and the devil is me."

Sammy sighed. "You don't have to protect him. And anyways, you can't. You think Joey hasn't been there before? You think he wasn't expecting it? I mean, A.B., it's all part of the Show."

He paused. "How is the Show anyway?"

"Long," I said.

"That's the whole point," he replied.

Home Stand

September 19   Tonight was National Bank of Washington/Armand's Chicago Pizzeria Calendar Night. Everybody in the stadium got a free 1989 calendar with color pictures of their favorite Washington Senators, suitable for mounting on the wall.

Most teams give out calendars in the beginning of the year as a way of drawing fans. It is indicative of this ass-backwards season that Beanie only got around to it this week. I don't know what the paying customers are going to do with their beautiful mementos, but I can tell you what the Washington Senators did with theirs.

Each and every member of the team, except Rump, Buck, and Billy, immediately blacked out all the games played to date and hung the calendars like shrouds over their lockers, where they sit salivating at the thought that there are only thirteen left to play. The clubhouse looks like it's in mourning. Somebody, it must have been Stein, even hung a black curtain over the mirror the way you do when you're sitting shiva.

No question: these guys are fried. Playing thirty games in thirty days two months in a row will do that to you, especially at this time of year. They could really use a rain-out now; instead they're still making up those six games from April. The only thing they can agree on are oldies and the weather, which refuses to put them out of their misery. The daily forecast: hot, humid, and another loss. This was Number 114.

Tonight, Fast Eddie, the old junkballer himself, issued his twenty-sixth wild pitch of the season, breaking Jack Morris's major league record, and immediately passed out on the mound from heat exposure. God knows, it wasn't from throwing hard. Mancusi doubled over with cramps, trying to field a bunt down the third base line. Monk had left him in the game after he pinch-hit for Billy in the sixth and had nobody else who could play third. Then again, neither could Mancusi. "First time the son of a bitch has bent over since June," MacKenzie said, which was just about right.

Stick isn't helping anything with his disgusting display of cheerful camaraderie. Every day his limp worsens perceptibly. And every day he hobbles through the clubhouse saying, "Way to go, guys. Let's get 'em, men." Tonight Stein told him to shove his fucking calf up his ass. Stick said, "Good idea. I ain't never tried that yet."

I finally reached René de Georges and told him I had decided to go with another agent. He said tartly the market for baseball books had pretty much dried up anyway. I guess I'll find out. I get my contract for my diary next week.

September 20 The legend of Dr. Deadline has a new chapter.

The story begins at the Carter Barron tennis center on upper Sixteenth Street. They have a tournament there every summer, a tune-up for the U.S. Open. But for a long time the courts were clay and nobody except Peruvians you've never heard of showed up, unless of course their agents had a "relationship" with the tournament. So they built a spanking new facility, which is unused fifty-one weeks a year. Thus was born the first annual D.C. Senior Satellite Mazda Tournament Challenge, with a field of fifty-year-old former junior champions, three of whom have gout.

There was no one in the stands who could actually be identified as a paying customer when first-round play began yesterday. But the Washington *Tribune* was there in the person of Dr. Deadline, whose increasing fear of flying has now grounded him completely. "I don't do travel," he told Sal last week.

So Sal gave him this plum assignment, which is almost as bad as getting sent to cover an ultramarathon in January.

The feature match last night was a scintillating two-setter between a guy who once reached the quarterfinals of the U.S. Clay Court Championships and another guy who was once an alternate for the Chilean Davis Cup team. I forget their names. They traded moon balls for three hours before the guy from Chile retired with blisters at 1–4 in the second.

This gave the Doctor approximately an extra hour to file and ten inches less to fill. He blew it. He actually missed the deadline.

Milo was telling us this up in the press lounge before tonight's game. He was in the office today—he's spending a lot of time in the office since Bette broke up with him—and got it straight from Sal, who was not amused. But Milo was, and Milo knows how to spin a yarn. Girard laughed so hard listening he got the hiccups, which lasted longer than Bobby Damn Jenkins, who gave up 7 walks in 3 1/3 innings and is a lock to break Bob Feller's modern-day record (208). Brenner and MacKenzie spent two hours pounding Girard's back, screaming obscenities, and pouring water down his throat while he stuck his fingers in his ears. So much for the working press.

But I digress.

When blocked, the Doctor likes to pace. He gets a lot of

exercise this way. So there he was with Rock Creek Park in front of him and three inches on his screen and he decided that maybe a walk would help. "Gotta exercise the muse," the Doctor always says.

So he turned off his machine and went for a stroll. It was midnight before he got back.

Now, this is Washington we're talking about, where white folks who travel up Sixteenth Street to watch old folks play tennis where black folks live expect some protection (as well as complimentary tickets), in this case five large trained Doberman pinschers. The guards who walk the dogs and patrol the grounds naturally assumed that two hours after the last ball was served nobody was still working in the press box. So they followed instructions and locked all five Fidos inside.

Along came the Doctor. He was humming now; ready to write and thoroughly in his own world, reciting his lede out loud to the moon and the stars.

In addition to fried chicken and deadlines, the Doctor is also allergic to dogs, especially big dogs. They make him cry. One whiff of canine flesh and he starts to tear up. So there he was in thrall to the muse and opened the door to an onslaught of paws and howls and seriously decayed bicuspids.

A cop picked him up three blocks from the tennis stadium. The Doctor has lots of curly hair and a somewhat swarthy complexion. In the dark, he could be mistaken for Hispanic, and he was. "Hey, José! Where's the fire?" the cop said.

Then he shined a light in the Doctor's eyes and saw this red-faced maniac with tears running down his cheeks pleading for Seldane. Now the cop figured he had a loony on his hands and started calling for medical personnel instead of backup. Milo says it took the Doctor an hour of showing the cop his Princeton Club tie and a phone call to Sal to persuade him to take him home and not to St. Elizabeths.

Milo says Dr. Deadline starts behavior modification therapy and driving lessons tomorrow.

September 22 Monk asked Stick to pinch-hit tonight. Bases loaded, no outs, bottom of the ninth in a 4–4 game. A hitter's dream. Son of a bitch had already been announced into the game when Rube returned from the clubhouse with the bad news. "Stick says he can't go," Rube reported.

Billy said Monk was so pissed he swallowed his chaw, which made him lots more pissed as well as more than slightly sick to his stomach. He was turning red and gagging and still there was nobody in the batter's box, a fact that soon came to the umpire's attention.

He meandered over to the dugout and Piggy began explaining the particulars. The whole time Monk was gagging and choking and Rube was pounding on his back. I guess it was proof positive that this is truly Monk's team because nobody made a move to do anything. Finally the ump said in no uncertain terms that he didn't give a fuck if Monk choked to death on the dugout floor but if there wasn't somebody in the batter's box in ten seconds, he was going to forfeit the game.

Our esteemed coaches at first and third were busy picking their noses and hadn't bothered to notice the delay. Piggy was busy attending to Rube, who was busy attending to Monk. So finally Rump told Stein to grab a bat and get his ass up there. Stein refused.

This was his first day back from suspension. The Players Association appealed his case and he's been reinstated while the commissioner's office diligently tries to uncover how many other American League pitchers are in debt to Stein. Charlene refuses to cooperate: she says she's saving the rest for her book. And Stein isn't talking on the advice of counsel. Suddenly he's into the letter of the law. He told Rump he didn't have the authority to send him up there and he wasn't going nowhere unless Monk said so. The umpire looked at his watch. Rump looked up and down the bench. Finally, he saw Brawn sleeping by the water fountain—I guess he didn't get much sleep last night on the training table—and nudged him in the ribs with a bat. "You ready to hit, Big Guy?"

Brawn opened his eyes and said, "Brawn is ready anytime, anyplace." Then: "Where am I, anyway?"

He struck out looking. Actually, that's stretching the point. According to the Rangers' catcher, Brawn was snoring in the batter's box. He became the first man in history to go down on strikes sleeping.

Naturally, the Rangers scored two in the top of the tenth when Boom Boom DeForest gave up his fourteenth home run in his fourteenth outing and the good guys lost Number 116 on the year.

When I got downstairs, Stick was standing in the middle of

the clubhouse hitting a bucket of golf balls in the general direction of his manager, who had dared to inquire why he had not been available to pinch-hit in the bottom of the ninth. "You tellin' me I can hit? I'm tellin' ya I can't!" Stick said, aiming another Titleist in Monk's direction.

Monk bravely took cover behind Buck. Lawson told Stick to knock it off and Stick hooked one past Brother John's nose. I think Lawson would have been in serious shit if Stick had not noticed me standing by the clubhouse door. I was a much more inviting target than Lawson. Stick began teeing off in my direction.

Balls were bouncing all over the place, ricocheting off the amber waves of grain and several parts of several anatomies. One got Billy in the ass. Another hit Pete King on his pitching elbow. A third whizzed past Rump's left ear as he came out of the shower. "Careful now, Stick, you wouldn't want to go and reinjure yourself with that backswing, now would you?" Rump said.

"Oh yeah?" Stick said and stroked another past Rump's ear.

Rump never flinched. He just stood there with his arms folded, shaking his head. "You take your best shot now, Stick, 'cause I swear to God it's gonna be your last."

Stick started in about how golf is therapy and if Rump doesn't believe it he can go ask Stick's personal physician. "Sure, Stick, sure," Rump said.

Stick got this hurt look on his face and put down his five-iron and said if that's how they all feel he won't make the final road trip with the club. His announcement was greeted with a standing ovation.

September 23 An hour before the game Stick limped out of the toilet carrying this towel rolled up like a long French baguette. He was very quiet and very ceremonious, which is definitely not the norm. So of course everybody noticed and followed him to the buffet table in the center of the room, which was loaded with Gatorade and cookies made by a first-grade class in Bethesda. Stick didn't say a word. He just put the towel down in the middle of the cookies and unrolled it as if he was about to unveil the *Mona Lisa* or something.

"Gentlemen," he said. "The world-record piece of shit."

Apparently Stick will go to any lengths to get back in his

teammates' good graces. They were impressed, all right, but they tried not to show it.

"So what?" Pentacost said.

Stick elbowed him in the ribs. "And you thought *my* twelve inches was good!"

They all laughed, but they still aren't talking to him. I can't believe he's going to play here next year. I think they won tonight just to spite him.

September 24   The last weigh-in before Judgment Day was this morning. And sad to say, the news was bad. With just a week left in our crusade to lose 400 pounds by the end of the baseball season, we have 42 big ones still to go. Sal was beside himself. He actually got up on the meat scale and berated his troops for failing to pull their weight. No sooner were the words out of his mouth than Pincus arrived with his jaws wired shut. Apparently Ross called him in three weeks ago and told him if he wasn't under 300 pounds by the end of the season he will never cover another college hoops game for the Washington *Tribune*. Pincus has lost 17 pounds since, which means he's only 19 plus for the season. That's 19 pounds the rest of us have to lose by next week.

If anything, Pincus smells worse than before because now in addition to not showering he is also wearing the same clothes every day. When the Doctor demanded an explanation, Pincus tapped out a note on his terminal saying there's no point in buying a new wardrobe until he's reached his new critical mass. The Doctor immediately circulated a new petition demanding that Sal buy Pincus a new pair of pants. Sal said he can't afford anything that big.

However, he did like the idea of the liquid diet and said, surveying several seriously pendulous guts, that the participation of any and all staff members would be greatly appreciated. There wasn't what you'd call an overwhelming response to his entreaty. In fact, no one said a word, except Rocky, who belched. So Sal volunteered Captain Fuck-up, who eyed his last cheese danish sadly and asked if he had to get his jaws wired too. Sal said no, that he would trust Zeke on this one.

I was surprised to find that I am exactly the same weight I was when I left for spring training. I feel so different now. I guess my weight is just about the only thing that hasn't changed.

I don't hyperventilate on deadline anymore. I don't go batshit if I miss a ground-ball out. I don't read every lede to Michael. And I don't get goose bumps every time the ump says, "Play ball!"

I think I'm beginning to take baseball for granted.

When I was little, I got depressed every fall. Mom used to worry about this, take it personally, like it was a reflection of her marital woes. She never understood it was just the end of the season. But then she never understood why I spent the winter scouring the newspaper for news of a blockbuster trade, a hint of a holdout, a note that some former great had signed with a Triple A team. These were the things that told me the earth still spun on its axis, that spring was on its way. This was what I lived for. I counted the days until the pitchers and catchers reported to Fort Lauderdale.

I told Milo this morning I think I loved baseball better from afar. He said everyone feels this way by the end of the season. "The legs go first," he said, "even for sportswriters."

God knows mine are shot. My shoulders ache all the time, even when I'm not carrying anything. I'm going through the motions. Another game, another sixteen inches, another day in the Race to Immortality.

Speaking of which, it looks like it's going down to the wire. After splitting today's doubleheader, the Senators are 38–117, one win less and one loss more than the Mets twenty-seven years ago. Those lucky bastards only played 160 games in '62, finishing 40–120 and $60 1/2$ games out of first. With three games left in Arlington and four at home against the Yankees and a perfectly wonderful ten-day outlook from the National Weather Center, it looks like the Senators are going to play all 162. Mathematically it's quite possible that the Senators can both win more and lose more than the Mets. So serious negotiations are in progress within the department concerning what does or does not constitute the worst team ever in the history of baseball. Captain Fuck-up says fewest wins. I say most losses. This morning, on the meat scale, Sal said he'll decide when the math becomes more clear, by which he means whatever makes a better story.

Seven more games. Then the play-offs. I've got the American League. I don't know who's got the National League. But Sal already told me I'll be writing lede from the Series. We haven't talked about next year and I'm glad we haven't because I don't know what I'll say when he asks. I haven't decided yet whether this is what I want to be when I grow up or just something I had to get out of my system. Besides, once this diary is published I'll never be allowed back inside any locker room in America.

Arlington

September 25 Interviewed Buck today about what it's like to be having a Rookie of the Year season. It was a piece of cake. This story will write itself.

Among other things, Buck said, "I seen *SI*. I seen *The Sporting News*. I seen TV. It's real. Everybody can't be lying. But I'm just going to down-key it anyway." He also said he wants to be "just another George, Dick, or Harry." On the other hand, he likes being recognized. "Walking down K Street is like walking down the main street in Nuba." He thought about that for a second and said, "I guess I'm kinda stuck between the both." With that, I closed my notebook. What else do you need to know?

I thanked him and got up to leave, but I didn't really have anything else to do and neither did he, so we just sat there together looking at the field. I love ballparks where they mow the outfield in a crosscut of light and dark. It always reminds me of fields just before harvest. I just wanted to sit and look at the grass and memorize it for the winter. Apparently he did too. "Maybe when we get home I'll have to get me another piece of that sod to keep me company this winter," he said. "I'll have to remember not to put it on no radiator."

Me and Buck have a lot in common when it comes to sod. Back in April when we first visited New York, I took a blade of grass from the Yankees infield and brought it back to the hotel and put it in a jar of water that I still keep by the side of my bed. I hadn't told anybody about that all season, except Michael. But I told Buck about it today and he smiled. I was thinking nice thoughts again about baseball and that maybe the gulf between those guys swinging the doughnut in the on-deck circle and the little girl who imitated them in front of the television wasn't so big after all when Buck said, "Can I ask you something?"

It's hard to explain why, but I was startled. Ballplayers never ask reporters questions. A question is an invitation to a conversation and a conversation is an invitation to a relationship.

A question is a definite risk. So I was surprised at the inquiry, even from Buck.

" 'Member that day back home last winter?"

How could I forget? This was in January, the day before the big press conference announcing his signing. Sal wanted a one-on-one, not this group jerk stuff, so he sent me out to RFK to look for Buck. It was a horrible day: like twenty below with the wind chill, and I was not dressed for the occasion. I'm a baseball writer. I don't do parkas.

So there I was wandering around RFK looking for this big black guy whom I've never met, who's not expecting me, and I'm wearing these little spike heels and a bomber jacket. The field was all ice and frozen mud. The groundskeepers had already torn up the Bermuda and rye football turf and they were getting ready to resod with bluegrass for baseball. My heels kept sinking in the ice and my feet were as frozen as my behind. Anyway, I saw this guy who I assumed was Buck and I started running across the field, slipping and sliding and sinking in the mud. "Buck! Buck! Excuse me, Buck!"

Buck took one look at me and took off. There was no way I could catch him. I mean, the guy only runs a 4.4 forty. By the time I got to the dugout, he was down the steps and had disappeared up the tunnel. At least, that's what I thought. Then I heard the toilet flush and I realized he was in the urinal next to the dugout. No problem. I've gotten some of my best interviews waiting outside men's rooms.

So I waited. And I waited. I mean, I was really cooling my heels. But Buck didn't come out. I banged on the door. No answer. I called his name. I even called him Mr. Buchanan. No reply. I yelled, "You might as well come out 'cause I'm not leaving till you do."

I figured he had to be as cold as I was. I figured he'd come out soon. I figured wrong. A half hour went by. Then an hour. We were at a complete and frigid impasse. I couldn't leave and he wouldn't. This is what we call legwork, right?

I stood there for two hours.

At the end of two hours the door opened and Buck stuck out his head. I said, "I'm A. B. Berkowitz from the Washington *Tribune* and I'm frozen solid and I'd like to ask you a few questions. Could I buy you a cup of coffee?"

And Buck said, "No comma."

I kid you not. "No comma."

It was your basic lesson in the power of the press. I had the power to make a grown man cower in a frozen urinal for two hours. Of course, he had the power to make me stand in a tunnel outside a frozen urinal for two hours. But I don't think he realized that. He was a rookie. He was new at this game.

Sal wanted a personality profile. I told him, "Sal, I read the clips. There isn't a single quote in them. What if the guy doesn't have a personality? What if all he's got is a batting eye?"

"Tough shit, that's what," Sal said. "Twenty inches by four o'clock."

Welcome to the era of personality journalism. Everybody's gotta be a personality. And if the personality is smart enough to know he doesn't have one or will sound just plain stupid trying to be one, that's just tough shit. We'll quote him the way he talks and crucify him with his words. "No comma." Sal told me to write it. "No comma."

Now Buck wanted to talk. His voice brought me back to the present and the dugout in Arlington, Texas. "So how come you're so diff'rent?"

"Different?" It was an act. I knew what he was asking.

"Diff'rent from the other writers."

I guess that's just about the nicest thing a ballplayer can say to a reporter, considering the general esteem in which we are held locker room-wise, not to mention worldwide. Truth to tell: other guys, though not the Washington Senators, have told me the same thing. I'm always embarrassed and I always tell them it has to do with being five-one and a girl, which is true as far as it goes.

Last spring when I was trying to decide whether to go over to sports, Milo took me with him to Pimlico for the Preakness. I wasn't writing or anything. But I was up in the press box watching when Milo and all the other writers went over to the infield to watch them put the wreath of black-eyed Susans around Risen Star's neck. There was this cluster of writers around the horse and the jockey and it got bigger and bigger until you couldn't see either the mount or the jock or the reason for the blob of humanity surrounding them. It gave me this terrible taste in my throat watching Milo's legs churning as he tried to keep up with the pack and hear what the little man was saying if he was saying anything at all. Milo was powerless to do anything else. We all are: running like mice to keep up to get the quote to get the story to get the piece of cheese. It's so demeaning. I understand why people fear the power of the press, but it's the powerlessness that ought to scare them. Because it's the impotence that makes guys go over the line and bash people in print just so they don't have to feel so demeaned anymore.

Sitting there in the press box at Pimlico, I had a bird's-eye view of pack journalism and I was so glad to be above it all. I promised myself I would never be like that. Now Buck was telling me I was different and I was getting embarrassed because I know it isn't true at all.

Still, he wanted an answer. "I was a little girl who loved baseball. One season I played Little League. But mostly I played alone. Girard, MacKenzie, those guys, they played high school ball, college. They're so busy trying to show you how much they know they don't bother to ask anything. I'm not competing with you. Just them. Also I'm cute and nonthreatening. People tell me things. When they're not telling me to drop dead, that is."

"I was so scared," he said.

"Me too."

Buck looked at me for the first time, puzzled. "Not then," I said. "My first time."

So I told him about my first major take-out for the Today section when I was sent out to do a piece on some hot-shit star of some hot-shit sitcom who ended up at the Betty Ford Clinic two months later. I can't remember the name of the show or the name of the hot-shit star. All I remember is she was fifteen and I felt even younger. "She was doing the PR tour—New York, Washington, Chicago, L.A. Everybody was getting a shot at her. God, I was nervous. I went out and bought a whole new Ralph Lauren outfit just for the occasion. I must have checked the batteries on my tape recorder seventeen times.

"There were five of us scheduled to do twenty-minute one-on-ones, one after the other. We were all sitting in this hotel suite waiting our turn. I was last. The *Trib* always is. They gave us these bios on her life so we wouldn't have to waste time asking dumb questions like her age or her hobby. I remember it said her hobby was cooking dinner for friends and her favorite book was *The Joy of Cooking*.

"Anyway, I got inside and there was this person, this pint-sized person, squished in the corner of this brown-and-orange-plaid sofa. She looked like she hadn't eaten in weeks, much less cooked dinner for friends. She was so small. It was like she was trying to get inside the cushions. The room was filled with dying flowers—three identical FTD floral bouquets—and baskets of rotting fruit wrapped in orange cellophane. The grapes were puckered. The apples were withered and the peaches smelled. She looked just about as good."

"What'd you do?" Buck said.

"I asked her if I could take off my boots, which I had bought specially for the occasion, and I put my feet up on the table next to the peaches and she smiled and we talked. I don't know if that answers your question."

"I'm getting married," he said finally and somehow it didn't sound like a non sequitur. "Right after the season. Back home in Nuba. My grandma's gonna cook up some red beans. My baby's gonna be the flower girl. I was hoping, I mean we was hoping, that maybe like, well, you'd come. Seeing how you was the one that brought us together and all."

Buck was so embarrassed he couldn't look up. He studied his spikes like he'd never seen a pair before. I studied my Joan and David's like I'd never seen a pair of them before either. "I'd be honored," I said.

Then I went upstairs and watched the Senators win Number 39 of the year, equaling the record of the 1962 New York Mets, who were also 39–117 on September 25. Buck won it with his twenty-fifth home run and his ninety-ninth RBI of the season.

September 26   Spoke to Ruth tonight. She paged me in the press box to tell me Michael isn't seeing Shane anymore. She got it from the Doctor, who got it from someone in City side who saw Michael sitting by himself at The Pit while what'sherface ate french fries at another table with some editor.

Ruth says I should call him. I told her this matchmaking business is out of character for her. She said this stubbornness is out of character for me. And besides, she's sick of listening to my ledes and my bitching. "At least sleeping with him isn't a conflict of interest," she said. "Think about it."

Think about it? I think about it all the time. I go home and find decorative purple cabbages growing in the garden outside my building and think of Michael, who pointed out the insidious trend long before I noticed there was one. I open the refrigerator and see mold multiplying inside a bottle of Mott's applesauce and think of Michael, who went out to the Safeway in his pajamas to get it. I don't know why: he always ate applesauce after we made love. I go to bed in the forty-eighth different bed I've slept in since February and dream of Michael marrying me at the pitcher's mound in Robert F. Kennedy Stadium.

"Hmmm," Ruth said.

"Jimy Boy was going to perform the ceremony. I was standing there on the rubber with the train of my dress dragging in the dirt, waiting for Michael. You know how the groom is always standing there waiting? Well, instead it was me, the bride. I kept reaching down for the resin bag and rubbing my hands in the dirt. I was stalling for time. I was wearing sanitary hose and stirrups and spikes and my bouquet was in the shape of a glove. Everybody was there; you and Sal and Milo. All the attendants wore baseball uniforms, even Mom. The organist played 'Take Me Out to the Ballgame' and 'Wooly Bully' three times each and still there was no Michael. Finally the umpire comes out to find out what's going on and starts jawing at me. You know—the way Earl Weaver and the umps used to go at it. So I kick some dirt at him and just as he's about to give me the heave-ho Rump appears at my side with a wedding ring between his thumb and forefinger.

"The ump says, 'Play ball!' The organist sounds a 'Charge!' And Jimy Boy begins: 'We are gathered here together.' Everybody's nodding and smiling and I'm the only one who knows that something's wrong. Mom keeps saying, 'Now, now, dear, it's just wedding jitters.' I can't make anyone understand *this is the wrong man.* It was awful."

"Then what?" Ruth said.

"Then I woke up."

"Call him," she said.

"You."

"You want me to call him, I'll call him. I'll tell him you're waiting for Mr. Right on the pitching rubber."

"Don't you dare."

"That's right. I don't dare. But the point is, neither do you. You won't even admit you were wrong in the first place, the night of Ross Mitchell's party."

I heard the sound of contact and looked up just in time to see Rump line a shot down the leftfield line, a triple for anyone with wheels. I groaned. "What is it?" Ruth said.

"Rump," I replied. "He just struck another blow for love."

Ruth held on while I watched Stein go down swinging to

345

end the game, the 118th loss of the season. "Rump was left stranded," I said.

"I'll say," she replied. "Call him. Call Michael. He's been asking about you. I've got to go."

The mathematics have never been so clear. Threesomes don't work. And the Washington Senators are 39–118, the same as the '62 Mets. It doesn't look good for any of us.

September 27 Marv Cox called in the top of the eighth. Marv is not a happy man. He has been shitcanned by the Stick. Seems like Stick was filming this commercial for a new Stick deodorant, a six-figure deal Marv put together for him, when they got into this fight on the set and Stick told him to take a hike. Marv's never been fired before by a guy in tap shoes and a top hat dressed up as a tube of Stick deodorant who happens to owe him thirty grand. "Just thought you'd like to know," Marv said.

Sometimes I can be a little obtuse. At first I did not get the import of the information. Here he was trying to unload the story of the year on me and I'm going, "Uh-huh, uh-huh, sure, Marv, whatever."

Marv was pissed enough to spell it out. "You listening to me, Berkowitz? He was wearing tap shoes. You get it? *Tap shoes.* He was singing this stupid song, 'I'm the Stick Man and I'm a sweet-smelling kind of guy,' and dancing all over the keys of a make-believe typewriter."

Finally the light dawned.

"What about the calf?"

"Calf? There is no calf. He's been sitting on his ass protecting his incentive clauses since the end of August. The guy is a dog. You hear me, Berkowitz? *D-o-g.* Dog!"

I sat up and started taking notes. "I hear you, Marv."

"His contract has three incentive clauses. The deal was he'd get an extra one hundred thou if he hit .280, 25 home runs, and had 90 RBIs. But he had to do all three to get the hundred thou, otherwise it was just ten thousand for each category. So he sat his ass down the day he got his twenty-fifth home run and his ninety-first RBI. The fuck didn't want to jeopardize his .280 batting average and his one hundred grand."

The dimensions of the story were finally and belatedly coming clear. I'd like to tell you that as an objective reporter the prospect of revenge never crossed my mind. But I won't. It certainly crossed Marv's. That's why he called me.

"That cocksucker thinks he's got the world by his dick. He doesn't need anybody. He's gonna go it alone. 'There's no percentage in it, Marv,' he says. 'The Stick is no man's but his own man,' he says.

"We'll just see what kind of man he is when this shit hits the street. You need anything else, you call me, Berkowitz. It's yours. I'm not giving it to anyone else. He'll hate it most coming from you. Be sure to quote me now, Berkowitz. That's Cox. *C-o-x.* Cox."

The line went dead and I went numb. I can't remember ever being handed a story quite this good or quite this way before. It was ugly. But it was mine.

It was getaway day and I barely had time to file my game story and the all-important Race to Immortality—Surprise! They lost Number 119!—and still make the bus. I called Captain Fuck-up from the airport. My fingers were dancing already. I was inspired, all right.

The Captain said, "No."

"Whaddya mean, no?"

"I mean no. I mean, don't write it. I mean, we gotta check it out."

Check it out?

I knew Zeke was a major league jock sniffer, but this was a whole new ballgame. He was telling me to sit on a major breaking story. His attack of ethics on behalf of my good friend Stick was enough to make me sick.

"What do you think you're working for, the fucking *New York Times*?" I demanded. I don't even think he got the irony or the allusion to himself.

He just said, "Thirty-nine and one-nineteen. Boys gotta win four straight from the Yankees," and hung up.

They were making the last call for my flight. Either I kissed off the plane and called Sal hoping he'd overrule Zeke or ran for it and called him from the air. I ran for it, figuring if worse came to worst I could dictate from the plane and still make deadline.

The on-board telephones were out of service.

I kept telling myself Marv hated Stick so much that he'd keep his promise not to tell anyone else. It really would hurt most coming from me. But sitting on a breaking story, thirty thousand feet up, crossing time zones while deadlines pass is like trying to nap on a bed of thorns. There's no getting comfortable with the situation.

I ordered a drink and I ordered another. An hour out of D.C., I calmed down. By the time we landed, I knew what I was going to do. I called Marv from a pay phone just inside the gate and told him my idea. He loved it. He hates Stick even worse than I thought. When I got home, I called Billy. "No problem," he said.

The Last Home Stand

September 28   Stick was soaking his largesse when I got to the stadium at 2:00 P.M. Billy gave me the thumb's-up, so I knew everything was going as planned. Game time was still five and a half hours away, but most of the guys were already in the clubhouse, playing cards, getting treatment. Monk hadn't said anything about coming in early, but for once they actually wanted to be at the ballpark. They do not want to be the worst team ever, and if that is their destiny they want to be it together. It's the most team spirit they've shown all year.

Their task is clear. All they have to do is win four straight from the Yankees to avoid ignominy. Mine was less straightforward. I had to smoke out the Stick.

If any of the guys were curious about what I was doing there two hours before anyone else from the press arrived, they didn't say anything. I was counting on the lassitude of my colleagues to save my ass and my scoop. They didn't disappoint me.

At 2:30 P.M., as promised, Billy got up from his locker and wandered into the whirlpool room. Stick was snoring like a baby. He never suspected a thing. Billy turned the temperature up to just short of frying and returned to his locker, where I was busy reading the album notes on Metallica's latest.

It didn't take long for Stick to wake up.

He careened out of the whirlpool on the dead run. He was beet-red and bellowing. I'd like to quote him exactly, but I'm not sure how. It went something like *"OohmyfuckinggodjesusfuckshithelpmeI'mburned!"* In and out of the shower he ran, back and forth across the clubhouse he hopped, until finally he collapsed in a heap amid a field of stars-and-stripes and rolled back and forth on the carpet as if he was actually in flames and moaned, "I'm burned. I'm fucking burned. Somebody get a fucking doctor."

Nobody moved. Except him, of course. Let me say right up front that he was no more burned than he was injured. But to tell you the truth, I'm not sure anybody would have made a move in his direction even if he had been.

After a few minutes, I went over and stood above him. It was as close to towering over anybody as I'm ever going to get. I'd be lying if I said I didn't like the view. Stick was soaking wet, as pink as a new pig, and shriveled. Flaccid, I mean.

"How's the calf?" I asked.

All around the room, heads began to swivel. Eyes met. Glances were exchanged.

"Whah?" Stick said. Though maybe it was closer to "Whaaa!"

"The calf. How's the calf?" I asked again.

Stick reached belatedly for the limb in question.

"I couldn't help noticing that your limp is gone. In fact, unless I'm very much mistaken, you were running back and forth across this room not three minutes ago."

"Yo," Mancusi said.

"Son of a bitch," Rump said.

"You gotta play hurt," Brawn said.

The clubhouse was mobilized now. The entire forty-man roster gathered around me. It was the sweetest and meanest interview I've ever conducted. Also the fastest. I had to get out of there before Girard or Brenner or MacKenzie showed up.

Stick denied everything. He whimpered and shriveled and said nobody knows his body like he knows his body, which prompted a fair amount of laughter in the clubhouse. Then he got mad and started calling me a cunt, which he had never done before, and that's when I knew I had him. "It's 'cause of the martinis. Everybody knows about the martinis, right, guys? So I slipped her a Mickey. What's the big fucking deal? You gonna let this broad get even like this? Who ya gonna believe, her or the Stick?"

The challenge was greeted with silence.

I told Stick that a story would be appearing in tomorrow's editions of the Washington *Tribune* quoting his former agent, Marv Cox, as saying that while the Washington Senators were trying mightily to avoid becoming the worst team since the 1962 New York Mets their allegedly injured designated hitter was taping a television commercial in which he tap-danced for five hours and approximately 108 takes. I also said that Marv had Fed-Exed a copy of the outtakes of the Stick deodorant commercial to the offices of the Washington *Tribune*, which I had screened this morning and which would be made available to any of his teammates who wanted to see the Stick dance. Then I asked if he had any comment.

I hardly recognized the voice as my own. Maybe that's because I had found it for the first time. It was my very own fuck-you voice. I always wondered what it would sound like: gruff like Bernie Squire's or petulant like Girard's or sweet like Milo's. It was none of these. It was just matter-of-fact. For once I really didn't give a damn how the other guy felt. And that felt great.

Stick said, "I ain't gonna respond to this fucking horseshit."

"Fine," I said. "Just wanted to give you a chance to tell your side."

"I'm telling ya," he said. "She's got it all wrong. She's *taking it out of context.*"

Stick was desperate. That's what they all say when they're desperate. But by then no one was listening. His teammates had turned away from him irrevocably. That left just Stick and me and Monk. I hadn't noticed him standing there, but then he never stands out in a crowd, shrunken as he is. Now I couldn't help noticing him. He was besides himself, as Buck likes to say. He was snorting so hard that the hairs inside his nostrils were standing upright. His beady eyes bulged and the phlegm got stuck in his throat. He gasped and wheezed and finally brought it all up, leaving a trail of Red Man all over Stick's newly healed set of wheels.

"Yo, Skip, pencil me in," Stick said. "I think maybe I can go today."

But by then Monk was down on his knees in his office praying to Jesus that Stick Fuller would get his red ass traded to the worst bleeping team in the motherbleeping major bleeping leagues, which of course is us. Nevertheless, Milo says, Monk swore on his mother's motherbleeping Bible that the Stick will never play for him again and I suspect that much is true.

Anyway, the Senators charged out of the dugout like a team that had finally found its context and beat the Yankees, 6–2, on Pete King's seven-hitter for their fortieth win of the year. At least now we know the Senators will win as many as the '62 Mets. Buck drove in his one-hundredth RBI. Rump went 3 for 4 and raised his average to .247. And Stick stayed on the bench.

I called Sal and told him what I had. "That's a Holy Shit story, Berkowitz," he said, which is the highest compliment Sal pays.

But that wasn't the half of it. Sal wouldn't have understood even if I had been able to explain. Maybe for the first time ever my insipid need to be liked hadn't prevailed. I hadn't bent over backward to be fair or nice or sympathetic. I had simply confronted the Stick with what I had. Finally I was one of the guys.

I topped off the story, most of which was already written, added some scene and some quotes, and filed by the top of the third. It was your basic tap dance.

September 29   They ignored me. I walked into the clubhouse and they completely ignored me. It's not like I expected a red carpet and confetti. But I didn't expect the silent treatment, either. Nobody even acknowledged I was there.

I wandered around, looking for someone to talk to. One by one, they all turned away. In short order, my chest felt like a meat locker.

Maybe the story was wrong. Maybe I screwed up the quotes. Maybe Stick really *was* injured or, worse, burned. Maybe someone set me up. Oh my God.

Everything I knew to be true suddenly was in doubt. I went over the story in my head, trying to find the error. It's amazing, and also embarrassing, how you can memorize your own words with such little conscious effort. I could see the whole thing laid out before me, all thirty inches of it, under the understated banner headline: DOG BLEEP! Suddenly I didn't care for my lede: "This is the portrait of the Stick as a major league dog." Suddenly I felt a great urge to sit down.

Every reporter on every beat has a safe harbor, someplace you can go when a guy calls you a cunt or tells you to eat shit and die and for once you can't shrug it off. Sometimes you don't even know it's a safe harbor until you get there. Thus it was I found myself perched on the stool in front of Buck's chair, hoping like hell he'd return from wherever he had gone and say something sweet about my story or his baby.

I opened my notebook and tried to look nonchalant. I tried

not to feel hurt. And I tried not to scream when someone came up behind me, placed one large hand across my eyes, and began feeling me up with the other.

When I say feeling me up, I mean just that. This anonymous hand made its way up one side of me and down the other. It rubbed my thigh and tickled my knee. I have very ticklish knees. And you know what I was thinking? That I wished like hell I had worn stockings.

It was an adventurous hand, a Columbus of a hand. It rubbed my calf, it caressed my cheek, it touched my neck, my shoulders, my arms. It came damn near close to a lawsuit and each time skittered away. But the one thing it did not do was stop. And nobody in the goddamned clubhouse made a move to do anything about it.

I started to laugh. A strange reaction perhaps, or maybe the only one under the circumstances. I mean, there I was literally in the dark with this big callused hand making tracks all over my person and I hadn't got the faintest fucking idea who it was or what I could do to stop it. All I knew was it was one of forty guys and that the other thirty-nine were waiting to see what the hell I was going to do. That should have told me something right there. But I was a little too preoccupied for logic.

The hand came to rest on my right calf. If there's one part of my body I do not like, it's the calves of my legs. They are not the kind of calves featured in stocking ads, upturned in that ancient gesture of sweet surrender. There is nothing great about them at all except perhaps their size, which is the legacy of so many hours on the baseball diamond. The only thing you can say about them is that they do not lack definition.

Calves!

Suddenly I knew. That was my clue. This was my test!

I had been waiting for this moment all year. How did I know? I knew because whoever it was kept going back and rubbing my right leg exactly the way Stick has been rubbing his for the last month. I knew because I know ballplayers and I know that they have their own strange way of accepting or not accepting you. I knew that whoever was attached to that meandering hand was trying to tell me that I had earned my chance with the story on the Stick.

I thought about what Ruth would do. Tell them to get fucked, write a story, and file a lawsuit. That's what they would expect. That's what an outsider would do.

I thought about what Michael would do. But of course a guy would never be in this position. Guys get shit in their shoes instead.

I thought about who it could possibly be. It couldn't be Rump. That would be too close for comfort. It couldn't be Stein. He wouldn't dare. I eliminated Stick for the same reason. Lawson was also out of the question, as were all of the blacks and Hispanics, race relations being what they are.

All the while, the hand was surveying a few more of my peaks and valleys. I laughed harder. I remembered Dave Dorsey, the former MVP. One time some years back, Dorsey hit a woman photographer with a crutch after she had dared to take a picture of him hobbling out of the clubhouse. Maggie Blum told me about it when I went over to Sports.

"It's Dave Dorsey," I screamed, hoping that whoever it was wasn't too young or too dumb to remember.

Billy Blessing dropped his hand from my eyes, stuck his thumb in his mouth, and whimpered, "She only goes with MVPs."

I made sure not to look in Rump's direction, and followed Billy across the locker room as fast as I could and wrapped my arms around him in a serious bear hug. "Don't worry," I said. "When you're MVP, I'll go with you, too."

Billy grinned and Big Foot said, "Watch out, A.B., son of a bitch'll hold you to it."

Then the Senators went out and took their second straight game from the Yankees. Billy went 2 for 4, Buck hit his twenty-sixth dinger, and Rump threw out two runners trying to steal. As a result, they are now 41–119.

For a change, I was really into it and thus a bit distracted when the phone rang in the third and I heard myself bark "Berkowitz" into the receiver. I never call myself Berkowitz.

The voice on the other end of the line was high-pitched and officious and too old for the person it belonged to. "I'm terribly sorry for the late notice," said the young associate producer of "Nightline." "We thought we had Cosell lined up for the show, but he had to cancel and we wondered if you'd be willing to come on and talk about the athlete as role model."

"When?"

"Well, tonight. Rump Doubleday is scheduled to appear and he recommended you. In fact, he said he won't appear without you. I'll tell you what we'll do. We'll send a limo to the press gate for you. Would that be all right?"

I allowed how maybe I could work it into my schedule and the young associate producer, who wasn't in the slightest sorry for the late notice, slobbered all over himself thanking me profusely, which I figured was the least he could do, considering he had been nice enough to inform me that I was second choice at best and forced upon them at worst.

As promised, the car was waiting for us at the press gate. There was also a chilled magnum of champagne in the backseat and a terse message from the officious young producer saying that the entire London Philharmonic had been killed in a plane crash and our segment had been killed along with it. The car was ours for the night and thanks anyway.

Rump shrugged. "I'm not in the mood for being a role model anyway," he said. "C'mon, let's go for a ride."

He had given me fair warning. I paid blissfully little attention. "Why not," I said.

Rump popped the cork and proposed a toast "to baseball, to things that endure, to the end of the season and the beginning of next, to the winter meetings."

I slurped a glass of Dom Pérignon and accepted a refill. It was only after my third glass that I remembered I hadn't eaten anything since lunch. By then we were cruising past the Jefferson Memorial. It was a beautiful night. The marble shone in the moonlight. The Washington Monument glistened in the reflecting pool. We drank again and again: to the Stick, who is no longer as hard as Chinese arithmetic; to Stein, who no longer eats Jell-O; and to Billy Blessing becoming the MVP. Rump said, "Yo." And we drank some more to brains and to Brawn and to Monk's vocabulary. Rump filled my glass again and again.

We were sailing now and a cool wind was blowing through the car. Rump had talked the driver into turning off the air conditioner. We circled the Capitol—the Dome looked a bit fuzzy—and glided back down Independence Avenue past Air and Space and the Hirshhorn. For a minute I swore the airplane dangling in the window was about to take off. But I was seeing things. Rump put his arm around me and proposed one final toast to us. I looked up at his face, which really is a very nice face, and, to be honest, probably would have kissed him if I hadn't passed out in his lap instead.

September 30 Once again I woke up in bed not having the faintest idea how I got there, who undressed me, or who was kind enough to tuck me in. At least this time I knew where I was. The clock beside my bed said 3:00. It has said 3:00 for the last month, which is about how long it's been since I've been home and attended to those niceties of life like winding the clock and throwing out the spoiled milk.

I did what I usually do in a panic. I called the office. "Calm down, Berkowitz, it's only noon," said Raoul, who has become inured to my disarray and my promises to buy a new watch. "You got a 2:00 P.M. start. They won't throw out the first ball without you."

There was plenty of time to get dressed, get sober, and get my ass to the ballpark. I managed two out of three.

Everybody was upstairs in the press lounge eating crab cakes by the time I arrived. At this point in the season, there isn't much left for us to ask and less for them to say. But food was the last thing on my mind, so I went downstairs and wandered around the clubhouse looking for gossip and Rolaids. "Wait! Don't move!" Buck said suddenly.

His voice was urgent but soft and froze me where I stood above the fiftieth star on the clubhouse floor. Buck tiptoed toward me, his index finger pressed against his lips. Then he reached forward, hands cupped, and touched my shoulder. "Got it!" he said. "I got it!"

"Got what?" I asked.

But Buck ignored me. Billy came over to look at whatever it was or was supposed to be. Buck whispered something to him and opened his hands just enough to give Billy a peak. "A beauty," Billy said. "A real beauty."

Then Billy cupped his hands and Buck gently handed over the thing and Billy began to waltz around the room, humming "Born to Be Bad" and clutching the thing to his bosom. It was a dudical waltz.

"Lemme," Brawn said. Billy gave him this exaggerated shrug and then his okay. So Brawn cupped his hands and did a turn around the room, stopping only when Stein emerged from the john to find his large naked teammate waltzing to unheard music.

"What the fuck is going on?" he said.

"Buck's been chasing butterflies again," Billy said. "It's a rare one. Found it sitting on A.B.'s shoulder."

Brawn handed off to Guttierrez and Guttierrez handed off to Mini-Doc and Mini-Doc handed off to Mug Shot. One by one, they all took a turn dancing around me, hands cupped sweetly in the air. All except the Stick, that is. He kept trying to cut in, but no one would let him.

Around and around they whirled like porcelain figures on a child's cuckoo clock; and just as fragile but naked and alive. Rump was last. He pirouetted once, twice, three times until at last he came to Buck's locker and bowed deeply before him. Buck cupped his hands again and joined me where I stood in the middle of a room full of naked men I sort of know.

He touched my shoulder and opened his hands wide. "I think I best let this one go," he said. "You take care now, A.B. This butterfly's gotta last more than just one season."

In the press box, I kept reaching for my shoulder. "Something wrong?" Brenner said. "Just the opposite," I replied.

The game started. I barely kept score. I don't know if I was more hung-over or more overwhelmed. Either way, I really couldn't concentrate at all. I'd watch a routine grounder to short and forget two seconds later what happened. "What'd he do?" I kept asking. "What'd he do?" "Six–three," someone would reply.

Luckily, the Senators took an early 5–1 lead, which was 8–2 by the bottom of the seventh, so I didn't really have to pay attention. It was the bottom of the eighth when Danno nudged me on the shoulder and suggested I might want to watch.

"Buck's up," he said. "He's going for the cycle."

I checked my scorecard. Sure enough: he had tripled to center in the first, gone deep in the fourth, and doubled into the gap in the sixth. But I was too hung-over to remember any of it.

No one on the 1989 Washington Senators had hit for the cycle all year. Apart from that, it was a completely meaningless at bat. No matter what he did, Buck would still be Rookie of the Year and the Washington Senators would still finish dead last in the American League East. It didn't matter at all. At least, it shouldn't have.

Buck settled into the box and took his warmup swings. They seemed more deliberate than usual. Each time he swung, he locked his wrists and pointed the bat at the pitcher and held it there in equipoise. Four, five, six times. Then he planted his back leg again and dug his spike in the dirt and curled his fingers around the bat handle, one finger at a time, the way you play an arpeggio on a piano, the way Joey Proud did the night he became a hero with a torn Achilles heel. I couldn't believe I had never noticed the similarity before.

The count went to 3–2. It was one of those at bats that become a game within a game, a duel between strength and surprise. Buck fouled off a pitch and then another and curled his fingers around the bat again as if he couldn't quite get a grip on something; as if he knew everything was one swing from flying out of his grasp.

The last pitch was low and away. Buck lunged at it and turned instinctively toward first. It was a slow roller to short. It had infield hit written all over it. My stomach churned and tightened. I put down the binoculars. You don't need magnification to see history repeat itself.

In moments like this, baseball forces you to make a choice. You can watch the shortstop charging, or the path of the ball, or the runner racing down the baseline against the geometry of aerodynamic flight. You cannot see it all. But this time I did. I saw a little girl wrapped in wool on a cool September night at Yankee Stadium, watching her hero and waiting for her grandma's chocolate cake. I saw Joey Proud reach for the bag, straining to beat out the inevitable. I saw Buck's leg cave in.

He collapsed in the baseline, a dancer in mid-leap, his legs extended beyond reach or reason. He hung there for an instant, or so it seemed, before the force of gravity sucked him to the ground, splayed in the basepath, covered with chalk. His fingers kept feeling for the bag. My fingers had no feeling at all. The violence of the injury, the symmetry of the present and the past, was oddly beautiful to see. It immobilized me.

Everybody but me ran for the TV monitor, watching the replay, the inexorable pull of fate, in slow motion. I couldn't look. I didn't have to. I had seen it all before and I knew I would see it again and again and again, the prodigious what if of history.

"Huh?" Danno said.

"What-if," I replied.

"Ain't no what-if about it. That sucker's dead meat. He's gone."

They carried Buck off the field on a stretcher. The crowd stood and cheered. A few reporters even applauded. The Senators won their third straight from the Yankees. But Buck was lost. He disappeared down the steps and the press box came alive with the adrenaline of occasion. Phones rang, wire machines clattered. Hoarse men shouted into fifty telephones. "Did you see that?" "Son of a bitch!" "It's a hamstring!" "It's a knee!" "It's bad."

I didn't even bother to turn on my machine. I touched my shoulder, and began to dictate. I was writing from memory.

OCTOBER

The End of the Season

October 1 Buck wouldn't go to the hospital. He told the doctor he wanted to be with the team on the last day of the season. One way or the other, he was going to be on the bench when the Washington Senators either did or did not equal the '62 Mets as the biggest losers in history.

It's hard to overestimate the impact this had on his teammates, the majority of whom have never been accused of placing the greater good above their own. They weren't just surprised to see him. They were jolted like livestock butting against an electric fence. They actually jumped out of Buck's way as he hobbled to his locker on a pair of crutches that were meant for somebody half a foot shorter than he. It looked like Moses parting the Red Sea.

By the time Buck lowered himself to his Naugahyde throne, the shock had worn off and his teammates began to venture toward him. I wouldn't want to get carried away and say they were actually rallying around him. The fact is, they didn't get the chance. A final moment of potential team unity was obliterated by the crush of reporters who descended on Buck's shredded right Achilles tendon. One guy actually rested his reporter's pad on Buck's leg and started to use his quadriceps as a desk. A radio punk crouched beneath his cast. And some TV cameraman, net-

361

work no doubt, ordered Buck to move his foot six inches to the left because it was ruining his shot. The Washington Senators didn't have a chance to ask him how he felt. We did it for them.

"How's the wheel, Big Guy?" Brenner shouted.

"Okay, long as I got my legs," Buck said, holding on to his crutches.

"When they cutting on ya, Big Fella?" MacKenzie called.

"S'afternoon, right after we win Number 43. Doc says Buck should be just fine by spring training."

I was standing behind Buck's shoulder and couldn't see the expression on his face. But I winced at his optimism. Joey said the same thing once.

"So, Buck, I guess this just about makes you a shoo-in for Rookie of the Year," Girard said. "Sympathy vote 'n' all."

Guys were standing in a circle three-deep around Buck, jostling for position, checking quotes. But Girard shut them all up. The murmuring ended. Sometimes a really tasteless question will do that. But this wasn't really even a question. It was an invitation to a duel.

Four months ago, Buck would have lost it for sure and everyone would have gone up to the press box laughing and snorting and repeating whatever he had said one hundred times until they convinced themselves they were that much smarter than he. But not this time. This time Buck didn't say a word and neither did anyone else, though I could think of a few choice ones I'd have liked him to use. In the uneasy silence, I thought back to that day in Texas with the rain obliterating his tears and how he struggled to find the words for what he wanted to say and the eloquence he finally managed. I thought about his straggly mustache and how much it has grown in and how his transplant hasn't. If ever I have rooted for anyone, I was rooting for Buck to find his voice now.

"Maybe it does and maybe it don't," Buck said finally. "But if I need your vote to win, Girard, I'd just as leave do without the accolation."

No one corrected him. And no one laughed, except maybe at Girard. Buck signaled the end of the interview. A couple of guys pleaded for a few more minutes, but he was adamant. I stood aside and waited for them to clear out.

"Guess this boy's gonna limp down that aisle for sure," he said when we were alone.

"Don't matter how you get there."

"That's what *she* says."

Buck gazed at his leg. When he looked up, his eyes were full. "Damn," he said. "Damn." I knew he didn't want to cry. Not then. Not there. I knew if I comforted him he would. So I started doing schtick instead.

"You think you got it bad? You should have seen my sports editor two hours ago. Spent the whole goddamned morning in the publisher's sauna. Son of a bitch has to lose four pounds by this afternoon or we're screwed. You remember, I told you 'bout Ross Mitchell, the owner, who says we've got to lose four hundred pounds by the end of the season?"

Buck nodded. "Well, as of yesterday, we had lost four hundred and one. Then last night this guy Pincus, who started the whole thing by getting stuck behind the wheel of his Lincoln, went on a binge and ate twelve Big Macs. Of course, it was understandable. His jaw had been wired shut for weeks.

"Anyway, he comes in this morning for Judgment Day and he's gained five pounds. Five! Sal went bonkers. Sal's the editor. Sal is six foot six and weighs maybe 140. Sal asks for volunteers. Suddenly everyone's on deadline. 'Sorry, Sal.' 'No can do, Sal.' So now Sal personally has got to lose four pounds by the 4:00 P.M. deadline and it's not like he's got any extra to spare.

"You should have seen him this morning, stomping around the office in this rubber suit, which is practically falling off him to begin with, screaming: 'So you think you're gonna sweat the son of a bitch? We'll see who's gonna sweat who!' Short of telling a guy he'll never write for you again, the worst possible thing a sports editor can say is, 'I'm gonna sweat the son of a bitch.' Pincus is doomed. Sal is still in the sauna. As of half an hour ago, he still had two to go."

Buck laughed and laughed until the laugh became a yawn he couldn't quite stifle and the yawn dissolved into laughter again. "Didn't get much sleep," he said, laughing some more.

"Me neither," I said.

Buck looked puzzled. I pulled a copy of the morning paper out of my briefcase and handed it to him. "I was at Yankee Stadium the night Joey Proud got hurt. He ripped up his Achilles tendon trying to beat out a bouncer to short. On a 3–2 pitch, low and away. I was nine. He was my hero. It was how I learned about vulnerability."

Buck stared at the picture of himself splayed in the basepath covered with chalk. "On a 3–2 pitch, low and away?" he said. He was almost whispering. "I didn't know."

Baseball players, the best of them anyway, become historians. They know that certain numbers—a 56-game hitting streak, 61 home runs, 2,130 games played—are not just statistics or records but the parameters of shared experience. They know about streaks and slumps. They know about Wally Pipp's headache and Lou Gehrig's demise. They know that the best of them fail two out of every three times. They internalize these things and respect them.

But what to make of two men two decades and light-years apart whose vast potential is forever compromised by a stupid, meaningless, honorable attempt to do their best on a 3–2 pitch, low and away? Coincidence? Perhaps. When you put nine men on a field of a particular shape 162 games a year, year after year, anything can happen twice, even two guys running out their potential in exactly the same way. And maybe that's all this was. But maybe I wanted Buck to tell me it was something more.

"Ain't none of us bulletproof," Buck said.

Seconds later the cloying scent of Clubhouse cologne once again announced the presence of the Reverend Jimy Boy Collins. His fleshy pink fingers grasped Buck's shoulder in what he hoped would be construed as sympathy. "Son," he said. "Son. Son. Son."

It was Jimy Boy's first clubhouse appearance since the Shaft, which is how we refer to his trauma in the elevator. It was also the first time I heard him call Buck anything but "boy." "Son, I have come to pay my respects," he said, which was bullshit because nobody knew Buck was going to be there. "And I have come to pray for your soul."

"Ain't my soul that's the problem," Buck said. "I'm right with my Lord."

Jimy Boy failed to get the point, or at least he didn't acknowledge it. "Son, the Lord giveth and the Lord taketh away. And I'm sure, as sure as I'm standing here before you today, a Christian man, a humble man, a man of God, that the Lord Jesus Christ had a purpose in this, your moment of tribulation, and that you need only pray to know His mind and His purpose. Remember, son, prayer heals."

Jimy Boy released Buck's shoulder and I couldn't help but notice the thumbprint left on Buck's neck. Ballplayers never rub. But Buck rubbed. He was still massaging his shoulder when Jimy

Boy mounted the buffet table, his Gucci'd foot perilously close to a plate of dehydrated Sloppy Joes, and began exhorting his team on to victory.

I guess I wasn't entirely surprised, just entirely grossed out, to hear what he did to Ecclesiastes. "Boys, 'For every thing there is a season, and a time to every matter under heaven: a time to be born, and a time to die; a time to plant, and a time to pluck up what is planted . . . a time to weep, and a time to laugh; a time to mourn, and a time to dance; a time to cast away stones, and a time to gather stones together; a time to embrace, and a time to refrain from embracing . . .' "

This produced a couple of muffled chortles around the locker room. Jimy Boy ignored them.

" 'A time to love, and a time to hate: a time for war, and a time for peace.' "

Here Jimy Boy took a deep and practiced breath while searching the room for a hint of transcendence. There was none forthcoming. So he plunged ahead. "A time to win, and a time to lose. And, yes, men! A time under heaven to kick some Christian ass!"

I guess maybe Jimy Boy was expecting the infidels to rise up with a whoop and a holler at this shocking and premeditated profanity. But it didn't exactly work out that way. The infidels were stunned. I mean, truly stupefied. They stood there looking at Jimy Boy as if he was out of his fucking mind, all except Lawson and Pentacost, who were truly appalled. Finally Monk came to Jimy Boy's rescue, clambering up on the table next to him—and, I might add, getting Sloppy Joes all over his long underwear and Jimy Boy's blue pin-striped suit. "I think what Rev. Jimy Boy means to say is we should go out there and win one for the Big Guy Upstairs. Is that 'bout right, Reverend?"

Jimy Boy beamed at Monk and Monk beamed at Jimy Boy and Piggy beamed at everybody, but that was about it for beaming. Everyone else in the locker room simply turned away and began getting dressed for the last time this season.

I looked around the room. It was all so familiar. But it felt as if I was seeing it for the first time: Billy's eye-black, Stein's JEWISH JOCKS FOR JESUS T-shirt, Lawson's cleats with the crosses on the toes, Rump's batting helmet turned backward on his head.

Rump always turns his batting helmet backward just before he goes out on the field. And he always stops at the door for a piece of sugarless bubble gum and taps the IN GOD WE TRUST sign over the threshold. This time he made a detour for Buck's locker and tapped his name plate instead. "I think what Monk and Jimy Boy meant to say is we should go out there and win one for the Big Guy right here. Right, fellas?"

I'd like to think that's what happened. But frankly I'm not quite sure you can attribute the afternoon's events to anything quite so lofty. Here's what we know. The rest will remain forever a matter of conjecture.

The Senators were losing, 2–0, in the bottom of the ninth with the heart of the order due up: Brawn, Rump, and Stein. Brawn, who was 0 for 21 coming into the game, managed to get himself hit in the head with a 2–2 fastball that would have knocked the shit out of anyone else. Brawn shrugged it off and trotted to first as Rump was announced.

The stadium erupted in a deep guttural roar, a wave of sound that bounced off the undulating façade and back again. I had never heard the place so loud except at Redskins games. It was not just Rump's last at bat of the season. It was perhaps the last at bat of his career. And even Washington, with its smug determination not to care, was moved enough to do the right thing.

Rump doffed his cap and hit the first pitch over the leftfield fence. The game was tied. Stein was up. The Senators' fate hung in the balance. Maybe they wouldn't lose 120 after all.

I watched Stein leaning on his bat in the on-deck circle. His name was announced and he stepped into the batter's box and reached down for some dirt. As he did, the Yankees' manager popped out of the dugout and signaled to the bullpen for relief. Stein turned and walked back to the on-deck circle, grinning. I hadn't seen him smile that much since the night he met Charlene.

Charlene.

I should have guessed right then. But I didn't. I didn't put the pieces together until the count went to 3–2 and Stein drove the payoff pitch deep into the centerfield seats. It was a payoff, all right, a waist-high batting practice fastball, and if it evened the score between Stein and his friend on the mound, it also gave the Washington Senators a 3–2 win. Stein skipped around the bases giggling and the Senators finished the 1989 season with a record of 43 wins and 119 losses, 3 wins more and 1 loss less than the '62 Mets.

I called Charlene immediately. But her number was disconnected. A blank sullen look was all I got from the Yankee reliever when I asked if he had ever had the pleasure of her company. "I hung one. So what?" he said. "Doesn't prove a thing."

He was right. It doesn't prove a thing and I can't prove a thing, but I'll go to my grave believing the Yankee reliever grooved one final pitch to Dick Stein.

As for the Senators, you'd have thunk they won 'em all. There was champagne everywhere. Torrents of champagne. Geysers of champagne. It dribbled from Mount Rushmore and oozed from the plush Dacron polyester custom-made stars-and-stripes two-inch pile. It obliterated every note I took.

I made my rounds anyway. At every stop at every locker, I got doused a little more. If pouring champagne on top of someone is a form of communication, I guess you could say they're all finally talking to me now.

Mancusi said, "Yo," and poured champagne on my head. Lawson announced his retirement and poured champagne on my head. Buck said he'd see me in Nuba and poured champagne on my head. Guttierrez called me La Conchita and poured champagne on my head. One thing about the cheap stuff, it blinds you just as good as Dom Pérignon.

Rump was the only one who was actually drinking the stuff. He was naked except for his red GO DEEP T-shirt and surrounded by the third wave of reporters who had come to hear about the mighty clout that tied the game. "Hit it off the fists." He shrugged. "Woulda been an out in Yankee Stadium. Oh well, that's baseball."

MacKenzie asked if Rump had thought about hanging 'em up, this being a good way to go out and all. Rump scratched his beard, took a swig, and looked at me. I could feel him looking for some clue in my eyes, but I couldn't open them enough to give him any guidance. " 'Pends what happens at the winter meetings," he said, but I knew I owed it to him to settle things before then.

Monk came over to shake his hand. I've never seen the manager of a 43–119 club so happy. "Unbe-fucking-lievable," Monk said. "Unbe-fucking-lievable."

I figured what the hell and followed him back to his office. I stuck out my hand and he spat at my feet. "Unbe-fucking-lievable," I said and walked away.

Just as the celebration was beginning to wane, Windy Bragg appeared at the door, followed closely by Beanie, who trailed him around the locker room handing out freshly Xeroxed copies of a press release announcing the trade of Stick Fuller to the California Angels in exchange for a player to be named later. *"Any* player to be named later," Windy said, and the champagne flowed again.

There was no need to ask the Stick to comment. His face said it all. It looked like a bat that's just been shattered by a high hard one. Understand: Anaheim is just about the last place on earth Stick wants to be, what with Charlene and his ex-wife in residence there.

Stick said, "I want an extension. I want to renegotiate."

Windy said, "Good luck, son."

I went to Stein last. I wanted to get him alone. It's not that I thought he would say anything I could use, but I needed to know. Just for me. "Nice pitch," I said.

"Nice fat one," he replied. "You could call it an 'insurance policy,' but I'll deny it if you quote me. Just say I did it for the team."

Then he pulled off his sweaty, champagne-soaked JEWISH JOCKS FOR JESUS T-shirt and handed it to me. "Here," he said. "Have a nice life."

Of course, there wasn't anything I could write except my suspicions, which weren't enough even for the Washington *Tribune.* So I went upstairs to write a nice little sixteen-inch game story about how the Washington Senators beat the rap of history. Sometimes you can't write everything you know. Not in the newspaper anyway.

Somebody, Billy probably, had poured another bottle of bubbly over my head as I walked out the door. There was no looking back. There was no looking at all. The stuff dribbled down my hair and into my eyes and I cursed myself all the way up to the press box for getting this damned perm, even if it does cover my bald spot.

I groped my way to my seat and felt something small and hard and slippery beneath me: a jewelry box wrapped in thick white paper. Blind as I was, there was no mistaking the sumptuous red leather box with the gold embossing. Cartier. Inside, on a bed of black velvet, was a watch just like the one my grandmother gave me when I was a little girl dreaming of a career in the bigs. Only the color of the face was different. But the time was exactly right, the present. And engraved on the back were my name and the NEW YORK YANKEES logo.

I rubbed my eyes and rifled through the paper looking for a card. But there was none. I checked the box and then the wrapping again. "Son of a bitch," I said.

"Maybe you ought to check your screen," MacKenzie said.

Sure enough there was a message. But I was damned if I could read it. The little gray LCDs were doing the fox-trot in a champagne haze. "Jesus, I can't read!"

"Much less write," Girard said.

MacKenzie and Brenner gave him a look and shrugged. "Fuck off, Girard," MacKenzie said. "I'll read it for you," Brenner said.

They came and stood by my shoulder and read aloud. "The Pit at eight. It's about time, isn't it? Michael."

"Hey, you know someone named Michael?" MacKenzie said.

I sat down hugging my side. The phone rang. As usual, Captain Fuck-up didn't bother to say hello. All he said was "You fucked up, Berkowitz. It wasn't a 3–2 pitch. The count on Proud was 2–2."

I started to protest. I was there. I was nine. Oh, what the fuck.

"Ain't none of us bulletproof, Captain," I said.

Final Statistics of the 1989 Washington Senators

Compiled by John Labombarda

PLAYER	BAT.	SLG.	G	AB	R	H	TB	2B
Boo Bailey	.167	.333	12	12	0	2	4	2
Guy Biggs	.136	.318	12	22	0	3	7	1
Billy Blessing	.145	.185	42	124	5	18	23	2
Al Brawn	.182	.260	63	192	11	35	50	6
Buck Buchanan	.311	.538	156	533	78	166	287	32
Rufus Doolittle	.000	.000	8	18	0	0	0	0
Rump Doubleday	.238	.401	117	357	32	85	143	16
Jean-Claude Duvalier	.230	.255	148	478	49	110	122	10
Stick Fuller	.282	.513	132	419	71	118	215	22
Geronimo Guttierrez	.200	.237	153	524	48	105	124	15
Mug Shot Hackett	.224	.284	143	415	27	93	118	10
Ricky Himeshi	.167	.222	32	90	3	15	20	2
Nick Isakoff	.306	.611	10	36	6	11	22	3
Benito Jones	.169	.195	28	77	3	13	15	2
D. A. Kindred	1.000	4.000	1	1	1	1	4	0
Willie Kluttz	.171	.237	32	76	5	13	18	2
John Lawson	.258	.336	80	217	18	56	73	5
Dante Mallia	.095	.143	8	21	0	2	3	1
Joe Mancusi	.243	.342	110	404	46	98	138	18
Demetrious Mourning	.204	.282	40	103	8	21	29	3
Riki Rini	.235	.324	14	34	1	8	11	3
Dick Stein	.229	.312	134	401	39	92	125	12
Fennis Tubbs	.193	.240	60	150	13	29	36	4
SENATORS	.233	.337	162	4,704	464	1,094	1,587	171

PITCHER	W	L	ERA	G	GS	CG	SHO	SV
Juan Arroyo	5	17	5.33	25	24	3	1	0
Charlie Bold III	0	4	4.85	21	0	0	0	1
Boom Boom DeForest	0	3	10.25	14	2	0	0	0
The Gooch	1	3	4.69	42	0	0	0	1
Big Foot Harrison	0	4	3.00	57	0	0	0	9
Fast Eddie Hernandez	9	19	4.75	32	32	13	1	0
Bobby Damn Jenkins	7	20	6.45	31	30	10	1	0
Pete King	4	4	3.35	35	4	2	1	2
Stretch McCarthy	3	7	4.49	30	10	2	0	0
Lefty O'Donnell	7	15	5.83	29	29	9	0	0
Rawley Pentacost	7	21	3.91	32	31	11	1	0
Henry Aaron Poussaint	0	2	7.80	7	0	0	0	0
SENATORS	43	119	5.07	162	162	50	5	13

3B	HR	RBI	HP	BB	IBB	SO	SB	CS	E
0	0	0	0	0	0	10	0	0	2
0	1	1	0	0	0	7	0	0	1
0	1	7	0	2	0	33	1	1	5
0	3	18	15	16	1	45	1	0	3
4	27	105	12	90	10	99	17	5	6
0	0	0	0	1	0	5	0	0	0
0	14	50	2	24	1	60	0	1	7
1	0	24	4	40	0	75	4	2	40
0	25	91	19	75	8	128	1	3	1
2	0	13	3	33	0	73	1	24	39
0	5	20	2	16	1	35	1	0	9
0	1	4	1	5	0	21	0	0	2
1	2	6	0	3	0	3	2	1	0
0	0	1	0	1	0	10	1	0	3
0	1	1	0	0	0	0	0	0	0
0	1	3	1	1	0	19	0	0	1
0	4	16	7	6	0	42	1	0	8
0	0	0	0	0	0	6	0	0	0
2	6	33	3	21	1	84	0	0	16
1	1	4	1	3	0	28	1	2	2
0	0	4	0	2	0	3	0	0	0
0	7	44	2	23	1	69	0	0	9
0	1	8	0	5	0	28	0	0	9
11	100	453	72	367	23	883	31	39	190

IP	H	R	ER	HR	HB	BB	SO	WP	BK
157.0	168	103	93	38	6	78	108	3	1
39.0	39	26	21	7	1	18	28	1	2
26.1	62	34	30	14	1	11	14	1	0
80.2	82	51	42	9	0	40	62	2	0
72.0	65	31	24	7	2	20	42	0	1
225.2	239	137	119	31	14	123	154	26	5
234.1	246	189	168	45	3	209	137	2	6
86.0	74	40	32	8	0	30	53	0	1
110.1	114	62	55	14	19	99	97	14	4
228.1	235	172	148	28	2	110	123	6	17
214.0	196	115	93	24	1	89	153	4	3
15.0	20	15	13	6	2	11	4	2	2
1,488.2	1,540	975	838	231	51	838	975	61	42

The use of the word "lede" to denote the beginning of a story dates from the era of hot type when newspapers were set in lead. Editors, sending instructions to the printers about how a story should be set, needed to be able to distinguish between the "top" of a story and the lead used between the lines of type to make the story fit its assigned "hole."

Author's Note

Casey Stengel, who knew a thing or two about managing a ballclub, once said, "I couldna done it without my players." I always assumed he was talking about my beloved New York Yankees. Then again, he could have been talking about the 1962 Mets or my beloved 1989 Washington Senators.

Writing a novel, I have learned, is a lot like managing a ballclub. They are both team efforts. If you're lucky, which I am, and you've got deep depth, which I do, then maybe, just maybe, you get out of the cellar.

My thanks to all those players, real and imagined, who have filled sweet summer nights with longing and joy. And to my personal 1989 All-Stars, all of whom played their roles to perfection: Sandra Bailey, Janet Duckworth, Grace Gabe, Herman Gollob, Mary Hadar, Gerri Hirshey, John Labombarda, Fay and Mort Leavy, Nancy McKeon, Dennis Roche, George Solomon, Sid and Diana Tabak, Rick Vaughn, Lois and Tom Wallace, Andrew Weiner, and most especially, my Murderers' Row, Dave Kindred, Lucy Herring, and Mr. Clutch, Peter Isakoff.

I couldna done it without you.